TO IGNITE A FLAME

PART 2 OF TEO AND ESTELA'S DUET

ENTANGLED WITH THE ENDUAR

DANIELA A. MERA

Golden Glow Press

DANIELA A. MERA

First ebook edition June 2024

Book Cover Design by Artscandre

Book couple art by Agnieszka Gromulska @aseriaart on IG

Map by Daniela A. Mera

Book Artwork by Daniela A. Mera

Edited by Sydney Hunt

Proofread by Chelsea Barton

ASIN (ebook): B0CLL26SPL

ISBN (paperback): 978-1-960343-22-2

ISBN (hardback): 978-1-960343-21-5

SUGGESTED READING ORDER

Entangled with the Enduar is a series of interconnected stories. Some are duets, others are standalones. While you do not have to read in this order, it is recommended for maximum enjoyment. (Note that not all books are out yet. Enjoy this sneak preview!)

Teo and Estela's Duet (Completed)
1. To Steal a Bride
2. To Ignite a Flame

Ra'Sa and Melisa's Standalone (October 2024)
3. To Defend a Bride

Arlet and Vann's Duet (2025)
5. To Beguile a Bride
6. To Enchant a Stone

Niht and Abi's Standalone (Spring 2026)
7. To Charm a Bride

SUGGESTED READING ORDER

Ulla and Thorne's Duet (2026)
8. To Trade a Bride
9. To Burn a King

Joso and Selena's Standalone (Summer 2027)
10. To Tame a Bride

Paoli and Si'Kirin's Duet (Fall 2027)
11. To Bewitch a Bride
12. To Bleed a God

PRONUNCIATION GUIDE AND LIST OF TERMS

Ceremonies

Grutaliah Bondyr (grew-tah-lee-ah bon-deer)—Mating Ceremony
Dual'moraan (do-al-more-ahn)—First Cut
Hlumrynna (hu-loom-ree-nah)—Parting Ceremony
Hlums'dor (hu-LOOMS-dore)—Travel blessing

Enduar Words:

Enduar (en-doo-are)—knowledgeable ones
Ruh'duar (ruh-doo-are)—cave-born Enduares
Hlum-scri (hu-loom-scree)—magical cards
Mihk daourn (meek dow-oor-n)—I love you
Pater (pah-ter) —Father

Elvish Words:

Cumhacht na Cruinne (coo-aht nah crun-neh)—power of the universe

Oscailte (os-lee)—open

Mo chuisle (ma-hushla)—my pulse/heartbeat

Vaimpír (vahm-peer)—vampire *heh* (also know to the Enduares as "cold ones")

Peredhel (per-eh-del)—half human elf.

de Bhaldraithe (deh bald-dray-hu)—name of the sisterhood Mrath leads.

Creatures:

Cave rat - **Ruc'rad** (ruck-rad)

Cave bear - **Ruh'Glumdlor** (ruh glum-dl-ore)

Cave bat - **Ruc'ciel** (ruck-cee-el)

Crystal wraith - **Glacialmara** (glass-ee-al-mar-ah)

Glow spiders - **Aradhlum** (ah-rahd-loom)

Glow wyrms - **Wyrmhlum** (worm-loom)

Crystal Dragon/Mother of the Crystal Wraiths - **Drathorinna** (dra-thor-ee-nah)

Characters

GODS

Grutabela—*grew-TAH-bell-ah*

Endu—*EN-doo*

Doros—*DOOR-ose*

Nicnevin—*NIC-neh-ven*

Yde—*EE-dee*

Khuohr—*KOR*

Abhartach—*OW-er-tagh*

HUMANS

Estela—*es-TEL-ah*
Mikal—*Meek-AHL*
Arlet—*ARE-let*
Aitana—*ah-EE-tah-na*
Abi—*Ah-bee*
Paoli—*Pow-lee*
Melisa—*Meh-lee-sah*
Luiz—*Loo-ees*
Selena—*seh-LEN-ah*
Carolina—*ca-row-lee-nah*
Salma—*sahl-mah*
Isaraya—*ee-sah-ray-ah*

ENDUARES

Teo/Ma'Teo—*TAY-oh/mah TAY-oh*
Vann—*Van*
Liana—*LEE-an-ah*
Svanna—*sv-AH-nah*
Ulla—*OO-lah*
Iryth—*EE-rith*
Neela—*NEE-lah*
Ra'Salore—*Rah-sah-lore-eh*
Fira—*FEE-rah*
Joso—*JAW-sow*
Lothar—*LOW-thar*
Dyrn—*D-URN*
Velen—*VEH-lehn*
Tirin—*TEE-reen*
Niht—*night*
Faol—*fa-OHL*
Keio—*Kay-oh*

Rila—*Ree-lah*
Adra—*ad-RAH*
Urira—*oo-RYE-ah*
Si'Kirin—*sih-KEE-reen*
Ner'Feon—*ner-fey-own*
Ka'Prinn—*KAH-prin*

GIANTS

Erdaraj—*ER-dah-rash*
Lijasa—*LEE-jaw-sah*
Laavi—*LAW-vee*
Rholker—*ROLL-ker*
Keksej—*KECK-se-sh*
Uvog—*OO-vog*
Fektir—*FEK-teer*
Marej—*mah-RESH*
Aksa—*ASS-kah*
Ezdur Eriekk—*ez-DURE ER-ee-ek*
Eneko—*EN-eh-co*
Rilej—*REE-lesh*
Veklor—*VEK-lore*

ELVES

Mrath—*Mu-rah-th*
Arion—*AH-r-eye-own*
Thorne—*th-OR-n*
Ayla Daecaryn—*AY-la day-CARE-n*
Elanila—*EE-lah-nill-ah*
Farryn—*FARE-en*
Glyni—*GLIH-nee*
Lusha—*LOO-sha*
Taenya—*TAYN-ya*

Thasinia—THAS-in-EE-ah

OGRES

Braareg—*BRA-reg*

OFFICIAL PLAYLIST FOR TO IGNITE A FLAME

Each Chapter has its own song!

I wanted to do a pithy dedication for this book, but it turns out I am way too sentimental.
So...
For April and her daughter.
Thank you for reminding me that romantasy books connect us in the most special ways.

WELCOME BACK TO ENDUVIDA!

Dear reader, thank you, thank you, *thank you*, thank. you.

The outpouring of love for Teo and Estela's story has been overwhelming and your excitement and well-wishes have literally fueled all my drive to not only finish this book, but get it out three months early.

Before we begin, I would like to set the stage. First, this book is adult fiction and includes mentions of sexual assault, crude language, violence/gore, harm to a pregnant person, misogyny, slavery, and death.

Please take care of yourself.

Second, this book picks up immediately from the end of book one. Hooray! Sweet relief from that nasty cliffhanger.

Allow me to provide you with a quick recap.

ESTELA WENT TO THE ENDUAR MOUNTAINS WITH HER HALF-BROTHER, MIKAL, TO ESCAPE THE GIANTS. THE ATTEMPT FAILED. SHE WAS BROUGHT BEFORE THE ENDUARES, WHERE KING TEO RECOGNIZED HER AS HIS MATE. SHE, AND ALL THE

OTHER HUMANS, REPRESENTED THE SALVATION OF HIS PEOPLE—A WAY TO REVIVE THEIR DWINDLING POPULATION AND GROW STRONG ONCE MORE. HOWEVER, AFTER STEALING HIS MATE FROM THE GIANT'S CLUTCHES, SHE WAS SEPARATED FROM THE SAME BROTHER SHE'D BROUGHT TO SAVE.

ESTELA WAS FRANTIC AND MADE A DEAL WITH THE KING; SHE WOULD STAY, AND THE KING WOULD SAVE MIKAL. PREJUDICES RAN DEEP AS SOME ENDUARES RESISTED THE HUMANS, BUT NO BIAS RESISTED MORE ARDENTLY THAN ESTELA'S. SHE TRIED TO ESCAPE AND CURSED THE HUMANS WHO INTEGRATED SO EASILY TO A SOCIETY SHE THOUGHT SAVAGE.

TEO CONTINUED TO WORK HARD TO SECURE PEACE FOR THEIR PEOPLE DESPITE HIS HUMAN BRIDE'S RESISTANCE. HE LIED TO THE GIANTS AND MADE A NEW TREATY, ALL WHILE LOSING HOPE THAT HIS MATE WOULD EVER ACCEPT HIM.

OVER TIME, ESTELA CHANGED. SHE REALIZED THE ERROR OF HER WAYS, BEGAN TO TRY TO MAKE AMENDS, AND FELL IN LOVE WITH THE KING. AFTER SO MUCH TIME STUCK IN AN UNCOOPERATIVE MINDSET, SHE CAME TO TRUST THE PRESUMED MONSTERS IN THE UNDER MOUNTAIN.

THE ENDUARES INVITED THE ELVES TO THEIR ROYAL WEDDING CEREMONY ON THE FESTIVAL OF ENDU, HOPING TO SECURE ALLIES TO AID IN MIKAL'S RESCUE. THE ELVES THEN BETRAYED THE ENDUARES FOR LYING TO THEM DURING THE FIRST GREAT WAR AND STEALING SOMETHING TEO HAD NO KNOWLEDGE OF. TO GET REVENGE AGAINST SUCH MISDEEDS, KING ARION TOLD THE GIANTS WHAT WAS TO TAKE PLACE BETWEEN THE HUMAN WOMAN AND ENDUAR KING.

SECOND PRINCE RHOLKER WENT MAD. HE KILLED HIS BROTHER AND FATHER AND SENT A SMALL ARMY TO RETRIEVE THE WOMAN HE HAD SOUGHT AFTER FOR YEARS. THEY DISRUPTED THE FESTIVAL AND TOOK ESTELA AGAIN, LEAVING

TEO ON THE STEPS TO THE PALACE, GRIEVING, AND DESPERATELY WONDERING WHAT HIS FATHER DID TO THE ELVES THAT WOULD CAUSE SUCH DRASTIC MEASURES.

FOREWORD BY ANTONIO CASTILLAS

Excerpt from Chapter 18 of *Ancient Mythology and the Giant Court*

As with all great things, the world started with a spark. In a time when the earth was a freshly formed sphere, nearly empty and inhabited by the most basic forms of life, there were gods who reigned from the skies above to the deepest crevice on the planet. Once no more than stardust observing the cosmic roll of time, they were now imbued with the power that none other than the Universe Divine could provide.

Grutabela and Endu begat the trolls, gods of stone and love. He was the severity to the soft beauty of her feminine figure, moving and crashing together across time and space to fill the world with a song only detected by their children.

They were immortal enemies of Khuohr, the god of the Giants who needed no mistress nor formal creed. Priests and prophetesses meant little to a blade. As the harbinger of war and torture, his doctrine was written in the scars on the bodies of his giant sons, and the tenets of his faith were sealed in blood, only to be delivered by axes—sometimes with blunt, punishing force, other times cutting precise as the weapon's pointed edge.

After being rejected and scorned by Endu, Nicnevin, goddess of the elves, ran into the cold, calculating arms of Doros, god of wisdom and fairness. They ruled from separate planes, never touching unless to bless their small, pointed-eared children with their ethereal, echoing voices that rang out long after their perfect mouths closed. They each planted a seed carefully designed for the children of arborescent songs and tapered ears.

Doros gifted a drop, a mere morsel, of wisdom into their corporeal recipe. Something small to remind them to whom they belonged. Nicnevin, however, cast a kernel of mistrust into their hearts. A reminder that love meant little when mortals were flawed and often dishonest. She put enmity between the trolls and elves, never to let the two peoples be mates. Cursed the very idea, as she herself sought comfort in the arms of any other being that would have her. One that would touch her with dark passion, instead of studying her with cold, analytical eyes.

The ogres of the north worshiped the very air around them, believing that their goddess, Yde, was guiding the stench of their swamps from the lowest farm up to the tallest castle. A hideous reminder that one might forget about the wind when it is no more than a gentle breeze, but it is still capable of mass destruction. At times, however, they were too trusting. Unlike their kin, the giants did not understand the neglect from the other ruling species of the land.

The most peculiar of all of these, perhaps, are the humans. A primitive people who let their creators be lost to time and lack of education. Little more could be expected from these creatures, who were believed to hide in mud huts and rat-infested caves. Indeed, whatever god or goddess they might have been borne from would be a pitiful deity in comparison to the great power held by the others inhabiting different corners of the cosmic pantheon.

The giants used this information to prove that humans were a lesser-than species. With such logic, they bound an entire people in chains and used their labor to build their great kingdom.

During its peak, after one hundred years of profiting off of enslaved workers, every young giant lord would have traded their own family to be a prince, as was only fitting in a primitive society where the most significant success one could achieve was amassing wealth. Honor was awarded through having the most land, the most gold, the most women, the most sons, and since the Great War, the most troll diamonds.

Considering this and the nature of Khuohr, it's crucial to understand that most families in the Giant Court knew of extra sons sired by the king's licentiousness. Surprisingly, it was a journal scroll abandoned in an old cave that shed light on such matters. These *Terksat*—or king's gift child—brought honor to the court by proving the strength of the king's seed in his younger days. Many might look back on the practice of sleeping with other men's wives as abhorrent, but the Giant Court was a cruel place filled with practices inspired by their hedonistic deity.

In fact, High King Erdaraj would be remembered for centuries as the most powerful giant sovereign thanks to his views around bearing children. He cemented his rule when he broke the laws by allowing both of Queen Lijasa's sons to live to adulthood, thus showing any of his rivals that trivial assassination attempts, like one poisoned leg of meat, would not result in the ruination of his official royal bloodline.

Official records indicate that he waxed poetic after the

death of Queen Lijasa, even going so far as to allow one half-human bastard to live in addition to the thirty-two *Terksats* and two princes. Unfortunately, as with all human slaves of the time, surnames and families were not provided. The name Mikal is all that is left to history.

～

Antonio's notes:

This makes little sense. Nothing else left to history? No names? No more stories? Anyone in Arrebol knows that our people came from humans liberated from the giants. Then we mated with these so-called Enduares, and the line of kings began.

The same question continues to plague me—how was such a relationship between troll and man forged in the first place?

The First Prince, Keksej, was the mirror of his father. Tall. Handsomely scarred by giant standards. Unafraid to complete the less savory tasks of life like using his famous knives to carve obedience into royal slaves, bedding the wives of unruly lords, torturing prisoners, and waging wastefully bloody wars.

Unfortunately, his brother, Second Prince Rholker, was never as strong. He disliked torture and refused to touch any of the women his father sent his way. He knew what he was—a backup plan.

If Keksej died, he would be there to fill in. Then and only then would he be required to engage in the art of war and avenge his father's name.

To say the Second Prince was uninterested in the king's title would be an understatement. Which only makes both his ascension to the throne and the following entries from his journal all the more surprising.

I've included them here to return to easily after reviewing

the other records. Was all of this over his attraction to a human woman?

~

Prince Rholker, Entry 1

My father brought his whore's children before the Giant Court today. The bitch and the bastard, he likes to call them. I had feared being forced to watch their execution, but something—call it divine intervention, call it human witch magic—appeared in the room and stayed his hand.

Keksej was furious, but I felt relieved. The thought of watching my half-human brother in the hands of my full-blooded giant brother makes my skin crawl... Humans are vermin, but a baby is still a baby.

Prince Rholker, Entry 2

I was assigned to work in the slave fields this morning. Keksej is sick after his last skirmish with our cousins, the swamp ogres of the east. I detest humans. They smell, and their skin is too smooth. It's unnatural.

Prince Rholker, Entry 3—One day later...

I saw the little bitch again. Her brother has shot up like a weed. But she...

It was by accident. I stepped on one of the human's mattocks, and it had to be removed from my foot. They brought me to the healing hut, and there she was. Her face rounded out, her hips spread, and her breasts grew in a pleasing manner.

Human women have never piqued my interest, but there was something about the way she wrapped my wounds that was surprisingly enticing. She and I don't share blood.

When I ran my gloved finger across her shoulder, she didn't run—merely stood very still. It was encouraging. I wonder if she remembers my father's decree.

Prince Rholker, Entry 4

I watched her foraging in the forest. When I approached, she seemed afraid. That was when I saw the blood running down her arms. I recognized the patterns from my own scarred flesh—this was my brother's work.

I suggested she remove her clothes to allow herself more freedom of movement. It took some coaxing, but she agreed.

She's very pliant. I've never seen a human

woman as beautiful as her. I would happily memorize the curve of her buttocks and the sweetness of her breasts every day for the rest of my life. I've been considering taking on more and more dangerous tasks just so that I can see her in the hut, and, for a few seconds, feel the ghost of her fingers on my skin while she dresses my wounds.

Prince Rholker, Entry 5

She's old enough to go to the breeding pens, the doctor told me. The thought of letting some other human man fuck her when she should be sharing my bed is infuriating.

They'll fill her belly with their disgusting children and ruin her forever. Her breasts will sag, and her skill will be marked by some other man's son. She won't be mine anymore.

It can't happen.

I don't ask my father for anything, I simply do as I am told. Surely he won't deny me the chance to have her. He made that decree twelve years ago, and he can't possibly expect me to uphold it since everything has changed.

Prince Rholker, Entry 6

I've waited for her since she became a woman. I have loved her, protected her, worshiped that bitch slave, and when I brought her home with me—where it is safe—she bit my hand and told me no.

No.

I saved her from those pits and a million other things. The image of her face twisted up in rage and agony is burned into my memory, along with the feel of her filthy skin. She looked at me like I was a monster.

I love her.

How could she say no after all I've done?

Prince Rholker, Final Entry

The troll king tells me she is dead. I vow on my mother's grave that the world will pay the price.

PROLOGUE

RHOLKER

Four Months Ago...

"**I** love my gift. It's so tantalizing to think that it came from those savages in the mountains," Prince Rholker's future bride says from the other side of their private table. They are hidden away in a secluded gazebo for their engagement dinner while the rest of their people feast. Lady Marej has light red hair, the color of strawberries mixed with gold, and when the firelight hits it just so, it gilds her smooth skin and decorative scars. Beneath the large diamond hanging on a braided chain are her breasts that she's gone through extra effort to display. Rholker notes that they pushed out of her tight corset, as if begging for him to touch them. By giant standards, she is everything that a prince would look for. For some reason, the Second Prince is not tempted in the slightest.

Rholker grunts in response. It's nearly swallowed up by the echoes of ravenous partying happening in the palace.

This trollop comes from the Fektir house, a high-ranking lordship that owns most of the northern fields. She's accom-

1

plished in weaving, hospitality, and the sexual arts. Lord Veklor told the prince that she could make even the most restrained men finish with two quick strokes of her pierced tongue. Even now, promises are floating in the air around them as she smiles up at him through her lashes.

There's a male slave at her side and a short whip in her hand, prepared to punish the human for any misstep toward her prince.

Rholker swallows. His bride's golden features only remind him of the impossibly tiny gold flecks in Estela's eyes. It should be Estela holding that whip and torturing one of her own kind for his pleasure. His pretty little traitor.

The image relaxes something inside of him, and he allows himself to dream—to explore his most luxurious fantasy. His human bride. Rholker's father has forbidden him from speaking about Estela in his presence, but that doesn't stop the prince from planning.

Especially since he will finally be allowed a comfort woman, and the king has been distracted by the court lately. Not to mention that Erdaraj has always told his sons that giant princes do as they please.

Rholker's gaze returns to Marej's breasts, and he wonders what it would be like to have Estela perched on her chair dressed in a tight, low-cut dress instead. The slave's curly hair would be oiled into gentle ringlets, her eyes and lips would be painted red with berries, and the most beautiful part of her would be on display for all to see—the brand he marked on her sternum. By this point in time, Rholker would have also found some way to erase or replace Keksej's awful twin-mark he imposed next to his.

The image has blood pumping through his princely veins, mixing with the alcohol he'd been guzzling throughout the night. He's drunk on wine and thoughts of *Estela*.

"Like what you see?" Marej says.

Rholker doesn't respond, and the silence stretches out between them until it is thin and taut. The woman promised to him stands up, grabs her whip, and crosses over to his seat. She pushes the wooden chair back and kneels between his legs. His jaw tenses.

"Are you shy, My Prince?" she says while reaching toward the bulge between his legs and tracing her whip against his thigh.

The prince reaches for his goblet once more, only for his fingers to knock the gem-encrusted gold right off the table. The human slave standing to the side flinches.

"Why don't you pick it up?" Marej demands of the slave.

The man drops to his knees and fumbles the cup even further away. When it is placed back on the table with shaky hands, there are dents and scratches in the precious metal.

Marej's face twists into a cruel expression as she stands and raises her hand. "Idiot. That goblet is worth more than your life." Then she lashes the human man twice.

Rholker hears his gasps under the weight of her forceful blows and watches the graceful arc of her tattooed arms. Precise and lethal.

It's over just as soon as it started, and she looks back at her betrothed for approval.

There is... nothing. No spark of pride. No lust, nor meager attraction.

Rholker pushes his chair back, and her red mouth falls open.

"My Prince," she calls sharply. "Where are you going?"

He waves his hand over his shoulder. "I wish to retire."

The sound of a fallen chair precedes her appearance at his side. She's holding her skirts up, showcasing her tiny, neatly groomed feet.

3

"Shall I join you?" she asks.

Rholker gives her one sharp shake of his head.

"But, My Prince—"

He halts and grabs her arm. She freezes at his touch, and her breath stutters as he drags his gaze over her face, hair, and chest.

Then his lip curls. "I will have to endure a life of you soon enough. If I want you, I will call."

The skin of her face blanches to white, and Rholker rolls his eyes. "Come now, don't be so surprised. Scurry off to my brother. I'm sure he'd love a taste."

Her jaw flexes, and she steps back while yanking her arm out of his grasp. "Perhaps I will do just that."

The prince continues down the stone corridor without another word. There's a masculine scream behind him—more of Marej's fun, likely—but he pushes on. The flames crackle on either side of him as he moves. Each step feels blessed because it will take him to the woman who has stolen his mind and trapped his heart.

Fuck my father and his rules.

Today, he will claim Estela for the rest of time. She will be grateful for it, and Rholker will keep her safe. He knows that she feels the same—she's spent years casting him sideways glances and healing his wounds.

How could anyone touch that gently and not be in love?

In no time, the prince is at the slave pens. It smells like shit and human sweat. He wrinkles his nose and pushes into her hut.

"Estela, come with me," he barks.

Her brother, Mikal is sitting in the corner, scratching charcoal across a wooden plank. Idiotic dolt. He is on his feet in a second but freezes when he sees the prince.

"Prince Rho—"

"Where. Is. She?" he demands slowly.

The slave's jaw clenches. "I don't know."

Heat pricks at the base of Rholker's spine. The bastard Mikal is loyal to Estela, but even if he weren't, he hates the prince. All Rholker knows is that if he touches Mikal, Estela will be furious. Maybe even stop loving Rholker.

So, Prince Rholker turns on his heel and stomps back into the night. He knows the places she likes to go.

More heat ripples up his spine as he thinks about what she could be doing out there... and who she might be with.

"Where are you going?" the half-human slave shouts. Rholker ignores Mikal and starts running. A guard at the edge of the pen sees and restrains the little pup.

"Leave her alone!" Mikal screams as he lands a punch on the guard's face, but Rholker is already nearing the forest. He keeps running until he cannot hear the slave any longer.

Trees stretch up around the prince, and he sighs when he reaches a thick patch. This area isn't meant for giants—the trunks are too close. He squeezes between two particularly tangled logs.

Branches and leaves whip at his face when he calls out, "Estela!"

No response. He tries again.

Above him, a branch snaps. His head stretches upward while he gazes at the moonlight filtering down through the leaves.

He can just barely make out the small form pressed against the strong redwood. His heart skips a beat. He doesn't need anyone to confirm it's her—he would recognize his perfect human from a mile away.

"My little Estela, come down please," he calls up.

She doesn't respond. He blinks.

"Are you hurt?" he demands.

Still nothing.

5

Rholker's fears from earlier return with a vengeance. "Is someone up there with you?" he snarls. Rage brews under his skin. He reaches out and wraps his arms around the tree.

He shakes with all his might, and she screams. Stepping back, he lets her tumble into his arms. Pride swells in his chest when he doesn't hear another voice—nor thud.

"Why were you hiding, my love?" he says down to her. She looks up at him, stunned and he realizes this is the first time he's ever felt her skin for more than the brush of fingers through bandages and poultices.

"Put me down," she says.

He pretends like he hasn't heard her and reaches up to cup her cheek. Soft. So soft. Supple, too, like ripe fruit.

He wonders if she'll bruise like an apple.

Something roars to life inside of him, and, before he knows it, he's bolting away, back to his rooms. Past the slave pens, past the party. She fights against him, but her blows might as well have been the kiss of raindrops.

He's high on the scent of her sweat and the smooth texture of her neck. When they arrive at his room, he locks the door behind him with one hand.

"No!" she screams.

"Shh," he says, pressing his hand over her mouth and placing her on the bed. Her eyes are wide, and he realizes that her cheeks are streaked with dirty tears.

"Oh, small one. Don't worry. I won't be in trouble; no one will find us here."

After an evening of that pathetic woman hurling herself at him, he feels he is where he's meant to be. His other hand trails to her bare shoulder, and he groans as blood rushes below his belt. He pulls the fabric down farther, exposing the entirety of her arm and her breast as it springs out.

Pain bursts through his other palm, and he yanks his hand

back. Red blood is pooling on his skin. The heat pulsing inside of him is doused.

Sobriety hits him like a wave of ice water.

Rholker's eyebrows scrunch together just as Estela screams again. Then there's an audible bang on his door. It's louder than a knock—almost like they've brought a battering ram.

"No," he breathes. *This is all wrong.*

Another deafening bang.

"I hope they punish you half as much as they'll punish me," Estela spits through her bloody teeth.

The prince looks up at the disgusting woman who is supposed to love him just as they break down the door. There is no kindness nor shyness in her gaze, there is *fire.* Flames dance in her irises that scorch his very soul.

He whips around to find Keksej standing next to a smug-looking Marej. Six slaves are behind them, as are two giant warriors.

Rholker glares at his future bride, Marej.

"You brought *her* here?" His brother, Keksej, pinches the bridge of his nose. "For fuck's sake. What the hell is wrong with you, Rholker?"

Rholker's senses had been swimming in Estela's skin, her smell, her legs, and then she was gone, leaving behind the sting of her rejection. The prince can't believe that his brother barged in on this moment. Keksej will no doubt add it to the pile of humiliating moments he's witnessed over the years.

The First Prince crosses the room in two strides and wraps one hand around his brother's neck. "What am I supposed to do with you now?"

Rholker shoves him off, but Keksej grabs the prince again.

"Act like a child, and you will be restrained as such," Keksej hisses.

Rholker can smell the wine on his breath.

Marej steps further into the room and laughs. "I was hoping that she was at least worth the trouble, but it seems you aren't quite as *capable* as I'd hoped." Her eyes drop to Rholker's now-flaccid groin.

The room fills with a sickening silence.

The Second Prince grits his teeth, and his hand flies out to strike her across the cheek. The slap echoes in the room, and Marej's responding cackle reverberates through his being. He can't stomach the audacity of her mockery, the injustice of her words. Golden-brown eyes flash in his mind.

Estela was supposed to love me.

Rholker's heart twists and convulses, a living, breathing fire of anger and betrayal.

Marej doesn't even touch her cheek. She casts him a sly smile, her deep yellow eyes glinting in the soft light of my room.

"Oh, My Prince, you truly are a pathetic excuse for a giant. I can see why they've had such a hard time finding you a wife."

"Go to hell, Marej," he seethes, his heart pounding with rage. He clenches his fists so tightly that his knuckles turn white.

"Take the whore to the king," Keksej shouts.

The guards drag a quiet, tear-streaked Estela out of the room, and Rholker is left with Marej and the rest of the royal entourage.

Marej continues smirking as she watches Estela being led away. Marej's peals of laughter play repeatedly in Rholker's skull, cutting deep, as if she's etching each ugly bark into his flesh.

Keksej steps forward, his face a mixture of disappointment and concern. "Calm down, brother. This is not the time or place for such a display."

"No need to protect me, Keksej," Marej coos, walking around the heir to the throne and tracing the back of his shoulders with her scarred fingers. "He's a beast without its claws."

Everything mounts on Rholker's shoulders: rejection, ridicule, shame. The next time that Marej opens her mouth to spew her poison, he lunges.

Every awful emotion swirling in his soul is channeled into his powerful blow.

When his fist collides with her face, it sends her crashing to the ground. The sound of bone cracking comes seconds before blood leaks crimson across the luxurious, hand-woven carpet.

The sight of the dented skull on the floor serves as a twisted kind of solace—proof that Rholker is not the pitiful, weak thing she despises. Time passes slowly as he waits for her chest to rise with another labored breath or for her eyes to flicker open. Nothing. He straightens and shakes away the pain in his knuckles. First Prince Keksej stares at his brother with a tight expression.

"Feel better?" Keksej sneers. He points to one of the slaves, and they hurry over to start cleaning the mess leaking all over the polished wood.

Rholker nods. "Much."

"And what are we supposed to do now? She was to be your bride," Keksej asks, more annoyed than angry.

Seconds pass, but Rholker's feeling of freedom doesn't fizzle into shame. He shrugs. "I believe she has a younger sister. She'll be even better for breeding." Not that he wanted to bed and impregnate the bitch.

Keksej purses his lips and stares long and hard. "That is true. But you'll need a new engagement gift since Marej has been wearing the last one around for the last week. Hell, she's even flaunted it in the lumber yards in front of the foremen. It will reflect poorly on Father's wealth if you reuse it."

Rholker's eye catches on the glinting diamond at the dead

9

woman's throat, and he nods. "Yes. I suppose it's time I finally go to the Enduar Mountains."

Keksej shakes his head. "No. You're shit at negotiations. I'm sure that Father will send me."

The Second Prince takes a deep breath, and then another, as if taking in new air can cleanse the blood on his hands. It works.

His older brother grasps his shoulder and guides him out of the room.

"Come, your new bride is at the party. I suggest lying with her before she discovers what has happened to her sister. It will make the marriage contract simpler," he says calmly, the heat of the wine in his system evidently cooling. Or perhaps not. Keksej is a convincingly sober drunk.

"What is her name?" Rholker asks, despite seeing Estela's face in his mind.

Keksej shrugs. "Who cares? When Lord Fektir asks, tell him that you found Marej rutting a slave. She was a slut. No one will question you."

It is a good plan, but unease still curls in his stomach. Keksej can play savior all he wants, but no one will deal with Estela but Rholker. He just needs time. He just needs to see her. He just...

PART ONE

CHAPTER 1

YOUNGITE

TEO

The cold stones of the palace steps dig into my knees as I picture the destruction of both the giants and the elves.

The fucking elves.

They made this happen. *They* sent the giants here. *They* are the reason my mate is gone.

Joso, the hunter, wraps another bandage around Lord Lothar's bloody stomach. Liana the wise woman and I help situate the stained fabric, trying to clot the brutal stab wound Lothar received while trying to prevent Estela's abduction.

"How many are dead?" I force myself to ask before they leave.

Joso pauses as he hands the rest of the cloth to Vann, my personal advisor. "My King, the warring crushed four houses, brutally murdered three hunters, and dispatched seven elders to Vidalena from either shock or a crude attempt to evacuate."

"Who died?"

"Teo, now is not the time," Vann interjects from behind me.

"Who *died?*" I insist.

Joso takes a deep breath. "Ma'Flari, Ik'Cia, Kra'Noki, Lif'-Suro, Suh'Yaryn, Me'Fyl, and Ti'Vhur."

"Thank you," I grit out as he picks up the council member. He gives me a nod before he sets off to the infirmary.

I stay there on the steps and force myself to see each face.

Two elderly women.

Five men.

From two hundred and ninety-one Enduares to two hundred and seventy-nine in the space of four months. Each precious soul that slides through my fingertips is a piece of my own being, torn from my insides and fed to the shadows that follow me from day to day.

Shadows that grow stronger while I crumble.

More features flash before me, of the men and women who remain. There aren't enough Enduares—not by any stretch of the imagination—to go after my wife.

I seethe, letting the bitter, acidic rage pour through my mind and leak into my thoughts. Slowly—one drip at a time. Intentionally.

Coldhearted bastards.

My fists curl tighter, and the nubs of my fingernails dig into my palms.

Murderous, blood-soaked images flood through my mind. I see elven dwellings burned to the ground, bodies littering the brush—decorating their forests with grotesque vistas as their beloved rivers run red. I'd never warred with the elves, but one day...

Amidst the tumultuous revelations, it's impossible not to reach out to my mate. The sacred bond nestled in my chest vibrates gently as my crystal wakes up. The mating mark on my neck starts to burn, almost tickling my throat.

My star? I say.

Silence rattles around in my skull. The absence of her

response is felt in the chasm of my heart. I strain every sense for some sign of her. The only thing I have is the proof of the bond itself.

The threads connecting us together are unsevered and strong.

For that I should be grateful, I suppose. There are few other comforts, especially with the scalding realization that we cannot leave to go after her. Not with a half-broken city and dozens injured. We need allies, but we are alone.

My left eye clouds, and then my right, and then tears are scalding the rims of my eyes and clinging to my lashes.

I blink once.

Hot splashes of salty liquid spill across my cheeks just as a hand rests on my shoulder.

"Ma'Teo. Stand," Mother Liana, one of the only remaining Fuegorra readers, says.

It hurts to see her. As a wise woman of our court, she was training my mate to do the same. I suck in a sharp breath at her command and draw up every ounce of courage to obey her words. My tail helps brush off some of the blood and rubble still stuck to my skin and clothing.

Motion merely stirs the ugly, murderous rage and grief brewing within my ribcage.

I feel more animal than Enduar. More demon than king.

Luckily, I am not alone on the steps. Liana and Vann still stand behind me.

"You need to rest, brother," Vann says.

I look at his grim face. He holds his arm out, almost like a specter of the past. Fifty years ago, he did the very same thing to save my life as my father exploded the continent with his cursed volcano. It was the very day that all four of our great cities sank into the ocean deep.

Unlike that day, I don't reach out to take his hand.

"No." My tone is clipped and impossibly low.

The tight line of his lips twists down. "Teo, we will get her back. I will sharpen my cleaver tonight, and we will go hunting tomorrow. But... you don't look well. You need to sleep first."

"I said *no*." I flex and close my hands.

"Vann," a soft feminine voice practically sings. Ulla steps into view. Blood is splattered across her cheekbones, and her soft blue eyes are filled with concern. "I know that look."

"What are you doing here?" I spit. "Lothar is dying."

Ulla chews on her lip. "There wasn't much I could do. He is being cared for by Luiz. I wanted to see Estela."

It's like a fucking dagger straight through my heart.

Liana steps between me and the others. "Ulla, the queen is gone. I suggest you all leave before something bad happens. Go back to tending to Lord Lothar."

Vann whips around to look at her, but what he sees causes him and the others to back away.

Blood, vengeance, and cruelty seep out of the surface of my skin as the intrepid wise woman grips both my shoulders.

"Teo'Likh?" she asks bitterly, citing my father's name and raising her eyebrow.

"What?" I growl at the name, his obnoxious voice laughing in the back of my mind.

My son.

My son.

My son.

"Get off me."

She is strong and doesn't budge. "You wear the face of a dead man."

I snarl and step away, feeling the pulse of the ground below me. A lick of my hot magic scalds my body, reminding me that I had been on fire an hour before I knelt at the steps.

Liana shakes her head. "You are exhausted—mind and body. I know how much the magic must've taken this time. If you don't feel like resting, then I will put you to sleep, but you must not continue to sit in this attitude. You are going to damage your mind and body."

I take a sharp breath. "I will go by myself."

She frowns. "I will come—"

I brush past her and start walking toward my room. The palace is a blur until I open the door to the king's suite, and a wall of sweet-smelling earth and flowers crashes against me.

Estela.

The whimsical scent brings back a dozen moments with my mate, each pounding against my ribs and drowning my senses in agony. She was here when they took her. I had just laid her down after making the sweetest love I'd ever experienced. My knees hit the ground again as my mind races.

Breathe.

I press my hand to my chest and search for those invisible mating bond threads yet again. They calm me.

She's alive, but the only way to get her back is to find help.

Exhaustion does tug at me, but I can't stay here. Standing and stumbling away from my cursed room, I go to the royal library. The scent of stone paper, both fresh and old, fills my nostrils and brings me back to life.

It is hard to choose to be lonely, laying in my bed when the written word provides the ability to find answers, perhaps even solutions. Better yet, I might even find the possibility of peace—of escape.

I walk the rows that I have spent a lifetime memorizing—from contracts to ballads, and both magic and royal journals—and, swiftly, the scenes of bloody death and murder are replaced with stories, morals, and the knowledge of a people.

One particular row calls to me. It gnaws at the back of my

mind, telling me that the time has come to visit. I look at the metal plate with the words:

Annals and Official Journals of the Kings

My father's legacy. Suddenly, the need to sleep is gone entirely, replaced with the need to unravel this mystery and formulate a plan. *What did my father do to betray the elves so thoroughly that they would seek vengeance against us?* Perhaps if I understand the history with the elves more thoroughly, I can mend our relationship for good and at least gain a couple hundred troops to retrieve my mate.

It's not hard for me to understand the giants' betrayal of our peace treaty. All I need to do is think about the meeting Rholker and I had to negotiate our laughable peace treaty. His haunted, shattered expression that came when I told him Estela was dead still plays through my mind. His motives make sense.

Power and desire are some of the most potent motivators known to any being's existence. Rholker is young, by giant standards. His obsession with Estela will keep her alive. My mate learned much during her time here, not even mentioning the power her Fuegorra has graced her with.

Rholker's a fool with a target on his back. His days are numbered, and they will end soon after I can find a few extra soldiers.

More rage fuels me and gives me strength to stop and walk into the row.

Phantom spider legs scurry up my spine as I gaze into the gaping maw of a literary beast. Here, in these rows, I will find my father's final writings before he ended the Enduar world five decades ago, along with part of the elves and giants.

Even invoking that awful day unlocks the memories I

actively cage. A few words he spoke sneak through the bindings, and I cease to be in the library.

"Orfka ir asuso, hlumgla estra..."

His voice, incanting above the din of death, slices my heart from tip to point. I struggle against bindings, planning to shake him out of whatever has possessed him. When I break the chains, I lunge at him. Then...

I blink.

It all fades, so I step forward and stack the scrolls I've spent a lifetime avoiding in my arms and head back to my table. One row of shelves, with glowing, unearthly songs and glimmering scrolls, calls to me. Sparing a glance at the precariously stacked tower of scrolls, I sigh and dip into the lines of sacred texts. There's a glittering, bejeweled scroll that my father read often. I can almost see it on his desk when visiting Enduvida in the winter.

Adding it to the pile, I continue my trek. It only takes a few moments for me to sit down and drown in blue-black ink and pearl-gray stone paper.

My mind wanders and flies away to the swirling cosmos, far from the pain pounding in my mind. I study the stories I watched with my own eyes long before the destruction of my people—the skirmish with the swamp ogres, Father's love for Mother, and their meeting.

It's surprising to find that his earliest words are a far better comfort to me than facing the nauseating pressure in my chest. If I think too long about Estela, the weight threatens to flatten my lungs and choke the steady beatings of my foolish heart.

Slowly, I pick up my father's final scroll—one I brought from Iravida myself. It feels different than any of the others. Tainted, somehow, by an oily aura that makes my fingers slip off of its end ribbon—as if it doesn't want to be opened. Blood roars in my ears as I unroll it.

It hits me at once. The smell of my old home is almost as powerful as Estela's scent. Old, diamond-spun fabrics—in a time before the diamonds were cursed—millions upon millions of my people and bright fires.

I look at more of my father's handwriting. So precise and familiar. Each letter is neatly formed. Efficient.

Ma'Teo has returned from the Giant Court. He seems unwell, and I have sent the healers to his room. The information he brings is invaluable, and I doubt that even he knows what it is. The Elvish Artifact is key in all of this, I am sure of it.

Once I find it, I will be one step closer to saving the continent from the darkness that threatens to fall on us all. No more will we be left waiting for the ax to fall, cutting off the beast's bindings and setting it free from its ancient prison. We will be free from this monster. If what the...

I shut my eyes, blocking out the following words. It stabs at something inside of me to see the way he feigns care for either me or his people. He sent me to lie with an evil woman so that I could break into her vault, steal her personal correspondence, and then kill her.

I had been so convinced that my father asking me to go to Zlosa and seduce the Giant Queen was for the good of my people. Back then, I was so sure that I could serve the troll court well, return home, and then move forward. I was taking too long to recognize a mate. What was it to seduce someone if it meant saving my whole world?

For so long, I kept it far from my mind, thinking I would

understand when I was king. Tirin's face appears in the hazy dark behind my eyelids. He was barely old enough to be a hunter when Rholker came, demanding I kill my own people or risk a war.

See? my father hisses. *You are just like me.*

I press my lips in a line and whisper aloud. "No, I am not. He offered himself up for something he believed in. You spent years, decades, fashioning me as your blade. You whetted me against cruel orders. I chose none of this—I could never ask someone I loved to make the same choices, *pater.*"

My father's voice doesn't respond. How could it? He's a figment of my imagination. I do not even know if a shred of his soul continues on in Vidalena.

When I was forced out of Iravida, my mother wasn't even dead—his brain was just addled with power. With a desire for something.

A part of me wishes that I had told my mother. She died before she knew what I had done.

What was done *to* me.

A vision of white skin, kept out of the sun to ensure an unblemished complexion, swooping scars around yellow eyes, and intimately bare feet forces its way to the forefront of my thoughts. Lijasa's pleasant face is framed by carefully arranged red hair and a golden crown of Enduar gems sits atop her head. She sits on her bed, smiling and watching me undress.

I slam the scroll down, and drag a hand over my face. My eyelids are heavy, and a yawn breaks through my defenses. Something deep inside of me nags at me to sleep, but my father's voice returns and grows in volume.

Weak.

Weak!

WEAK!

"Gods on their stoney thrones," I growl and pick up another

scroll. The words of Ta'Reht dance before my eyes as I search for solace in the divine. Somewhere. Anywhere—for it is in times of calamity that gods take on their truest uses. Divine beings could purify the righteous indignation of their people with terrible power, or to avenge the honor of their own names. Sometimes, they might graciously seal the sorrows of their followers with a thousand salty tears and simply provided hope.

We need some fucking hope right about now.

As my eyes scrutinize each word with careful detail, my father's voice goes quiet and Lijasa's slow smile fades. One line in particular directed at the humans sticks out to me.

Which god or goddess begets a race and leaves them without power?

Which god, indeed, I think, continuing my perusal of the scroll. I had nearly forgotten about the swamp ogres, as it had been so long since once had been mentioned.

The story of Nicnevin and Endu feels important, deep in my soul. Awareness pricks at the back of my neck as the words blur together, and understanding takes the forefront. The weaver of my inner consciousness is nearing the satisfying zenith of a thought.

The library clock's song strikes a gentle tune, marking four in the morning. It shocks my thoughts back to the elves.

I realize that Liana was already serving under my father when he decided to steal this *artifact*.

My mind lights up, and I stand, delighted to finally have made it somewhere, anywhere. Grabbing my father's scroll, I push out of my chair, half mad with exhaustion and not caring when the chair crashes to the ground.

When I find Liana and the other council members in the throne room, I lean against the doorframe.

"Why the hell aren't you asleep?" barks Liana when she sees me.

I feel Ulla, Fira, Salo, Vann, and Svanna's eyes snap onto me, but I only look at the bejeweled elder.

"What was the Elvish Artifact?" I demand.

Recognition flickers over her face, then her mouth falls open, and her eyes grow wide.

CHAPTER 2
OCEAN JASPER
TEO

"What do you mean?" Liana asks.

My gaze is discerning as I look at her from across the room and study her features. Slowly, I hold up the scroll and stalk closer. She tracks the movement, confusion clouding her clear gaze until the moment where Teo'Likh's name is on clear display for all to see.

"Some light reading, I see," she says with a frown.

I glimpse Vann's deep glower as I move in front of Liana so she can see the words. The others cram closer, namely Ulla and Svanna, who read the text with silent, moving lips.

"Yes," I say firmly. "I was told that we betrayed them by not giving sufficient warning about the potential dangers of using the volcano. That we went to war to expand our borders and put an end to our land war with the giants for good." My skull rattles with all the things I thought I knew, but I continue, "Except, this personal record shows a much different story. He speaks of darkness and mentions the wise women's involvement."

Liana nods thoughtfully. "If it mentions the wise women, he'd be mentioning Mother Urira."

I take a deep breath, still not quite understanding how Liana connects into all of the pieces. Searching for tactful words is an impossible task in the face of my bone-deep tiredness. "Yes. So, what did you do?"

Liana shakes her head. "Mother Urira was my mentor, but that did not mean me or the others were her protégés. She was nearly three hundred years older than me, and she was a marvelous teacher, but she worked for the king. As I work for you. That affords a level of privacy and decorum, especially when entrenched in the old ways."

Her words carry the metallic clarity of truth, so I take another fortifying breath to help me steady my thoughts. The others continue to look on, silent as I plunder past whatever they'd been discussing.

"But surely you knew something," I insist. "When I mentioned the Elven Artifact, I saw the recognition in your gaze. The elves hating us for not disclosing the severity of the power always made sense to me—they died in droves during the eruption like anyone else—but that was only part of the story."

Liana shakes her head. "And I'm telling you—Urira was the one who knew about that. It was something whispered among us while we painted and shaped the star cards."

I grit my teeth, and the pulsing in my head intensifies. "*Tell me what you know.*"

She worries her lower lip. "The elves have a much different way of viewing magical artifacts. We don't need to exhaust power. There always is enough. Our gods taught us that nothing is lost, merely shifted. And with time, it shifts back, like the cycles of the stone and the earth beneath our feet.

"While we view everything as imbued with this power, they have a... penchant for finding, harvesting, and enchanting

25

objects. Trees are alive in a way stone is not. Elves are selfish and can only be convinced to share power through hierarchy of power. All that power came from one place—their godly artifact. That artifact was split in three, their holiest number, but the magic was not split evenly."

"How so?" Svanna asks, listening just as intently as me.

"In the Elvish tradition, women mean little. But... between the three orbs, one is given to the king, the other to his firstborn son, and the final is bestowed upon his firstborn daughter." Liana's face turns downward.

Svanna's eyes narrow, and gazes thoughtfully at the scroll. "I take it the weakest part was for the girl."

"Precisely. Merely a few drops of power, in comparison to the whole goblet-full of power given to the heir. The king, of course, would have power that surpassed them at all."

As I watch the wise woman's expression, it darts back and forth, as if she were trying to find something long lost. Her eyes study the stones beneath our feet, flitting between each crack and juncture.

At last, Liana speaks again. "I remember that your father needed more power to control the volcano. Your Ma' family line has always been strong, but he found the abundant blessings poured out from his Fuegorra and the main Ardorflame Temple insufficient. Urira herself spoke less than a handful of times about something called the *Cumhacht na Cruinne*.

"It translates roughly to... the power of the universe. It was a gift from Doros at the dawn of the elves. But I didn't know your father ever went for it. I recall... the undertaking to remove it forcefully from the elven capital would have accrued exorbitant casualties."

The words I've studied pass before my eyes quickly, in flashing motions. Liana's attempts to deflect do little to squash the feeling deep in my gut—the one that tells me I just *know*. My father had nine personal battalions dedicated to guarding his riches. Nine thousand soldiers. I'd bet they were all guarding that artifact.

I push past everyone and slump into the throne, allowing myself to bend slightly under the weight of exhaustion.

My father stole one of the oldest artifacts from the elves.

A sour bile rises in my throat. It is hard to pinpoint the moment when Father's madness began. The ramblings I read sounded little more than the musings of an old fool playing the part of a savior.

The true price of leadership is the willingness to place the needs of the many above the needs of the few, his voice whispers to justify his bloody crusade.

Memories of the elves' murderous rage from hours ago return. His choices are being paid for in the safety of my mate. My woman, who should be nestled in my arms as her heart beats in time with my own. Perhaps...

"Teo—" Ulla starts.

I interrupt her with, "How is Lothar?"

The healer, Ulla, shakes her head. "He is sleeping. Iryth is tending to the worst of his wounds."

My ears almost prick up at that as I look at Svanna, Iryth's mate. They have a small baby together. "And Sama?"

Svanna's lips quirk up at the corner, clearly grateful for something lighter to speak of. "I'm sure she left him with Lyria. She's one house down from us and loves a cuddle."

I exhale, still not feeling much better. "If Lothar isn't available, send for Turalyon. We need to contact the elves." Turalyon was sent with Lothar on the mission to visit the elves. Hopefully he will be able to tell us something useful.

Salo speaks up this time. "My King, I don't think that's a good idea."

I hold up my hand. "Peace, Salo."

The words cast a bit of frosty dissonance in the air.

"I would be called Ra'Salore," he says. Salo had always been a quiet, somewhat dissenting member of the personal advisors, but he is a talented stone bender and has served his people well. His brother was the one who sacrificed himself to the giants for peace, and I can see he will never fully forgive me for it.

Weary, I drag my gaze to his. "That is how you were *once* called. We changed our customs."

He straightens his back. "Unlike some, I am proud of my family name—the one my brother Tirin also carried before his death. I wish to carry it on."

Exhaustion makes my flesh sag against bone. I don't have time to argue.

"Very well, Ra'Salore. I merely want to know what Turalyon found out during his time at court. I don't intend to go racing off to the men who just orchestrated the abduction of my mate," I say wryly.

He nods once. It's a sharp, jagged movement, and with his old name restored, he almost looks different. Hardened.

Fira, who has been quiet to this point, excuses herself to find Turalyon. The silence weighs in the room.

My body wilts into the stone throne, when Liana clears her throat. "If you refuse to sleep, will you at least let me help?"

My head barely moves, which is the best agreement I can give at this moment.

"Ulla," she urges softly. The two of them approach the throne and rest their hands on my head. I hardly protest when they start to sing in tandem. Energy pours out of the crystals around the room and flows into my very soul. The vibrations wake me up, and my mind feels more alert—it seeks out the bond once again, stroking its shimmery brilliance.

Then they move back, and I adjust my position on the throne.

"My King, I ask again, you wish to court the elves once more? Perhaps this time they won't just kill a few of us—they'll finish the job properly," Ra'Salore says.

I shake my head. "We will wait for Turalyon, and then we will make a plan to seek out more soldiers. Yes, *perhaps even from the elves.* While I understand your concern, we must go for my mate. The giant court has been restored to its full glory. If we don't seek out help from someone, we would still risk dying out for good."

I open my eyes again, the blurriness gone, now replaced with the downturned concern from those before me.

It's strange to be familiar enough with a group of people to hear their words through the slightest curve of their mouths, both up or down, or the wrinkles around their brows and eyes.

Vann stares at me, eyes full of bitter, almost reluctant, understanding. His vows of allegiance are apparent in his confident, straight-up posture. He is willing to follow, to trust.

Ulla's eyes are full of thinly veiled concern as she frowns and bounces her bright blue irises from my disheveled hair to the patch of skin under each of my eyes, and the spectacles that rest on the crook of my nose.

Ra'Salore watches me with distaste. Loudly voiced disagreement is apparent in every sharp angle of his nose, chin, and ears.

Liana is thoughtful as she meets my eyes, unflinching. Wise. Slightly horrified as she considers what her mentor might have done to the elves.

Svanna... Svanna is unwaveringly steady. Eager to watch, to correct where she sees fit. That is why it is strange to me she has not yelled at me for my lack of sleep, too.

Another part of me knows that she understands. Her love for Iryth is unmatched. I can almost hear her mind churning, knowing without a doubt that she would also take risks if her family was separated the same way mine had been.

Thank the gods for each of them.

The silence is anything but uncomfortable when Turalyon's footsteps return to join us. The young Enduar bows before the throne, and I extend my arm, gesturing for him to approach.

"My King," Turalyon says again, this time bowing further.

"Thank you for coming, Turalyon. I realize that there hasn't been much time to do a full debriefing after your return from the elves..."

I trail off. When he arrived mere days ago, with the elf King Arion, we spoke of nothing more than the festival. Of my wedding.

Pain slashes across my body. I keep it locked away under the need to know. To learn more about what we are up against.

Turalyon clears his throat. "Yes. There was much to report, and Lord Lothar was hoping to organize everything into a presentation for the whole council." He scans those around me, then straightens his back. "I assure you, I will be able to answer any questions you might have had for him while he is healing."

I nod once, pleased with the man's honor. "How would you classify the health of the elvish court?"

"Excellent. Their capital is entirely rebuilt, and there appears to be enough citizens to maintain the general population. It is a beautiful place, as far as forest cities go. A pleasing waterfall is located in the center of the—"

I frown. "They are doing well? Then why stir up a war between us?"

Turalyon pauses. "Your Majesty, I don't know. Half a dozen archers escorted us from the gate to the palace, but we were never verbally threatened. After our initial meeting, King Arion showed us their woodworkers, gave us gifts of cloth, and let us listen to their musical instruments. The trees, it seems, do sing back as our stones do. We dined on their breads and leafy foods."

The only time I'd ever gone to Shvathemar was when I was still a child. The memories are fuzzy, and mostly incomplete.

"What were their military forces like?"

Turalyon's eyebrows draw together. "There are more archers than I could've anticipated. Very few women though, it seems they restrict them to their homes." At this, Turalyon frowns. "Come to think of it, there were whispers about a group of women living in the woods."

I sit up. Just what I was hoping for. Those who place their misogynistic ideals over the happiness of all their citizens deserve a gods-damned female-led rebellion.

"What? Where?"

He shrugs. "I'm sure Lothar would know more about it. His hearing is better than mine."

"Lothar is two inches from death right now. I suggest you think harder," Svanna pipes up. Her sharp words pierce, but I can't fault her.

Turalyon frowns and thinks for a moment. The silence is electric. "I think there had been skirmishes or something of the sort. They are in the northern forest, closer to the border between the giants and the elves."

"Excellent. Then we will go there." I nod once, pleased to have a lead.

Those around me agree, and Vann starts for the door just as Turalyon shakes his head.

"No, we shouldn't try to go there. They don't use archers and diplomacy; they are assassins skulking through hidden shadows. They'll kill us on sight, and we might not even see them coming."

I raise an eyebrow. "They'd kill us, or the elves?"

Turalyon sputters. "The elves said—"

"Exactly. They spoke their misguided words into existence

without anything to support it. An enemy of our enemy can only be our friend—we just need to introduce ourselves."

Ulla steps forward. "Not until you sleep."

Turalyon looks helpless, but I am not about to let a good idea go to waste. Surely, we can handle something as perilous as this without coming home in a box. Turalyon is a little younger than Velen, the singer, but he remembers the old days.

Turalyon has voiced his hope for a family like the rest of the hunters. If he wants it so badly, he should understand these are the risks and sacrifices we take to forge a better future.

I wave Ulla off. "I feel much better now. In fact, Ulla, why don't you come with us?" My gaze filters around the room. "Ra'Salore, the stone bender, Ulla the healer, and Turalyon the budding diplomat. We'll make an excellent team."

Ulla shakes her head. "You need more hunters."

I raise my hands. "So, I'll bring Niht, too!"

Vann steps forward, mouth open, but he's interrupted by the wise woman.

"Ma'Teo." Liana's prickly tone makes me turn around, slowly. I look at her, lips pursed and arms crossed. "You will sleep this time. No reading." She snatches the scroll out from under my arm. "I will check."

Vann lopes over to my side. "I'll take him."

I let out another breath and submit to my fate. As we walk, the weight from before returns. No sooner than we pass the familiar passageway that leads to the scrying grotto and the bathing pools than Vann speaks again.

"I doubt you would appreciate my lullabies, brother, so I suggest you seek slumber as quickly as possible."

I let out the first semblance of a laugh in the last six hours. "I don't think I've ever heard a musical note leave your lips."

He smiles. "Ahh, but the sound of steel leaving my belt is sweet enough for me to resist the art of crystal singing."

I, somehow, smile again. "What if your mate appreciates a kind song to ease her into sleep?"

The easiness is blotted out by a large, looming emotion.

"You forget I will have no mate," he growls.

I look back at him, somehow also angry. "I think you will, and I grow tired of pretending you don't already have her. I don't understand the intricacy of why a Fuegorra would or wouldn't sing, but I feel—"

"My crystal will never sing."

I stop just before my room. "Vann, the humans are here to stay, and we are dying. If it's not Arlet, I am sure it will be someone else. Though, there is something in the air between you two. Perhaps I could ask Liana to look at you and find out what is amiss."

My friend's face is as cold as ice. "I will speak to her if I wish."

The guarded, roughness of his face troubles me. "Has something happened to you?" I ask.

The flicker on his face comes seconds before the denial, but it is too late. I've already seen his truth.

There is a small nudge in my gut, pushing me towards solving whatever this is. But, another part of me knows that I can only solve one problem at a time.

"You won't go with us tomorrow," I say. "There is no one I'd rather trust this city to than you."

"I'm not so wise or level-headed as you," he says.

I smile sadly. "You have been around the throne just as long as I have. You can do this."

Vann opens his mouth to resist again, but I shake my head. He knows I'm right. Besides, a part of me isn't settled with his love life. If there is some problem preventing him and Arlet from being together, I will be able to solve it when I get back.

"Sleep well, brother," Vann says, reaching out and putting a hand on my shoulder. "Would it help you if I stayed nearby?"

Even upset, he offers to be a friend. Without thinking, I pull him into an embrace.

"Thank you, but I am all right," I say as he eases himself out of my grip.

When he turns to leave, I feel like I can finally sleep.

I just pray the gods will keep Estela until I return.

CHAPTER 3
UVITE
ESTELA

T*eo?*

My mind can't help but continue to search for my mate despite knowing he will not hear. It feels like a small eternity, but I know it has only been a day or two.

Uno, dos, tres...

I cut off abruptly. Counting doesn't help me. Not anymore.

There is a sensation in my gut that connects to the glittery magic from my Fuegorra. That bond shows me that he is alive and well. Surely, he must be planning to come for me, but I am not stupid. I know how many Enduares there are—not enough to launch an attack—even if he might wish it.

He has already done enough.

The last day has given me time to think about my time under the mountain. In my head, I relive the cruel words spewed from my mouth and the deaths I witnessed.

First, Tirin, the young hunter who believed in matehood and sacrificed himself so humans could continue living under the mountain.

Then... Dyrn, the noble hunter protecting his people from

the cold ones who attacked me. I still remember watching him on the table, bleeding out. I called for someone to grab herbs, only to find that I had used up the precious ingredients for a poison meant to kill my mate.

I am the link between the misfortune that's fallen upon the Enduares of late. I was selfish when I tried to escape. Even though I didn't want to hurt innocent people... I'm learning that intent doesn't equal culpability.

Even thinking about what the giants could've done to get me here makes my heart race. I was unconscious, but I am sure they damaged Enduvida. Perhaps they killed some of the Enduares.

Their deaths wouldn't have happened if I hadn't walked into their lives.

The responsibility to escape should fall on my shoulders—I must pay them all back for everything I took for granted.

My head tilts back against the bars in my cage.

There are no windows. No light seeps through the door. Not a single soul had crossed the threshold into the small cottage since my last conversation with Rholker, and the torch has long since burned to ashes.

I'm as hungry as the day I was rescued by the Enduares. Time stretches on, muted in this pitch-black cage as I discard plan after plan. Searching, grasping, for any thread of inspiration while so utterly, chest-crackingly *alone*.

Sadness pricks against my skin with the same intensity as getting a branch of fresh pine needles whipped repeatedly across my bare back. There's no voice in my mind, no palpable presence to scoop me up and hold me until the emotion passes.

There are other sounds, though. Slave foremen and giant warriors shouting, the laughter of my people, the gentle lilt of the human tongue, and the occasional scream. They all filter through the walls like a nightmarish ballad.

The cottage must be somewhere near the lumber yards—but the exact location is harder to discern.

I have tried to call to them by kicking until my bare feet became bruised, scratching until hot blood streamed down my painfully cold hands, and screaming until it felt like I swallowed a pile of stone shards, but it made no difference.

At least I have a few reminders of home. The Fuegorra heals my broken skin, and I rub my ring with one hand and slide the necklace from its hiding place in my pocket with the other.

Amor[1], the ring says. A message of love from *my* love.

And the necklace says...?

I don't know.

Without light, I cannot inspect the stones well enough to know their names, but I can recognize a few energies—amethyst, sapphire, emerald, ruby, obsidian, and moonstone. The first letter of each word appears in my mind, and I draw them on the dark, dusty ground while I hum single notes just to hear them bounce off the gems and warm my insides.

Depending on where I hold the necklace, it feels different. But mostly, it feels like home—*my* home.

I was just starting to learn the ways of peace. Of planting seeds and laboring for their growth, of healing, of caring for others, of being loved in a manner previously unknown to my selfish, armored heart.

Now I have been yanked out of the quiet, welcoming place and put back in the hell that is Zlosa, with Rholker threatening me to take my agency, body, and burn everything I love. It fucking hurts.

And Mikal... Mikal is somewhere here, in this same city. Does he know that I've come?

Tears burn my eyes as I listen to the rhythmic chopping of wood. I cry for all the humans who have withered in this damned place, enslaved from birth and expected to chop, to serve, and to be grateful enough for their scraps to never fight back.

And if the giants can't have their gratitude, they will gladly take their fear. I think of the merciless deaths—whipped to shreds, torn apart by spreaders, or simply rammed through with spears.

More threads of dread weave together and wrap around my now-chilled heart. The princes only left Mikal alone because of their father, King Erdaraj, and the decree that Mikal should remain alive and I should remain untouched. Now he only lives because of Rholker's obsession with possessing me.

Luckily, when Rholker came into my cage after I awoke, my Fuegorra provided a new protection for me. How long that will last, I cannot say.

Rholker has the power to change his mind quickly.

He controls my food, my future, and my light.

This room is dark like I thought the Enduar Mountains would be—cold, and without even a sliver of heat to warm my cage. No mushrooms light the crags of the space, nor does the Ardorflame guide the way back out of the abyss in my mind.

I sit on the ground, atop smelly furs and straw, and think of things I could say, ways to slip through the bars, or, better yet, manipulate them. If only I were a metal bender, or, better yet, had worked with the smiths instead of Ulla.

The floor is uneven and catches along the calluses on my hands. A new idea blooms. My magic is too unpredictable, like a lyre string stretching and snapping when I'm in danger. But if I could make a weapon, I could kill him and run.

No guards come with him to my cell. It would be the perfect plan.

Tearing at the ground, I peel a long splinter from the boards. I do my best to sharpen it against the metal bars in the dark.

When the door cracks open again, I leap back and hide the

makeshift tool behind my back as I see the large shadow in the doorframe. My heart stutters in rage and grief to see Rholker. His long hair is tied up atop his head, and a new crown is resting on his brow.

The traitorous king takes one purposeful step into the room and stops to strike a match. A sharp hiss heralds the warm yellow flame between his stout fingers. His cruel eyes and powerful form are lit up as he guides the small pulses of light into a glass lamp.

The oil catches the spark and blazes to life. My gaze dips for a second to look at the letters I've left on the ground.

A S E R O M.

Nothing of use, but I am missing thirty-four letters. I scrape my barefoot across the Enduar markings so he won't see.

My eyes return to Rholker, only to find a trail of six women behind him. They are hidden under dark cloaks with long, flowing sleeves that cover their hands and long hems with short trains that obscure their feet.

Rholker smirks. "Estela," he says, drawing out the word as if he were savoring the syllables the same way he'd like to savor my flesh. The oil lamp is held up closer to his face, and I see his ugly, scarred smile stretch upward. A few of the puckered lines are new—still red. I wonder where he got them.

"Thank our guests for traveling all night to see you."

I press my lips together in defiance. Then I brace myself to accept whatever punishment he has planned for me today with these women.

Rholker takes another step forward and moves to light a fire as the six women line the space beside him.

"This is the daughter of Aitana?" one woman asks. Her accent is deep and guttural, not at all like the soft notes that come from my human tongue. *And she knows my mother's name.*

Rholker grunts his approval.

39

One of the women makes a sound so inhuman that I find myself inching toward the back of my cage. Presumably, the same woman holds up her arm, bringing the sizable billowing sleeve with her, and a long, pointed fingernail peeks out from beneath the black-stitched hem. My mouth falls open when something slithers to the point of her digit.

A snake.

Its lithe, forked tongue darts out.

"If Mistress Dahlia ssspeaks, you will ressspond," it hisses. The voice echoes in my mind, rattling around at the base of my skull and making my shoulders inch upward. I file the name away.

Dahlia.

Rholker raises his chin, puffing out his chest as he turns to the women. My grip on the splinter tightens.

"You are in my court now, and I have something you want. Do not think that since I have given you honors my father with-held that I am one of your thralls," he spits at them.

One of the women makes a disgusted sound, but the one called Dahlia cocks her hooded head to the side as her companion speaks.

"Do not forget that we are not the sole benefactors of this deal. We came to provide a service for you—"

Dahlia cuts her follower off. "Very well, Young Rholker. I would like to begin."

Rholker frowns but doesn't offer any retort; he merely gestures toward my cage.

I press myself back further as Dahlia reaches the bars. The others fill the space behind her, making my only view their dark cloaks and absent faces.

My breath is ragged as it escapes my chest.

It surprises me when Rholker is the next one to speak.

"Give them your hand." His command rumbles through my

being—pure dissonance—and I am frozen in place. It strikes something so deep in my soul that I would be foolish to ignore it.

Apparently I am that foolish because I say, "No."

A hissing sound comes from the shadows in front of me. I move until my back is flush against the cold bars.

"Do you think you can hide from us, little one?" Dahlia says. Her voice is heavy and ancient and *frozen*, like the chunks of ice scattered along the way to the Enduar mountains.

I keep my mouth shut, but it doesn't stop the thud on the ground or scales scraping against wood. My whole body starts to tremble as I look down at the viper in my path. Its muscular body coils to the left and right before reaching my foot.

Biting down on my lip hard enough to draw blood, I grasp onto the iron bar with one hand and pull myself up, all while wielding my weapon. The sudden movement agitates the snake, causing it to bare its fangs seconds before it lunges. I strike at it and miss. The second its teeth connect with my bare foot, a chill spreads. The ice crawls through my insides, icing over my muscles, stomach, lungs... heart.

"*Stop. Fucking. Touching. ME!*" I rage.

A blazing warmth spreads across my body as the Fuegorra fights against the darkness. The light grows bright enough to burn my eyes, and I squeeze them shut. There is a garbled sound from Rholker, and I expect the glow to scare away the damned serpent, but instead, the heat freezes over.

Black edges my vision, and I fall to the ground.

THE SENSATION OF TEO'S FINGERS TRAILING DOWN MY SCARRED BACK brings me back to my senses with a stinging, disorienting stab through my ribs. Even though the memory is sweet, something in it has been twisted—I shouldn't be here right now.

I was... in Zlosa. With Rholker. The rest of the specific details fizzle out and lay in razor-sharp shards at my feet.

There is something dark in the shadows of the cave that didn't exist before. Something that lurks behind the glow-glitter dusted stones and between the luminflor and lumicaps. It doesn't speak or try to interfere—it watches. Studying every detail of my nude form, and memorizing the trail of my mate's finger.

Suspended between time and thought, I am unable to resist the shudder of his rough fingers and gentle touch. The gasp that escapes my mouth is as loud as thunder. I see the scene from all angles, finally brave enough to tip my head over my shoulder as he takes in the scars representing my shame. It hurts to see the rage in his eyes. But... it melts away to sadness. Then resolution.

My Teo. Always analytical, so often disciplined. This memory is too private, so I try to tear it from before my eyes and lock it in some gilded box, never to be touched again.

I can't.

He takes my hand again, squeezing and leading me into the pool. What comes next is burned into my mind with excruciating detail, like the stone artwork etched all across Enduvida. This should belong to me and him alone, but the lurking presence persists. I try to black out my mind to shield Teo from anyone seeing us in the water. Small, brilliantly colored particles of blue and green dance around us as we move.

This memory was pure heat and bliss, but I thrash against the intrusion my lover isn't aware of. Far too late, I think of the windows in my mind that I used to keep Teo from reading my thoughts.

Teo's teeth graze against my neck, and I grasp at the corners of those windows. My fingers slip as I fight for purchase. The memory continues in horrifying detail, prying apart the most sacred moments of my life.

I slam my fist against the shudders, closing them for good...
And wake up gasping for breath on the cold hard ground. The dryness in my throat causes the gasp to turn into a sputtering cough. Gods, it feels like I've swallowed stone shards and hacked them back up.

Clutching at my neck, my eyes focus on the tall, metal bars caging me in like a wicked, dark hand holding my body in place —as if I were no more than an insect. Near my head, a small, forked tongue flicks out and hisses. Every muscle in my body coils tight and then springs away from that spot.

I look up to see the six hooded women watching with hidden eyes while Rholker stands behind them. His face is hard, but a glimmer of concern flickers with a twitch of his lips.

My heart continues to race—did he see all of that? He'll kill me. He'll kill Teo—

"Well?" he asks, clearly annoyed and clueless.

A splash of relief covers my innards.

"We found what you sought," one of the women says. "She fucked the troll in a hot spring."

The second of relief is dashed to pieces. My body tenses, every nerve on edge as Rholker's face contorts with a mixture of confusion and fury.

Those yellow eyes trail to the side of my neck, now clearly visible. My hand flies to cover the scabbed-over bite marks I know that I'd find there.

"Estela," he starts, his voice rumbling through the tension in the room. "What have you done?"

His tall, powerful body reaches for one of the room's chairs, picks it up, and throws it against the wall. I flinch as it splinters into pieces. My eyes track them as they fall to the ground, and I am painfully aware of how he wishes that chair was my body. Under his calm, obsessed exterior lies a predator.

Mikal. I need to find Mikal.

"Tell me how to get the stone out of her chest so I can touch her again," he growls, reiterating the lie I told him when I first arrived.

He steps close to my cell, and I crawl toward him, body aching. I grab my sharpened piece of wood again.

The women pause before they answer, and I find myself holding my breath as I stare at Rholker's large ass. He's too tall to stab in the heart, but a bleeding ass is still painful.

"We require more time to sift through her thoughts," they say in almost perfect unison.

Blinking back hot tears, I stab through the bars. The sharpened wood punctures his left thigh.

He makes a strangled noise.

"What the hell?" My tormenter whips around. He looks at me like I have stabbed him in the gut and forcefully torn out each of his organs, not merely given him a flesh wound. If only he knew how much I would've enjoyed the former.

"You are a memory slicer," he says darkly, no longer addressing me but still holding my gaze as he pulls out the stick and throws it across the room. "Slice apart that memory for good. Leave it until it is nothing more than threadbare ribbons in her mind. I never want her to think of it and find pleasure again."

Each word is slow and perfectly articulated.

The women communicate with only the slightest shift of their faces, hidden in their deep hoods. The snake, curled almost gracefully around one of the bars, slithers to its mistress's outstretched hand.

Pierced with a new level of fear, I fight the tears welling up, and I push into the grip of cold metal.

I close my eyes and try to focus on the memory, memorizing each detail so that it feels like it's carved into my very being.

They won't touch it. They can't. It would be like trying to remove the scent of humidity from a room after a thunderstorm, nearly impossible to erase. The memory is a tangled web of emotions, desires, and sensations, all woven together in a tapestry of love. Mine and Teo's tapestry. Our matehood.

The memory isn't just a snapshot in time, but an experience that is alive, constantly shifting, and forever imprinted in my consciousness. How could they ever steal that?

But then, as we reach the moment where his fingers touched my back, something new slides into the image. The dark eyes, watching, analyzing... insidiously probing.

My eyes fly open once more, and I find the women watching me. The leader, Dahlia, turns to Rholker.

"We will return this evening to finish. This time, you will not come, Giant King," she speaks for the first time. Her voice is as silky, dark, and cold as a snake's.

Rholker frowns, the twisting of his lips mostly visible in the near blackness. Then, the women leave.

The door shuts, with Rholker remaining. He sucks in a deep breath.

Slut.

Bitch.

Little Flea.

Whore.

All the titles that I've been called over the years pass through my consciousness, and I shove them all away.

"You shouldn't have let him touch you," Rholker says, his eyes dropping to the floor as if he could feel anything approximating sadness.

My whole body tenses, preparing for him to spew a cloud of vitriol. I turn my sights to the ring on my finger. *Mi amor.*[2]

"I touched him first," I say, my voice much stronger than it feels, and look up. I refuse to let this memory be anything other than the damned miracle it is.

He moves the torch to the back corner. It lights those ugly, yellow eyes seconds before his body tenses. Then he reaches down, picks up the other untouched chair at the table, and throws it against the bars. The metal rattles upon impact before splinters scatter across the ground.

"Now where will you sit as you watch them torment me?" I say sardonically.

He snarls.

Closing my eyes again, I focus on the cage, feeling the icy cold from the metal seep through my skin and enter my bloodstream, grounding me. Then I return to the image of Teo's fingers trailing down my scarred back, the sensation of the water surrounding us, and the memory of his lips on my neck.

"Estela," Rholker shouts, trying to pry my attention away.

My mind feels like it's being pulled in different directions, with the perfect images of our love-making clashing against the hatred and fury in Rholker's eyes.

He can't steal this from me.

Another crash against the cage has the bars shaking, zinging in my teeth.

"Why did you let him fucking touch you? You are mine. You never understand, you—"

Something sharp scrapes across my face, and my eyes fly open at the exact moment the Fuegorra in my chest glows to life. The brightness from before returns, and this time, I realize that it is no mere glimmer, but a blaze that lights up the entire room. Brighter than the fire in the corner.

Rholker slinks back at the light, as if he weren't responsible for the smashed wood littering the floor.

I stand, seething and indignant. The Fuegorra makes me feel like I am a million times more powerful than I am.

"That's right. Cower. You are a weak, pathetic man. I told you that you would regret bringing me here," I say, each slicing insult shooting off my tongue with expert precision.

Gone is the fearful woman from before. I can do this. I can go back to my love unbroken.

His face sags, almost as if he were about to cry.

"No, you little slut. You think you can threaten me? You couldn't even save your brother."

My fists tighten, as a malevolent smile spreads over his face.

"We whipped him when he came back. He was so sick he couldn't move for months. Every time he was on the brink of death, we would call the healer and bring him back. All for *you*."

A pit forms in my stomach, and this itchy need to see Mikal returns with a vengeance. It feels like I could peel the flesh from my bones.

Rholker watches me, waiting for the moment when my resolve breaks. "When I first felt that power of yours, I thought you'd been turned into a witch. The truth is much worse, and it is you who will regret everything you've done in my absence. Slaves do not find new masters." His face twists and morphs into something monstrous. "In the name of Khuohr, I'm going to kill everything you love. Slowly. Finger by finger. Limb by limb."

He continues his rampage of words. "When the world is lying at embers at your feet—when the body of your troll is hung up in the streets to rot and the Enduar children's bodies are scattered in pieces across their enormous tomb of a mountain—then I will bring Mikal to you so you can either watch his final breath or succumb. You will be so steeped in contrition that you will fall at my knees and beg me to take you."

My heart hollows out with each bloody, sadistic promise. The poison drips off his tongue like acid and burns holes in my resolve. *Mierda*[3].

"When that gem is out of your chest, it will only be the beginning of your remorse, *my little love.*"

A part of me recoils at his new name. My love doesn't belong to him. But a much larger part of me crumbles with each word, and he watches it all.

"The last time we saw each other, you were to be married. Did you kill her too?" I ask, my voice much quieter now.

Smiling like the ugly thief he is, he says, "We didn't marry, but I have my uses for her."

While I have never felt much sympathy for a giant, I fear for her. His words shatter my heart into countless pieces. He relishes in my pain, believing that he can break me.

He smiles, turns on his heel, and walks from the room.

When I shift to lie down, I find a small cloth with something, round and slightly pliant. The second I pick it up, the smell of bread fills my nose, and hunger takes over my thoughts. Pressing it between my hands, the smell grows stronger, followed by a delightful crackle.

Logically, I assume that the women brought it for me. When I don't smell the sourness of poison, I tear off bits and pieces and stuff them into my mouth. The loaf isn't large, but my stomach hurts when I'm done.

With a bit of food in me, the ache in my stomach subsides. Unfortunately for me, I'm stuck in a dizzy headache. Fragments of memories swirl, and I close my eyes, helpless but to watch them pass.

One in particular is clearer than the rest.

"A human queen will bring the light of hope
To those in the shadows, forgotten and alone
The strength and courage of a noble soul
Will be the catalyst for a new tomorrow"

I recognize it, mainly from the voice that speaks the words. Liana. Even thinking her name brings me more peace and eases the dizzying throb behind my eye sockets. She spent so many days alongside me, teaching me how to use my magic and how to be something more than I was. Her stern expressions and gentle hands helped me change.

Dissecting the bits of her poetic song, I consider each line. Certain words stick out to me: hope, catalyst, shadows, alone. I realize... that Zlosian slaves live in the shadows, mostly alone. We don't congregate as friends. We don't hold onto ceremonies or traditions.

I just came from a place that was a dream compared to life here. I hate Zlosa, but so does everyone else. Mikal shouldn't be here, and neither should the other slaves. If Rholker wants me so badly, I'll stay. I'll find Mikal, make friends, and I'll take a few back with me.

I have the opportunity to bring hope. Teo is so good at inspiring such an emotion. I could act like a queen and be a good shining light in the darkness. The stones have already sung it.

I can do this. I just have to be strong.

CHAPTER 4
HENMILITE
TEO

I reach out my hand across the bed, feeling for the smooth, furless form occupying the other side of the mattress. Supple skin rewards my search almost instantly, and the lazy, contented hum of the crystal in my chest turns to an insistent melody.

My thumb runs over one of the jagged, bumpy lines left from an old scar and, for a minute, it is hard to let the past be the past. I remind myself that the harsh tokens the giants left her with couldn't be solved at the moment, and I comfort myself with the surety that I would exact payment for each one.

Drawing my mate close to me, she makes a slight sound of protest, trying to curl further into the bed, and her long, disheveled hair sweeps off her neck, exposing two small bite marks.

Mating marks.

They don't glow like mine, but they awaken something primal. A shiver of pleasure rumbles through me. Brushing my fingers over the marks makes her stretch her long, delicate neck, as if hoping for more touch. I'm more than happy to oblige as my hand circles around her throat, and then she grabs my hand, bringing it down to her breast.

The pointed peaks are soft and electric against my palm, and she sighs.

Such brazen movements please me. But not so much as when her eyes flutter open and she looks up at me through her pretty, long lashes. Her smile breaks my heart.

Every harsh, defiant line of her face is smoothed away with an openness that terrifies her. Her want is painted in the mauve of her cheeks and the slight part of her lips.

"Buenos días,[1]" she murmurs, greeting me in her people's language.

My fingers edge toward the stone in her chest practically vibrating in my palm. Her eyes close again.

"How do you feel, my star?" I ask, and something pricks in my mind. It's a small awareness that this isn't real—that this isn't the morning after our wedding.

But it should be.

Estela is predictable, still too shy to care for herself in the way she desperately needs and deserves. With her eyes closed, she wraps her hand around my index and middle finger. The shifting of the blankets causes the heady scent of her arousal to perfume the air.

If I could drown in the smell of trees, sunlight, berries, and her, I would. I certainly will try.

An ache blooms in my cock, twisting and braiding together in anticipation as she brings our hands lower... lower. I reign in the need that insists I move faster as my fingertips brush the soft curve of her belly.

"Estela," I all but growl, pressing my forehead to hers. She sucks in a gentle breath. "You still have to tell me what you want. Though, I'm a curious creature. I'll settle if you only tell me how you feel."

Her eyes open again, and her brows draw together. "Hot. Every-where. It only gets worse with your small touches. I want—need—you to ease this tension inside."

I smile, pull back, and brush my lips against her forehead, but she *has other plans. Her hand pulls me into the sweet, wet heat between her legs. The soft hair pads my hand as she guides me exactly where she desires.*

The gentleness inside of me fades as my other hand moves to support me while I catch her mouth with my own. Her lips part for me without any coaxing. Desperate. Tasting. Tentative, but maddening.

The slickness on my fingers helps me glide to the small bump at the apex of her thighs. I remember it well from the night before.

So small, just like her, and utterly different from the body of an Enduar woman.

Just the motion makes her hips move, and I smile through our kisses, proud of the trust she shows in me with each shifting sway. I would spend the rest of our long lives ensuring that I make her feel safe enough to abandon every fear and show this unblushing creature as she works in time with me to find her climax.

I pull back when I feel the small shakes in her thighs.

"You're close," I say, and she nods as her beautiful chest rises and falls with heavy huffs.

"Don't stop," she pleads.

I shake my head fiercely as I lower my mouth to her nipple. She arches when a broad stroke from my tongue escalates her pleasure. As her fingers thread through my hair, I'm encouraged to continue. I could never tease her.

"You are such a marvelous woman. You take each movement so well," I murmur.

The taste of her on my tongue is beautiful, but not as beautiful as the desire I have for my tongue to take the place of my fingers. And then to fill her up to the point of ecstasy.

"Every part of you is so song-shatteringly perfect," I murmur as her hands grip my head tighter, and then my index finger slides further down, its noble duty replaced with my thumb as I insert one digit into her canal.

She moans. Loudly. The perfect harmony to our song.

From there, it takes a mere moment for the delicate muscles inside of her to take flight, fluttering around my finger as every part of her tightens and pulses.

"Teo," she begs. "Come inside me. Now."

I suck in a sharp breath but don't hesitate to remove my hand, despite her protesting whimper, and promise to make it right as I position myself at her entrance. Every part of me is ready to satiate my own ache in her giving body. Slowly, I savor the feel of pushing inside and...

A loud, insistent beat stops the moment. It isn't a gentle fade, more an abrupt shutting off of the moment as the lights turn on in my room.

I bolt upright, immediately sore and groggy. My head thrashes from side to side, and I feel the uncomfortable stickiness on my thighs. I lift my blankets to find my undershorts coated in seed.

Dragging a hand across my face, I let out a long exhale and grab the partially soiled blanket. When I reach the bathroom, I peel off everything and run it under the water before I start scrubbing the cloth and leather with soap.

Once it's hung up, I reach the tub in the corner and lower myself in. Soft ghosts of dreams brush across my skin, but I force myself to hurry.

I need to help the others pack, and I need to leave. Leaving means finding the elven assassins that Turalyon told me about. Finding them will permit me to gain their trust, find allies, and go to rescue Estela.

Once clean, I finish using the bathroom, tend to my pack of clothing, armor, and weapons, and head out and down the hall-way. Ra'Salore is waiting near the bioluminescent fountains at the tops of the steps.

I pause, take in his traveling gear, and he nods to me. I nod back.

"Good morning," I say as he bows and murmurs a quiet, "My King."

We walk in silence, across the moving walkways, past the residential area, and into the mines. As we descend the tunnels toward the *glacialmara* stables, I focus on breathing.

For the first time, I allow myself to consider what it would mean to be leaving Enduvida for more than a few hours. The last time I laid down and rose with the sun's cycles was when we were at war five decades ago.

As the crystals around us glint in time with the stunning metalwork of our ancestors, I get lost in the past, when the city housed a metal bending academy. It isn't until I hear the familiar tinkling sounds of *glacialmaras* that I'm drawn away from the memories. The crystal wraiths have been our mounts since the dawn of civilization for the Enduares. They are long, floating serpent-like creatures with razor sharp tails and eyeless faces.

Coan, the stablemaster, gazes at everyone with hard, steel-colored eyes.

"Ho, Your Majesty," he says brusquely as soon as he spots our approach. I force myself to be polite and smile as I wave my hand. He's one of the elders and has a particularly comforting, paternal air about him.

Liana, Ulla, Niht, and Turalyon are strapping on saddles made of *Ruh'Glumdlor* leather. A small chorus of everything ranging from, *Ma'Teo* to *My King* fills the air. I look each of them in the eye, knowing every potentially awful outcome of this trip. They could die.

I could die.

A pang of despair comes when I realize that Vann did not come to say goodbye. I didn't think he was still particularly upset about the discussion we had before I fell asleep, but perhaps I had not seen the signs of his irritation.

It feels uncomfortable to leave without saying anything.

The *glacialmaras* are restless as we load them up with packs of supplies. They buck when leather straps are wrapped around their middle sections, and their melodic chimes sound discordant. One comes up to me with its unseeing eyes, somehow studying my being.

"We call her Rahda," Coan says with a smile.

I raise an eyebrow in the face of the creature's scrutiny. I knew that *glacialmaras* were a female-only species. But the name...

"You named it after a rat?"

Coan nods. "She likes to steal food from the others. And she's much more mammal than crystal beast."

To prove the stable master's point, her head pushes into my hand, and Coan huffs a laugh. I run my palm over the smooth section of hard stone, gazing down at Rahda as I ask, "How is everyone?"

She nudges me again, and I swear a voice inside of me says, *have a little faith. Not everything will end in disaster.*

"Better, now that I see you have slept," Liana says.

I make a sound by sucking on my teeth. "Glad I could help. Will you be joining us, too?" *Please, no.*

She makes a face and places a hand on her back. "I'm too old for these small creatures. My back would be squealing before the sun begins to sink in the sky."

I fake a laugh to hide my relief. "Perhaps we should bring *drathorinna*," I half-heartedly tease, bringing up the mother of all *glacialmaras*. She hasn't been seen out in the open since the first Great War, and she is only ever ridden by Fuegorra readers, like Liana or Estela.

"Ha," Liana muses. "No, I must keep the crystal dragon safe for her new rider."

"Very well," I say, suddenly serious and turn to the side,

where Ulla hums a tune that displays her nerves. She checks that all of the packs weigh more or less the same before our small party departs from the caves.

Last night, I felt sure in choosing Niht the hunter, Turalyon the diplomat, Ulla the healer, and Ra'Salore the stone bender to accompany me. It's a balanced decision, accounting for every need. And yet, the weight of asking people to head into dangerous territory presses down on me this morning.

I finish strapping the last crystal beast and straighten, wiping my hands on my leather riding pants.

"How long has it been since you left the caves, Ulla?" I ask, still thinking about the massive distance we'll have to travel. Leaving without a healer would be foolish, but she seems unsure and that makes my nerves spike.

She stiffens, silver-blue eyes meeting mine before she brushes a stray strand of gray hair behind her ear. "Since Sama's blessing."

I raise an eyebrow. "For more than a morning."

She presses her lips together. "Never. I was born in Enduvida before the wars."

My lips press together, and acid pools in my stomach. It is strange not to know that about her. She was one of the few who had lived in this city before, but I always assumed that she had spent more time traveling around the world. I desperately wish there was another healer with more experience leaving the caves.

Vann grumbles behind me, surprising me out of my worries. I straighten to find him sauntering in from the tunnels. Gratitude flowers along my rib cage. I shoot him a half-heartedly sharp look through my grin.

"Perhaps you should take someone who knows the overlands better," he says.

I shake my head. "Ulla is a healer. That will be vital. Besides, she's also a better cook than you. You must stay and work with Svanna to keep everything running smoothly."

Vann lets out a noncommittal "*Bah*" which makes me genuinely smile.

Ulla smirks, not showing any sign she still feels even a fraction of my anxiety. "Stay away from the plants and the pots. Luiz knows what he's doing well enough."

The momentary lightheartedness evaporates like mist meeting a flame. My heart clenches as I think of Estela working in the kitchens. I see the plants... plants she brought to the under mountain.

Life that my mate brought to this dying place.

Life that now blossoms in my soul, climbing up the walls of my stoney insides and wrapping themselves around my fleshy heart before carving her name with a thousand thorn pricks. Gods, I just miss her. Even though I slept through the night, my weariness returns.

I compose myself and reiterate, "There isn't anyone I would rather trust to take care of Enduvida than you and Svanna, my friend. Though I appreciate your willingness to come with us, I need to know our home is safe in my absence."

Ra'Salore speaks up as he finishes packing his creature. "I would remind you that I am not so willing to visit our betrayers."

I grind my teeth. "Remember what I said yesterday—there aren't enough of us. If what Turalyon says is true, then we aren't meeting with those who betrayed us. This is an off-shoot group of considerable size which could give us hundreds of soldiers."

My gaze travels to Ra'Salore, and he nods, subdued but not convinced. "I will follow you."

"High praise," I return. Silence follows as we all mount the creatures.

"Not so fast," Liana says.

She reaches toward the reins and brings me close to her, producing a clump of smoky quartz from within her dressing robes and holding it up to my forehead. She moves it back and forth, singing a simple *hlums'dor* song. The small ritual is familiar, a parting blessing for travelers to find safety on the road. One by one, she blesses us all.

Then she places two pieces of swirling, green sardonyx in my palm. "These are speaking stones. I didn't have time to prepare more. Each is only good for one message, so be careful with what you send."

I put the gems in my pocket, nod, and whisper my thanks. She pats me on the shoulder and then gives me a playful shove.

"Go!" she calls after us, and we push away. The rush of air is instant as we follow the warm tunnels around their twists and turns, emerging in the open air.

Sunlight beats down on us, reflecting off the snow with blinding rays, and I hold up my hand to shield my eyes from the assault. A thousand new smells whip past my face as the clear, fresh air swirls around us in abundance. To one side, the frozen sea glitters in the sunlight, and to the other side, the forest with snow-dusted tops.

As riders, we must be the eyes for our *glacialmaras*. I turn to look at Ulla, and find her frozen, mouth agape as we hover several feet above the ground. Niht races up behind her reaching out to tap her on her shoulder.

She makes a surprised sound, and then laughs, leaning forward and racing after him. Unlike the two of them, Turalyon and Ra'Salore wait for me to move. Our clear crystal steads take on a blue hue as we nudge our mounts forward and fly down the mountain. We whip past the spot where Estela was attacked by a cold one, where her blood seeped into the ground, and onward. I see the trail the giants used to travel to our mountain.

It could still carry her scent, and I push aside the urge to go and smell her. We race on to the east, toward our cousins. I shudder as I think of the cold ones that threatened her life and came into our tunnels, changing those with their black bites.

I just pray we don't find any more along the way.

AFTER RIDING FOR SEVERAL HOURS, THE FIVE OF US SET UP OUR FIRST camp amidst the icy forest. Ulla and Turalyon light a small fire, and I unpack the dried supplies while Ra'Salore keeps watch in the corner. Niht roasts a couple of small beasts he shot with his bow.

I watch Niht bite down on a leg of meat while I tend to a roasting creature.

"I swear. I saw a rat this large in the middle of two bushes," he boasts, holding his hands far enough apart to accommodate a small child while Ulla shakes her head.

"That was a fox or a wolf, you giant fool," she says, but she's laughing.

I smile when Niht shakes his head. "I come from seven generations of the most respected hunters in our history. Do you think I wouldn't recognize a... what did you call them?"

This time, I can't help but chuckle along with Turalyon and Ulla. For a minute, the catastrophizing stops, and I don't think of every horrible outcome. I can picture all of us making it home with my mate.

"A wolf, oh, great hunter," Ulla mocks.

Niht shakes his head before looking up. He points into the snow. "Look, there?"

We all scramble over the fire to look exactly in the direction he points and see...

"Gods on their stoney thrones, Niht. It *was* a wolf," Ulla

starts laughing hard enough that the furry beast spares one last look at us before dashing off.

Ulla claps him on the back, but the tops of his cheeks are slightly purple.

"You haven't spent much time out of the cave. I heard you say so yourself earlier. Animals love me," Niht says.

Ulla smiles. "That doesn't mean I don't know anything about animals. I do read quite extensively. Some Enduares are excellent artists." She extends her hand and hums a few notes. A few small white rabbits peak out of a burrow beneath the snow.

Everyone watches her, and the rabbits tentatively come forward to snag a few of the dried leaves that we brought. They sit on the ground, listening to her song.

I smile, warmed by the fire and those around me.

It isn't until Ra'Salore takes a step towards her that Ulla stops singing and the rabbits dash away. She brings a gloved finger up to point at him.

"No hunting, my friend; we have enough meat. You too." She shifts the accusation to Niht.

Niht puts his hands up. "Fine, fine. I promise, cross my heart and turn to stone." One of the rabbits comes over to him, and she gawks. He laughs and reaches down to stroke the creature. "I cannot help it if they come to me, though I kill their kin."

Ulla smiles. "You are a big child."

He grins. "Yes. I'm hoping when I find my human mate, she doesn't fear my age since my soul has retained a certain youthfulness."

Ra'Salore snorts. "You are an immature dolt."

"It surprises me you think you would find a mate amongst the humans," Ulla says, ignoring Ra'Salore.

Niht shrugs and takes the spit off the fire. "I met the queen. She's fiery and talented. Very proficient. The one with red hair is beautiful, too. I like their small heights and ample bottoms."

I growl at him, and his eyes go wide.

"I only meant—"

"Nice to see you don't think Enduar women are enough for you," Ulla says bitterly through downturned eyes.

That eases the tension, and I feel a twinge of guilt, but Niht crosses over to her slowly, swishing his tail behind him.

"I am also named after Lo'Niht. The greatest scholar on love in our history, my dear," he all but purrs. "If you were interested, all you had to do was ask."

Ulla rolls her eyes. "You would be so lucky."

He grins, a wicked thing spreading across his face. "Oh, I would count myself amongst the luckiest."

"And I would count myself amongst the cursed."

Ra'Salore chokes on his food, but Turalyon and I start to laugh. I throw my tent down atop the snow as Niht lets out a few huffs of his own.

"That was very clever, Ulla," Niht says, grinning.

"Thank you," the healer replies with her own smile.

Turalyon sits down next to me on the leather mat I've put down to keep away the chill of snow. He smiles up at the stars.

"Thank you for bringing me, My King."

I reach around and pat my hand on his back. "This is the easy part, friend."

He stills. "My King," he starts. "Permission to speak my thoughts?"

"Of course, Turalyon," I say, reaching out to pick up another piece of meat.

"I know that you've entrusted me with several missions the last few months, but do you really consider me a friend?" he asks.

I nod. "Of course I do."

"Then, as a friend, can you tell me of the war?" he asks. "I remember the bloodshed, the lava. I had just finished the *dual'-moraan* when we realized we might die."

My smile fades.

"What is there to tell of war? It's a gruesome business that sometimes cannot be prevented. My father fought every surrounding species in search of power."

"And the war we seek to start?" the observant Enduar asks.

I flex my jaw. "This war will be fought to right wrongs."

Turalyon nods thoughtfully. "That's a good way of putting it. I see your many years alive have brought you wisdom."

I look over and elbow him in the ribs. "Are you calling me old?"

The hunter grins. "As a friend? Yes."

I shove him and he rolls away, laughing. Forcing another smile on my face, I stand, bid everyone a good night, and head to my tent. I am not offended, and I don't wish to bring down their mood. Not when they are all doing me a great favor.

Better to be bitter and alone.

CHAPTER 5

ENARGITE

ESTELA

If there is one constant in life, it is the inevitability of filth. Yesterday's blood crusts my fingers, though they are long since healed.

The space between bars is little more than a hand-width wide. When I tug at them again, they still refuse to budge. This cage is impenetrable, so I have spent the last few hours racing through possibilities.

Now, my plan has four parts: play Rholker's pet, find Mikal, speak with the other slaves, and convince as many as possible to escape with us.

While I know that playing his pet means explicitly not escaping before the time comes—whatever time that may be—I need to make contact with some of the other humans. So, walking around the perimeter of my cage yet again, I run my hands along the rough metal and wait for the torch to run out.

Eventually, with no immediate actions to be made, the thick darkness takes over. I'm left with a hauntingly empty, excruciatingly cold room as an ugly prelude to the return of the memory slicers.

There's an oily, black energy to them, nothing like Liana and her singing and scrying. If I am still, it's almost like I can hear the wise woman's chiming dresses, covered in stones that hit together every time she moves. When I hum to the stones around me, they are weak. I should have listened more carefully to her lessons and poems, maybe then I wouldn't be discouraged so easily.

Words about monarchs and power swirl around in my mind. Holding my legs to my chest to preserve warmth, I absentmindedly rub the stones of the necklace Teo gave me.

More tears drip down my cheeks. They don't freeze, as they did on the trek to the Enduar Mountains, but they leave behind wet trails that seem to attract the cold air. It keeps me in a heightened state of awareness.

That is how I am able to hear the footsteps outside this shack long before the door opens.

An inevitable hell.

Each crunch on the gravel walkway sounds louder than it did with my merely human ears—before the Fuegorra.

Slowly, the creaky, dilapidated door swings open, revealing the moonlight-soaked night. The silver rays illuminate the tall trees just beyond the six raven-black hoods. They enter without a word. The air in the room grows thin, and my chest heaves, trying to keep up with the lack of breath that's causing my hands and feet to tingle.

They walk in a triangular shape, presumably with Dahlia heading the front, two flanking her, and three in the back. They stop in front of my cage, and the temperature seems to drop when they close the door.

White, puffy clouds of labored breaths form in front of my face, just barely visible before the light is shut out again.

I close my eyes, choosing to believe that it doesn't make a

difference whether or not I see their ugly vipers. My grip on the windows to my mind is tight.

"Estela," Dahlia's voice says. "I see you got our gift."

Stiffening, my ears strain to hear her nonexistent breaths. It was assumed that she would know who I was, but hearing the name slip from her lips is as strange as watching a lake burn to a crisp. Everything about these women is unnatural, and I wonder why they gave me bread.

They are too small for giants or Enduares. So, I assumed they were elves, but I am still not fully convinced, as the elves seem to despise women. Giants hate humans even more.

"Open your eyes," Dahlia's voice commands, it sounds sly and guileful.

They gave you bread, perhaps you should see what they have to say.

"Human, we have brought you food and a blanket," she says. Suddenly, the hiss of a match precedes a light flickering through my eyelids. This time, I do look. I watch as they light another torch, and warmth returns.

She looks around the room, and I feel the displeasure radiate off her in waves. She snaps her fingers, and the chairs and tables knit back together, setting themselves in their original places. I watch, wide-eyed.

"Who are you?" I ask.

Dahlia pauses. "We are the Six."

"Aside from that. Why are you helping the giants?" I ask. "What have I done to you?" Despair laced in that futile question—I know very well people hurt people for no good reason every day.

"You haven't done anything to us... yet," Dahlia says. "And we have worked with the giants in the shadows for a long time. Mostly to alter your memories."

I freeze. "What?"

She shrugs. "Little things to keep you in line. A few tweaks, and you forgot something you weren't supposed to see, or perhaps you saw something much more awful than you really had."

My eyes grow wide. "And you've worked on me?"

She nods. "Yes, but only once. You were young."

The dream I had the first night I arrived in Zlosa lingers on the edges of my consciousness. I saw my mother save Mikal and I but I thought it was an error. "Please, there was a dream I had last night. It—"

"Enough, we did not come to speak of what has or has not been done." Dahlia holds up her hand, but my mind continues to race. The dream was *reality*.

One of the women from the back row approaches the bars of my cage, carrying a small bundle in her hands. From here, I can see the animal fur. Its neat folds are testament to how the leather was processed to be soft and workable. I can also see the basket, with hints of color peaking back at me: orange, reddish pink, green...

Food.

My stomach growls.

I force myself to look back at the women. Even with the fire, their faces are mere shadows. I take a sharp breath at the sight of their strange forms.

"Do you not desire these things?" one of the women says.

I laugh inwardly. Of course, I do, but it wasn't that long ago that they were forcing their way into my mind, slithering through my most private thoughts and watching. Rholker had called them mind slicers.

"Why bring simple comforts to the woman you've come to destroy?" I ask.

There is a long pause that hangs in the air between us.

"You have something we want. The giants are no strangers

to our coven, and we met with Erdaraj before we met with Rholker. We agreed to come in exchange for what we seek," she says simply.

Her voice has a slight echoing quality to it as she lays out the facts. As if she were the logical one, as if she were helping me.

I'm left wondering what she means by coven. *Is it some kind of court?*

"You agreed to shred my mind," I seethe.

"What are a few memories in exchange for freedom?" Dahlia retorts.

"Those memories are worth my humanity."

"One night with a man, and you think his prick a magic wand that will save you with one hard thrust. You are mistaken. Come with us, and you can have a hundred men, each just as well equipped as your azure monster," Dahlia shakes her head, and for a second, I swear I can glimpse the planes of the face below. Not enough to make out pointed ears, but... it's something.

"Out of respect for who you are, we offer you this exchange. Let us do our work, give us the thing we seek, and we will help you escape this gods-awful place," she says.

I raise an eyebrow. "Who I am?"

There is a pause, and another woman steps forward as the room fills with a slithering hiss.

"Will you help us?" Dahlia asks again.

"Why not just assist me in my escape and leave my memories intact?" I ask.

Dahlia pauses. "The contract was written in magic. We cannot forego that part without inciting a punishment."

I purse my lips, wondering how someone could punish these shrouded women.

My plan plays through my mind. If I go with them, then I will once again be far from Mikal; it will also take me further from my people. Perhaps I once would've been a person who struck such a deal. But the under mountain changed me.

"*I see things with my magic. We need a queen, and your people need liberation,*" Liana had said a month ago. The seed was planted, and it's already starting to grow.

"I cannot," I start. "But—"

"She has sufficiently refused," another interrupts with a deeper, more ominous voice. "We will begin."

Sweat breaks out on my palms. One heavy heartbeat passes, and another woman steps forward as the room fills with a slithering hiss.

"*Wait.*"

"We have waited long enough."

Fear races through my veins as I watch them gather around the cage. The torchlight dances off the silver threads of their cloaks, giving them an otherworldly glow. I can feel their eyes on me, studying my every move, every breath.

I grab onto the windows of my mind and hold tight, bracing myself as they reach into the folds of their cloaks and retrieve small, slithering snakes, with eyes that glint in the dim light. My heart pounds in my chest as they circle my cage, their movements synchronized and eerie.

Invisible hands grasp at my legs and feet, hoisting me up into the air. The pressure on my back gives me the sensation of being laid on a table. My feet are inclined above my head, and that unsettles me as I thrash against the unseen bonds. The more I move, the more my movements are restricted with invisible bindings that cut into my flesh.

Fear gives way to a surge of determination. I refuse to let them invade my mind again, to strip away my memories and leave me hollow, without the time I shared with Teo.

As the snakes slide toward me with their forked tongues darting in and out, I take a deep breath, summoning the power of the stone. The Fuegorra at the base of my throat pulses with ethereal light, but they are far from deterred.

The snakes move faster, somehow crossing the distance in the air, circling my legs seconds before latching on. Dizziness starts to take over as I watch them curl around my ankle. Then, also summoned from some far away place, water pours over my head. The frozen bite hardly registers when the water goes up my mouth and nose. I sputter and gag as more water pours.

Pain burns across my lower body while I lay there, desperate and sputtering, as one of the serpents bites down. Hard. Instead of saving me, the light dims, and I fall to the ground. The pain is immediate and searing, coursing through my body like wildfire. My vision blurs as the venom takes hold and my muscles convulse in agony. The women surrounding me hold up their hands, revealing pale-gray skin.

Then, they plunge into my thoughts.

I fight against them, desperately trying to hold onto the doors of my mind, and by extension, my memories. We return to the royal pools. To the glowing images of my mating mark still healing on my neck. Of declarations of love. Images of Teo's laughter, his touch, and the moments we shared flicker like fragile candle flames in the midst of a hurricane. I cling to them with the strength of a drowning soul clinging to a buoy.

My grip was never strong enough.

Their hold is iron-clad, their intrusion relentless. They shred through the tapestry of my mind with an eerie efficiency, unraveling the fabric of my past like ribbons torn apart by the wind. That intimate connection I had with Teo is ripped asunder, leaving behind only fragments of what once was.

As they delve deeper into my mind, they penetrate the recesses of my memory, ripping away the tender sweetness of our linked fingers and passionate kisses.

My soul mourns the loss. But amidst the anguish, a flicker of resistance ignites within me. I refuse to let them completely erase our love, our connection. I muster every ounce of strength I have left and push back against the invading force.

With a surge of power, I summon the remnants of my memories, weaving them together into a barrier against their onslaught.

It is a mistake. The barrier I create flickers and weakens, unable to withstand the assault. A pain so exquisitely sharp rams straight into my skull, and I fall to the ground once more.

I gently prod at the memory as another bucket of water is dropped across my face. The details are blurry, but my body's reaction is clear. I convulse against the thought of Teo touching my skin.

Horror leeches away my thoughts. Another stream of water hits my throat, but when I try to reach up and brush away the slick dampness, I find myself still bound.

Another splash, right on my throat.

Then another.

My breath comes out as white clouds.

"We warned you, daughter of Aitana. Remember, as you writhe on the floor, that we offered you a way out," Dahlia's voice whispers with a voice that reverberates around the room. "We will return for more when the Giant King calls upon us."

They leave after draping the blanket over my prone form. Warmth instantly returns, but I wish for a flame, for anything to chase away the frozen shadows now taking up space in my heart.

CHAPTER 6

AZURITE

ESTELA

"**V**elen! *A new song. One for me to dance to with my bride,*" *Teo calls.*

The memory takes on its normal path, with Teo drawing me close as Velen, the Enduar Singer with the stone-like face and gods' gifted voice begins his melody.

Shit, I groan. This was the first time I let myself give into the attraction with my mate, before I knew what we were.

The eyes of the Six are still watching from a distance. I turn my head to look at them, but Teo's hand gently brushes my back, and regret radiates through my soul as I remember how I punched him in the face when he tried to help me.

This memory only serves to show just how fucking imperfect I am—how many mistakes I've made. But it is still precious to me for reasons I don't have to give to anyone.

No one else needed to know that the memories were shredded—the moments lost to the cold, bitter magic of the Six —were compounding, addling my mind so that the ones left untouched were extraordinary.

I hold my love closer. Savoring the clean smell of his skin, and the way his strength feels supporting me. In a few moments... it will all be gone.

As if on cue, Dream Teo reacts to my deviation from the past. His arms tighten to the point of pain. I look up just in time to see his features twist into a monstrous mask.

I try to pull back, just as a slit appears across his throat. Blood spurts out to the beat of his heart, coating me in the hot, sticky liquid seconds before he stumbles back and falls to the ground.

One of the Enduares screams. Then another shouts, "*The human bitch killed the king!*"

The room darkens, and the metallic scent of blood is everywhere. I look at my mate dying at my feet as screams fill my ears.

I sink to the ground while the memory takes another turn. Sharp pain rakes through my head as the scene is ripped to shreds before my eyes, simply leaving a bloody scene in front of me. Slamming my eyes shut, I do everything I can to keep myself from touching the memory and ruining one of the only ones I thought I had left.

The screams, the pain, the blood all subside. Leaving me in the present. Blood rushes to my ears and they ring as my brain squeezes. Then the water comes.

Ice, like dozens of needles, goes up my nose and into my mouth. I choke, waiting for the sense of drowning to pass.

Teo isn't dead.

But you did try to kill him... You deserve the pain.

My heart stutters.

Everything inside and out of my body is raw. Swollen, even, despite how starving I am. I scramble to collect the blanket as soon as my limbs unfreeze, but my legs move slower than I would like.

The snake bites along one leg are clearly on display, as

Rholker and the Six watch me. Dahlia's hooded face is turned down toward me, and for a few moments, the silence is piercing. Then, the women turn, and start to leave.

"Well?" Rholker says at last. "Can I touch her?"

Dahlia pauses, a snake now curling around her black, cloaked arm as if it were a long, elaborate armband.

"No. But she is sufficiently docile for you to bring that pretty little collar you showed me," she says.

I spent my life wearing harnesses... but a *collar*. Even through my chilled shivers, a new sickness pierces my empty stomach. I wonder if Rholker knows about how eager they were to help me escape.

Remember when you called Svanna a monster? You deserve to feel pain for every cruel second you inflicted on those you yearn for.

The voice in my head pops back up to poke at my wounds.

I take a shuddering breath.

Rholker, however, visibly relaxes. "That is good enough for now, I suppose."

"Since we have achieved this for you, we expect payment on our doorstep this eve," one of the other women says.

Dahlia nods.

Rholker purses his lips. "In good time. Your job is not finished yet, and we agreed upon a lengthy visit to Zlosa—at least until the Winter Feast."

My ears prick up, as a memory swirls. I was taken from the under mountain on the Winter Solstice. If Rholker is having his feast now, it's likely to celebrate something like a victorious battle, or perhaps, an actual wedding.

"Your coronation will not be misssed," Dahlia's snake hisses at Rholker.

It takes effort to conceal my shock. Rholker is not the official king yet.

Everything makes sense all at once—Sure, he killed his

father and brother and replaced the coronet with a bejeweled pinnacle of a sovereign, but that never meant the others accepted him.

My eyes trail between the Six and Rholker, wondering what their relationship truly is. Are they elves?

They must be.

Or, maybe they are something else entirely.

King Erdaraj hated all humans, despite using them for his pleasure and service. He would've never worked with one of us, even ones with magic that we call *Brujas*.

Rholker has done something dangerous to forge this alliance. And, like the bumbling Second Prince who once pursued me relentlessly, he has done it poorly. From where I stand, it looks like he's drowning.

For the first time, hope blossoms in my chest, despite the shredded memories and the aches that keep me shivering even in front of a fire.

The Six leave for good, but Rholker remains, looking at me with unveiled conviction.

I meet his stare with unflinching strength.

"Estela," he says softly and reaches out to brush his hands against the bars of my cage. "I'm sorry I've treated you poorly. I promise to make it all right."

Then he turns and I am left staring at the spot he occupied seconds before the door reopens. The prince playing king returns, this time with a much smaller, curvier human form.

I stiffen. This woman is familiar to me, from the silkiness of her dress that hugs every pleasantly round part of her frame to the plush furs draped across her bare shoulders. Her hair is raven black, a popular preference among human men, and it is clear she has eaten recently and often.

Her smile is saccharine sweet, something men love and never detect any irony in.

This is a comfort woman, but not one of the royal ones. She was given to a lowly lord or, perhaps, a human slave foreman.

And she's carrying a bundle of fabric and a wash basin... and a collar hangs off her arm.

"Your Majesty," she says with a slow, dipping bow.

Her painted red lips curve up at the sides into a demure smile. A woman very practiced in her craft.

Rholker nods and watches her as she approaches my cage. She withdraws an iron key and slips it into the lock. I feel each click of metal as she turns the mechanism and the bar slowly slides out.

Then she opens the door and I look up at her from the ground—vulnerable and wounded. My head pounds and pulses as she steps closer to me. I feel frail.

"Estela, my dear," Rholker starts, then studies my blank face. He laughs. "Well, shit. Those bitches didn't lie. You really are subdued."

I don't say anything, and neither does the woman. My eyes study her again. I don't know whether she is friend or foe. It's all too familiar to me that slaves don't necessarily stick together by virtue of being the same species. Some, like Sergi who walked with me on the trek to Enduvida, offered no comfort when Rholker whipped Mikal's and my back. The other slaves called me a whore.

"Sadly, I have matters to attend to." He nods to the comfort woman he's sent to attend me. "Clean her the best you can. Make sure she eats everything, and leave the fire."

My heart squeezes. *Warmth.*

I keep my breathing normal as he leaves and the door closes behind him.

Only then do I look up at the comfort woman and find her eyeballing my dress. I ignore the smell of actual food and look down. Despite the torn strips of the gown and the dirty, wet hem, it is still vibrant in color and beautiful.

Glittering curiosity comes to the forefront of her eyes before quickly fading.

"It's stone silk," I say gently. "From the Enduar mountains."

She pauses, looking me right in the face, and then unlocks the cage with one hand before placing everything on the ground while she pointedly ignores me. The way that sweet smile fades and is replaced by a blank expression is eerily similar to what my mother would do after returning from Erdaraj's bed.

It's almost enough to forget to stare at my cell door. Wide open.

Almost.

I clear my throat. "The other woman slave who went with me to the mountains, Arlet, learned how to weave it. Did you know her?"

Arlet was always better at getting to know others. My heart aches at the memory of her.

The woman remains silent and dips her rag into the water. Her bronzed skin shines in the light of the fire, like the most polished metal in Enduvida. Everything about her is beautiful and alluring.

Then she holds out her hand, waiting for me to extend my arm.

"Will you not speak to me?" I ask, hesitantly lifting my arm.

She shakes her head, silky black tresses swaying around her shoulders.

"Is it because Rholker commanded you to remain silent?" I try again.

Nothing.

I swallow and think of every nightmare I've heard about those who find themselves misfortunate enough to spend time with the Enduares. She probably believes that I was enchanted by their songs and have gone half mad.

Her hands are warm, but the water is warmer. She's not rough, but she is tentative—like I could lash out at her any time.

"The stories they've told you about the Enduares are lies. I'm not bewitched, I'm... married to one of them." My throat is still burning with each word, but they are important words to speak.

The comfort woman freezes, and a lock of her dark hair falls in her face. "You married one of the flesh eaters?"

My lips quirk up at the corners, partially because I understand her, but also because I have been so desperate to talk to someone and this feels fucking divine.

"No one died in the under mountain. The Enduares are gentle with us. They offered us homes." I gestured to the stone embedded into my sternum. "This helps me heal. It was a gift from them."

She stares at the gem, but doesn't say anything else and just continues to clean.

I want to tell her everything—about the rituals, the songs, the comfortable caves, albeit with slightly sulfuric smells—but she doesn't show signs of wanting to know more, so I close my eyes and let my words turn into tears that slip down my cheeks.

The stinging pain in my nose and throat fades as the small cottage continues to warm up, and the warm water is dragged over my skin.

Then the woman raises both of my hands over my head. My eyes open as she starts to work the stone silk dress off of me.

"No," I say furiously.

She frowns. "Didn't you hear the prince? He wants to start taking you with him tomorrow. You can't wear this anymore."

I think of the beautiful memories I've shared in this dress. Of my wedding, and then of—

My mind pulses, and I double over in pain as I gently brush against the torn memory. There were supposed to be sacred moments after our wedding, not blood-soaked horrors.

But all I feel are jagged edges, slicing through my invisible fingers as I prod. It's a peculiar duality to feel nothing but the agonizing absence of something that was once marvelous and to know, deep down, it was incredible despite not having any evidence.

Small mercies from the stone in my chest, I suppose. More goodness from the Enduares.

The woman scrambles away as if I were going to hurt her. I hold my hands up.

"No, I'm sorry. I just—they took—"

The woman opens her eyes, horrified at me, and then looks directly at the door. She hurries to her feet, and then rushes out of the cage. She locks it, leaving me with the food, clothes, water, and collar. Then she darts out of the cottage.

I stare at all of them as I sit there on the ground in pain. Too weak to do anything just yet, I rest my head against the bars.

"*Mamá, ayúdame*[1]," I whisper, sighing. At least she left the fire going.

Then I slowly turn my memories over to the dream I had when I first arrived. One from my youth, with the vision of my mother stopping Erdaraj and his men from killing my brother and me.

Opening my eyes, I gather up every drop of strength I can, and reach for the tray of food. There isn't much, but there is water, bread, and a few *bolas de hoja*[2]. I sneer at the food I used to prepare for Mikal.

It's almost like Rholker is playing on some intimate secret between me and my brother.

I eat the bread, drink the water that has a slightly acrid flavor to it, and stare at the steamed plants. Time passes, my stomach rumbles, and then...

"You are a short-sighted thing," Liana's voice from the past reminds me.

Fuck Rholker and his games. He will pay for every single one. He will lose his kinghood, kingdom, and every last one of his slaves.

"I will teach you how to be a queen, and you can lead our people to fighting for a better world."

I tear off a few more strips of the cloth from the hem and work on ripping off each of the gold buttons from the panels on the back. I want a physical reminder of my wedding if my memories are fading.

After braiding the thin pieces of fabric together, I fashion a small necklace and turn my attention to the new clothes the comfort woman didn't have time to put on me.

Letting out a deep breath, I pick up the fur dress.

"We need a queen, and your people need liberation."

There are battles I will fight, but what I wear won't be one of them. Not yet.

CHAPTER 7
LABRADORITE
TEO

I've wrapped fur around my face, leaving only my eyes uncovered as we fly through the woods.

While there had been easy conversation over the fire last night, it didn't carry over into morning. As soon as the first pink-gray streaks of sunlight artfully painted the space where horizon meets deep black sky, snow started to drift down from the heavens, and we sank into silence. Even Niht. It was as if the air shifted into something darker—far more menacing.

If our sleeping and waking habits weren't already in line with the overland's daytime hours, I would've preferred to sleep through the sun's intense radiance. It drains us after long hours riding.

The *glacialmaras* have grown tired as well, and their song shifted from pleasant twinkling to shrill pinpricks of sound in my ears, their color has shifted from clouded blue to dull grey. Even Rahda no longer soars above the treetops, so we are forced to dart between brown trunks as we move along.

I eat to keep from fainting, but the food sits heavy in my belly. My bond is silent, though perfectly intact.

It was unknown to me if our communication would sustain across the forests between us, and I am sad to see that we truly are separated for a time.

I wish that I could feel everything she was suffering through. Even if me standing in her place couldn't spare her, at the very least, I would know exactly how to comfort her and mend her scars.

Especially because the trees remind me of the past. If there was someone who could understand the twisted games that giants play, it was me.

In fact... If I listen close enough, I can almost hear Lijasa's voice call from a shadowy thicket, saying, *You've teased me long enough. Tonight you will come to my bed.*

Fighting away the memories of endless months spent in Zlosa is tiring, and I am already exhausted.

The darkness around us thickens as the sun disappears completely. The sound of the *glacialmaras* fades, and Rahda slows. There's a low, ebbing hum—almost like waves of music —that reaches out to us.

"What's that?" Ulla calls out, and looks at me with her piercing silver eyes showing through her scarf. Her breath manages to escape the furs and paint the air with puffs of white.

"I know that sound from the war," Niht grumbles.

I stiffen. Of course...

It is one of the altars the Enduar hordes would stop at to rest.

No one else says a word as I yank on the reins, and let Rahda veer towards the sound. The billowing song crashes into me, and the nausea that has been plaguing me fades. The Fuegorra in my chest starts to beat and sing in time with the beacon, and it feels like coming home.

But not home.

It is merely a moment of peace. One I experienced dozens of

times during the Great War where I could lay the death and bloodshed at the feet of my gods and rest for a night.

When the smooth, marble altar comes into view, I let out a long breath. It's been five decades, and it still looks new. It doesn't take long to recognize the carving: my goddess, Grutabela reaching down from her stoney, starry throne to Endu, who is the crag beneath our feet—the fissures in the earth, the mountains, the volcanoes.

Rahda halts, and I don't bother to usher her on before I lift myself out of the saddle, ignoring the chafing between my legs and approach the icon.

There is a single white step, dusted with snow and I drop to my knees. The Fuegorra in my chest starts to glow, burn, and hum with recognition. My eyes burn from relief and the image of the lovers before me—reaching out toward each other—calms my restless soul.

My gods.

Without thinking, my fingertips brush the scene and I whisper, "Protect my mate," in the old tongue.

"I think it would be best if we set up a camp here," Ra'Salore says, and Ulla voices her agreement.

The moment between me and the icon settles, and I turn around to watch Turalyon tie Rahda alongside his *glacialmara*.

I get up, and help them clear away patches of snow to set up tents. More small creatures run past us, and I even allow myself a smile when one of them clings to Niht's pant leg.

In no time, a fire is started, the tents are pitched, and we are eating dried supplies in silence. I pretend not to notice how Niht feeds the small squirrel more bits of his food.

It is harder to ignore when he tries to climb the tree after the creature.

Ulla laughs, but I turn back to my tent and close the leather flap behind me. It is lonely in the small space, but I need to rest better if we are to make it to the rebellion's hideout tomorrow.

The dim light is alive with Ulla's idle singing, and I sink into the bittersweet melody like some might sink into bed after a long day of hard work.

My eyes flutter closed after mere minutes, and I offer another prayer for Estela, also asking for a speedy trip to see our cousins.

A SCREAM WAKES ME. I'M OUT OF MY TENT IN A SECOND, STILL FULLY dressed, with a knife at the ready. Ra'Salore is there too, followed closely by Niht and Ulla. I count them, with my brow furrowed.

"Where's Turalyon?" I demand.

Niht's eyebrows shoot up and another scream fills the open air. This time, I take off running in the direction of the noise. I can tell the second we leave the perimeter of the protected camp because the nausea returns. A few more feet, and I see the large, red stain on the forest floor.

Turalyon's scream is abruptly cut off, and a few tendrils of mist curl towards us from the trees.

"Shit," Ra'Salore says from my side.

Every muscle inside of my body coils and tightens as I recognize the signs of the cold ones that nearly killed Estela and invaded our caves.

"Get back to the camp, Ulla," I shout over my shoulder before tightening my grip on the knife.

My ears pick up on the sound of crunching snow behind the tree to the left. I peer into the mist as Ra'Salore and Niht join me on either side.

"Watch out for the teeth," I say, thinking of Dyrn, the

Enduar who was bitten and came back to life as one of those awful creatures.

From the shadow of the mist, a succubus emerges with something in tow. It takes very little time to identify it as Turalyon's body.

A dull roar sounds in my ears as I take in the limp features of his body. Rage builds up like boiling water in a kettle, and I explode. For a moment, I regret not bringing Vann, as he and I have spent our lifetimes syncing our fighting strategies. Luckily, Ra'Salore moves with me. He isn't as perfectly intuitive as Vann, but he has good instincts.

The stone he bends swirls around him, causing my hair to blow back.

The cold creature hisses at us, and I realize it is overfull. Its movements are slow, and it's almost too easy to cleave my dagger through its throat seconds before I retract and Ra'Salore slices cleanly through the meaty conjunction where neck meets shoulder with a perfectly honed slice of rock.

The head falls to the ground, and we wait for signs of other creatures.

None come.

"What do we do with our brother Turalyon?" Ra'Salore asks.

I look at him, heart still racing, and chest pumping. He isn't prone to niceties. He's rejected such notions in the past, and I thought his brother's death would only make him more of a hermit. But it seems his name is not the only thing that has changed since his brother sacrificed himself for our people.

I take one long breath and then dip down to pick up Turalyon. His throat is mostly ripped out, and his eyes are wide open, frozen in glassy fear. I reach down to gently push them closed.

"The best option would be to burn both bodies to make sure neither of them come back to life," I say.

It's a gruesome thought to burn one's friend. But this friend is indeed dead, as is his wisdom and experience with the elves. The kindest gift I can give anyone is to ensure they stay dead after being subjected to the cold one's poison.

Niht approaches and takes the creature and its head. I watch with dread curling in my gut. Did they follow us from Enduvida? I don't know what this means, but I can't dwell on it now.

When we approach Ulla, I already find her building the foundation for a much larger fire. "How did you find so much wood?" I ask, detached from the world around us.

She shrugs. "I gathered for quite a while before we went to rest, and I brought dried starter mushrooms. Highly flammable, and highly successful in creating hot flames. You must be quick though, I don't know how long this will burn when there is so much snow."

I nod sharply and approach the scorching heat. When I kneel down, I look back at our blood soaked friend, Turalyon. His blue skin has gone ashen, and his eyes have somehow slid part-way open again. I close them once more.

My eyesight blurs, and I force myself to take in every gruesome detail, from the body to the pyre.

Turalyon was on this trip because he had gone with Lothar to visit the elves, but I was the one who asked him to come. He was clever and hopeful—I saw a future councilman whenever I spoke with him.

I mourn that future, especially since he will never have a mate.

Niht helps me remove the last bits of metal and armor, leaving him in nothing more than his undergarments.

A tear falls down my face, just as Ulla starts to sing the *hlumrynna* song. Every Fuegorra in the camp lights up, as do the two short towers of quartz Ulla brought to amplify her songs. It holds none of the vibrato of the Parting Cave, where we usually hold death ceremonies, but we use the same words.

"Far away, in Vidalena's embrace,

Amid mountains warm, a sacred space..."

I close my eyes against the onslaught of tears. Two hundred and seventy-eight Enduares now.

Ulla's song continues, and Ra'Salore and Niht's voices pick up with the Enduar words.

"To our family, gone but not lost, we gather to say our last goodbye.

To express our love, and forever cherish them,

In our stones, their memory won't dim."

The melody reaches its end, and the time has come to say goodbye. Despite the blood dampening my clothes, it is a hard thing to place the body amid the flames. The heat licks at my arms, but I have long since learned that the heat doesn't bother me as it should. Dealing with lava and magma has given me a thick skin.

"Say hello to our family in Vidalena," I say down to the dead hunter, and lean forward. "Go with the Stone."

Once his body is laid to rest, I stand and watch. I wonder how many may have been buried in this place—this old altar with a blessed camp space for soldiers. How many Enduares came back from battle half alive, and gave up their ghosts as soon as the song of home touched their sharp ears.

Having spent my days slicing, and my evenings trying to forget, it fell to me more than once to return back home and tell their families of their deaths. Two years into the Great War, we stopped visiting homes and started posting lists in the city centers.

My heart still hurts for their brothers and sisters who longed for their return. I hope the fallen are resting well.

We stand in quiet reverie, save Ulla's humming and the gentle throb of the beacon.

When I look up, I meet Ra'Salore's gaze. It is... softer than normal. It moves me to compassion. I wouldn't want to force a soldier to sleep in a haunted place.

"When would you like to leave tonight?" I ask. We have had only a few hours of rest, but now that we have lost our guide, it would be worth it to leave earlier.

His jaw tightens. "If you say the word, I will go, My King."

That isn't a yes.

When I look at Ulla and Niht, I see the weariness etched in the lines around their eyes and mouths. "Never mind. This place is safe. We shall stay the rest of the night."

Ulla visibly relaxes, but I don't catch the rest of the conversation as the three of them move to burn the creature that killed Turalyon. Normally, I would have abhorred the idea of having their ashes anywhere near each other, but we simply don't have enough wood for two fires.

It will have to be sufficient.

The tent flap closes behind me again as I crawl back in, and I sink to the ground atop my bedroll. The hole in my chest feels a little wider.

The ground shudders and moves under the weight of Ra'Salore's stone bending. He buries the ashes, the memories... the lost souls.

I wonder if loss will be the tune my life is written to for the rest of my days.

CHAPTER 8
EMERALD
ESTELA

Two days pass, and the metal collar chafes against my neck. It's made of silver, studded with rubies, and I swear, it feels harder to swallow and draw breath.

Huddled in the corner of the cage, I have my new gown on. Rholker stares at me from the other side of the room as the comfort woman pours another bucket of steaming water into the bath. The sound makes me sweat.

"The Six instructed me to let you rest for a few days before I bring you back to stay in the room I've prepared in the palace," he says.

The words flow over me, *past me*, without ever really sinking into my mind. He took me out yesterday for a short walk. It was cold, and there were patches of snow clinging to the trees.

I'd been right about being near the lumber fields. A few of the humans snuck glances at our party—but all turned away quickly, grateful that it was not them paraded around by the prince like chattel.

"The bath is ready, My King," the comfort woman declares. She wears a tight-fitting leather dress today, and her silky raven hair is half-tied up with a vegetable-dyed ribbon the color of autumn leaves.

I groan, preparing to be thrust into the water *yet again*. Ever since I was tortured, I can't touch it without feeling like I'm going to drown. It's just water, and yet...

Rholker's eyes dip down from my face to the bare expanse of my chest. Giant women wear deep, square necklines and corsets to push up their breasts, which are typically scarred by artists to enhance bulk and shape—this one is more modest than most because the tip of the Fuegorra barely sticks out from behind the fabric. Rholker doesn't want anyone to see that I've been marked by the enemy.

The joke is on him, and he hates it. I can feel his gaze snake up to the still-healing mating marks on my throat even after I return my eyes to the dirty floor. He wants to remove them. The cruel brute won't rest until all markings of my time with the Enduares are erased.

Obliterated.

"Come, Estela," Rholker says, walking over to unlock my cage. I stand up, suddenly very aware of his size. "The water is warm," he adds, as if that would appease me.

I hesitate, reminding myself that he's seen me naked before. Hell, he has made people bathe before.

But... I've changed. I'm not just some slave that he can torment and threaten into his bed. If Rholker touches me, my Fuegorra will burn him with light and he knows it. *My* body belongs to *my mate* because *I* gave it to him.

You can endure this a while, escape, and exact revenge with Teo at your side.

I wince even thinking his name. It's wrapped up in too many ruined memories. The pain makes me take a deep breath, turn off my feelings, ignore all sounds, and keep my eyes fixed on the floor. Whatever words pass between the woman and Rholker are lost.

Moments later, I feel her warm, soft hands guide me to the space next to the tub. I look down at the water, and blood rushes in my ears. The fire in the corner used for heating the water suddenly feels too hot.

The laces at the back of my dress start to loosen, one by one, with sharp hissing sounds. It almost reminds me of dragonflies buzzing through the air in springtime, which is a better alternative to snakes slithering into my cage and paralyzing me with their bite.

But delusion only lasts so long. When I grab hold of the large metal tub for stability, a bit of the too-warm water splashes on my knuckles. It doesn't even touch my face, but the room tilts sideways all the same, and I shove away as hard as I can.

A part of me registers that I hit the soft body of the comfort woman, but it feels like I'm back in the cage, tilted at an odd angle, and water is forcing its way up my nose, down my throat, restricting every airway.

I'm drowning.

Gods-damned *drowning*.

I focus on sucking in air since it's become a scarcity. I gasp and tremble as the layers of fabric are removed from my body.

Don't die. It's just a bath. You won't die.

But it might be good if you do.

"What's wrong with her?" Rholker has the audacity to ask, as if he hadn't spent a week watching the Six torture me.

The comfort woman gives an apologetic response that I don't fully hear as she guides my naked form back to the side of the tub. My skin presses against the warm brass metal, and I pause.

This time, the metal actually reminds me of my idyll home

TO IGNITE A FLAME

—of Enduvida. The place I have to get back to... after I get Mikal.

I hold my choking breaths and lift one of my legs to place it into the tub. The water is warm like it was on the night of my wedding.

As fast as a tidal wave, I smell blood. Terror. The damaged memory.

The sensations from before return tenfold. Water in my mouth, throat, and lungs.

I twist to run away, but my foot gets caught, and I fall. I land atop the comfort woman once more and she shoves me off, shouting, "*¡Quítate!*"[1]

I push away from her, my back flat against the wood planks beneath me, while my chest heaves. Rholker's face appears in my view, looking down at me with worry. He reaches out and hesitates when my gem starts to glow.

Rholker says, "Pick her up this time. She'll need to be put in like a babe."

My head whips back to her. Her dress is covered in water stains, and her cheeks are flushed from pushing, hauling, and then catching my fall. She doesn't deserve this. Finally, I speak to her.

"*Por los dioses*[2], no. Please."

Her eyes are hard, but her arms still wrap around me and lift me up. The comfort woman is stronger than she looks, or perhaps, I've lost weight again.

When I try to fight or push away, she makes a labored sound, but she doesn't let me go. She doesn't so much set me in the tub as she does drop me in. The liquid sloshes and splashes. My lungs seize again, and I fight to breathe.

Red and orange light bursts from my body, and the woman cries out, shielding her eyes.

"Estela!" Rholker yells. "Stop moving, or I will slice the head from your brother's shoulders *today*."

The words cut through the panic, and I freeze. Air still fights to get into my lungs, but my limbs stay close to my sides. The light fades to nothing more than a persistent glow.

A minute passes as I suck in tiny breaths, and I meet Rholker's yellow eyes. It doesn't matter how vulnerable I am before him.

He looks worried.

"Mikal is... alive then," I pant.

Rholker looks down at me with an almost earnest expression. He doesn't respond, but he doesn't have to.

I hold my breath. The last time that I saw him was when Keksej was restraining me while one of the giant warriors hit Mikal over the head and took him away. My world was torn apart. Even the thought of it causes an icy pit in the middle of my stomach.

I'd seen a vision of him sleeping, dirty, after my Fuegorra was put in. He was growing thinner from the giants' abuse. Alone. He's a strong sixteen year old, built like an ox, but he can't break free alone.

Teo was right. He wouldn't kill Mikal right away when he could use my brother as a bargaining chip.

Tears prick my eyes and urgency to act thrums across my nerves. I could touch Rholker and let him burn. Maybe sear off his face with a swipe of my hand and brand him the same way he held me down and branded me. Then I could run—fucking *run*—and be at Mikal's doorstep.

"Will you take me to see him today?" I ask again slowly, fighting to keep the raging thoughts at bay.

Rholker scowls. "No. We are going to court today."

"Take me to him after," I beg, clutching onto the edge of the tub, trying to ignore the squeezing in my throat. I haven't drowned yet. I won't. Not today.

Rholker's eyes narrow as he steps closer to me. "Prove that you can behave yourself, and I might let you see him soon," he says.

It's enough for me to remain still, despite the pain coursing through my body as my head is roughly tilted back and water is poured over my long, curly hair. I close my eyes, grimacing, and let the soap be lathered in.

Uno, dos, tres...

Pulling on old habits, I imagine my table. The plants in the small greenhouse that Ulla cared for. I think of their leaves, of selecting the perfect amount to be crushed for a small stomach sickness brew. I smell the minty leaves release their scent in the boiling water.

A swipe of the bathing brush passes over my skin, and I swallow hard, clenching my jaw, and think of healing with the crystals. The Fuegorra warms. This time, it is comforting. As if looking for something to sing to.

From the corner, where my clothes are discarded on the floor, a few small notes permeate the air.

A melody.

A song.

It's not a quiet ringing, but a song. At last.

Rholker's eyebrows knit together, and I panic. With my limited singing ability, I start to hum an off-tune melody that I hope won't resonate with the crystals. It covers the sound well enough, and he looks away.

The metal collar still clamped around my neck warms for a minute under my singing. It's a strange sensation, but when I stop humming, it fades.

The comfort woman helps me out of the tub, wraps a thick

DANIELA A. MERA

cloth around me, and picks up another length of fabric to start drying my hair. She has a blank face, with just a hint of bitterness. I worry that I hurt her, and think of the small necklace I made.

It was meant to be a reminder of my wedding... but I have a ring and a necklace, and I need to work harder to find a way to help my people. Everything can't only be about Mikal.

If only we were alone, I would show it to her. Perhaps... we could be friends. I could convince her to come with me, once I can tell her the truth of the trolls.

A new dress is placed over my head and fastened. My hair is brushed until it dries by the heat of the fire, and it is curled and pinned in the style of the giant women. A powder that smells like bark and resembles my skin color is pressed atop my mating marks, then red makeup is smeared over my eyes.

This dress is thinner than the one I wore this morning. Whereas yesterday's dress had proper sleeves, this one has thick straps connecting to the boned, silk bodice. It's shiny and revealing but better than the mere scraps of fabric my mother wore to see Erdaraj.

When the comfort woman reaches down to retrieve my old dress, alarm bells ring. I thought they would leave it be—it still has all my jewels. I turn, hoping to talk to her somehow and tell her not to throw the things away, but Rholker is already wielding my leash, ready to clip it onto the collar.

My heart races as he clips it on and opens the door. I turn back to the comfort woman with one last frantic look. She catches my gaze, clearly confused, before I am taken outside.

The sun is brighter than it was yesterday, and it is still morning. I reach my hands up to shield my eyes as a sharp yank forward has me stumbling and coughing. Rholker turns around abruptly.

"Are you well?" he asks, seeming worried as if he hadn't considered how disorienting a *neck leash* might be.

94

I glare at him, hacking one last cough into the crook of my arm. His red hair and yellow eyes seem harsher in the wintry light, but he doesn't wait for more than a few moments before we continue on.

We pass the fields and make it to the palace. White marble pillars are everywhere, a stark contrast to the woodland cabins and cottages in Zlosa, and a testament to the elevation of the royalty. A depiction of Khuohr, the god of war, is painted across the ceiling, and his consorts line the outer walls. Each holds a gold basin, as if offering some gift to him above.

We are quick to make it into the throne room, which is at least ten times larger than I remember. A long row of furs is laid on the ground for us to walk upon, while rows of giant lords and their wives fill both pews and carefully carved chairs.

Earthy tones are everywhere, along with mountains of brown and auburn hair. A few stray yellow eyes turn to glance at us, but most of the conversations continue as normal. They are a dull roar in my ears as the royal giant warriors congregate around us.

One of the warriors steps into the hall first and pounds his spear against the stone with a loud crack. All speaking ceases.

My eyes move to the end of the walkway to see a giant figure seated next to the throne, and a blue head is hung above where Rholker will place his flat ass.

An Enduar head.

I suck in a breath. My heart pumps loudly and my fingers go numb. That has to be the one who sacrificed himself and let Teo kill him.

Rholker stoops down to whisper, "Remember, if you wish to see Mikal, you will behave today."

I look up at him, feeling raw and anxious, but I nod.

The entirety of the court stands, then bows. When every head is cast downward, Rholker starts to walk in.

I take in the men from afar. A part of me knows that this is my chance to get information that would be precious to the Enduares—but I hardly know where to start. I wasn't raised to understand politics.

Right now, with their enormous heads bowed, even if not explicitly to me, something new stirs in my bones. The Fuegorra in my chest hums.

A snippet of a vision. A promise—they would all pay.

I am a queen. Perhaps not one that they recognize, but that kind of endowment comes from within.

My thoughts trail off when I get a good look at the wooden throne at the end of the walkway. There are cushions on either side of the carved seat. One is already occupied by a young giant woman, wearing a white dress similar to my own. She also has a collar on, but in place of being pulled by Rholker's firm hand, she is attached to the throne. Her head is also bowed into submission, showing off her reddened eyelids and scarred forehead.

She looks like a high-bred giant. Her auburn curls seem healthy, and her skin is otherwise unmarked by the sun, as many giants prefer for their women.

I recognize the gems on the thrones instantly because they call to me from the other side of the room. They don't sing, they weep. If the others hear, they don't show it. Liana once told me that the songs are louder to those with stones, but only Teo and I could hear our song.

A few of the giants angle their heads to see what is happening and Rholker gives my leash a tug, causing the Fuegorra's light to sputter out as I choke.

When we reach the seat, the new king pauses and gestures to the cushion on his right side. I look up at him for a mere moment before I take my place, remembering the way he used

Mikal to threaten me moments ago. It just makes me more angry.

No sooner have I lowered myself than he sits on his throne —the one no doubt carved by the bloody hands of slaves past. We gaze out at the audience, and I see others who look vaguely like Rholker—his bastard brothers, from the decree when every royal lord would gift his wife to High King Erdaraj to sire a son. I'm surprised they let the *Terksats* into the court.

Unlike the general friendliness that Teo conducted his entire court with, Rholker is aloof and full of rules of conduct I couldn't begin to guess.

One of the royal court members sitting on a gilded chair at the front of the room stands and opens a book. He clears his throat.

"Gentlemen and members of the court, this session is prepared to begin. Long live High King Rholker!"

Not every member of the court repeats the sentiment. Rholker stiffens at my side, and the silence feels much wider and more ominous than it should. It almost shocks me to see how much dissent there is, despite its not being openly declared.

"We have come to discuss the mid-winter feast. High King Rholker's official coronation is of utmost importance to each and every one of us."

One man in the second row looks furious as he watches. His clothes are some of the richest I've ever seen, and his wife also wears those cursed Enduar diamonds—*blood* diamonds formed from the lava that ravaged the continent.

My eyes stick to the gems and their shine as the other giant reads out a list of matters that will be attended to first. Everyone else likely sees the brilliant rainbow of lights reflected from the diamond, but I see the darkness when the light hits it just so.

There's a flicker of recognition when the name Nandi is mentioned. That was Keksej's wife before he died.

Wasn't she also executed by Rholker's hand? My palms start to sweat when a side door opens, and a giant woman is brought in.

The best way to describe her is haggard, from the dirty red hair that hangs around her face to the clothes that look like they've seen weeks on her body. It's hard to resist looking up at Rholker as half the ladies in the room gasp.

When the female prisoner spots King Rholker, she starts screaming in giantese.

I make out the words "pig fucker" and "my son" before they wrap a cloth around her mouth and hit her with the long end of a staff. Her stream of insults is silenced with a whimper, only for one of the men at the back of the hall to stand up, positively indignant, and resume shouting. It's a sharp contrast to the general ambivalence coming from most of the giant lords.

"What's the meaning of this?" he has the audacity to demand. "Unhand my sister!" His silk clothes look expensive, and his burning yellow eyes look just like those of Keksej's widow.

Rholker doesn't move from his seat, effectively ignoring the outburst until the man stands up. "Lord Eriekk," he starts, but the man starts to make his way out of the row. "Ezdur, be seated or you will join your sister."

The man casts a look hot enough to sear through metal to Rholker before slowly returning to an empty seat and lowering himself.

The woman has started sobbing as she kneels before the king.

The rest of the court looks on. Silent.

They spent so many years making my people no better than animals, but they don't have a miniscule scrap of conscience they could use to protect one of their own kind? Giants are the worst of us all, and my hatred burns hot within me.

Rholker stands up. "Some of you had begun to doubt my legitimate claim to this throne on the grounds of my nephew's continued breathing. When I succeeded my father and brother, I thought that leaving my nephew in the court would be a merciful action."

Rholker's eyes scan the crowd, and my skin crawls.

She was screaming for her son. Something primal inside me blinks to life. It's just *a child*.

"Hell, I felt the same mercy for the lovely Nandi. But you all don't want a merciful ruler; you want an iron fist," he says harshly.

My stomach drops into my ass, and I can't take my eyes off of Nandi.

Her face is agony and hopelessness.

Rholker stands and holds out his arms. "Do you see Nandi's son in this court? Son of my brother, the *great* First Prince Keksej?"

No one answers his mocking tone.

He points at a man glowering in the second row. "Lord Fektir, do you see Nandi's son?"

The giant lord sticks his chin out. "If you are asking me to play your dirty game, then I will answer that I see *my* child chained at your side. And that I used to have a second daughter mere months ago."

Understanding blooms.

He's speaking about Rholker's bride. The one he was meant to marry when he took me to his rooms. But... I saw her. Marej, they called her. She hated me, and she definitely isn't the person chained to the other side of the throne.

If Rholker has taken two of this lord's daughters, then this must be the other—Marej's sister.

Did Rholker kill Marej after I was escorted from his room?

Rholker holds out both hands. "Keksej's heir is gone. He will never claim his right to the throne."

Nandi lets out another gods-awful sound as the realization that her child is dead sinks in.

Rholker rubs his head.

"Remember that I tried to be merciful," he calls out to the crowd. "Warriors, *come.*" The room is silent as they approach, and one holds out a sword. Its sharpness practically sings in the air.

Rholker takes the weapon and steps forward. He moves down the stairs slowly, one at a time, until he is in front of Nandi.

"Please, Second Prince, bury me next to my son," she sobs, all layers of vicious brutality stripped away to tear-streaked desperation. Her hands tremble as she holds them out in front of her. Guards press down on her shoulders, keeping her kneeling.

I adjust my weight on my cushion, my mouth uncomfortably dry. I take a deep breath and hold it as my slightly jagged fingernails cut into my palms.

"What did you call me?" Rholker demands.

She lets out a sob, then the guard grabs the back of her head and pushes it down. I hurt for her, and I feel ashamed to watch this and do nothing. For a moment, it doesn't matter that this woman's husband whipped my back until it was torn to ribbons. She just wants her baby.

"King Rholker," she says at the floor, her voice muffled by hair and grief.

While her family had tried to speak when she was first brought in, no one speaks for her when Rholker kicks her in the stomach. The wheezing cough she lets out makes me flinch.

Rholker raises the sword and turns around for all to see.

"I am your High King," he calls. Then, in an uncharacteristically theatrical movement, he points at the guards. "Move her hair so that my blade might slice clean through her neck."

I utterly freeze as the moment draws close.

Weeks ago, I was in a similar place, watching Teo kill his own hunter. The young boy had volunteered, and it broke something in Teo to do it. Rholker just looks furious. More of Liana's words return. *True rulers fight for their people, not against.*

As the sword slices through skin, sinew, and bone, I gasp. The woman on the other end of the throne shushes me, but I can't stop the tears from gathering.

I look up at the severed head of the Enduar on the wall. His glassy eyes look savage and feral as they stare forward into some unseen abyss. He was *arranged* to look that way, but I know the truth.

He wasn't hunted like a beast. Teo's man offered himself for his people; Rholker kills this woman because she threatens his fragile kinghood.

Disgust coats my tongue as bile rises up my throat.

Nandi's blood leaks out of her, and the smell of it makes my stomach churn.

Rholker doesn't clean his blade when he lifts it again. Nandi's blood drips down the steel, past the handle, and onto his hand. It stains the white cuff of his shirt.

"Anyone care to join her?" he calls to the room.

The father of the woman chained alongside me stands.

"This is cow shit. We did not come to watch an execution —you invited us here to announce your coronation." He shakes his head hard enough that some of the strands in his well-bound hair come free. His face is red. "Did you bring us here to murder our daughters before our very eyes, you limp dick?"

There's something about his passionate speech that almost

sounds like fatherly care. That evaporates when I remember that he *traded* Rholker two of his daughters to marry.

Rholker's chest heaves, and he slowly lowers the arm holding the sword.

"I would sit down if I were you, Lord Fektir," he practically whispers, voice hoarse with adrenaline.

He turns to one of the warriors and hands off the sword. It is traded for a spear.

Another giant stands up in the pews.

"We will not sit, we will not be silent to your toying." He thrusts a finger in my direction. "You brought that human bitch to court, you killed one of your own to sustain your throne before the royal court, and you—"

Rholker cocks his arm back and hurls the spear straight into the lord's chest.

The woman at his side screams as the man is impaled into the bench, like a needle through paper. His mouth hangs open, trying to speak his last words as Rholker's guards flood in from the side doors.

Seconds later, every exit is closed off.

"The human woman is valuable," Rholker says. "She is the queen of the trolls."

I freeze as a roar of male voices cascades through the hall, shouting, threatening, anguish, and pure rage. Rholker descends into the crowd, shouting at those who oppose him.

"Oh gods, he's going to kill me, too," a voice near me sobs. I look up to see Lord Fektir's daughter pulling against the short leash attached to the throne. When her attempt to break free fails, her mouth starts moving in rapid succession. Praying, I realize.

What good are prayers to a god of war?

My eyes squeeze shut. The smell of blood is everywhere, and the shouting persists.

"He won't kill you," I grit out, feeling ridiculous having this conversation when the sound of wood being shoved across marble makes me open my eyes. Rholker has moved farther back into the hall, away from the throne. A small group of guards surrounds him as he shouts in giantese about his divine right as heir to the throne.

I turn to look at the woman with glossy red curls. Her entire face is clearly visible over the throne. The metal leash loosens on my neck as I lean toward the armrest, but she doesn't look at me.

"If he kills you, your father will never accept him as king. Your father is important, yes?"

The woman stops praying and blinks, finally looking down at me. Her eyes are full of fear and sorrow, just like Nandi's.

"Yes."

I swallow, the same compassion stirring in my gut. It's ridiculous to feel bad for a giant again, but... while the military seems to be loyal to Rholker, his social power is low. I don't think he would kill another daughter of Lord Fektir. Perhaps she, too, needs a little hope. "Then you are too valuable to die."

The woman finally looks down at me with glowing amber eyes. "Giant women have no power."

"You do."

"I thought that slaves were as stupid as rats."

"What an interesting thing to say to someone trying to comfort you."

She frowns. "Does the troll king possess you to come into our court and ensue chaos, human whore?"

Anger and embarrassment flush through my cheeks. I was a fool for thinking she could be anything other than what she is.

"Tell me why you bring the human here!" a giant calls.

"I'll fucking show you," Rholker responds. My eyes snap

onto him and my heart races as he barrels toward me, face red and fists clenched.

He grabs my short chain and tugs me to my feet. I scramble and choke on the collar. Then he grabs a knife out of his belt and carefully uses it to cut away part of the silk in my bodice, revealing the Fuegorra. "You doubt me once again. She is married to the king!"

Each gaze is heavy, and many grow quiet while others continue to grumble angrily in the corners of the closed-off room.

Lord Fektir is the one who speaks. "You can use her to get to him?"

My skin burns.

"Why should we care about a king who leads a court that is practically a handful of vermin?" Someone else shouts.

"They killed my mother! It is in my right to seek vengeance," Rholker shouts.

"You will not bring up your displeasure at the murder of your family when Nandi's blood still soaks the stones at your feet." Lord Fektir glares—studies Rholker.

When I look up, I see a bloody king standing before his throne, wielding his women in chains. It must be quite the sight for everyone else.

Rholker tilts his chin up and thrusts my chain forward, causing me to take another step. "If vengeance is not good enough for you, then know I also see this siege as preventative. She is proof of their ability to mate with humans. What if they breed an army to fight against us?" He continues, "If they are gone, they would leave behind a city full of riches."

The silence that follows is full of churning thoughts, and it makes my insides twist.

"If you could finish off the cave rats, every last one, then we could have free access to their mines in addition to our own," Lord Fektir says.

Rholker nods, panting. "Precisely."

Diamonds are of paramount value to the giants. Their usage and resale have built the entire capital. I didn't know that they already had mines, though. Where?

"We have more than enough humans to mine them, and I have already sent more women to the breeding pens to increase population," Rholker says.

I am preternaturally still.

My people.

My *godsdamned* people.

The gem on my chest begins to glow. No one shies away as it shines through the silk bodice; they all stare.

"I will not sustain your coronation before then," he says.

Rholker shakes his head.

"You must. The feast has been scheduled! All of our allies are already invited and have agreed to come."

Lord Fektir remains silent.

"Lord Fektir, if you wish to be counted among those who make it to the future, to the next great dynasty of giants, I suggest you attend my coronation."

Fektir raises his chin, mouth in a tight straight line, and a new wave of murmurs spreads across the room like a flame through a dry forest. The threat is heard clearly, but he doesn't respond. After a moment of silent deliberation, Lord Fektir gives a firm nod.

"I will come to your coronation, Rholker. Then, you will slaughter every last Enduar. Do this, and you will have my continued support in your campaign as king."

I swallow hard, but when this man is finished speaking, it's as if most of the room settles into agreement. My mind squeezes as I try to comprehend the threat.

This is no longer a silly infatuation with a female slave.

This is... war. Genocide. Complete annihilation of Enduvida —my home.

My mate.

My future.

Humanity's future. The Enduares' future.

My breaths are shallow as the meeting around me begins to conclude. The doors are reopened, and dozens of well-dressed slaves rush in to clean the two dead giants.

I look at Rholker. It's clear I had underestimated him this entire time.

As if sensing my attention, he turns to look at me and raises an eyebrow.

"What, my dear Estela?" he murmurs.

My breaths are uneven. My mouth opens and closes in rapid succession, trying to find words. "Will you take me to see Mikal now?"

A slow smile spreads across his face.

"I told you to behave. I don't think using your troll magic is behaving."

I open my mouth. "But—"

"Enough. I am growing tired of you. Let us return to the cottage."

He leaves Lord Fektir's daughter on the other side of the throne, watching us with an expression that gives away nothing. Her father doesn't even make a move to unchain her.

Dozens of my people avoid my gaze as they work to mop up buckets of blood and carry out bodies easily three times too big for one person to bear.

A memory flits through my mind, another of Teo. One untouched by the memory shredders. I try not to focus on it, lest it triggers whatever evil magic they'd used against me, but I think of his tall, calming presence.

He was such a large person—in stature and kindness. He made me want to be bigger.

And so I would be—and the giants will pay for every inch I grow.

Before we make it out of the enormous room, one of the lords stops Rholker. He's got graying hair, and I recognize him as the advisor to late King Erdaraj, Regent Uvog, but he doesn't look at me as he leans in to whisper in Rholker's ear.

I don't hear what is said, but there is movement around the corner.

Green flesh just barely sticks out, and my head cocks to the side.

An arm and a foot poke out seconds before a large head covered in moss and twigs gazes over at us. Large yellow eyes are the defining connector to the giants.

My brows furrow. I haven't seen a swamp ogre in years.

Rholker shakes his head at the man who is speaking and then proceeds to drag me out of the palace. But not before my gaze meets the ogre.

There's a strange noise that fills my ears as it does, like being transported away from the wintry forest and to a warm, wet nest surrounded by feathery trees and the ballad of insects singing to the fire.

When the contact is broken, the sounds still echo in my mind. The swamp ogres were volatile and not allowed in the giant court. If Rholker is seeking a relationship with him, it could be dangerous. When I glance up at the ruthless king, I wonder just how much further he's willing to go.

CHAPTER 9

DIANITE

TEO

I t took us five days to travel through the forest and find the general location that Turalyon had marked on the map. We each switched off coaxing along Turalyon's old *glacialmara*, and it slowed our progression, but none of us would leave one of *drathorinna's* spawn to the elements.

We're still in the Northern Forest, just barely outside the borders of the Elvish capital, Shvathemar, but everything about this place feels crowded and ominous. We don't soar or race here, we move slowly—cautiously.

The elvish lands are enchanted to be in a state of perpetual spring. Deep brown and golden trunks stretch up all around us, with luscious leaves in nearly every shade of green. Their tops press against each other, fighting to get enough light to keep surviving. The odd patch that leaves don't obscure is filled with sprouted flowers in pastel hues.

Insects fly in a peculiar way—more hovering than soaring, unlike the birds. They dart back and forth before diving toward the ground at some unseen target.

One of the fowls I'd been watching earlier with iridescent

red feathers lands on Niht's shoulder. He coos to the creature, and it chirps back before flitting away.

When it returns, it brings friends. Some of them land on Ulla, who laughs in delight.

"No killing these little ones, either," she tells Niht sternly.

He smiles. "Of course not. They wouldn't give us anything other than a morsel of meat."

Ra'Salore is peculiarly quiet as he studies the forest, only pausing to curse and swat at some bug.

There's no sign of a sequestered rebellion led by women out here, no grand castle, not even a shack or the ruins of an old house.

I take a deep breath, drawing in the scent of moist ground and fresh trees to help steady myself.

"Are you sure this is the spot?" Niht asks, and I hear the rustle of a scroll as Ulla takes out the map.

Again.

Rahda seems to let out a long sigh as she twists her crystal head to look back at me. I stroke the smooth stone once more as we slow our pace and fall into place alongside Ulla.

My glasses are still resting on the crook of my nose, so I see the hand-drawn expanse that Turalyon left us. I study the trees around me, then return to the carefully measured marks and the artful illustration of Shvathemar.

There is no hum of the ground to guide our paths. I almost worry that we have been going in circles in these trees with nothing more than the rising and setting sun to guide us. But we haven't strayed. A hill stretches up to the eastern side, just as it should. I remember crossing the river, deviating from the road leading to Arion's territory. We had followed everything down to the carefully painted letter.

"Yes," I say.

Niht makes a sound a few paces away. "I need to stop to take a piss."

I look up and see his hair spilling out of his braid. He shifts his weight to his back leg, puts one hand on an armored hip, and raises the other to his shoulder, where a new bird is perched.

"Will you leave me in peace, little one?" he asks. The bird squeaks and flutters away. He smiles and disappears behind the tree.

Sighing, the rest of us dismount and our *glacialmaras* float together, curling in comforting motions and expressing their weariness.

I riffle through my pack, pulling out a spyglass. Switching the crystal in the lens to look for hidden magic, I study the landscape.

Nothing.

All of us are quiet, resigned.

"Maybe we missed a turn—" Niht starts upon returning.

"No," Ra'Salore bites out. He crosses to Ulla, who is still reading over Turalyon's notes. "I propose one final scan of the area. Perhaps there is some hole in the ground, covered by leaves."

I look at the golden sunlight shining through the tightly packed leaves as the sun dips into the horizon.

"No more than an hour. We need to set up camp before dark."

To be honest, I don't know much about the monsters that lurk in these forests. It's possible that the cold ones followed us to this point. There are also tales of large creatures lurking in Elvish lands: wolves the size of men covered in moss and thickets, and dryads who protect the land from those who would seek to destroy their sacred space.

As the others scour the region, I ensure the *glacialmaras* are tied up. Rahda's twinkling chimes grow louder as I approach.

She separates from the others, who appear to be playfully crashing against each other and tangling up their leads.

"Shh," I murmur as I stroke my hand over her head. "You have flown so well during this trip. It would be foolish to be so loud that you give up our location." My words are scolding, and I am unsure if she understands, but the tip of her long, jagged tail whips out behind her.

I sigh, leaving my friend, and walk deeper into the forest. The peculiar structure of the trees still disorients me—unlike the expanses of crystal that followed me everywhere in Enduvida.

One thing I know with my whole being: they are alive. But I do not hear their song, and they seem to have little concern about making their secrets known to me. They just watch. Study me and my every move. Neutral in this moment, but in the next? Would they be our enemies? They certainly hadn't been my enemy in the past.

Their leaves are different from the elm trees in Zlosa. Normally, I try not to think about the giant capital, but being surrounded by a forest has made me pensive.

When I had first arrived on my mission, I wore my finest doublet and jewels. Walking up the marble steps was odd, as I knew the giants cared little for stones.

My father had spent years describing every inch of that place in excruciating detail.

It was almost as if his voice had been whispering in my ear, guiding me behind doors I was not shown. Mistrust was every-where, even in my own heart, despite my relaxed smile. It wasn't until I was escorted into the throne room that the first lick of fear chilled my innards.

The image of High King Erdaraj sitting on his great wooden throne and his wife, Queen Lijasa, seated on a smaller chair at his side still makes my stomach clench.

Lijasa's room was on the top floor of the giant palace. It had massive windows that overlooked the capital city and the surrounding forests. After I finished servicing her, when she was sleeping, I would stand and watch their leafy tops sway in the wind.

Sometimes, their violent whipping felt like the pieces of my soul I'd given away to that cruel woman.

The flutter of wings to my left draws me back to these forests we are in now. Swallowing hard, I glance back up at the sky and see how far the sun has sunk. We aren't searching for ghosts, we are searching for allies.

Though, perhaps they are ghosts because these allies apparently don't exist.

Taking one last sweeping look around, I turn on my heel and head back to the clearing. Only Ra'Salore is there, and he is already undoing the pack on his *glacialmara* to set up camp.

I follow suit in silence. My head is full of monsters. His might be as well—as the tension between us never truly abates.

Ulla and Niht soon join us. Before the last rays of light fade into inky darkness, four leather tents and bedrolls are neatly arranged a safe distance from a modest fire. Ulla sets up a few crystals to mask the flames and smoke.

The truth hurts. There's nothing to be found out here.

The warmth seeping into my hands, legs, and clothes helps keep away some of the chill of failure. One must celebrate the small things to bear the weight of the future.

A new idea has been percolating in the back of my mind. If there are no women to meet, we must be flexible in our strategy. We simply don't have time to scour every inch of the forest when Estela is still with the giants.

A familiar panic claws up my throat, and I stroke the bond. When I do, that channel right below my heart stirs, and I gasp.

The sensation fades quickly. But feeling her, if it's just her soul, is enough for me.

"Tomorrow, we will go to the Elvish capital, and we will request an audience with King Arion," I say, trying not to sound like I am choking on the words despite them sticking to the back of my throat. It would be painfully humiliating to go back to him and ask for help after he is the reason my wife is gone in the first place.

"Teo, no," Ulla says immediately, stopping her gentle singing and dropping the handle of the spoon she was using to tend to the dried meat softening in boiling water.

I meet her gaze. "We can't go home empty-handed."

She frowns, but Ra'Salore's face has turned sour.

"Groveling at the feet of those who betrayed us is not something I can support."

I watch him stand up and follow suit.

"What other choice do we have? We came this far because we need assistance to free my mate."

He sneers. "Perhaps the humans are more trouble than they are worth. You only had her for a few short months. Just let things be—there are other matehoods. Soon, there will be children. As king, it is your duty to place the needs of the people above your own. Always."

The air is electric, and Ulla's face darkens. "King Teo has sacrificed—"

"*We have all sacrificed,*" Ra'Salore practically shouts.

I've never seen him so angry, not even after his brother's death.

"My brother was beheaded for the cause of the humans. I know that was his choice, but he and my mother were all the family I had left. My sisters were killed in the eruption. My father gave his life as a member of one of the king's battalions. I have come here out of duty, but my family's headcount has not been improved by the humans—not yet. I won't die before I can carry on my line. Perhaps my loyalty to the crown has been misplaced." The words are tumbling out of him, like years of unspoken confessions.

Each word lands its blow, and I feel a deep shame in the pit of my stomach.

Niht stands next to him and puts his hand on his shoulder.

"Ra'Salore," he says as the other Enduar yanks his arm away.

"Do not try to placate me, old man. I'm going to sleep, and in the morning, I am going home. As I think all of you should," he says.

The sound of laughter fills the air, causing everyone to freeze. It's a jarring, foreign sound in the wake of our fight.

A second later, a form appears right next to Ulla. She gasps as arms wrap around her, pulling her close. A knife is pressed to her throat.

"Ulla," I choke out as the figure is fully revealed.

A tall elf with short, well-combed white hair that sticks out around sun-tanned skin, pointed ears, and piercing green eyes stands in the middle of the camp. His garb is dark, nearly black.

I draw the knife tucked into my waistband, lamenting the armor and sword lying in my tent. Ra'Salore and Niht are more prepared. They point their blades at him, and he makes a tsking sound.

"Now, now, gentlemen. While you are a fearsome sight, with your heavy metal and azure skin, be careful where you stick those blades, or you'll find your companion bleeding out on the ground faster than you can swipe me with one of your tails."

"Are you one of Arion's assassins?" I growl at him, and he turns his perfectly straight nose toward Ulla. Her eyes are wide, and she clutches the arm holding her immobile.

All of his attention fixes on Ulla. He is only slightly taller than her. If she were to turn and look at him, it would almost look like a warm embrace.

His expression hardens. Then he jostles her, eliciting a soft whimper, and gives me a simple "No."

"Then who are you?" I demand.

"My apologies, my dear," he says to her, ignoring me. "You have quite a lovely singing voice, so I sincerely hope your king doesn't do something brash." His eyes find mine once more and narrow. "Something that would compromise your lovely neck."

"You've been watching us," Niht spits at the elf.

The man smiles. It's a charming, pointy curve of his mouth. "Yes. Though, you're all rather boring if I'm being honest. And criminally uncreative."

I take a step forward, which he doesn't seem to react to, though Ulla flinches in his arms. If he were going to kill her, he would've by now. While I don't see mercy flickering in his eyes, I think his capture of Ulla is more for show than anything else.

He wants us to be afraid, but he is also curious.

"Do you know anything about an enclave of elvish women?" I ask, trying to cut through the tension around the fire.

He looks bored. "You're looking for elvish women in the woods? I didn't realize how stupid you... *Enduares* could be. I haven't seen a female elf outside of her humble dwelling since... never. Don't you know that the pinnacle of feminine bliss is tending to a husband? They're very well-domesticated," he nearly purrs as Ulla gains her footing and starts to shift. "Perhaps this lovely lady could learn something from them."

Ullas face turns purple with her flush, so I keep talking. If I can just distract him from Ulla, I could tackle them both and get that knife away.

"Then why are you here? I'll ask you again: are you one of King Arion's assassins?"

He actually laughs this time. "I'll answer you the same: *gods, no.*"

I take the opportunity to take another step, feeling everyone's eyes on me, and his laughter dies.

"If you want me to release your delicious friend, tell me what you want with the sisterhood."

"My human mate was stolen by the giants. We have few options left for allies in this fight, so we've come here, hoping to speak with the sisterhood."

The elf all but rolls his eyes. "Trolls seeking out the help of the elves to deal with the giants. A tale as old as time—and one that I've already grown benumbed to."

I take a deep breath. "I've also come to offer my people's services. If you aren't with the king, you are against him. Once my wife is safely secured, I will ensure a new sovereign sits in Shvathemar."

His eyebrows shoot up. "Friend, I'm not sure if this is the place for you to spout treason. Though, I am dying of curiosity. How did you hear of these... women?" the elf asks.

"After one of my councilors came to reopen communication with Arion before the festival. While he was here, he heard of a small rebellion of women brewing in the forests."

If this man isn't with the king, he might be with this rebellion despite being a man.

"We have brought gifts and an offer of help in any way we can. We also might have information about an artifact that my father stole."

The elf watches me with a blank expression.

"You're not lying," he says after a second.

I shake my head. "No, I'm not."

Slowly, he lowers his hands, and Ulla stumbles forward.

Niht crosses the fire to help her. The newcomer spares her

one final apologetic glance, and it's then that I see a familiar roundness to his features—particularly the ears.

One that speaks to a human background.

"You're half-human," I say boldly. My eyes grow wider. Of course, he would not be in Arion's court. The elves were just as concerned with racial purity as my father.

The man frowns. "Thorne the *Peredhel,* not at your service," he counters.

I recognize the parts of the word, practically a slur among elves as it translates to *half-human.* They are defined entirely by the undesirable half of their lineage.

He studies us for a second longer.

"If you aren't liars, I suppose I will let her decide what other dark intentions you might have."

I straighten my shoulders as my hope soars.

We've found them.

"Take us to the sisterhood, and I will heartily promise to help dethrone, kill, or otherwise imprison Lord Arion," I say, hoping to solidify my stance further.

Thorne lets out another jarring laugh. "Very well, my friends. If you desire to inculpate your court to aid us, who am I to reject you?"

He raises his hand, and a small spark lights up the tip of his finger.

In a second, the forest around us begins to rustle and twist. Some of the trees themselves animate, and their long, fluffy branches sink down to become arms and hands. Eyes open on once unseeing bark, and their mossy green orbs study us with blank expressions.

Niht gasps, but one of the trees hones in on Ulla.

"My lady," an ethereal voice slides through the air. "You may come first," the dryad says.

Thorne gestures toward the trees, and Ulla casts him a sharp, mistrusting look, which he almost seems to smirk at.

She takes the branch's hand, and Ra'Salore, Niht, and I start moving to join her.

Thorne raises his hand, and a billowing shadow hits each of us in the forehead.

Most of my strength blinks out like a light. Struggling to move, I look back at the *glacialmaras*, which are yanking at their tethers.

An awful, gurgling sound makes the earth beneath us shake and sink. One of the dryads picks up my limp form, and I see a face grow from the ground, like another tree. Large, glowing eyes blink open amidst leaves and branches. It opens its mouth and says something in old elvish. Something even I do not understand, though it sounds like a question.

Thorne steps forward, and the rest of my awareness fades.

CHAPTER 10
M⬭NSTONE
ESTELA

For several days, my life follows the same pattern. Cold, shivering nights filled with nightmares and partial memories, and then frigid mornings with the comfort woman preparing me for Rholker and his strange, little parades with me around the lumber yards.

During this time, I am reduced to a pitiful foreign creature that others sneer and gawk at—particularly when I am given a dress with a low enough neckline to show off the Fuegorra.

My move to the palace has been delayed because he still cannot touch me. When we return to the cottage each day, I ask him to take me to Mikal. He denies me, hands me a strand of hair from my brother's head as "proof" of his continued living, and then leaves.

I braid the black hairs together, desperately wishing that I knew they were actually his, and use the empty spaces in my day to memorize information I can take back to Teo. Everything I learned will be both a gift to my new people and an apology for the sadness that has followed in my wake.

Lord Fektir is the driving force behind the court, while

119

Regent Uvog is the one who has been tending to some unknown business with the swamp ogres. The Six are here, though their presence mostly causes worried whispers in corners and dark rooms that I barely catch. I saw Dahlia once, waiting in one of the palace rooms. She dipped her head to me while I trembled in my chains.

There are twenty-seven families in the royal court. A majority must agree to Rholker's coronation for him to stay in power, and at least ten families are loyal to Lord Fektir and will follow him in whatever decision he makes. This includes Regent Uvog.

The stakes are high for my sadistic captor—but even higher for me. The Six told Rholker that I would need to remain untouched for several weeks. That healing period ends on the night of the mid-winter feast.

His coronation. If he wins, then...

I try not to think of what it would feel like to be in his bed. The fractured bits of my consciousness are held together largely by ignoring my reality. Spiraling into the depths of my future if I fail is foolish.

I always have a plan. Gathering information and finding a way to save as many humans as possible—including Mikal—is the best I have right now.

Lost to my thoughts, my door opens. Like clockwork. However, only one form shuffles in, bearing a humble meal.

I look up at the comfort woman from the back of my cage, leaning against the bars.

"*Hola*[1]," I all but croak.

She looks at me, all that friendliness she puts on in front of the giants wiped away. She places a large bucket near the door full of my bath water, and then places the food on a table while she lights a fire.

Once the flames are warming the chilled room, she takes the

TO IGNITE A FLAME

waste bucket, goes back outside, and then returns with a mostly clean recipient.

"*No debes hacer eso,*"[2] I say. "If you would let me out, I'd clean it myself."

She snorts. "Nice try, but your shit isn't the nastiest thing I've had to clean."

Then she washes her hands in the water bucket and comes over to unlock my cage door. She places the individual dishes in front of me. *Bola de hoja*[3], eggs, bread, and tea. Eager to speak to her, I sit up and cross my legs.

"*Gracias,*"[4] I say, picking up a piece of mostly fresh bread.

I tear it in two and hold out the other half. It is an old offering of peace between slaves—gods know that I've coaxed more than words out of fellow slaves by giving up my food. When Mikal and I had gone on the trek to Enduvida, I convinced seven of the others to keep quiet while I sabotaged a cart.

She eyes the bread as if it were a dead rat. The beginnings of a sneer tug at her top lip as she glares at me.

But she doesn't leave.

"I'm Foreman Eneko's comfort woman. You think they don't feed me? He's not the kind who likes to rut a skeleton," she spits out.

The words are intended to scare me off, but I've been prickly enough times in my life to not run away when someone shows me their thorns.

I raise my eyebrows. "Why would the foreman let his comfort woman babysit me all day?"

"Probably because the king asked him to." She folds her arms, watching me carefully. "How old are you?"

"Twenty-five," I say. "And you?"

She purses her lips. "Older than twenty-five and younger than thirty-two."

I huff a laugh. "Does Eneko have a relationship with Rholker?"

"Eneko had to seek permission for me to become his comfort woman from Rholker," she says bluntly.

This conversation is coming to an end, but I like talking to her.

"Do you know who my mother was?" I ask casually.

She narrows her eyes.

"All the slaves know who you are." She takes the bread from my hands, tears it in two, and puts one half away. The action makes my chest hurt. We humans are always saving a bit for later. Just in case.

"You are the lucky, beautiful bitch who was spared rounds with giant lords and breeding pens because of her *mamá*'s legendary work," she says.

I nod slowly, but then, I gesture at the cage around me.

"I wouldn't say I was spared all the rounds with the giants. Keksej's favorite hobby was tearing my back apart and... You see what Rholker does."

She snorts, looking down at the bread as if considering whether to take another bite.

"A cage where everyone brings you food and you can sleep alone. Untouched."

My mother's face flashes before my eyes. I see her looking down at me in her short, silk green dress. She kisses my cheeks and whispers a prayer before she waves goodbye and joins the giant escorts. The only reason I'm untouched is because she went willingly into the king's bed.

I can't forget that.

"You're right. I don't want it to be said that what I experienced is worse than what you've been through. I respect you for the choice you made, and it kills me that it's necessary to survive. I merely want to show you that I hate the giants just as much as you," I say.

She pauses as if just now considering this. When her eyes flick back to me, her guardedness has faded.

"So, did you marry the Troll King because you wanted to escape? Or did he force you?" she asks, though I know she's supposed to be pouring a bath. The bucket she brought with her is still by the door, and the fire remains unlit.

I won't complain.

"I proposed the idea to Teo because I wanted his help to save my brother," I say. There's so much more to say, that I am trying to escape, that I was made a queen. She doesn't even know about the two powers in my chest—one from the Fuegorra with the ability to see the future and heal my body, and the other, a gift of light that burns others.

She raises an eyebrow. "I'd say you made a bad deal."

I take a deep breath.

"Teo will come for me. I know it—and he'll help me get my brother back. I just might have to help him out a little." It's a heavy gamble to reveal so much to her, but there's curiosity on her side. It's a risk I'm willing to take if I can have an ally.

"Did you consummate your marriage?" She decides to eat the rest of the bread.

The question prods at the ugly, broken memories, and I furrow my brow against the pulsing pain in my mind.

"I..." I wince against the pain in my head. "I fell in love with him. They have something called mates in the caves—it's like your perfect other half."

She watches the pain on my face but reveals nothing of her own thoughts. Then she looks at the marks on my neck.

"So you did."

I nod.

"Ahh, so that is why Rholker was so mad. Gods, men are all

the same—they get whoever they want, but the second you touch someone else, they start a fucking war." She reaches into the cage and takes another piece of my bread.

I say nothing.

"Something like that," I say, feeling that familiar helpless rage peeking up at me from its dim hiding place. Everything in Zlosa is cold, wet, and bitter. I just need to get out of here and go *home*.

"But the Enduares aren't such jealous, fickle beings. They were all respectful. Even the king. He waited until I came to him." I wince again in pain, trying to keep the panic at bay as false memories of blood invade my senses and the sensation of choking settles around my throat. "You might think me half mad, but the stories they tell you about trolls are lies. It took me... too long to realize that."

She gives me a sideways look.

"It is a place where slavery doesn't exist. Where you are given a choice over your life—where you can write your freedom on your heart for all to see. For you to choose. I wish I could paint you a picture of the love between the people, the hardworking community, the gentleness met with stone-tempered strength when necessary."

The woman scoffs again but then reaches into her pocket. She pulls out a handful of jewels. They sing to each other, and my whole soul fills with the light of home. Not so much memories as *feelings* of memories, ghosts in my mind that are untouched by the slicing.

It's impossible to contain the tears that well up and slide down my cheeks.

"Easy there. I found these when I was taking your dress to be burned," she trails off. Then she holds them through the bars. "You should do a better job of hiding them."

Our hands brush when I take them from her. "Why are you

doing this? You could've kept them... or traded them for something better."

She grows irritated that I've offered her anything. "You overestimate my relationship with most other slaves. Many comfort women are my friends, but many are merely pets to their masters—little songbirds. Someone would run their mouth, I would get in trouble, you would get in trouble. Besides, my things are searched regularly."

I watch her, acutely aware of how precious this tentative allyship is between us. "By the foreman?" I ask.

She lets out a bitter laugh. "By his wife."

My mouth drops open.

"I'm sorry."

She shrugs.

I hold up the stones and then hum a note—one that Ulla used to make while we worked together on plants.

One of the stones on my necklace sings back, and the Fuegorra flickers.

Her eyes grow wide. "What the hell was that?"

I smile.

"Trolls get their magic from the hard things of the earth: metal, stone, and crystal. It's beautiful. Each has a different purpose—I'll be honest, I don't know most of them. But I know this."

I hum a short melody, and it's amplified in the room. The woman is absolutely mystified. Before she can stop herself, she copies my clumsy tune.

They sing back to her, and her mouth falls open.

"That's..." She trails off into stunned silence and when she speaks, she murmurs mostly to herself. "How did I not know this was possible?"

I pick up the small necklace I had made of gold buttons and stone silk and hand it out to her.

"Here. I made this after I saw you looking at my dress. It was my wedding dress. There aren't any gems for you to sing to, but you should keep it."

"So you wish to bribe me?" She rolls her eyes, shaking off the wonder from moments before, and stands, walking to the fireplace. She kneels down and begins to light sparks with a flint.

"Please," I try again. "There's a place near the eastern slave pens where I used to live. I have a hollowed-out tree where I keep herbs and supplies—keep it there if you wish. It was a place for me and my brother when we were young."

She eyes my hand for a minute longer and then takes the necklace and stuffs it in her pocket.

"Herbs mean little when you don't know how to use them, but I will happily steal them for other reasons."

I shake my head.

"It's not stealing if I am giving them to you. I can tell you how to use whatever you need." My eyes drop to her wrist, where there is a faint cut stretching down to her forearm. I gasp, my insides twisting. Gods only know where she got it from. "*That* for example. You want to keep it clean. Even in the winter, there are trees, a type of elm, that have small pockets of sap scattered across the bark. Pop the bubbles and use the sap to create a bandage for the wounds at night; it will help prevent them from getting infected. Even better if you can put some moss on top of that, but it will be harder to find in the winter."

She looks down at me, wary.

"I'll come back later for the dishes. Consider today a day to yourself."

She leaves the fire running but picks up the bucket by the door. Something inside of me relaxes at the thought of not having to be bathed.

The door opens.

"*Me llamo Melisa.* And you don't have to keep annoying

Rholker with your incessant questions. Your brother is alive—I know where he's kept."

Then she closes the door. More relief bubbles up, joining the relief from not having to take the bath. I press the gems to my chest, letting their songs mingle with my Fuegorra as I smile.

Thank you, thank you. Thank. You.

I need to get her out of here and show her just how precious the gift she gave me is.

CHAPTER 11
EUCLASE
TEO

M y few moments out of the waking world were filled of nightmares with large, haunted faces appearing in the ground and endless chatter.

When I gather enough strength to reopen my eyes, there are trees above me that have grown into a dome shape. It's impossible to tell where one starts and the other ends as they reach across the clearing and form an arch.

My brows furrow, and the voices of a crowd continue to hum in a river of unintelligible noises. Instead of cutting down trees like they do in Zlosa or Shvathemar, it looks like they've used magic to shape them according to their needs.

The knotty bulges in the trunks look like carvings, and the wrinkled brown bark has been manipulated into the appearance of flowers and butterflies. Like a painting. Blinking away the crusted moisture in my eyes, I see squirrels, spiders, and ugly creatures with fangs sharp enough to tear a grown man's throat crawl through branches and leaves.

The roar of hundreds of different voices makes the pounding in my head intensify, so I stay prone for a second longer.

I roll to my side and groan at the soreness. I flex my hands which is greeted by stiff pain that radiates through my arms and chest. Looking to my left, I see that the other Enduares were also laid out on the unnaturally plush grass.

My attention is drawn away when the words *Enduar King* rises above all others.

Taking a deep, aching breath, I slowly lift myself onto my elbow, ignoring the pulse of my brain against the confines of my skull. I rub my brow.

We are surrounded by tables with both bare elvish feet and leafy stumps on full view. My heart skips a beat when I also see ten large giant toes.

My eyes swivel up, and I blink at the giant woman who stands side by side with a dryad and an elf. When she catches me looking at her, she nudges her companions and points at me with a toothy smirk.

Just slightly behind her is a whole damned bear, though it is nothing like a *ruh'glumdlor*. It lacks black fur, blind eyes, and spiky armor plates on its shoulders and elbows. These are all soft brown angles and razor-sharp claws.

If it weren't for its paws, it might be considered endearing.

My head twists from side to side, and the room goes silent. There are hundreds of elvish women, maybe even more than a thousand just in this room with many more outside. I don't see Thorne, but the dryads I presume who dragged us here are lined up behind a thorny throne at the front of the space.

This is not a small enclave. The sisterhood isn't a small group of dissenting women.

It's a whole civilization apart from Arion's rule.

"Welcome to the Sisterhood de Bhaldraithe, Enduar King," a female voice calls out. "Pity, I was hoping you'd wear your glasses to our meeting. I've heard they look quite striking upon your face."

It's curious how they call us by our new name.

As I gaze upon the woman, I am met with rigid, elegant beauty. She has silvery blond hair, and she bears a striking resemblance to Arion. There is no doubt that he is her brother, though his practiced decorum is nothing like what she exhibits.

Liana's words about brothers and sisters in elvish courts return to me as I take in her smooth tresses. They are braided in a dozen smaller strands that knot over her neck and shoulders. They drip off one armrest while her legs hang over the other side of the throne.

This woman is a picture of cold, comfortable indifference—of danger. Daggers are laced up her legs, and she has one out that she twirls between her fingers.

I hurry to rise, despite the stiffness in my muscles and joints. It's a feat to keep myself from going light-headed and falling over.

I dip my head as Ra'Salore, Ulla, and Niht rise as well.

"Thank you," I say.

She stares at me with unblinking eyes.

"Are you... Lady Mrath?" I search for the appropriate title, ready to invoke the artifact, *Cumhacht na Cruinne*, as bargaining leverage.

I will be able to give this deal a clean shot at success.

One corner of her mouth tilts up.

"No need for formalities here, Enduar. I have no set title—some call me a nightmare, others call me friend. Some truly idiotic men once called me princess. But I'm sure you knew that." She swings her legs back over the edge of the throne with predatory grace and reaches over for a goblet of wine being offered to her. "My sisters call me Mrath."

I look around as she holds up her goblet, and the rest of the room toasts to her.

"Very well, Mrath. Where are my mounts?" I ask.

"Back at your camp," one of the dryads says.

"Well, then, would you be so kind as to tell me what this place is?"

Mrath dips her head and smiles. "You are very polite for a man. I am sure that you heard of us as a band of murderers. It is not entirely incorrect, but it is also not right."

I listen intently, not bringing up the rumors of their rebellion.

Mrath continues. "The Sisterhood is an escape from the bondage of our old lives. Yes, there are assassins in our midst —those who were not allowed to be trained with the king's archers and assassins. But there are just as many healers. Weavers. Travelers." She cocks her head to the side. "We have even been known to protect a select few. For a price, of course."

I nod. "Thank you for welcoming us into your enclave. I have urgent matters to discuss, and I have news that might be of interest to you."

"Have we welcomed you?" She stares at us long and hard, her eyes passing from me to Niht, then Ulla and Ra'Salore, and then finally back to my face. "What has my brother done to have you sniveling and crawling to my doorstep?"

I straighten my back.

She's goading me.

"Recently, we were seeking an alliance against the giants, so we invited King Arion to the Festival of Endu. It was my... wedding night. He told the giants of the plan, and they invaded my home and stole my mate. I need help getting her back and killing Rholker."

She purses her lips. "Such miscare on your end, but I must admit. I already knew all of this—I wanted to know if you would lie." Her lips curl upward. "Spying is also one of our specialties."

I tighten my fists. "It was foolish for me to be so trusting, but I never intended for any harm to come to Estela."

"Es-tell-ah," she says slowly, drawing out each syllable. "Lovely human name, but I thought the giants made it a rule that humans belonged to them and them alone."

I purse my lips. "King Erdaraj mended the agreement, but—"

"Then he was killed by his son," she finishes. She lets out a single laugh and shakes her head. "Lucky bastard."

As we speak, one of the squirrels climbs up Niht's leg and clambers to his shoulder.

Mrath watches, displeased.

"The purpose of the Sisterhood is the betterment of our people. There are neither Enduar nor human women in our ranks, yet you want our help."

I clench my fists. "We did not know of your existence, we are barely alive ourselves. And as for the humans, others have come in search of the elves—you never met any of them?"

Dread twists in my gut when she shakes her head.

All those who came before seeking freedom with the elves... Did they all die? Arion did not know much about humans, so I assumed they would not have gone to the capital.

Mrath carefully watches my expression as the realization sinks in. We likely didn't save a single slave we freed.

"You want access to my help? Then you must be as one of us," she says after a few more moments. "You will learn to steal, cheat, and murder to earn your place." She's still spinning her knife over her fingers and letting the drops fall onto the throne. Where her blood touches, small red flowers bloom.

"Those are the rules for you to help us?" I try to clarify once more. All of those things sound like they will take an exorbitant amount of time, and ten days have already passed with Estela in the giant's clutches.

She tilts her head back and laughs. Her spiny crown doesn't budge.

"No, *Teo*. That's what you'll do if you want to live long enough to see your pretty little human. You came here without my permission, and there's only one rule of Sisterhood de Bhaldraithe: don't fuck with Mrath."

I stare at her, watching the way her cold eyes take in our small group.

Slowly, I nod.

"I wouldn't dream of it."

She reclines on her great, wooden throne again.

"If you want our help, you'll have to prove yourself someone worth helping. It's a fine and pretty thing to say that you'll slit my brother's throat, or give back an artifact your father took, but I have no point of reference to know whether or not that is even true."

My fists tighten. Thorne told her everything.

Ulla speaks up. "Our king was once called the Butcher of Giants, and his father had the ruthless brutality to blow up most of a continent. Surely that is assurance enough."

Mrath's chin tucks against her neck and her lips curve down slightly. The air around us feels charged with warning, and the dryads behind her creep closer.

"Words and rumors are valuable—many are even true—but I want to see you in action. Tonight. I have some rubbish I've been meaning to deal with for quite some time."

Cheers erupt around us with all the women banging their goblets against the table.

Ra'Salore speaks next, clearly surprised. "You want us to kill someone tonight?"

Mrath angles her chin upward and smiles. It is a lethal look.

"How long has the king's mate been with the giants? Ten days? I hear he's been dragging her around... on a leash."

Rage burns hot inside my body, and my tail flicks out behind me angrily. She knows far more than she was trying to let on earlier. She knows that Estela is my mate; she has spies in Zlosa.

"Of what do you speak?"

She shrugs. "Rholker brought a very strange group of women to handle her. She seems quite docile these days, which is a shame. I was hoping to see what kind of fire she spits out when threatened."

"So, she's alive and unharmed?" I ask, desperate, fighting the shaking anger inside me. There are no crystals to calm me down, no gentle embrace of the caves. I must control myself.

"Alive, yes. Unharmed? Well, you'll have to see for yourself. *If you pass the test,*" she says with a grin.

A thousand scenarios pass through my mind. I see Estela's back, the scars, the bruises. I think of her hands, her fingers. Her hair. Her feet.

Gods on their stoney thrones, what have they done to her?

"Are we in agreement then?" Mrath asks again.

I blink, looking up at her. She wants me to kill one of her targets to prove that I can help her with her brother. Killing is nothing new to me. I've killed enough people that my hands will be stained red forever.

My people are my redemption. I have done awful things for them—to keep them safe. To keep them alive. Estela isn't just one of my people—she is my mate.

I look up at Mrath and stare straight into her smirking face. She looks as if she doesn't believe I will agree to her terms.

"When we were married, I spoke a vow to my wife. I told her that I would protect her with my power, influence, and my own body. You think I am too noble to do this thing—I see it written over your face. You think The Butcher has grown soft." I tighten my fists. "Give me your target, and I will finish it before morning."

Mrath's mocking smile fades. She stands up on her throne.

"Very well. Off you go—you will find your instructions in your camp."

She snaps her fingers, and then the enclave fades. Seconds later, the camp appears around us. I look at the *glacialmaras*, which are untouched, as she said they would be.

Pinned to my tent with a dagger is a bloody note and a map.

The map marks something not too far from where we now stand, and the note reads:

You will deal with a woman named Laavi under our protection. Her house is marked on the map I've attached—I'm told she sleeps on the second level. Be wary, if she is alerted to your presence she has some nasty enchantments she can trigger that will make you all beg for a swift death.

Laavi. That name... it sparks something in the back of my mind.

"What the hell happened to this place?" Niht says, breaking the thought before it reaches completion. It's likely just a coincidence, anyway.

I look up and see the enclave right in front of where we were camped. The forest does look different, with four or five grand houses visible through the trees. They aren't close to each other, but it's hard to believe we didn't see them at all when we arrived.

Powerful glamour.

There's much I have forgotten about the elves.

"It seems as though our eyes have been opened to this hidden place," I say.

Ulla lets out a short melody as she comes over to help fold up the remains of our camp. Our fire has long since gone out, but our vision allows us to see quite well in the dim light. Her face is open, shining, clearly in awe by all she has seen. I forget how new this is to her.

"Are you ready?" I ask, reluctant to break her brief moment of marvel.

She lets out a breath. "How long will it take to get to the... target's house?"

Pursing my lips, I say, "Not long. It seems it is one of the women she herself has sworn to protect."

I point in the direction of a house with black windows just beyond the hill.

"Can we trust Mrath if she kills those who pay her for protection?" Ra'Salore asks at last.

I look at him and see his eyes dark. Deep lines bracket his mouth.

"You have been displeased with every path I have taken since I left Enduvida. I understand why you would be frustrated, but I do not wish to have a companion who questions my every move. You may go back home now, as you wished to earlier, and I will do this alone. Hell, go wherever you want."

He says nothing, just stares intently at me.

"I—I will stay with you."

I drag a hand over my brow. "Why? Why do you do this to everyone?"

Ra'Salore looks at Niht who is silent. Then he takes a deep breath.

"I want to see the human women when we rescue Estela."

Ulla rolls her eyes.

"You want a mate, but you asked me to give up my own," I say slowly. Loneliness can do awful things to one's mind.

"I do not have to explain my desire to you again," Ra'Salore bites out. "Much less if you all will mock me."

I shake my head and wave off his comments. "Very well. If you complain once more, I will banish you from the mountain.

I'm not lying." The words are heavy, but Ra'Salore nods once with a tight jaw.

I show them the map and the note.

"Ra'Salore, you will climb the northern wall and scope out the inside. There is a window there," Niht says.

Ra'Salore nods. "It won't be a problem."

I nod and then look at Ulla. "You will stay outside and alert us if anything goes wrong."

She looks visibly nervous. "I would prefer to stay with you."

I frown; she is not cut out for battle. "Whoever comes with me will need to watch everything that happens at my back. There's a mention of enchantments, so we'll need to be extra careful."

Ulla reaches into her pocket and pulls out a crystal. "This detects magic, along with your spyglass. I can use it to help you."

I open my mouth when Niht speaks.

"I will stay outside. If you hear the bellow of a caught *ruh'glumdlor*, you will know that something has gone terribly wrong."

I look at the sky. It is still the middle of the night, but we don't have long. "Let us go."

CHAPTER 12

AQUAMARINE BERYL

TEO

I blink into my spyglass as I look up at the house.

We stand in the shadows behind the trees. A faint red magic shimmers along the door handle and glows from deep inside the house. We are stripped to dark-colored leather under armor garb grown stiff after days of wear. Waiting for Ra'Salore to scale the side of the house feels like being forcibly submerged underwater.

Like the houses in Enduvida, it is cylindrical. However, this dwelling also has dark, leafy green paneling up the side. Glamour had covered such a vast space. Clearly, our crystals can't pick up every trace of their magic; otherwise, we would've seen the enclave.

A seed of respect for these women is begrudgingly planted, despite what they are forcing us to do.

I hold up my hand, and our strategy is set in motion. Every inch that Ra'Salore scales feels like a mile. I'm on high alert, anticipating something just beyond our sight that could reach out and hurt the stone bender.

Ra'Salore looks over at me, hanging on the balcony of the

second floor, primed to act as soon as I give the signal. A feeling deep in my gut holds me back.

We've waited for over a half hour, and there has been no movement from the inside. A part of me wonders if there really is a woman in those curved walls, or if the queen of tricksters has merely sent us on a wild spider chase. The note said that she sleeps on the second level, which is why we chose the window to break into.

The hairs on the back of my neck rise, and I look over my shoulder to see what creature watches us—but there is no bear nor dryad. It is likely one of Mrath's spies ensuring that we make good on our word.

I take a deep breath, listening to the rhythmic sway of the trees in the night breeze, and nod to Ra'Salore. Like an expertly tightened spring, he swings his legs up and climbs to the window, latching onto the side of the house and using his tail to steady him. Faster than the strike of a serpent, he holds out his hands, and the Fuegorra in his chest lights up through the fabric.

In seconds, the cloudy window melts away. When it is completely gone, his tail adjusts position again before he swings and ducks inside the house. Even with our strong hearing, I can detect neither the creak of a floorboard nor the scrape of furniture against a polished floor.

The passing time is measured in my racing heartbeats, and I find myself holding my breath until he comes back. When he does, he slides out of the window, clutching to the side of the house with the ease of the most experienced crystal harvesters.

Ulla and I look at each other.

"I'll go first, then help you. Are you ready?"

She has a hollow paleness to her complexion, but she nods and slips her crystals into her lace-up pockets.

We don't speak as we approach the space. I try to follow the exact path Ra'Salore had taken up the wall, but I falter. When I slip, it makes a loud groaning crash, but thankfully, the wooden panel on the side doesn't break.

Ra'Salore reaches out and helps me into the room. As I roll onto the ground, I take a second to breathe before righting myself and spinning around to help Ulla up as well. Once all three of us are inside, a loud snort from another room breaks the silence.

I freeze, and the choking sound recedes into a deep, labored breath. The house isn't enormous, so it is easy to pinpoint the woman's location. Fingering the dagger in my waistband, I draw as much air as possible into my lungs as Ra'Salore and Ulla return to their positions on opposite ends of the room.

As my eyes adjust to the dark space, void of the harrowing light from the moon and stars, I pause. Everything is much larger than the average furniture, and there are paintings of the Zlosian forest.

My heart skips a beat when a stench hits my nose—old blood. I flinch when Ulla touches my elbow.

"Teo," she whispers in our language. "What's wrong?"

Another wave of prickling premonition passes over my skin, and I look up, searching for the spy in the shadows.

I take a deep breath and shake her off. "Do you smell that?"

She looks at me, her nose wrinkling. Then she blinks, "Yes. Is the target already dead?"

I shake my head, pulling her toward the room with the closed door and the loud sounds.

Ulla holds up her crystal and shakes her head to confirm there are no enchantments waiting to burn us alive or alert the target.

Strange.

Mrath told us there would be.

Despite the voice in my gut telling me to stop, I put my

handle on the knob and twist, opening it up inch by inch and then all at once.

While my friend stays near the door, I step into the room. The sour stench hits me straight in the face, and I gag.

It's human, and whoever it is is definitely dead. What in the gods' holy names happened here?

I raise the knife in my hand, holding my breath, and then stop when I see the large woman lying on her back.

A *giant* woman.

I turn back to the awful smell and see the illumination of a male form. I can make out a little more than the extent of his wounds.

"Who would do this?" Ulla whispers, just low enough for only me to hear. She crosses to the space where he is laid out and gasps.

"Ulla, later. Let's finish this first," I say through gritted teeth.

I adjust my grip on my weapon, and creep to the bed.

Moonlight spills over her face, showing off bright red hair that has been smoothed back into a tie. From the shape of her body in the lacy white nightgown to the sound of her snoring, she is the spitting image of Lijasa.

I am once again transported to Zlosa. To that opulent suite at the top of the palace. The curtains are drawn, and I don't glimpse a single leaf as I retrieve the knife I'd hidden days ago.

The evidence of Lijasa's passion is scattered around the room from the clothes on the floor to the drained wine glasses on the side table. Gods only know that it would take several glasses to willingly lay with such a woman.

Lijasa is sprawled out. Naked. Drugged.

And I hold a knife over her chest where her stony, wicked heart pumps out its last few beats.

There's no way in all the dark corners of the earth that she should wake when I draw near, but somehow, as my hand hovers over the bed, Lijasa opens her eyes and looks at me with a wanton lust. Terror scorches through my body, but I only allow her a second before I plunge the dagger into her chest.

She doesn't have a chance to scream.

The sound of the knife clattering to the ground draws me back to the present and causes the *very much alive* woman in front of me to stir. Her face turns toward the window, but it becomes clear she isn't Lijasa.

It's her sister—*Laavi*. They are similar, but I know her. She was supposedly executed when she tried to kill her sister on her wedding day.

I don't have time to reach down and pick up the knife before I hear a soft thump behind me.

Quicker than a cave-in, I twist around to find a dark, black-clad figure stalking toward me, knife in hand and pointed at my breastbone.

I don't have a chance to move, shaken as I am, and it's nothing short of a miracle when Ulla stumbles in front of him from a shadowy corner.

The attacker halts in his deadly course, knife a hair's breadth away from Ulla's long, blue neck.

"No," she breathes, fumbling at the space on her hip. Feebly, she holds up a short Enduar blade between them. "No more death."

"Put that down before you hurt yourself, my dear," a low, theatrical voice grits out.

Blood roars in my ears.

Mrath sent us here knowing of my past and sent an assassin to kill us before we could return.

And not just any murderer in the night...

"Thorne?" Ulla asks as he stands there, frozen.

He reaches up and pulls back the mask covering his angular features and reveals a tight jaw and bunched shoulders.

Thorne doesn't respond, and I take the opportunity to scoop up the knife, returning to the woman.

"Forgive me, Ulla," I say.

"Wait—"

"No, she's a monster, just like her sister," I say. "May your gods save you, for I cannot."

I bring the knife into her chest. *Hard*—for giants have much stronger bones than humans or elves.

She wheezes her last breath as her eyes flash open, and her arms flail out, one knocking me straight in the stomach.

The sickening crunch of her rib snapping under the force of my full body weight echoes in the room while her spine bows in agony.

Only when she stops moving do I remove the dagger, dripping with the stink of her life essence.

Panting, I look at her unseeing eyes. The only one left in her family is her nephew Rholker, and he's next. Lijasa's whole circle was full of slavers and liars. Those who take pleasure in pain.

I turn back to the lifeless body and summon a spell light. A table lined with sharp, clean tools is positioned next to the bloody corpse sitting in a chair.

The poor human was tortured to death.

Hot tears gloss over my eyes, and rage flows through my veins. Turning back to the dead giant in the bed, I see red. She died too fast. Perhaps I should have made her suffer longer.

The Butcher lives once more. Next to the pain I feel over the human, there is no dark corner of my soul that harbors space for mourning another giant pawn in a cruel dynasty, nearly ended.

I hurl the knife at her throat, just for good measure. More viscous liquid leaks onto the nightgown, staining the collar deep crimson. It doesn't spurt, more proof that her heart has stopped.

My blood pumps through my veins, filled with adrenaline and rage and *pain*. My voice is ragged as I gasp for breath.

This damned trip. I was free from these tortuous ghosts. Why do they now stand in the room watching me war within my wretched mind?

It isn't until I hear Ulla's gasping that I turn back around. Her chest heaves as she looks at the dead giant. I drag my hand over my face, smearing a bit of half-flaking blood from my face.

Her hand reaches up to cover her mouth, and I see it tremble.

Thorne covers it with his own steady palm.

"Ulla," I say, reaching out to rest my hand on her shoulder.

"I said no more death," she chokes out. We stand there, enemy and friend, comforting the healer. She is no stranger to death, but this was... different.

Seconds later, Ra'Salore creeps in, only to stop abruptly.

"What the hell is he doing here?" he demands when he sees Thorne. Then he makes a gagging noise and covers his nose when he sees the other deceased figure.

Thorne rips off the entirety of his mask and his silver hair spills out in short, strangely well-styled curls. His eyes are practically burning, and I get the sense that he's not a man easily restrained.

Though, he was by Ulla.

Ulla, who cries over the vicious murder of an evil woman. A bead of shame blossoms in my throat as Ra'Salore reaches over and draws her into his arms, away from Thorne and me. She folds into his arms and Thorne tilts his head to the side.

"Has she never seen a dead thing before?" he asks, completely ignoring the fact that he just tried to kill us.

I frown, not wanting to anger him if he has a tie to Mrath. I feel raw, exposed, but those emotions can be felt later. When I don't have so many foreign eyes on me.

"Millions of our people died in the Great War. She's a healer, she's seen death often."

He looks at me with a sour expression. "Then why does she weep over that damnable creature?"

"I've... never seen someone killed before. It was shocking," she hiccups. Then, as if she had forgotten her terror at the death moments before, she meets my eye. "Are you all right?"

No.

I nod. "I've done what needed to be done."

Thorne's expression softens. "Well then. Enough talking, let's go back to Mrath before you drown us all in your misplaced tears."

Her cheeks glisten, and I look at Ulla with nothing but respect. She stood in the way of the blade meant for my flesh in my weakness and was soft enough to weep for my soul, as I have seen her do for any of her friends.

Did our people appreciate her enough?

I turn away from them, break the chains holding the man to his death seat, and hold him in my arms.

Mrath let this happen.

The suffering sings in the air of this bedchamber. I care not if the filth left over from his human vessel gets on my clothes. Let the world know that this treatment of my wife's people ends today.

Thorne says nothing as we move down the house. He disables every ward, and we exit through the front door, which slams behind me.

My chest is rising and falling as my blood boils. The power I keep a tight hold on stirs in my veins, overheating my flesh and calling to the channels of molten heat deep below.

When Niht spots us, he looks utterly confused as to where

Thorne came from, and why Ulla is crying. Thankfully, after one shake of my head, he is silent.

"Ra'Salore!" I bellow. "Dig a hole."

The stone bender obeys immediately.

He kneels down, legs crossed beneath him, eyes closed and hands on his knees. The ground before us lifts and starts to rearrange itself. I listen to the sound of the moving dirt.

When the grave is ready, I kneel down.

Ulla starts to sing, her voice laced with grief.

I close the man's eyes, and say, "Far away, there is a place where there is no slavery or death. Go now, and tell the gods of what a wretched thing it is to live."

Stepping back, I raise my hands, feeling the dirt thread through my fingers as I weave him a shroud of earth and stone. I only wish to protect his body from further defilement.

The pounding under my skin doesn't subside. So I call on more power, reaching deeper and deeper to places that the forest doesn't know of, in the molten core of the earth. I sit with the angry heat for a moment, and then with a tortured growl, I pull it all up. The house behind us is engulfed in lava within seconds.

The Enduares do not flinch or try to leave. They watch as that awful house is reduced to a shower of sparks and ash.

When it is finished, I weep for the man dead in the ground and the woman tugged around on a leash. For the children murdered before they had a chance to grow up and for fathers who ask their sons to sacrifice more than they should.

The world has fallen—so I will burn it to the ground and remake it.

When I finally bring myself to stand, Thorne looks at me with burning approval and guides us back to the entrance of the enclave.

The air is heavy when we reach the wooden door with a great, beautiful face and green eyes.

She speaks in old elvish, and Thorne bows before her.

"Oscailte[1]."

"Bím i gcónaí ar fáil duitse[2]," the door responds in a low, lilting accent.

With the groan of heavy wood, the door starts to open slowly, revealing the way into the enclave.

Thorne continues to watch Ulla with a strangely intense gaze. His confusion is written on his face. I'm not the only one who notices.

Niht steps in front of her, blocking Thorne's view with one of the damned birds who has nestled into his hair.

This time, we are shown far more access to the entrance of the place than before. I take time to study my surroundings, from the rows of rooms with wooden doors to the hallways made of interlocking evergreen branches. It's impressive how everything works similarly to our system of tunnels in Enduvida. It succeeds in pulling my thoughts away from the exhaustion of murdering in cold blood.

Emptiness swirls through my mortal vessel, carrying me forward until we reach a place where there is a perfect view of the first streaks of dawn.

As I look up at the stars, celestial rocks in the sky, I think of my earthly star and whisper another prayer for my love. A woman now chained by the progeny of my own abuser.

I recognize the arching dome of trees above us making up the meeting hall's roof.

As we enter, everyone is still continuing their party, though the night has faded into loud lyre music and the laughter that comes from drunken dancing.

They ignore us. In fact, even Mrath seems unphased by our return despite her having sent one of her assassins to kill us.

The most dramatic reaction we get from the leader of this sisterhood is a frown when her gaze lands on Thorne. Without another word to us, he walks up the steps and sits on her thorny arm rest.

As soon as he draws near enough, she reaches over and strokes his arm.

"Well, pet? I'm assuming they passed my little test from the fact that they are here and not bleeding out on the floor of Lady Laavi's home," she drawls.

Thorne makes no expression, but his eyes trail to Ulla's bowed head and tear-stained cheeks.

"They did. The king is quite talented with a blade." Thorne leans back on the throne, playing with a thread on his carefully sewn tunic. "And then he buried the house in lava."

A pang of worry resounds in my chest. My father used that power for incredible evil, and I don't think that the would-be Elf Queen will look kindly on me just wielding it in her backyard.

But then, Mrath's eyes glitter and a slow smile spreads across her lips. "So you can still use the volcano."

"I don't use it unless it's necessary," I say.

She grins. "You've offered to help me get the artifact back, take down my brother, and you can wield the volcano? This is delicious."

"Let's hope it's an appetizing enough offer for you to finally assist us," I say firmly. Her ambition is dangerous.

She laughs, and the sound twinkles in the air around us. All the severe lines of her cold features light up. "Tell me, Enduar King, how did it feel to kill the sister of the woman you assassinated during the war?"

I glower in her direction. "You knew about Lijasa?"

She laughs harder.

"That's hardly a secret! But yes, I have reports detailing how much you suffered during your time in the royal giant court."

My heart races but I don't let on anything else. This woman must have had eyes everywhere from her childhood to present day.

"Lijasa was a monster. Most of the giants were when I lived there—they killed on a whim and took advantage of anything with two legs. I feel little remorse."

Mrath grins and leans forward.

"And a monster she was. Though she did pay us so much gold that it *still* fills our coffers. Her story is quite juicy, for it seemed that she had wanted to be a queen in place of her sister —I always had a soft spot for that. A bounty was placed on her head, and we kept her safe, giving her a human every now and then to satiate her needs."

My stomach roils and bile coats my tongue as I remember the slain human. His face was resigned to pain even in death. I pray that every god gives him a better life than the one he was given in this world.

"You chided me for keeping humans, yet you would sacrifice them to appease such an awful female?" I growl.

She shrugs. "The lawless are so because we don't have the luxury of civilized customs. It was either he died in that house or on the fields."

But there is one law: Don't fuck with Mrath.

The woman before me is still a snake... Can I really hope to believe she'll be loyal to me?

"How long have you been leading this enclave? I only knew of your father, the old king."

She smiles, not needing to sing lullabies to her conscious. She knows what she is, and she's thriving.

"I will give you information about anyone but myself." She leans back, her hand still on Thorne's knee. He doesn't freeze, but he makes no move to return the affection.

"Very well," I grit out. "At least tell me if you accept our deal."

After a few moments, she claps her hands and gathers as much attention as possible.

"Sisters! It seems we have a new ally. Everyone raise a glass for the trolls!" she calls out, laughing.

The drunken stupor follows suit, and something akin to relief softens my shoulders. Allies were allies, even if it was feeling less and less like this would be a permanent solution.

As if reading my thoughts, Mrath extends a finger and bids me draw closer.

I do, feeling nausea grow with each step.

"I am a woman of my word. You and a team will go after your bride first," she says.

Tension that's been knotted tight in my chest for weeks starts to unravel.

"We will need several hundred to get her from Zlosa and—"

She cuts me off with a tsking sound. "Never forget that I know far more than you. Rholker is preparing to hold himself a coronation."

I blink. "And you wish to kill him during his coronation...?"

She shakes her head. "I think we should take your pretty mate home first. He's quite obsessed, and I think it will weaken him to have her taken again. Then, we'll give him a few weeks of him wallowing in loneliness to make a fool of himself in front of the giant court..."

"And then we relieve his body of the burden from his big head."

She smiles and nods. "I like the way you think."

I take another step closer. "Just how many of your assassins will you send with me?"

She taps a pointed fingernail to her lips. "Two dozen."

"Twenty four women? That's not—"

"It will be enough because I say it. Do you understand?" she all but growls.

I glare back at her, flexing my jaw. "Of course."

"*Of course,*" she mocks gently. Then she traces her finger over my cheek and across my lips. "Never forget that I am your only hope."

The movement shocks me, it takes a second for the seal to set in.

Bound by magic.

With the ritual complete, she waves me away and relaxes on her throne. "So, dear king, please elucidate the facts for me— exactly what do you know of the *Cumhacht na Cruinne?*" she asks suddenly.

I swallow, thinking back on Liana's words. Before I'd left, the wise woman had explained the three orbs of power given to the king, the heir to the throne, and his firstborn daughter. The one with the most power would be declared sovereign.

Mrath looks over at Thorne, who nods. She winks at me.

"He can smell lies. Good thing you chose to be honest without forcing me to castigate your friends."

"I know that it's the greatest portion of gods-given power your people possess. Typically, it was meant for the king while the lesser potions of magic were given to the two royal children," I say, repeating what Liana had told me.

Then she leans back on her throne of thorns. "Well well, you *are* studious. Do you also know that was what your father stole from us during the Great War?"

I nod.

She smiles, pleased. "The court of the elves is a game of power—the one with the most wins. Arion wants the orb returned to him to solidify his rule. As the firstborn son, he has the greatest portion of power from my father. We will assist you with the giants, and you will bring me that artifact, which we will use to establish me as the new Queen of the Elves."

I take a deep breath, still deeply mistrustful of the woman.

She laughs, exhilarated.

"Can you imagine?" she says to Thorne who looks down at her dutifully.

"Yes, Mrath," he says, voice flat.

"Perhaps it wasn't such a shame that you showed up on my doorstep tonight. You've been most diverting. Go, rest. You will leave in the morning."

I look around the room, unimpressed with the revelry. "May we go back to our camp?"

She rolls her eyes, clearly annoyed with my request, but waves me off.

"Whatever you want, just leave me alone now. I intend to be thoroughly mussing my sheets with my gorgeous pet in the next quarter hour."

She points her finger at one of the dryads, and they move forward, prepared to take us out. Thorne leans over and bites her pointed ear, and she lets out a giggle. She casts him a heated glance before capturing his lips with her mouth.

I turn, tired of the display, and wait for the dryads.

It isn't until we've left the enclave that I take my real first breath.

I look around the camp and sigh. Then I fish out one of the stones that Liana gave me. Its black sheen gleams in the light.

Raising it to my lips, I say, "We've secured help. Tomorrow we ride to Zlosa."

I watch the color shift from black, to red, and then yellow and gray. The message must have been sent because the stone turns dull and lifeless.

I drop it to the ground and walk to my tent.

There are only a few more hours until the sun comes up, so I plop down a pillow and lay my head upon it—entirely content to let the emptiness consume me.

CHAPTER 13
NUUMMITE
ESTELA

It's fucking bath time.

Again.

At least Rholker isn't here.

"What, exactly, did those women do to you?" Melisa asks me as she pours another bucket of heated water into the tub.

Though she showed me kindness and did not force me into the water during her last visit, Rholker is not an inconsistent man. He wants me pristinely clean every time he takes me into society. Yesterday was a reprieve; today is a trek back to the depths of hell.

The sound of the water gives me chills and puts pressure on my lungs as my stomach churns.

"They... Rholker has always wanted me for himself. When he realized that the Enduares had taken me, he tried to get me back. When he finally brought me here, it was too late. I was already in love." The words burn my eyes.

They are things I never said to Teo, sentiments I never thought I'd say, and now even his name causes my throat to tighten and my eyes to fill with tears.

"Bah. *Love*. Rholker oft declares his love to you in this very room," she says. "It hasn't done you any favors."

I shake my head. "This is not love. He wants me to be an appendage that gives him whatever he desires."

She frowns. "Yes, yes, that I understand. So what did *they*— those black-clad women—do?"

I swallow, prodding at the shredded bits of my mind, and think about last night's nightmare where Teo moved in to bite me, but not for pleasure. To kill.

Sweat breaks out across my body.

"They are called Memory Slicers. They would hold me in the air as a snake bit me. I would retreat to my thoughts, and they would follow. They sorted my mind like how a doctor would sort through herbs until they found a precious memory of Teo and me. Then they would... shred it. Twist it. The memories hurt —burn. And they aren't real anymore."

My throat feels so raw that I can hardly breathe.

She tilts her head to the side. "Then why do you still love him if all the memories where that love blossomed are now ruined?"

I swallow and tap the gem on my chest.

"Rholker miscalculated. Teo is still my mate—a divine gift. That's magic that is more powerful than whatever those women possess."

"But they broke you," she insists, studying the way my clothes hang off my shoulders despite being fed often. "Aren't you at least angry they did it?"

I let out a mirthless laugh. "*Me siento jodidamente furiosa.*"[1]

Her expression changes, and she nods, pleased.

Melisa is familiar to me in an almost uncanny way. I recognize the masks she wears for different people and understand her soul, which is worn down to a blunt. She's angry, numb, lashing at whatever she can without getting punished.

My mother dealt with all the whispered words of other women, the verbal and literal lashings from those who were angry that someone with power gave her morsels of privilege.

"How dare she?" they would say openly. She was a human woman. A *slave.*

When Teo took me, I was angry and afraid. I was barely surviving. I realized just how much of that was my anticipation to experience everything my mother went through.

My mother's mother was dead before I was born, but she was cruel and everything my mother didn't want to be.

I've wondered about my grandmother. Her family. Her friends.

I look around the room as if I could see the generations of slaves past, standing at different corners. It is as if I can feel the angry spirit of all those who came before—the ones who watched my every move and felt justified every time I lashed out.

Anger will pass down from person to person, demanding to be felt until someone finally feels it—and fixes it.

"What are you thinking about now?" Melisa asks, drawing me out of my thoughts.

She seems insecure, as if she's trying hard not to let on how much it irritates her that I got lost in myself.

I frown.

"I'm still thinking about how angry I am."

She lets out a hearty, unexpected laugh, turns from the tub, and kneels in front of the cage. "Fuck yes. Tell me why."

My eyebrows draw together, but I can't help but smile.

There isn't a friendship between Melisa and me, not yet, but there is an understanding. "You know about my brother, Mikal. When my mother died, we were all each other had. I raised him like my own child. He's sixteen now, and they have him somewhere, torturing him."

"When was the last time you saw him?" she asks carefully.

"When I was left in Enduvida, maybe... five months ago. It kills me to walk around the lumber yards, scanning for his tall frame, and never catch a glimpse. It's like there's this ball of fire churning in my belly, waiting to explode and burn Zlosa down. *We shouldn't be here.*"

A heartbeat passes, then another. I feel my heart crack open a little wider as I swallow hard. "It doesn't matter to me that he's half-giant; I raised him. I fed him while he shot up like a weed, taught him to walk, and mended all his wounds. Caring for someone else is the hardest thing I've ever done, but the love that I experienced was also one of the purest things I've ever felt. That kind of love doesn't blossom in Zlosa, and it is horrible. *Tragic.*"

A hot tear splatters on my cheek when she reaches through the bars and grabs my shoulder, forcing me to look at her. Her dark brown eyes are glowing in the dim lighting. She's never looked at me so intently.

"Good for you. I mean it. I..." Her throat bobs. "Anger gets me up in the morning, pushes me to walk through the snow in barely adequate clothes, and forces me to lie flat on my back when Eneko decides he deserves a release. It fuels every smile, every flirtatious quip. Anger keeps me safe and warm at night when I hear the lashes of other slaves outside the doors." She keeps going, and I feel the weight of every word. She says it like a joke, but I know the reality of her words.

"You're right—anger is not evil, but it is dangerous. Anger is what will give us the tenacity to get out of this place, but if you let it burn too hard and hot for too long, it will burn away everything inside of you."

Every stony layer guarding her true thoughts and feelings falls away, and the grief turns her tanned skin ashen.

She moves back out of my reach.

"This is the second time you've mentioned escape. I think that's something for you—but not me."

I tilt my head to the side. "For all of us, one day."

Then her eyes flash back to me. "Not all humans deserve freedom."

My mouth opens and closes, and I think of the foremen who join in whipping, who take comfort women, who use us just as the giants do.

"You're right. Those who sided with the enemy are the enemy—but the future of the humans is freedom."

She doesn't scoff; she just looks at me with mistrustful eyes.

I wish I could say I didn't understand, but I've been selfish. My whole world was Mikal for so long, but being in the under mountain changed everything. Now, the world is Teo. Svanna. Arlet. Iryth. Liana—it's expanded to fit her, too.

I pull my hair over my shoulder and say, "If you come with me, you'll notice that all the men wear braids."

That draws her out of her thoughts.

"Don't they worry about whatever their version of woodlice is?"

I shake my head, thinking of all the times I had to shave Mikal's hair before working hours. "No. I think the lice might fear such mighty warriors."

She laughs. "You said they were gentle."

I look up at her. "They are. And the unmated women wear their hair in a bun— like a twisted loaf of bread atop their head."

"No braids for the women?"

"Only when they're mated. Then their mates will braid their hair."

She cocks her head to the side. "And what of the women who love other women?"

I smile. "There's a mated pair like that in Enduvida. Iryth and Svanna—they braid each other's hair. There's also a pairing of two men."

She draws her brows together and touches her own locks. "So those couples are allowed?"

I nod. "They are *loved*."

"Say your words aren't just nonsense, and, one day, I'm actually taken back to these caves. What if... my heart is pulled both ways?"

"Everyone in the under mountain has one of these put in their chest," I say, gesturing to the red-orange gem embedded in my sternum. "It will heal you and let you hear the song of gems more clearly. When you meet your mate, it will sing a new song only the two of you can hear."

"It looks like it hurt. I can see where it attaches to your skin," she says.

"I don't remember. I was dying when mine was put in."

"May I?"

I nod as she reaches over and presses her fingers to the stone. The lyre string of heat in my stomach flexes, and I panic, not wanting to burn her. I stop breathing, and she senses the shift.

"It doesn't hurt?"

"Not at all."

I don't think I can adequately explain how my new strain of magic appeared in Zlosa without first talking to Liana, so I resist the urge to explain that too.

"And you can hear music?"

I nod. "I can't guarantee you that the Fuegorra will pick someone for you, man or woman, but I know it wouldn't choose someone you wouldn't love," I say with finality. "But the Enduares are dying out. There are less than three hundred of them left. When I get back... I think I will have a child. Maybe more than one."

She balks at my admission. "And you'd want that?"

"I raised my brother," I say. "I've seen how the Enduares treat their children, and it's nothing like the breeding pens. It's nothing like how the giants treat their offspring, either. Everyone helps, even those without babes.

"They adore the younglings—they are their future. If I had a child, it's not like I would be sequestered in a hut until that poor creature was old enough to work. I wouldn't even stop my duties in the caves if I didn't want to. I could still be a queen, grow my undermountain garden, and learn my letters. Having a child in Enduvida means adding to my life, not subtracting."

Melisa takes a deep breath, processing my words.

"That does sound... different." She opens the door of my cage.

I don't even worry if the water has gone cold. It feels good to talk to Melisa—it chases the shadows away. A part of me wonders if it is the same for her.

"You're learning to read?" she asks as she helps me out of my clothes.

I nod. "Enduar letters. There's still a lot I don't know."

She doesn't guide me into the tub, nor does she pick me up and plop me down. She watches as I approach the water. I tremble when I reach the metal lip, and take a deep breath.

Then I step in.

The panic crashes over me again, and I thrash a little as I fight to breathe, but then, sitting in a ball and squeezing my eyes shut, I'm able to handle it.

Not enjoy it.

Endure it.

Melisa is right behind me, ready to wash my body. Each

second feels like agony, and then, she tugs on my shoulder and pulls me up.

Relieved, I burst out of the water and start to breathe again.

Stepping out of the tub too fast, I nearly slip, but Melisa holds me in place and slides a towel around my chest.

"No more falling on me. I'm afraid you'll break in two."

"*Gracias*[2]," I say.

The next few moments are a blur, but all I know is that the fire is warm, and the new clothes feel nice on my skin. Then she holds something out to me.

I look down and see the glittering jewels in her hand.

"Sing to them. It seems to help you," she murmurs.

I reach out at the exact moment that the door slams open.

Faster than lightning, Melisa shoves the jewels into her pocket as Rholker makes his way into the space, visibly upset.

His yellow eyes land directly on me. "Good. You're ready. Come, we're going to dinner."

I brace myself for the leash, but he doesn't have one. He seems to notice this, too, because he curses in giantese under his breath.

"Get out, whore," he barks at Melisa while staring intently at me.

A part of me feels the loss of her and the stones she carries, but she's proven trustworthy. I can only hope to see her soon.

I let out a shaky breath as the door closes behind Melisa. Rholker watches me.

The hulking giant king steps further into the cottage, taking up every inch of space and stealing the breath from my lungs as I look up at him without the bars to keep me away.

But it's the fact that we are without anyone to look upon us that makes me feel much, much worse.

"There are many things that I can bear, you know. But something about ingratitude makes my blood boil," he starts.

I force my hands to my sides, despite how hard they shake as I look up at him. My stomach churns with nervousness.

"Did something happen in the court?" I ask, trying to chase away any opportunities for him to reach out and touch me.

He lets out a strangled laugh. "You could say that."

When he doesn't elaborate, I step back.

That movement triggers something inside of him, and he follows me. His hand seeks my waist.

Por los dioses[3].

I curse when my back hits the bars.

This is it. This. Is. It.

I can hardly stand his desperation, so I squeeze my eyes shut, dreading the graze of his fingers.

"Estela, you look so lovely tonight," he says seconds before the pad of his thumb brushes over my clothed shoulder.

Every part of my body rejects the movement, and the Fuegorra on my chest flares to life.

The light is so bright it hurts my eyes when they fly open. I pour all the anger and pain into that magic, hoping it burns off his whole damned hand. While the magic is usually taut and hard to reach, I feel it give and expand. It's a lyre string, and I play it louder, pushing harder until the light brightens.

"This must work," he says through gritted teeth.

Instead of shrinking back like he did the first night I'd arrived here, he tries to grab me with both hands. His grip bruises my flesh and I try to push him off. One fingernail presses into the skin near my neck with enough force to draw blood.

I shove again, and the gem in my chest burns brighter, trying to heal me.

Finally, he lets go, holding his hands in front of him.

They are a mess of bright, red skin, and puffy welts. I take a deep breath and smell the stench of burned flesh.

"Damnit," he roars. "They told me it would be fixed by now."

Gracias[4].

I whisper to whatever gods will hear me.

Rholker fumes, reaching out and flipping over the tub. I can only imagine how much that hurts his hands. Water spills onto the floor, sloshing against the walls and barely splattering above the iron bars on the floor, protecting my cage. My feet are soaked.

I yelp and try to step back.

Our eyes meet, and I can see him searching. I put on my best shocked face and open my mouth.

"A-are you okay?" I choke out.

He could give me his whole kingdom, and I still wouldn't give a shit about him, but I need him to think I care so he keeps taking me outside.

He doesn't answer. Another string of curses falls from his mouth, and then he yanks open the door to my cottage, kicking water out. He doesn't so much as look back at me before he leaves and slams the door.

I turn to look at the chaos.

The fire still crackles in the fireplace. I can only hope it lasts long enough to dry the water or that someone comes to clean it up.

I walk through the small puddle and then look back to the open cage. I'm... loose. My eyes go straight to the door.

Is it... unlocked?

I suck in a deep breath, still acutely aware of how it feels like I'm drowning no matter how deep the water is, and force myself to walk some more through the finger-deep pool. Then I grab the handle on the door.

When I try to twist it, it makes a metallic sound but holds strong.

"Shit."

Then, I grab all the extra cloth around the space and start to sop up as much of the moisture as possible before holding it in front of the fire. I sit there, soaking in the heat.

It's not true freedom.

But it's a bit more than I had a few hours ago. I will savor it, and tomorrow, I'll try to figure out what made Rholker want to visit me.

CHAPTER 14
DUMORTIERITE
TEO

The sun is already high in the sky when we wake up in the bright forest. A part of me says that it's fine that I slept in, considering the events of last night, but I bolt upright nonetheless.

Two dozen women with sharp ears have joined our meager camp. They are eating our food and talking with Niht.

He laughs at something one of them says, and I can tell the exact moment when he flirts—not because she laughs with him, but *at him*. Niht seems blissfully unaware of her mockery and the bored, dangerous eyes of her group.

My tail flicks behind me as I'm surprised to note the group is not merely made up of elvish women. I stare at a pack of wolves, several bears, and one alce. I haven't seen an alce in decades, but it towers over all of us, and its proud antlers stick out around its head, demanding to take up space. A tall woman is brushing its fur and adjusting its green saddle.

As I stand, several eyes swivel toward me.

"Good morning," I say in my best approximation of elvish.

They don't react.

The woman tending to the alce steps forward.

"Teo, King of the Enduares," she says with a very shallow bow. "I am Ayla Daecaryn, leader of the Faefurt Assassins." She gestures behind her and continues, "My greatest work was when I infiltrated the swamp ogres as a courtesan and killed their Shaman Ogre King while he walked the astral plane."

She says nothing about her mount, but it huffs a snort and stamps its great foot.

I nod at both her and the creature as well. Hearing her speak so openly of her bloody exploits isn't surprising. After all, they made me kill someone to prove that I could be trusted enough to help. Perhaps this is their custom.

The one whom Niht was flirting with steps forward.

"I'm Glyni. I killed my father, High Lord Oakfeather."

Niht's face nearly makes me chortle, but I give my attention to our newest allies.

We're introduced to both elves from the sunny, tropical islands in the east and those who've grown up in the Faewilds of the far south. Thasinia, a woman with skin darker than my Estela, speaks of her murder of a giant family, while Farryn and Elanila, a set of elderly twins, talk about how they took out a member of my father's court eight decades ago.

My eyebrows rise. My father had spoken of the tragic accident that had befallen the Reh family line—never in a thousand years had I expected to be standing face-to-face with their murderers.

Despite trying to focus more on the names than the kills, I find I can only memorize Lusha and Taenya's names before anxiousness claws at my gut. I don't know if these women will be right for the mission, but they certainly are capable.

Cocking my head to the side, I think of their leader, Mrath, who refused to share any information about herself at the party.

"These stories are fascinating, but I can't help but wonder: what of Mrath? Who did she kill?"

Silence greets my question, fizzling in the warm sun as birds and insects flit between the trees.

One of them looks back at the smoking black mound in the distance, the house of Laavi. She swallows and says, "Sister Mrath killed her father, the old king."

I blink, frozen. It makes sense, I suppose, why she wouldn't tell me.

From the left, I hear one call out, "I've never bedded a human. Is it worth all this trouble?"

That's all it takes for Ra'Salore to growl at them.

They laugh, and the introductions continue. When the last name has been spoken, I give them a deeper bow.

"We are grateful for your help." The words aren't lies, per se, but they burn my throat. Gratitude might exist, but the trust between our people is non-existent.

They watch me.

"We are ready to leave when you are," Ayla declares.

My eyes fall on an empty pack that held dried supplies. "Have you eaten a hearty breakfast?"

Ayla smiles, showing the fangs that mark our two peoples as distant cousins.

"Yes." She walks over to her alce and leaps atop it with impossible grace. She shouts a few words to her women that I don't quite catch, and they all move to their mounts.

I go to the *glacialmaras*, which Ulla is watering as she sings a ballad. When I approach, she smiles, but her expression is tinged with sadness.

"Are you well?" I ask her.

She nods.

"Last night was awful. I just thought that he..." she trails off, glancing at the elves. There is one particularly bloodlusty elf who won't be joining us.

"Be careful with him," I say under my breath in our language to avoid someone overhearing. "Mrath called Thorne her pet."

She nods, then looks up at me with glassy eyes. "I don't think he's as awful as Mrath. Thorne hated what that woman did, you know. And you... gods, did you have to deal with that before you came home? I thought you had told me everything— I thought—"

I shake my head, wondering how she knows what Thorne does or doesn't hate.

"The past is dead. Let it stay buried."

Rahda continues to nudge my side, and I look down at her. "Yes, yes, you have been so impatient all night. What was I to do?"

Another ram to my hip makes me laugh as I stumble. Ulla joins me in laughter, and some part of me feels wrong. My mate is still missing.

It's going to be all right. We have the allies, and today we ride.

Soon, we will rescue my wife. The Fuegorra sings to life in my chest, and I let it fill me up as we clear this vicious place. It sings to Rahda as she pushes above the trees for the first time in days. The other Enduares follow me, but the elves remain confined to the ground with their beasts.

I stick my hands out wide as the air brushes past them like threads of silk against my skin. It slips through my fingers, and my hair blows back. I suck in breath after breath of pure sunshine.

I'm coming, Estela.

I push through my silent bond, hoping she can feel me, even if she can't hear the words. Together, she and I can chase away the ugly shadows littering our world.

I will always come for you, my love. No matter the distance.

CHAPTER 15

NEPHRITE

ESTELA

R holker takes me to the library. He keeps my chain clamped onto his chair as he studies title after title about the history of his people. It's unsettling, but at least he doesn't try to touch me again.

As he reads, I sit on the floor and look at the shelves that extend from the ground to the high ceiling. The rolling ladder before me looks like something Teo would adore—and then I wince.

He also had a royal library, full of scrolls. One that he cherished.

An hour passes as I wait, and the only sound is the loud slap of pages made from wood pulp.

I sit there and watch, thinking about the next few days. By now, I've amassed a list of names of the major giant court families. Most of the eastern lords don't trust Rholker, and I think that Fektir is still on the fence, even though he said he would accept him as king if he killed the Enduares.

So far, he hasn't made any advancements on such promises. In general, he can't seem to do anything without thrusting the daily tasks on Regent Uvog. He denies meetings, ignores letters and audience, and insults people constantly.

Many in the court view him as inexperienced. They do not agree with the involvement of the Six, and they hate seeing him bring me to court functions.

To quote Lord Rilej, *"Whores are for beds."*

His greatest weakness, besides his obsession with me, is his lack of attention to detail. He thinks that brute force will solve every problem, but doesn't have the heart to kill every dissenter. It makes no sense.

Soon, Rholker switches to writing. The quill on paper grates against my ears. Writing in giantese is as foreign as having wings to fly, so I just look at the bright bindings and gilded letters, guessing at their tales.

As I stare at a picture of a knife, Rholker shifts in his chair to look at me.

"It's late," he says, putting down his quill. "You need to sleep."

His voice has turned on that dreadful, gentle quality that it often does when he wants to fool himself into thinking he's being good to me.

I continue studying the inked image as if I were as mindless as a doll.

"You know, you aren't the first slave to come to this place," he says conversationally.

I hum an inquisitive sound and refrain from saying *"obviously."* Everything needs to be cleaned at some point.

"You don't look pleased at being here with me," he observes. "Would you like it if I read you some of my words?"

I look up at him, wide-eyed, mouth open. What the fuck was I supposed to say to that?

"No?"

I still don't respond.

He frowns, stands, and disappears into one of the rows, leaving me alone. I could run. The chain at my throat heats at the thought.

Freedom.

But he returns moments later, and I have to console the disappointment pooling in my gut.

He sets down a stack of small books bound in strange papery leather and grins. "Since you seem bored, meet the first rebellion."

Then he passes me one of the tomes.

I flip it over, clearly confused.

He laughs at me. "You know what I keep wondering?"

"No, not in the slightest," I respond tartly.

His smile fades. "I keep wondering why the Enduar King thinks you would be a good candidate for his queen. You can't read, you're too weak to fight, and you are impulsive. Your only redeeming quality is your pretty skin, and even your pleasing flesh has been ruined with scars."

I stiffen. His words should mean nothing to me, except he is... not wrong.

Rholker picks up a book of his own. "Selena, weaver. Executed for trying to hex the king, and skinned on the seventh day of the harvest month," he reads.

I blink.

Skinned.

Skinned.

I drop the book in my hands with a yelp. *Hostia puta*[1].

"These are bound with the skin of women?" I demand, forgetting to be docile.

He smiles down at me. "There you are." He thumbs a few pages. "I thought you'd forgotten how to feel. And yes, you are correct." Then he cracks the book open further and shows me the space between the pages. "And this is hair braided and twisted to make thread—just like the strands of hair I've been giving you off of Mikal's head."

Without thinking, I reach out, and stroke that lyre string in my chest. He acts as if it were some great achievement. As if I would *enjoy* this. Well, little does he know, I would *enjoy* scratching his eyeballs out.

A part of me says to discard this blasphemous book, but instead, I pick it back up and close it, not wanting to damage the remains of a slave further.

"What did they do to deserve this?" My grip on the lyre string is strong while I try to keep my breathing even.

He closes the book he was looking at and slaps it down with the others.

I flinch.

"They plotted to kill my grandfather. For a time, they were displayed on poles for more of your kind to see, but we found that hurt morale. Labor efficiency decreased, and all that. Why punish everyone for one woman's sins, right? Or... in this specific case, a group of women."

He looks directly at me with his yellow eyes.

I hear the threat loud and clear. If I don't do as he wishes, he will hurt Mikal.

I raise my chin at him and finally pull on the lyre string in my chest, reminding him that I have my own weapons. The light starts to glow, and it's worth it to see the fear in his eyes.

"Come now. You won't have magic in a few short nights. If you burn me, I will make sure to give both you and Mikal matching marks. Though, my hand might slip with your brother."

Narrowing my eyes, I consider this. On the one hand, he might be right about my magic being taken away. On the other... I haven't noticed the fire dimming.

"Do you honestly think I want anything to do with you?" I ask.

He smiles. "I think I have ways of making you love me."

"Bullshit."

"How about this: I will let you see your brother the week after my coronation. I must take a short trip, and when I return, you can go to him as often as you'd like."

I sit up straighter. "Alive?"

"Alive and well." He settles back and studies me, eyes passing from my styled hair to my scandalous dress and the light in my chest. He's hungry for the power that leaks out of my pores. "But, I'm sure you know that he only stays alive if you agree to be my comfort woman."

My blood chills to a stop, and my throat contracts but the light grows brighter.

Run.

Poke his eyes out!

I hold up my hand, dying to touch him and feel his flesh sizzle. He deserves it.

He sits forward again, testing me. His eyes bear into my own, waiting to see if I will burn him and risk injury to Mikal or put my hand back down.

The answer is clear, but gods, I really want to char his flesh.

"I don't belong to you," I say slowly.

He grins, clearly pleased when I fold my arms. "My little love, you are wearing a collar. Your flesh-eating lover knows he can't steal you away again. Don't you realize that is why he hasn't come to rescue you yet?"

I tighten my fists and clamp my mouth shut. Explaining what I feel would only put him on alert for Teo, or my plans of escape. The best course of action is to look hopeless.

It works.

"Now, I need to take you back to the cottage. Are you finished flexing your magic?" Rholker asks.

I let out a long breath, loosening my grip on the light. "Yes."

"That's it. Why don't you keep the book? Think of it as a present," Rholker says, turning to my chains he's wrapped around an armrest.

I clutch the tome to my chest, but don't answer as I stand.

Rholker finishes unchaining me just as Regent Uvog walks in.

The heavily scarred giant is larger than I remember, and his dark hair hangs around his scowling face. The sound of swamp insects fills my ears.

"My King," Lord Uvog says, not even sparing me a glance.

"What now?" Rholker says, turning away from me.

My eyes go back to the book. I take a deep breath.

"Shaman King Braareg is demanding that he be admitted to speak with you at last," Uvog says. "I tried to restrain him, but he threatened to leave."

"So you ambush me in the library?" Rholker says, pinching the bridge of his nose.

Heavy thuds of a weighty creature echo through the library.

The Shaman King comes into view, all moss, vines, and hand sewn leather. He has been put into proper clothing, but his green skin is a stark contrast to the pale, fleshy pinks of the giants.

"High King Rholker, you brought us here, promising an alliance your father long denied us. Do not insult us by keeping my people locked up in rooms. We are not—"

I don't wait for the next words, I snatch the small book Rholker was writing in off the table while they speak. Stuffing it into the folds of my dress, I wait a beat before looking up to see if anyone caught me.

Rholker holds up a hand. "We can discuss this in an appropriate place. Perhaps the throne room? I need to take this human to her cage."

Uvog and Rhokler are absorbed in conversation about the swamp ogres' king, but when I look up, I see Braareg isn't looking at the giants, he's looking at me.

My heart skips a beat, but he tilts his head down, and then my vision is invaded by a swamp. It's a wholly unique power, one I've never encountered.

All images cease, and Braareg returns his attention to Rholker, who continues to speak to Uvog.

"Very well, Giant King. But do not keep me waiting if you wish for my support," Braareg interrupts.

"Understood. Estela, come." Rholker tugs on my leash.

"My King—"

"Later, Uvog."

Regent Uvog gives me a sneering look, but says nothing more as Rholker pulls me past.

My thumb spreads across the top of Rholker's Journal. I wish I could read it tonight, but I'll have to wait until Teo can translate it for me.

Teo.

The name causes a slice of pain across my skull, and I think about what Melisa and I spoke of—the anger that scorches my soul. I regret not burning Rholker when I had the chance.

EVEN IN MY DREAMS, I GRASP AT MY COLLAR AS IF I COULD LOOSEN ITS iron grip on my neck. Gods, it makes it so hard to breathe.

It holds me tight while the memories I try so hard not to prod during my waking hours come to life before my eyes.

A strange light burns in my eyes, and when I finally let them open, I see Enduvida all around me. I stand near the

Ardorflame Temple, but the light doesn't come from the pulsing, red shrine.

No, it's a woman. A gilded form. Her deep brown skin shines in the light, as does the crown atop her head. It's as if she stands in a lightning field of energy—of love.

"*Mamá*," I say, the word falling from my lips and filling the air around us with more light.

She smiles and holds her arms out.

I don't think, I *run* to be with her. When she folds herself around me, I luxuriate in her softness, and the smoothness of her back. She clicks her tongue, like she did when I was a child. "Estela, my brightest star. *Mi vida*[2]."

I look up at her. "Why are you here?"

She smiles.

"The goddess sent me to wipe away your tears."

"What goddess?" I ask, my throat dry. "Grutabela?"

She presses her face to mine and shakes her head.

"No. *Our* goddess, *mi amor*,[3]" she whispers, brushing the hair from my eyes.

Everything about this is so familiar.

I look up at her, her white robes seemingly made of pure starlight. She brushes the tears from my cheeks, and the motion is so tender that it makes more spill.

"She's content to lie in obscurity in this land—for now. Worry about such things later. I've come to help you tonight, and then I must go back."

"Please don't leave," I whisper to her.

Her face scrunches up with emotion as she gives me a tender "Oh." She presses a warm kiss to my forehead.

"*Amor*[4], I never fully leave. I'm a part of the song your crystal sings to you and every bright thing that touches you."

Looking at her feels different. The lines of anger and anguish in her face are gone. Her face is smooth with love and sweetness. I hadn't realized it, but she is right about the song. While there's always been a melody for Teo and me, there are a few notes, perhaps even a feeling, that remind me of her.

"Are you in Vidalena?" I ask.

It's an Enduar heaven, but it belongs to all of us—and decidedly to my mother.

She beams down at me. "Yes."

"Good." I brush a hand over her spectral form. "Is it better than life?"

She tilts her head to the side, sad.

"Death is kind to us all. It is a gift to move on into something else, something more. But life is also a gift—it demands to be lived until the time comes."

I think of the senseless death that has surrounded me for so long. Helplessness, shame, pain. I survived so that Mikal would not be alone.

And then I found out that life was so much more. Not merely excellent lovemaking or a day free from aching joints and lashes on my back. It was harvesting plants and nurturing family.

It was growth.

She seems to read all of this on my face. It brings a smile to her lips.,

"I didn't think it would be this hard to come." She presses kisses all over my face once more and then pulls back. "Mikal is alive. Please, get him. You need to escape the night of the coronation."

Tears pour down the sides of my cheeks. "But my collar. That's the worst night. I'll be at Rholker's side and—Oh gods, *mamá*, he'll take me to his room, and..."

Perhaps, then I will stop feeling bad about the pain I've caused to those I now miss.

She shakes her head. "No, no, no. *Mi amor*⁵, calm down."

I bite my tongue hard enough to draw blood and wonder if she heard my thoughts.

"You have the power to break free. Take this," she presses something to my hand. "Labradorite," she says in Enduar. "Sing to it, and it will free you from the chains, but wait until the night of the coronation. You can't leave before then."

I look down at the blue-black stone that shines iridescent between yellow and orange. It reminds me of a distant place in the sky—nearly a star.

"Estela, listen, if you use it before then, it will break. Crystals can only absorb so much. Be careful."

I nod to her. "But I don't know the song."

She pulls me close once more and touches the Fuegorra. As she does, a new song sings to life. "Sing this."

As the music plays around us, my mind starts to clear. Instead of a crumbling place full of broken memories, it begins to build itself back up.

Not completely, but enough.

When she pulls away, the song remains.

"*Te amo,*[6] *Este,*" she says. "Please, release yourself of this pain and forgive."

And then the dream fades.

When I wake up, I'm still in the cold cottage, specifically, in the corner of my cage near the dying fire, and the tub, which has been fixed.

But now... when I look down at my hand, there's a crystal resting atop the book I cradled in my sleep.

I gently set the book atop a blanket and wonder if it's one of the gems on my necklace. I pull it out of my pocket, where it's been since Melisa gave it back yet again.

Closer inspection shows me that there are no other pieces of labradorite. But I recognize a few others, like opal. An unharmed memory surfaces, and I see lepidolite, which is a brilliant, sharp purple.

I write down the letters I already had.

A S E R O M.

Suddenly, more names come: morganite, tiger's eye, iolite.

I write them as fast as I can.

I look harder at the letters in the dim light of the Fuegorra, frustrated by my lack of learning. My stupidity. I should've...

And a message starts to form.

I will always come for you, no matter the distance.

It's Teo's voice..

"Dioses míos,"[7] I say, dropping the necklace in my lap.

He had given me that necklace as an engagement gift—but he was promising me something long before.

He endured my attempt on his life, my ignorant fear, and my foolish escapes.

Teo knew the meaning of forgiveness long before I did. He exacted justice when necessary, protected those he cared for fiercely, and forgave them all.

He let go of the awful things that Lijasa did to him before we met. He became someone in spite of his cruel father. He healed, and opened himself up to me.

Fearlessly.

I desperately want that.

For the first time in weeks, I hear his voice without pain. Not a memory.

A message.

CHAPTER 16

OPAL

TEO

I
t took us merely four days to reach a snow-blanketed Zlosa.

We rode every second the sun was up and slept just long enough for our beasts to rest. Luckily, the motley gang of wolves, bears, and one towering alce didn't hold us back in comparison with the speed of the *glacialmaras*.

"My tits are going to freeze right off," one of the elves says, followed by a round of hearty laughter that I don't join.

We are positioned on a nearby hill overlooking the royal palace. I should be searching for my wife, but my eyes follow the point of the towers, up to the top room. I stare at the spot where I was subjected to Lijasa's attention for months on end. It's insane that I can see the spot where her bedroom once was amidst the massiveness of the city.

When I finally have time to distance myself from the cruel memories, I bottle the torrent of emotions coursing through my body. Too many feelings will only make me sloppy.

The palace seems so big in my mind, but truly, it is small compared to the lumber yards and slave pens that stretch out endlessly in either direction, over hills, and into the trees. They have their perfectly manicured gardens a mere ten paces away from the pitiful gates that hold back their slaves.

I see no woman dragged around on a lease, so I take a moment to gaze into the city. Only a few great manors are in view, surrounded by the dozens of smaller houses for those in the lower classes. I spot the bathhouses, the barracks for the giant warriors, and the dining halls.

It is all unfamiliar to me.

All I know is the palace and all the horrors that went on there.

Is the reason that she's not out in the open now is because she's trapped somewhere inside the palace? Is she subjected to Rhokler the same way I was subjected to Lijasa?

It's almost too painful to entertain.

"You look at trees as if you've never seen one," a voice says behind me, much closer than expected.

I turn around, thinking they are speaking to me, but instead, I see Glyni and Ulla holding baskets full of scavenged food.

I sigh. These elves are not so bad. They have been kind enough on our treks, which is not what I expected.

Ulla shoots Glyni a wary look. "Before this trip, I saw them for mere moments and never so up close. Didn't you know that most of our cities were underground?"

Glyni laughs. "Yes, I'm very curious as to how you survive without the sunshine."

Ulla shrugs and taps her crystal. "I'm *very curious* how you survive without crystals to sing to."

As if on cue, Niht starts to sing a common working song.

The quartz towers Ulla had set out for goodwill and peacefulness hum back—granted, he's no Velen, but it's a pleasant reminder of home. I know that the large crystals will soon reverberate our battle songs, but for right now, I let the elves marvel.

"Ulla, come back, please. He's got a voice worse than a badger," Farryn laughs.

Niht stops. "Badgers can't sing. They just bark and hiss."

"Precisely," her twin Elanila says.

"Enough," I bark, almost guilty for the irritation swimming through my veins.

They quiet and look at me.

"We are here, and now we must find Estela," I say, practically breathless. As if to soothe me, the song that has been quiet for the last month starts up. It causes my Fuegorra to vibrate and the mating mark on my neck to burn.

I stagger, clutching my stone, and whip around to look back down at Zlosa.

I see nothing.

Estela?

Silence.

Ra'Salore steps out from behind a cluster of trees.

"We have a plan, one that you agreed on last night. Soon, I will go down to collect one of the humans. We can ask him what he knows of Estela."

Ayla scoffs.

"Where was I when that was agreed upon? We are a part of the sisterhood. Mrath already has humans that she uses for information."

I tighten my fists, trying to ignore the hum of urgency in the song. It needs me to go to her, but I don't know where she is.

"Then why have you not brought one of them here?" I hiss.

She raises an eyebrow and crosses her arms. "I sent Taenya a quarter hour ago."

I grit my teeth. "I suppose it is my turn to inquire why *you* didn't tell *me*?"

"I don't answer to you. I was called on this trip to help you, not serve you," Ayla smirks.

"And what would've happened if I'd sent Ra'Salore down after you'd already sent Taenya?" I press.

She steps forward and points at me, her wavy brown hair blowing in the winter wind.

"If you want to know my plans, you ask me. I will not make the first move." Ayla says.

I consider her words and concede. This is the fire I was expecting to deal with.

"Very well. What happens when Taenya comes back with your contact?"

She smiles. "We have fun."

There's a darkness in her look, one that I don't trust. It reminds me that she is an assassin and not a paladin of some sort.

"You will not hurt the human," I say with finality.

She raises her eyebrows. "He won't be in pain, he'll be dead. If we leave him alive, then he can be found and interrogated, and then he will certainly wish he had died swiftly instead of under the weight of a thousand beatings by a giant's boot."

I shake my head. "Let him free."

Ayla scoffs.

"No."

"We have freed dozens of slaves over the years through trades," I say.

She appears genuinely amused. "Oh? And have any of them survived?"

I purse my lips. "The humans believe that the elves take them in."

A few of the women listening to us now laugh.

"And you believed them?" one says.

I take a deep breath.

"When I first heard that you had no humans, I thought perhaps they had died. But I don't think so—maybe not in your

183

enclave, or in King Arion's city, but humans are stronger than they look. If they didn't find some other elvish town to spend their days, they surely would have made a place for themselves." Saying the words feels good, even if Ayla curls her lip at Arion's name.

I don't fault her.

"Have it your way then," Ayla says at last. "We won't... *dispose* of the contact. We'll let him free."

Ulla nods approvingly. "I'll make a pack for the man to take. We don't need so much, especially since we will return to Enduvida soon."

Ayla shakes her head and walks away, cursing our *bleeding troll hearts*, but no one says anything else.

I feel satisfied like a small weight is lifted off my chest. Now, we simply wait for Taenya to return.

Then I'll be one step closer to tearing Rholker to shreds.

CHAPTER 17

WILLEMITE

ESTELA

The morning of the mid-winter feast is cold enough to freeze my toes off. I know because I am currently being led through the snow by two giant warriors. Even with my boots, my feet are numb. It feels like it takes an eternity to make it past the lumber yards and slave pens and reach Rholker's rooms.

He won't be there yet.

I remind myself over and over and pat the large pocket in my underskirt that houses the small human skin-bound book, Rholker's writings, and my jewels.

The preparations for this coronation have been arduous, so much so that Rholker is still stomping around, ensuring every last detail is perfect.

I haven't seen his scarred face and crooked nose since the library.

In fact, no one has visited me—not even Melisa. The lack of her presence has caused an ache in my sides. She helped me forget the gaping hole in my chest for a few hours, like Arlet once did.

As I walk, something stirs in my chest that sends a jolt of adrenaline coursing through my body. Pressing my hand to my chest, the familiar song leaks from the stone and out through my fingers, making my eyes burn.

Teo?

I wince in anticipation of pain that never actually comes. It's then that my mating melody picks up again.

The air shifts as I gasp, and I can practically smell my mate approach in the distance. I thought that humans wouldn't have such a strong, animalistic pull to their mates, but the reaction of my instincts says otherwise.

I breathe for a few moments, but the sensation doesn't intensify.

He's still far away.

I need to leave before Rholker and his armies can hurt him.

Looking around as we arrive at the palace gardens, I am disappointed that there is no blue-skinned king, only hordes of giant warriors positioned on every corner.

When one catches me staring, I quickly look away.

Rholker must be worried. If his kinghood is not supported, this ceremony could turn into a fight. Depending on how angry the lords are, someone might even try to kill him. All in all, there's a real possibility that this will be a shitshow of a party.

The biting cold and too-loud crunches of snow beneath my boots soon end as I am taken through the back door and up three sets of stairs to a place I have only been once before.

Rholker's old room.

The door is still closed, but even seeing it from the hallway causes memories of the night of his engagement to come back. I breathe through each one.

When the door to the former Second Prince's room is pushed open, I am surprised to see that it has been expanded.

Melisa stands in the middle of the room, clad in her familiar shade of red, waiting with her head bowed. She's flanked by two women who smile with hardened eyes as the giant holding my leash pushes me in.

I stumble and grab hold of a gilded red chair.

The guards stop at the door. "She must be prepared by the time we come to collect her."

Then the door is shut tight, leaving the four of us alone together.

"*Hola,* [1]Melisa," I say with a smile.

"Estela." She returns the gesture with a familiar smirk—the kind she shows when the giants leave. "This is Abi—she belongs to Foreman Juan, and Paoli belongs to Lord Rejok. We three met in the breeding pens years ago before we were plucked up by our masters."

Each of them nods before straightening to stare at me.

"I'm Estela," I say slowly.

Three comfort women, soon to be joined by myself.

Both of the newcomers are beautiful, but Abi has a scar on the right side of her face that covers her cheek and stretches down her throat. Her full-bodied frame is squeezed into a dress similar to Melisa's, though it is blue over red. The curves of her hips and breasts accentuate the curve and roll of her belly.

I flinch, picturing how such a scar could be made.

Paoli is silent, but not unpleasant. She looks at me as if she could hear my thoughts, but doesn't wish to broadcast them—merely to store every secret away forever. Her hair is long enough to graze her bottom, and her cheekbones sit high and sharp on her face.

"I was never sent to the pens," I say.

"We know, but we won't hold it against you," Melisa says. "I personally only participated one round before Eneko came for me and made me take brews to ensure I would never be with child. Not something your Enduares can likely fix, though I am hopeful for Abi."

Her voice is light, but hope blooms in my chest.

Something tells me that she's going to come with me when I escape.

Abi smiles as Melisa throws her hand around her shoulders.

"This perfect creature wants all the babies, and her own house, and everything dreamers dream of," Melisa explains.

Abi glares at her. "Don't make fun of me. You told me she said there's such a thing as mates with the trolls."

"Enduares," I say, trying not to sound defensive.

Melisa shrugs, but Abi looks at me, her lips twisting downward.

"It all sounds like a fairytale, to be honest. But I can't help but hope. Juan isn't cruel to me like some of the other foremen are, and it was a fair trade for the freedom I'm allowed, but I want more," Abi says.

"You don't have to explain yourself to me," I say quickly, taking a step toward her. "And, yes. Everything I told Melisa was true." I look at the other woman, Paoli, and ask, "Did you have a child in the breeding pens? Is your lord cruel to you?"

"We don't know." Melisa says.

My eyes don't leave the silent watcher, but Paoli doesn't seem like she wants to offer the information.

"We can talk while we work," Melisa says before guiding me to the polished oak wardrobe with carved images of spear-wielding giants on the doors.

I look around the room and find a sparkling white outfit hanging next to a wardrobe covered in diamonds. The presence of the stones makes my skin itch. It almost looks like—

"A snow pixie?" I say, turning around. It sounds like a prettier version of the nickname the late First Prince Keksej used for me, *tiny flea.*

Melisa nods. "He ordered it just for you. Now you get to be his adorable little toy."

Paoli gives me an apologetic look, then moves her hands rapidly at Abi.

"She wants to know if you can get in the water," Abi says quickly. Her voice is gentler this time. "Melisa told us you had... issues."

I ignore the question and look at Paoli, who is expertly avoiding my gaze. It's not that she won't speak. It's that she can't.

"Did they...?" I gesture at my tongue, hoping that I wasn't being too candid.

She nods and opens her mouth, revealing an empty stump at the back of her throat. She makes a sound, and I am stunned.

Tongue removal happened to hundreds of slaves, but Paoli isn't a disgruntled man. She's a beautiful woman.

"I'm sorry," I say, truly meaning it.

She shakes her head and presses a hand to her chest.

I want to ask how it happened, but instead, I gather all my strength and courage and use it to fuel me as I strip off my clothes and get into the tub.

The giants used us for all we were worth. They scarred our backs, our faces, our necks, our tongues, and our hearts. They gifted us to those we never should've belonged to.

We just wanted choices. Choices over our bodies and our own lives.

That was all Teo had given me.

I need to find a way for them to have that freedom as well.

While Melisa is washing my hair, Abi shaves my legs with a sharp knife and Paoli polishes my nails.

The touches don't feel begrudging; they are kind—understanding.

When I meet Abi's gaze, she pats my knee.

"Try not to move. I don't want to cut you," she says.

"Everything you said earlier—You are going to come with us tonight, yes?" I ask.

She worries her lower lip and then nods. Paoli nods, too.

I lean forward, heart racing as they drop their ministrations.

I look back at Melisa. "And you?"

She stares at me without responding. Melisa can joke about coming all she'd like, but I want to hear her say she'd like to come.

"Eneko wouldn't like it," she says.

I grit my teeth. Is this the same woman who told me how angry she was days ago? I take her hand.

"None of you have to stay in the under mountain unless you wish it. You don't have to have a mate unless you wish it. Just, please, come with me."

Melisa's face takes on a strange expression. "You are absolutely sure that you are leaving tonight?"

"Yes. Will you come?" I press once more.

The time she takes to respond feels agonizingly long.

"Fine. We will travel through the harrowing cold together, like one little happy family," she says at last.

My heart soars upward into the skies. I lean forward and hug her, suds and all. She lets out a surprised laugh.

Abi makes a sound. "You moved again! Don't ruin my masterpiece. You have to be perfect if you want to avoid extra attention. Now, what is the plan?"

I know the look on their faces—it's the same one that Mikal gave me when we left Zlosa the first time. Pure, bright hope.

It's a bear sitting on my chest, demanding I succeed because they deserve a better life. Unfortunately, I didn't succeed before, but I will this time, especially because I can feel Teo's approach deep in my bones.

I nod once. "Melisa, there are some... items in my dress. Will you bring them?"

"Of course."

"And you know where Mikal is?" I ask, holding my breath.

She nods as she crosses to the dress. "Yes. He's near the whipping racks. There's a prison below."

I exhale. It wasn't hard to deduce that he was being tortured, but the confirmation feels like a blow to my gut.

"I think it is best that we leave during the feast, when everyone's drunk out of their minds. Melisa, meet me outside the kitchens, and you," I point to the others, "Wait in the trees near the northern steps. Just far enough away from the palace that the guards won't catch you."

"And if I bring friends?" Abi says.

I bite my lip. "I can't plan for them. There are too many unknowns."

She shakes her head. "Leave it to me."

"Bring them, but do it safely," I say, and Melisa's eyes grow wide.

One day, we'll come back for the rest. Every last pen will be torn apart.

Melisa is watching me, almost surprised.

I take her hand and look at the others. "Pack any supplies you can carry without getting caught."

The plan is sealed between us four with whispered words and the excited beating of our hearts. I've never known any kind of friendliness like this between laborers. A year ago, I wouldn't have ever even imagined it.

Soon.

I will be free.

Hope instead of anger sustains me as my hair is brushed, painted, and twisted.

It takes hours to turn me into an almost comical sight. I'm

showing far too much skin, but at last, it is done. My dress puffs out around my hips and doesn't fall lower than mid-thigh. My legs, stomach, shoulders, and arms are bare, save the glittering paint. There is little place to hide anything.

I pull out the labradorite stone, the books, and the jewels, and hold them out to Melisa.

"Can you keep these safe until it's time to leave?" She nods, taking the items in her hands but I immediately feel the heaviness of the diamonds clinging to my skin. "But wait, I need to bring that gem."

Melisa eyes the crystal as it shines and glows. I gaze at the shiny surface. My mother gave me that gem in my dream, and the echo of her song still plays in my mind.

"How?" she asks.

"Can we sew it on?" I offer.

Then she sets down the other objects, which both Abi and Paoli are studying, and pulls out a bit of thread. She then ties the stone around the short breast band covered with small diamonds.

It fits in perfectly.

I hug Melisa, counting the seconds until I can get rid of this cursed dress. She turns me to the mirror.

"You're a superb present for a pompous ass king. Isn't it such a miserable thing to behold? I hate that they feel entitled to whatever pretty thing sits at their feet. A part of me is sad I won't be there to witness his rage when he realizes we've all gotten the fuck out of this place." Her expression grows bitter.

"You're right. And I hate it too," I say, looking at the glossy sheen of my skin.

Abi steps forward, looking at her scar. "I wish that I never saw my face or knew what beauty I had before... I wish my image was merely a distorted reflection in the river—because then I wouldn't have to mourn what was lost."

"You are worth more than what you see when you look in this mirror." I step forward and push the gilded, polished metal over. It crashes to the ground, denting and distorting in the middle.

"Fuck the giants and their court," I say, seeing so much more than a pleasing set of eyes and well-combed hair.

I see desperation, passion, *courage*.

Each emotion licks against my inside. The Fuegorra begins to sing into the air, and the women around me gasp. Despite my fragile, mending mind, my eyes see a flicker of the future with perfect clarity.

Snow. Shiny, armored tails. Metal.

Hope, brilliant and as pure as freshly fallen snow.

The image is interrupted by a knock on the door.

A guard looks between me and the fallen mirror.

"Time to go, whore."

CHAPTER 18
MELANTERITE
TEO

The spy that Ayla had promised me is a middle-aged, weathered man with the fear of the gods written plainly across his face. They've sat him in a chair that was conjured by Farryn.

"There's a slave, a short one, with curly brown hair and brown skin," Ayla says, leaning over him and pointing a knife at his throat.

He trembles, and I would protest the cruelty of it all if I hadn't already won him the chance to live.

"There are many slaves that fit that description," he says, with a slight tremor in his voice.

I roll my eyes. None looked like my Estela.

"She will have been guarded, maybe even paraded around by Rholker," I say, not deigning to use a title for him.

The man's eyes widen with recognition.

"*Oh.* Her," he whispers. "Is she really your queen?"

The anger bubbling under the surface of my skin boils over.

"Yes, *her*," I grit out and he shrinks back. "And she's your queen, too."

"She was taken to the palace this morning. They are preparing her for the mid-winter feast. High King Rholker's using it for his coronation."

The words start to blend into each other from his fear. Even I am surprised at the speed with which the words tumble out of his mouth.

"A feast?" Ayla says, almost appearing more intrigued by that than our actual task.

The man nods rapidly. "Yes, it will begin in an hour or so, as soon as the sun dips behind the mountains. Everyone is here— the elves, the Cursed Six, even some of the swamp ogres."

Ayla purses her lips. "He has quite the horde, doesn't he?"

The slave just stares at her with his wide, terrified eyes.

"Do you know exactly where she was taken inside of the palace?" I demand.

The man shakes his head, and I let out a disappointed breath. It is difficult not to let every piece of bad news bring down my spirit like an avalanche.

"We will wait until the feast begins," Ayla says with finality. "We have glamour; we can easily dress up as lower-level guests. We'll have to go after everything is settled, and the alcohol is flowing freely." She must sense my doubtful look because she says without turning, "Yes, we can change even you large abominations."

"What of our tails?" Niht asks.

Taenya crosses her arms. "You could... I don't know, tuck it into your pants?"

Niht's tail curls around her arm.

"Believe me, there isn't enough room," he purrs.

She gives him a heated look, but I walk away, exasperated.

I know that we cannot charge yet, but every cell in my body is lit on fire as I walk back over to the spot that overlooks the city. The bustle of preparations for the feast flits and buzzes before. I see the carts drawn by cattle, and the lights already set on the palace.

When something stirs to my left, I see Ra'Salore. His mouth is pressed in a line.

"I know I'm not Lord Vann, but I hope to bring you a bit of comfort all the same."

I sigh.

"Thank you." Then, after a moment, I continue, "It's the waiting, no matter how short a time, that makes my skin feel like it's peeling off."

"I promise you, all will be well."

I look at him. His face is thoughtful, and not as hard as usual. It strikes me how little I truly know about his life, especially since his brother Tirin sacrificed himself.

"Thank you. It will. Let us prepare to ride."

I look back at the camp, where my armor is, and catch a glimpse of the man they are attempting to set free.

"No, I want to go to the mountain," the slave insists.

For someone who has spent most of the time sick with fear, he seems awfully excited to come to a place his people once considered hell on earth.

I push forward, and Ra'Salore follows close behind.

"What did you just say?" I ask.

He looks at me.

"Your Highness," he says. "News of Enduvida has been spreading through the slaves. We all know the stories that your queen tells. It started with one of the comfort women, but now a promise of a better life is whispered around every nighttime fire. I do not wish to go run into the woods—I want to come with you."

My mouth drops open, and I'm just about to respond when he continues.

"It is a place where slavery doesn't exist. Where you are

given a choice over your life—where everyone is kind and I can write my freedom on my heart for all to see. For me *to choose.*"

The words echo Vidalena's parting song. But knowing Estela said those words, to spread my home—our home—as a place of peace, makes a lump form in my throat.

"Then you shall come with us," I say.

Ayla looks at me, confused.

"Hmm, perhaps I would like to come to this mountain, too," she says through slitted eyes.

I nod.

"You all may come to my home."

CHAPTER 19
YUGAWARALITE
ESTELA

I don't know what I expected from the coronation, but it wasn't *this*.

Six women are seated around the back of the throne, flanked by the strongest warriors in the giant army, all clad in their finest uniforms.

One look suggests that some of the women are gifts from neighboring countries or giant lords, as I see two green-eyed elves, two humans with light hair, and even an ogre with skin the color of moss growing on tall elms.

All of them have been stuffed into the same pixie outfit that I wear, though their costumes are gold.

We are all little trinkets for the new king.

My shoulders tighten as I observe them kneeling upon velvet cushions with gold tassels, their heads bowed, and hands folded neatly in their laps.

The Enduar head is still positioned behind the back of the throne, and it adds heat to the boiling in my blood.

I force myself to take another long look at the face of the young man who sacrificed himself for his people.

For me, and my right to a better life.

So help me, I'm going to snatch the grotesque display away and burn it. His body was already given a proper burial, and I don't ever want his family to have to look upon such an awful decoration.

As I plot, the diamonds on my dress mess with my head. They play a low song, too quiet for the others to hear, that makes my brain pulse.

"Oh gods, that is stunning..."

"...a hundred diamonds..."

A few giants take up a discussion of my outfit when I pass, and I can feel their gazes hot on my skin. It's a special kind of torture to maintain my composure and sink onto my feather-stuffed cushion when I hear the tail end of a comment about "small tits."

Aside from the white color of my dress, I am also the only woman with a chain and leash. My cheeks heat as the tether is attached to the throne.

A part of me wonders if Lord Fektir's daughter will join us as she did during the court meeting. In truth, I do worry that she was murdered after that meeting. She wasn't kind, but I have a hard time wishing death upon her when she was chained up, just like me.

It isn't long after I've sat down that the rest of the guests are ushered in.

I sneak glances at their finery and am shocked to see the long, sweeping swathes of fabric glittering in the light of the polished chandeliers. For a culture that values wood so much, it is shocking to see how many gems are there—far more than the Enduares could have ever sold in fifty years.

It almost makes me curious.

That is, until Lord Fektir walks in with his wife in tow. My heartbeat takes off galloping when Fektir catches me staring at him, and he nods once with a mocking smirk while Lady Fektir glares at me with undiluted disgust. Her artfully painted red makeup pairs well with the scars on her forehead and neck.

I look back down to the hands in my lap, but soon, his voice filters over.

"My my, I didn't realize our daughter would be the only queen in attendance tonight."

"Oh, stop," Fektir's wife says.

That makes my head snap up.

The lord is grinning with a feral look in his eye—the look of triumph. The curve of his lips tells the tale of a man who got his way.

And what did he want?

One of his daughters to marry into royalty.

The night in the library returns to me.

Rholker had threatened me, yes. But perhaps telling me I would be his comfort woman was also his sick way of assuring me of my continued presence in his life after he was married.

It makes sense why he hadn't come to me in a few days. He was wrangling his bride.

Which is why... tonight...

I staunch the panic, trying to claw its way out of my body by taking several deep breaths. The music clashes with voices, but there is a gaping silence in my heart. There is no mating song. I am totally alone.

My mother was right—there would be no way to kill Rholker tonight unless I went to his room. And even then...

I think of my promise to the girls and ball my fists.

The will of the many over revenge.

I will kill him later with Teo at my side.

Right then, King Arion of the elves makes an entrance, still without a queen and ignores me entirely. I see his people take up several rows, in addition to the swamp ogres lining the walls without a proper place to sit.

The Six are not in attendance, which is strange since I know they are still in Zlosa. Perhaps they will be at the feast.

When the song changes, everyone goes quiet and stands.

I keep my head bowed, not wanting to give Rholker the satisfaction of seeing me stare at him as he struts down the aisle. It isn't until he ascends to the throne that I see he is not alone—a second pair of feet is at his side. There is no throne for her so she stays standing at the bottom of the steps. A priest of Khuohr, the giant god of war, comes over, and only then do I look up.

Rholker is dressed from head to toe in white while his bride wears blood red that matches the makeup over her eyes. Gold and silver are decoratively stitched over his battle garb, and he carries a large ax. His hair is neat, but every visible tattoo has been darkened, in addition to a new tattoo on each of his hands.

Giantese is shouted throughout the space, echoing off the walls and emboldening the giants to shout terrible war cries as drums beat to the rhythm of my pulse. I understand enough to make out the bloody promises. Time drags on as the priest holds up a crown and speaks bloody blessings upon Rholker's head.

It isn't until the crown is placed firmly on Rholker's brow that the giant men in the audience stand and retrieve shields from under their seats. They beat them in time with the drums as the priest's attention turns to Lord Fektir's daughter.

I remember her sniveling next to the throne, and now she stands there, sneering at me as if I were a smudge on her perfect silk dress.

"Lady Aska, bow to your husband, High King Rholker, and rejoice in your secured queenhood. May you produce heirs quickly!" the old giant calls out, in the common tongue, supposedly for the comfort of the invited guests.

She nods graciously as she falls to her knees, the first to bow to her husband.

Rholker leans down to take her hand and pull her up, then a circlet is placed on her head. It's nothing in comparison to the diamond jewels embedded in his crown.

The coronation is finished just as soon as it started, and it takes little time for the new royalty to exit the throne room, hand in hand.

When I look at Fektir again, he grins at me like a champion. I don't know exactly what he thinks he's won. If it's Rholker, I would've given him gladly. If he thinks it's victory over the Enduares, then he is the greatest fool of them all.

I let go of the hold on the lyre string of my magic, and it stretches out, expanding further than it ever has while the gem in my chest starts to shine. I imagine myself a burning star in the sky, my power mixing with Teo's to entomb him in a casket of lava. The cushion under my feet starts to smoke under the heat of my body.

His eyes grow wide, and his smile dims. I look up at him through the loose curly strands of my hair and smile.

There are a few gasps at the display of my magic, but everyone seems to think it's some sort of party trick. They murmur in the rows, almost excited.

They have no idea what maelstrom of rock and crystal lurks in the dark, ready to swallow them into the earth.

"Stop that," a warrior grumbles behind me. Another comes up and points a spear at my throat.

I listen only because of the women who will be waiting outside, primed for escape. The magic doesn't leave me, it merely reverberates under my skin—out of sight.

The panic amongst the guests wanes, and they begin to stand and file out, starting with Lord Fektir's row first. One of the guards steps forward and unchains me. The other women are left there, but I am taken out one of the side doors with barely enough time to look down at the singed velvet fabric from where I was seated moments before. The other women look at me with wide eyes.

"Where are you taking me?" I ask, twisting back to look up at the giant.

"High King Rholker wants you to sit with him at the feast," he grunts.

Unease swirls in my insides as the sounds of the highest lords and ladies in the land make their way to the feast. I wonder what Aska will think of my attendance—surely Lord Fektir will be furious.

"Will the other... gifts to his majesty be taken?" I ask, thinking of the elvish women, the ogre, and the other humans.

He doesn't respond, clearly not feeling the need to stoop to my level with a response.

The smell of meat and spirits hits my nose as we enter a side room. We pause for a few moments, waiting for a sign before we are led through another servant's passageway that spits us out into the great hall. I immediately spot the opulent table arranged in the center of the room. Rholker sits there with Aska Fektir at his side. The new giant queen.

Colors of every hue swirl before me. It's almost hard to take in all the richly dyed stripes and intricate patterns. The sparkle of gems threatens to blind me in a room already illuminated by floating candles and torches.

More music plays from a group of ogres positioned at the back corner of the room. After seeing their king, I don't feel like they are friends.

I've seen more of them in the last few weeks than in my entire life, but even I have to admit that their harpists, flutists, drummers, and lyrists play in perfect harmony.

It's not Enduvida, but it's pleasant. Especially for those

making their way to the long, wooden feasting tables. A woman is at the front, singing in old ogrese. It's... beautiful.

However, the space left for dancing is still, unsurprisingly, empty.

The giant waits for a pair of male elves from Arion's court to pass, and then we walk up to the throne. A roar of voices still chatters on, but I can feel eyes on me.

The frilly costume I've been given moves against my body with each step. The stiff skirt rubs my hips and the diamonds on the breast band chafe my underarms, as if the energy of this awful ensemble wasn't bad enough.

Sweat collects on my forehead and back, and I hope it causes the glittery powder to slide off my skin and make me a little less appealing.

"Come now, pretty slut. Show me a smile!" one of the giant lords calls as I pass, seconds before he reaches out to grab my ass.

On reflex, I yank on the lyre string of my magical reserve and light bursts out of me. I turn to hiss a curse upon the giant's head, but he cries out and holds up an injured hand. The flesh bubbles on his palm from the burn, and he slinks back, running from the room.

"Your Majesty," the warrior holding my chain says. He eyes me with palpable disgust. He knows I'm dangerous.

Good.

Rholker's nostrils flare before he looks back at us. At me. His yellow eyes meet mine, and his pupils dilate.

"Ah, yes. Give her to me," he says casually as he reaches out for the chain.

The warrior draws the links closer to his chest. "My king, I—
"

Rholker raises a brow.

"Has she been causing trouble?"

204

The man glances to either side. "I think she's using her magic."

Rholker's expression stiffens, and he grows angry. "And? If anyone dares to touch her, let it be known that even the High King's pets have sharp teeth!"

His raised voice makes all turn to look at us.

Yanking my chain away, he lifts it in the air.

"Behold! My secret weapon against our enemies!" he shouts.

The crowd cheers his toast, and he yanks my leash.

The movement automatically draws me closer to him, and Aska's red head turns toward me. Her amber eyes are filled with disdain as she looks at the creature her husband has brought to eat with them.

I wouldn't like to be here either.

Rholker pulls me close enough for the stiff skirt to press into his white pant leg.

I breathe, reigning in my magic with an iron fist. The string tenses and relaxes.

The flames abate.

If I hurt him now, there will be no chance to leave.

"Come now, Estela," he says, slapping one hand onto his lap. "Sit."

Aska's eyes widen in horror.

"*Rholker*," she whispers, enraged. "At least wait until after the party to fondle your plaything."

His face darkens as he turns to look at Aska.

"As you sit at my side, remember you have gotten what you wanted—a crown. You won over your sister. Take pride in it, but *know your godsdamned place.*" He pats his knee once more, a silent command.

Aska isn't finished. "You barely got what you wanted, my king. And you and I both know that if you openly disrespect me tonight, my father might do something... *unpleasant.* Marrying me was only the first part of your deal." Her eyes are glittering, and her smile curves into something sharp and cutting.

Rholker opens his mouth, and I assume he'll tell her to go to hell, but he surprises me and closes it. Aska's father didn't seem supremely worried about her receiving disrespect before, but the threat works well enough.

I would prefer not to be on his lap, especially since it means risking my escape plan.

Rholker looks back at me anyway, not hiding his hunger as he takes in every curve of my body and stretch of exposed skin. It makes my flesh crawl.

Then he nods his head once.

"Perhaps my new wife wouldn't begrudge me a little show," he says.

Aska lets out a long breath.

"As you wish," she grumbles, waving her hand at us while she brings a bit of roast venison to her mouth.

"Dance, Estela," Rholker says.

Every joint in my body stiffens. I know nothing of dancing.

Rholker twists the chain around his hand, waiting for me to comply. The tension between us is rising, but my mind is drowning in my plans, in everything I need to do before the end of tonight.

Escape.

It isn't until his eyes drop to my breast band where my mother's stone is carefully sewn that I panic. Falling into action is the easiest way to distract him from noticing the stone.

I bring my arms out to the side as graceful as I can, and begin to move my hips. It likely looks as awkward as it feels, but Rholker doesn't mind. He watches the path my fingers take through the air and smiles.

It's only then that he picks up his wine and starts to drink, relaxing into the chair and loosening his hold on my leash so that I can move more freely. As I twist from side to side, I let my eyes unfocus, unwilling to look at the crowd that no doubt is watching me from the corners.

Thinking of them will only make me angry, and that would make me—

"High King Rholker," a smooth male voice says behind me.

It takes effort not to drop my arms in embarrassment because I know that voice.

Rholker's eyes drag away from me and toward the newcomer. "Ah yes, King Arion. What a pleasure."

My giant master does not nod his head, nor does he adjust himself in his seat.

I lessen the width of my movements and finally turn to look at the king who betrayed my husband.

My mate.

He is the reason I am here right now.

I can't keep the crystal from glowing, but luckily, he doesn't appear threatened.

"Thank you for inviting us to your... exquisite celebration," Arion says.

Blood rushes in my ears as I see his long, silky hair arranged similarly to how it was the first day we met. His wooden crown gleams in the torchlight, and his piercing eyes sink into mine.

He doesn't smile or incline his head. This man stood at my wedding, watched my vows, and betrayed us.

"I must admit, I share your fascination with human women," he says conversationally as I continue to dance.

Rholker pauses and gestures vaguely toward the room.

"Perhaps you would like to select one for yourself," he says.

Arion nods, pleased.

"Actually, there is one that I met in the troll caves. She was quite... intoxicating. When you lay siege to Enduvida, I would consider her a gift of your highest respect."

My heart rate picks back up. He's talking about Arlet.

Rholker chuckles. "Your confidence is reassuring. Consider it done."

It's the last straw for me. Talk of the death of my people, my home, my kidnapping flows through the air like notes of music. Somehow, it feels like rocks have crushed me while the rest of my body implodes.

I lunge at Arion, nails first. My fingertips barely graze his green robes when the collar around my neck is jerked back. I sputter and choke, but the sudden movement makes me fall, and I knock my head against Rholker's throne.

"Good hell, I told you that bringing an animal to the dinner table was a bad idea," Aska says. "Our greatest apologies," she directs to the king while I wait for the blurriness in my vision to clear.

The light emanating from my stone makes it hard to see.

Arion stares at me in horror and then steps back, just out of reach.

I clench my hands, wanting another chance.

"I await my pretty red-haired gift, King Rholker, and I—" he says, still staring at my chest, with the slightest tremor in his voice. "Should I come back to discuss more later?"

"Get her out of here, *husband*," Aska demands. "She's ruining everything.

Rholker's jaw is clenched, but he doesn't let go of the tightness on my chain.

As if on cue, six dark-robed women also approach the throne.

It takes a second to register, and the room is quiet while I am forced against the side of Rholker's throne. The music starts to sour, and the lights above us dim.

"Essstela," Dahlia's haunting voice hisses.

Everyone at the king's table stiffens, and I feel her unseen eyes on me.

Arion looks at the women with alarm. "Who, exactly, are you? And why do you cover yourselves like assassins in the night?"

The five women that flank Dahlia turn toward the Elf King.

"We are the Sssix," one says simply.

Strange that he doesn't recognize them. Aren't they elves?

Arion seems unimpressed. He turns back to Rholker.

"Do you make it a habit of inviting those who entirely conceal their features from the other guests? How can I be sure they aren't sent straight from the trolls to kill us?"

The Six are silent, as is the king, but a giant completely oblivious to the tension walks by with three goblets of wine in two fists. His cheeks are ruddy, and he stumbles near the woman at the back of the flank. The two tumble over, and the black robe is yanked away.

She hisses and screeches, but wine splashes over her face, and whatever magic was keeping her concealed under the pitch-black fabric is revealed.

She's no demon. No elf.

She's a *human.*

I gasp. When the Enduares asked me about humans with magic, I told them about a legend among slaves: the *Brujas.*

They are real.

"A human?" Arion says, turning back to glare at Rholker. "Why are slaves attending the party the same as us?"

"We aren't slaves," Dahlia hisses, her voice low and strong.

She also yanks her hood off, revealing more elaborately painted greenish-black symbols over her pale skin. There's a haunting allure to her gaze, but she appears unashamed. Her eyes are entirely black, as is the paint around the sockets.

Straight black hair is braided into six sections tied at the back of her head with what looks like hollowed-out spinal bones.

The music stops entirely, and Aska has begun whispering furiously to Rholker.

Other elves are approaching, hands on their weapons, which causes several warriors to flock to us.

"What is the meaning of this?" another giant says as more and more draw near to see what's happening.

I can see their fiery questions as they see Dahlia and wonder why six humans who don't belong to the king can walk freely.

"Guards!" Rholker calls, clearly blanched.

His grip loosens just as Dahlia's bewitching face flicks to me. Like a snake slithering into my consciousness, I hear a voice in my head.

Prepare to run, Daughter of the Light Weaver.

I blink, and then one of the giants grabs the woman attempting to stand.

"You look like a child smeared cow dung over your face. I'll take you back to the pens. Maybe we'll find a frozen river to dunk your ugly face into," he laughs.

There is no warning before he goes straight as a plank, his eyes roll back into his head, and he falls over. Blood streams from his nose, mouth, and eyeballs.

Someone screams, and the giants move to grab the memory slicer.

It's mere moments before total pandemonium breaks loose. Screams fill the air, and all music stops.

The second that the lights go out overhead, more screaming comes.

The stone.

I reach to the familiar spot on the breast band and yank away the labradorite.

Lights flicker on long enough to see the spilling of more blood and carnage.

Rholker begins to bellow. I bring the stone to my collar and hum my mother's melody that's followed me for days. I feel the metal heat against my skin, but it doesn't burn. It just becomes... pliable.

I tear at it until it slides away from my neck. My heart is racing.

Metal bending.

As soon as its duty has been completed, the stone in my hand crumbles to dust in my hand.

The flickering lights barely illuminate the way to the servant's door, which is optimal since all the guards are now in the hall, and the lords and ladies are fleeing from the main entrance. I run as fast as I can in the dim light until I reach the familiar entrance to the throne room.

My gaze lands on the Enduar head mounted on the wall. The slippers on my feet are nearly as good as bare feet, and they serve me well as I rush past pews and the artwork of tyrants.

When I reach the wall, I use the textured column to the left to climb up. Being a tree climber has always served me well.

I shove at the head, and it falls to the ground. I retrieve the profane decoration and run toward one of the many statues of Khuohr's courtesans and consorts that bear flames.

Taking a long breath, I place the remains inside. The flame begins to lick at the wood and skin, and I sing the few words I remember from the parting cave as the wood crackles and skin burns.

There's a crashing sound at the door. I fall, scramble to my feet, and start to run. Never once do I stop praying for that poor Enduar boy who sacrificed himself.

As I dash out of the palace, I head to the whipping racks near the back of the castle, where the palace guard sleeps.

The snow bites into my skin, but the movement will keep me warm enough for now. When I dart through the arched hallways, I hear the pound of metal-armored feet running.

Chills pass down my spine watching more guards run to the feast hall. I press myself against the cold marble and wait.

As soon as the sound fades, I continue to run. The tall, carved trunks with beams that support dozens of bloody chains come into view two dozen footfalls later.

I slow, taking in whipping racks with bloody chains dangling from the tall wooden beams to hold slaves upright. I nearly vomit at the stench that clings to the spot after decades of use, but I hold my breath and search for Melisa.

I don't see her anywhere.

"Melisa!" I half whisper, half shout, completely desperate.

My heart is pounding loud enough to give me away—if this damned, sparkling white outfit doesn't do the deed first.

My friend emerges from behind one of the columns, and runs over to me. Relief floods my body. Her eyes are wide, and she is dressed in dark cloaks.

Her arm stretches out with a length of the black fabric. "Cover yourself, it will make it easier to remain unseen."

I nod, and start to push past her.

"Estela, wait."

Her voice is serious.

"What's wrong?"

Melisa shakes her head, and I see the tears on her cheeks. "I'm so sorry. He's not here."

I freeze.

"What are you talking about?"

"Mikal, your brother. They... moved him. I went to check after you left for the feast," she says. "Everything is awful, but the others are waiting for us. We have to go. It wasn't easy for them to escape—more warriors will be after them soon."

My brain can't comprehend what is happening.

"*No.*" I shake my head. I lost him once before. I watched the giants take him from Enduvida. I had a dream that he was here. He was safe. "NO!" I shout at her when she tries to reach me.

My breath is coming out in shallow pants in the cold air, and my head squeezes. I can't feel my legs.

"*Go,*" a voice from deep within urges. "*She speaks the truth.*"

The Fuegorra in my chest heats as a new vision blossoms before my eyes. Mikal's body lies in the back of a cart. He is thin, dirty, and bruised. One of his eyes is completely swollen shut.

Before the surroundings come into view, the vision fades.

My hands tremble as the weight of the world crashes in. I try to step forward. "*We have to—*"

Melisa grabs onto me, and covers my mouth.

"*Estela*, we have to go now—before someone finds us. I truly am so completely sorry, but I did bring your things. Please. Come on," she begs, dragging me.

It takes a few feet but I start running with her, only half conscious of what is happening.

The palace blurs around me, and the further away we get, the more I hear the shouting. I can *smell* the blood that soaks the air as they try to heal whatever awful thing is happening inside.

Wind blows back my black cloak, chilling my body to the bone as we run to the meeting place. Thick patches of trees hold cloaked bodies. Not a single guard is anywhere in sight, but I see the huddle of people from here. Not one or two—at least thirty.

I slow down.

"Mierda."[1]

Melisa slows as well, looking at me.

"You told her that she could bring friends." Her tone is careful like she expects me to say no. To turn her away.

As we near the group, Abi and Paoli wait for us. Abi smiles so brightly that it makes my heart hurt for another loss of Mikal.

"Rholker had sent these women to the breeding pens recently," Abi starts.

I notice the blood across her neck and face.

"What happened?" I step forward, grabbing her.

She swallows. "We had to kill the watchers."

"Are you okay?" I demand.

Her eyes dim.

"I—We—We got enough out."

There are so many questions rumbling around in my skull, and I think of what Rholker had said about wanting to increase the production of humans.

I look back at the women. "Were you followed?"

She shakes her head.

"No, many guards were called away to the great hall." She looks behind me, and an explosion breaks the glass on the front window.

A steady stream of people still flee from the palace

Good.

I will take away something more from Rholker. I will slowly bleed him dry until he begs me on his knees.

I take Abi's and Melisa's hands, pulling them forward.

"Let's go. The trees are too close together for giants to walk through. We don't have much time."

"Wait. A few of them are pregnant, some are mourning, some are furious at life itself—I don't know what they will think of the Enduares, but I..." Her voice cracks as we move through the trees. "I had to get them out."

I nod as I listen, but then the words run out, and they are waiting for me to respond.

Sucking in a deep breath, I say the words, "How many are there?"

"Thirty-six."

"Bring them all. The Enduares are a good people; they will be safe. They will find a place to heal."

The other women watch our progression, and I wave towards them, signaling our time to sneak off. They are silent as they all push forward.

The feeling in the air is as electric as the way before me parts. I dash forward, running ahead of the group. They follow behind as we hurry past sawmills. Past the graves of our people, the pitiful huts, and the latrines. We dodge through fields of budding trees until we reach the end gate.

My eyes widen in horror as I see a group of three giant warriors. They must've already heard us because they are waiting, spears drawn.

"What is this?" the one at the front calls. "Are these the ones that attacked the breeding pens?"

I step forward, out of the cover of the trees, knowing we can't win. But damned if I won't try.

I just hope the others aren't all visible.

"You are mistaken. The doctor sent us into the woods to search for herbs," I shout back. "There's an outbreak of disease."

One giant sneers, "Disgusting lying, bitches. Step back."

I don't move, but a gust of wind blows back the corner of my cloak, revealing my costume and naked legs. *No, no, no.* My entire body freezes.

"Wait," the one pointing a spear at me says. Then he approaches.

My skin tingles.

I can feel him studying me, but my anxiety mounts due to the dozens of women behind me who are unarmed and unprotected. What are we against spears and axes?

What are they against your magic?

Ever since I arrived in Zlosa, I've burned Rholker several

times. I burned the man at the party. My consciousness fumbles with the string in my chest, trying to get a firm grip.

He reaches out his spear further, using its tip to part the cloak and revealing the white pixie costume. He steps back and curses.

"You belong to the king," he sneers. "Men, kill the others. They're trying to escape!"

"Over my dead body," I shout, spreading my arms wide and pulling back the magical trigger.

One single note vibrates inside of me and the white-hot glow is instant. The magic stretches as far as possible, but it's too hard for me to hold. It richoches back and causes waves of light. They ripple through me and out into the open air.

It's like a falling star has exploded.

Just as the giant lunges toward me, something flies through the air lodges itself firmly through his neck. He topples over with a gurgle as I hop back and inspect the arrow.

One of the women screams and starts to run toward the fence, only for an ax to cleave through the air, parting her in two.

More screaming starts, and more arrows fly through the sky.

I turn, heart pounding and see another spear being aimed at a slave. I race in front of the sharp tip before it can touch the woman. The flare of my light causes him to lose balance, and his weapon falls to the ground.

I pick it up, and, *damn*, it is heavy. Every muscle groans as I aim. Then, with as much force as I can muster, I charge forward and ram it into his chest.

He slides onto the wood, gaping up at me, his yellow eyes glinting in *my* light.

Another giant spits on me. Then his hand reaches out and grabs me, the spear falling back into the snow.

I smell his burns, but not before I'm thrown to the ground.

I slide through the thin layer of snow and ice before ramming into a tree. Bones crunch. Pain blooms through my middle, and I cry out.

The thumping of heaving feet comes from the left, and four more giants are heading over.

I try and fail to sit up. Above all sound, the crystal in my chest begins to sing.

My body goes rigid as warmth lights up my insides, mending the bone as the sound of windchimes fills my ringing ears.

I whip around, and see the riders descend from the hill.

Four *glacialmaras* cut through time and space with a rider leading the rank.

Teo.

The bond is no longer silent. It is filled with deathly rage as the embodiment of carnage races toward us, sword extended and eyes burning.

DON'T MOVE! Teo screams in my mind.

Behind him are two others, Niht and Lord Salo. Then there are dozens of elves riding upon a stag of enormous magnitude, bears, and even wolves. They let out a battle cry, and the ground cracks open beneath the feet of the giants.

They are swallowed up as Teo rides on. When his *glacialmara* flies over the gate, he stops and holds out his hands. His eyes shut, and his head is thrown back. Red magic pours from his fingertips, reaching into the earth.

Out of the split ground, three columns of lava rise up, lighting up the entire forest. One smashes through the gate, another destroys the guard's hut, and the third swings towards the giants. They scream as their flesh is charred to a crisp.

It isn't until trees start to sway that I start screaming for the women to run out of the gate.

"Go!" I yell until my voice is raw. I see Abi and Paoli holding hands as they shriek and evade the lava spreading across the ground. The Enduares and elves start to grab them and haul them further away from the giant's land, leaving me behind.

I push myself onto my knees, face burning in front of the heat. An entire section of the forests collapses.

"Teo!" I scream. He doesn't move, just continues to wield more magic than I had ever seen. For the first time, I realize how this kind of power destroyed an entire continent.

Taking another heaving breath, I reach through our bond. I'm met with a heat so intense I almost shy away. He's a conduit for the earth itself, and it burns.

Teo, stop, I beg. *Please, you'll burn down the entire forest. There are slave pens nearby.*

Finally, I feel the magic ebb away. The crack in the earth starts to close, causing the ground beneath me to rumble. I scramble out of the way as another tree falls.

When I look up, Teo is no longer floating in the air. He's dismounted and races toward me.

"Estela." His voice is haggard. "You're alive."

I don't have a chance to speak before he snatches me up.

I'm overwhelmed by the feel of his armor and the smell of his skin.

Metal. Blood. Heat. *Home.*

Every part of me sings, and I collapse into him, only vaguely aware of us remounting the *glacialmara.*

"I knew that you would come," I say through sobs. "You made it."

His arm tightens around me, but the raging storm within him doesn't calm.

I feel him slice through someone, but I close my eyes and clutch to him as my injuries continue to heal.

Everything is too much. Too much death. Too much gore.

My eyes squeeze shut to it all, and for the first time in weeks, I let someone else hold me.

After endless days of torture. Of humiliation. Of outfits and chains and leashes, of spells and literal drowning.

A ray of light.

One that I don't deserve but that I run into nonetheless.

"We need to get the women away before any others are hurt," I call up to him. "I—I did all I can."

"Shh, you did enough. No more putting yourself in danger." His hand cups the back of my neck. "We will get them all out unharmed."

The elves' arrows and blades cut through bone, and their armored beasts tear at flesh until the small troupe of giants is reduced to a mount of steaming death.

The Enduares and elves crowd behind the women, herding them forward. They run, and their frightened faces pull at my heart.

"Let me run with them," I call up to my mate.

He shakes his head firmly, and his grip tightens.

"They can have you tomorrow."

I see the tightness of the muscles around his unbound face, and he looks ahead, terrifying power leaking off of him.

"Tonight, we leave this place for good."

You are safe. Teo's voice also speaks into my mind as the Fuegorra sings to me with mind-cracking joy. *Finally safe.*

Then he raises something to his mouth—a stone, I realize—and speaks into it as it starts to glow.

"Lady Estela is with me. We're coming home."

My heart soars.

PART TWO

CHAPTER 20
RHOLKER

"Where the fuck is my personal log?" Rholker demands as he shifts books and papers around his large, mahogany desk.

"My King, please. This is serious. There were seventeen deaths and more than a hundred casualties," Regent Uvog says from the other side of the table.

He is still wearing the ceremonial garb from the coronation, though his hair is now unbound, and there are bloodstains over his blue doublet. Displeasure radiates off him in waves.

"Fine." Rholker sits back and rubs his left eyebrow, pressing into his eye socket. "How many giants?"

"Eight, but the—"

"How many of them were high-ranking officials?" Rholker's words are short and clipped.

Regent Uvog's hand falls from his face, and he grits his teeth as his eyes pass from Rholker's blood spattered shoes to his stained white shirt. "Two were minor lords, and six were warriors."

Rholker lifts off his chair. His hands flex under Uvog's scrutiny, but his shoulders remain shoved back as he holds his head high.

"And what of Lord Fektir?"

"He is furious about his daughter's arm," the regent replies.

Rholker clasps his hands behind his back and begins to pace back and forth.

"It's a broken fucking arm. It's not like she was in any real danger."

"Your Majesty, some say it was you who shoved her on the ground when the Elf King tried to stab one of *your* witches," Uvog says.

Rholker is silent.

The only sounds are the crackling fire in the corner and the feet shuffling outside the office door as slaves clean up Rholker's mistakes.

"Look, the individuals of substantial meaning are fine. Arion, Fektir, the Shaman Ogre King, I don't understand why you are—"

"The ogres lost more than any other. I've given you dozens of chances to speak plainly with them. You have refused to forge a relationship at every turn," Uvog practically shouts, slamming his fist on the desk.

"They are our distant blood kin. We do not need to play diplomacy!" Rholker shouts back.

Uvog shakes his head. "For Khuohr's sake. I believed in you when you proved your prowess by overthrowing your father."

Rholker's eyes narrow. "I would be very careful with what you intend to say next. I am still your king, and you have already promised to march upon the Enduar caves."

"You are worried about the Enduares right now?" Uvog starts to laugh. Then he straightens, looking directly at Rholker.

"Tell me, did you know that your comfort woman took a whole quarter of the breeding pen when she escaped?"

Rholker's throat bobs.

"Yes," he grits out.

"You thought that keeping her separate would prevent her from poisoning the well, but you were wrong. Tales of the Enduares are spreading through the ranks like a disease. Now that a few dozen are gone, you can expect a rebellion," Uvog seethes.

"That's an easy fix—I punish those who try, and we fortify the guards," Rholker says simply.

Uvog shakes his head. "That won't help. A diseased limb must be cut out."

Rholker's head cocks to the side. "How?"

"You are the sovereign. Why don't you tell me?" Uvog says through gritted teeth.

Rholker stares down at the map strewn across his desk.

So many plans... they all swirl before his eyes. Riches, power, land. Everything was working.

He needed more slaves, not less. And yet, he also needed the support of his court.

"Culling the population will be the first step," Rholker says quietly.

"Precisely." Uvog displays the first modicum of agreement since entering the room. "We can poison food supplies, execute those that speak openly of revolt, and burn slave pens."

Rholker pauses.

"Would it not be more effective to bring back Estela? Surely, seeing her plan thwarted would squash any hopes. We'd show them there is no true escape."

Uvog's face drops, his eyes darkening as his fists clench.

"Enough of that woman," he growls. "Lord Fektir thought you stole her to gain an advantage over the Enduares. You

assured all of us that was the case. You made promises. Now...
Gods."

Rholker looks up as Uvog shakes his head.

"You are a love-sick fool starting a war over a *woman*. How many people have died and will die for one bitch?"

Rholker snaps. He strikes Uvog across the face.

"She belongs to me. Don't think I don't know the lengths you've gone to secure the prizes in your pleasure house, you filthy hypocrite."

"I've never started a war." Uvog steps back, wiping blood dripping from his mouth. "Is that why you are working with the witches? Did they give you the power you wanted to get her back? Rholker, tell me that you aren't that idiotic. There was a reason your father never deigned to work with them beyond minor memory altering."

"You know nothing of their power," Rholker growls.

"They own you now, don't they?" Uvog sneers.

Rholker's eyes are burning, but he doesn't respond.

"Tell me, *My King*, what did you agree to?" Uvog says.

"That is between me and them," Rholker says with finality. "I suggest you don't pry if you want to leave here alive."

The tall, burly giant swipes his arm across the table, spilling ink wells and ruining paper.

"You would threaten your regent?" Uvog shouts. "Is this what you think will work, Rholker? That you can just kill everyone in your way? Soon, you will find no one is left to manage your kingdom."

"I killed my brother and father, and now I am king. Eventually, the others will learn to fear me."

"You lied to us when you said you bested them in a fight," Uvog pushes. "You used filthy power. Khuohr would not be pleased with such blasphemy. He is a jealous god."

Rholker pulls a knife out of his waistband.

Uvog's eyes glint, and he mirrors the action by pulling out his weapon.

"Your pretty human has quite an impressive power, just like her mother. Did you promise to give her to the witches?" Uvog searches his face, angling the knife at his throat.

"I am your king. As regent, your job is to advise me. If you cannot do that, I suggest you step down."

Rholker is practiced with a blade, as was his brother. Those years of training have made him skilled at murder.

Uvog doesn't back down.

Before either of them can lunge, the door bursts open, revealing Lord Fektir.

He strides in, fuming, with several guards behind him.

Rholker attempts to straighten, but Fektir grabs him by his collar and throws him onto the ground.

The hot fire in Fektir's eyes doesn't match the cold expression on the rest of his face.

"You have some nerve," Fektir says down at him.

Rholker scrambles to his feet. "What the fuck is wrong with you?"

"The only reason you are still alive is because you made my daughter a queen," Fektir spits.

"A woman will never hold the throne by herself," Rholker bites back. "Divine decree has appointed my blood. That is *untouchable.*"

"Precisely, which is why you will give her a son. If you have not rectified your sins before then, then our land will welcome the rule of a babe," Fektir says.

His ambition lights up the room, seeping out of every pore. He wants the crown and all the riches that he was denied as a simple lord.

Rholker shakes his head. "I won't touch your disgusting daughter."

Fektir grabs him again, this time pushing him into the wall.

"You will, and I will make sure. When her arm is healed, you will visit her bed every night for three months."

Rholker opens his mouth, only for Fektir to slap it closed.

"I will be there. I will ensure you properly plant your seeds and water her garden until a new sprout begins to grow."

For the first time, Rholker's haughty expression fades. He has no plan and no great supporters in this room.

Fektir pounds the king's back against the wall once more. "Do you understand?"

Rholker looks into his eyes, full of hatred for those who think they can bend him to their wills. "Yes."

Uvog watches the exchange from the desk, chest heaving and mouth still bleeding.

"What is your plan? And I swear on the god of war, if you mention that damned woman, I will kill you right now and harvest your seed from your lifeless corpse," Fektir shouts.

Rholker refuses to appear weak any longer.

He fights back, pushing off Fektir.

"We are going to begin the process of culling the slaves and visit the Ogre King. I will go to the Elf King in the morning."

Fektir steps back. "I will go with you."

Rholker begins to protest, but Fektir shakes his head. "No. I won't let you ruin this, too."

Uvog nods once.

"I shall come, too."

Fektir nods tightly. "Excellent. Shall I call a slave to straighten your appearance, or do you wish to leave now?"

Rholker seethes at him. As if giving him such a meager choice could make up for the humiliation.

"We will go now," he says.

The three exit the door, push past the ruins of the great hall, and then head to the rooms for the ogres.

When they reach the door, the metallic scent of blood is everywhere. Two giants lay dead at the entrance.

Pushing the door hanging on its bent hinges, they step inside. In the middle of the room, four slaughtered giant warriors are propped up against the chair. The careful precision of the ogres' blades is haunting.

The stacked bodies can only mean one thing; the ogres have made enemies of the giants.

Fektir lets out a garbled sound. "If I could kill you and take your throne right this second, I would."

Rholker takes in the gore of the room, utterly helpless. "I can fix this."

Uvog laughs, but Fektir says, "No, I will fix this through you."

Rholker turns to him.

"I am your king," he insists with the same fervor as always. "You are a fool."

Fektir spits the burning words as black mist begins to pour into the room.

"You will not touch that which we protect," the hissing voices of The Six, the human witches, declare.

The two giants appear worried as they watch the entrance of the women.

"Rholker made a deal with us, an irreversible one. We are the only ones that can stop his heart," they say in unison, adding to the cold blackness with every second.

Uvog looks at Rholker, who watches smugly.

"You have ruined us," the regent laments.

Rholker shakes his head, and the mask on his face begins to fall. The fear in his eyes, the helplessness, the worry, it all fades into something dangerous.

"No, I will bring glory to our people." He steps forward, unbothered by the ominous black power.

229

"Your advice was welcome, Uvog. Fear not. I will indeed cull the slaves and rescue our alliances. I'm sure that your successor will be pleased." Rhokler pulls out his knife stabs Uvog in the gut.

The man makes a garbled sound and then sinks to his knees.

Fektir watches in horror.

"Would you like to add something, Fektir? I wouldn't like to lose you and your advice as well," Rholker says, entirely unbothered as he wipes the bloody knife on Uvog's blood-stained shirt.

Fektir grits his teeth.

"And what you said about Aska? I won't sire a child with her, not ever." Rholker continues.

Fektir lets out a roar, which echoes off the walls of the room, stinking of death.

"I won't support this. I'll go to the other lords," Fektir threatens.

"No, you will not. You will uphold the deal inked in magic the night I married your daughter," Rholker says with a grin, and his eyes glow red for a moment.

Fektir staggers back.

"That—that wasn't magic."

Rholker smiles as the witches flank him.

"Oh, but it was. Who do you think etched our marriage tattoos?" He holds up his hands with the black ink scrawling across his knuckles.

"I won't support a march on the Enduares until you fix all your other messes." Fektir bolsters his strength.

Rholker tilts his head to the side.

"Very well. Tomorrow, we will hold a meeting and invite the Elf King." He straightens his neck. "Never say that I haven't done you a favor."

Fektir gazes at the dark magic swirling in the room, the

yellow-red eyes of Rholker, and hateful stares of the witches. All the while Uvog's words about ruination echo through the room.

"You have tricked me, Rholker. Do not forget just how many of the lords I control," Fektir says.

Rholker smiles.

"Never. But do not forget how I can control you. What good is power if you are dead?"

CHAPTER 21

HAUYNE

TEO

Progress back to Enduvida is slow. With such a large party, what would've taken us one or two turns of the sun has easily turned into three or four.

While no one would fault the women who have come with us, it is a burden we are all happy to bear. There is a desperation that comes from having Estela back with me and not having more than a few moments alone. Adding in thirty-three women has made privacy a long-lost luxury.

All the tents that were brought have been sacrificed to the humans.

Niht has taken to going with the elves daily to hunt in order to supplement the stolen slave supplies. It takes a lot to feed around sixty people, especially when most are not yet sufficiently healed to assist with food preparations.

It's quiet most days, much quieter than I would've expected. Everyone is tired and cold, and I can see many are drenched in pain, both emotional and physical. Estela spends every stopping point healing those she can. Several have infections, four are pregnant, and, just like the slaves from before, they are all malnourished.

She worries about herbs and fevers, and I worry about the cold. This has raised tensions in the camp and...

Estela.

She is returning to Rahda after hours of bandaging wounds.

Every thought always comes back to her.

She told me Mikal was gone when she went to save him, and now my beautiful mate looks... different. Not only has the hollowness returned to her face, but the look in her eye rips up my soul. I know the look of torture. I know fear.

In many ways, I worry that we are in a worse place than where we started.

I finish helping Ra'Salore set up the tents for the women to huddle inside.

One of the women approaches and gives us a long look. Her long dark hair is drawn over the side of her shoulder, and Ra'Salore eyes the unbound locks like a starved man seeing meat.

"You are very warm, as a people," she says. "It would be nice if you would sleep inside the tents to raise the body temperature."

Ra'Salore shakes his head. "We are too large."

"I wouldn't mind lying on top of you to help save space." The woman grins.

The silent stone bender sputters. "I—"

Niht comes over, a squirrel on his arm.

"Melisa, look!" He holds out the squirrel. "You said you liked these fluffy tail devils. Though, if you ask me, they are more rat than pet."

The woman named Melisa laughs and holds out her arm. The pet scampers up and wraps around her neck.

I turn away from the chatter and find that Estela is gone. She's likely back with the women.

I frown. We need a quiet, warm place to speak.

A part of me is frightened to peel away the layers of her mind and find out whatever is lurking beneath. Not because I am afraid to take on her pain, but because I worry about what it means to confront such emotions when this journey has brought out a great deal of brokenness in my own consciousness.

My one hope is that the two of us may carry each other's pain together.

I wander away from the tents. When I find what I'm looking for, a cave with a warm, slightly sulphuric smell leaking out of it, my heartbeat increases.

As I push into the entrance, I find it mostly clean. It takes little time to use a discarded branch to sweep out any mess and tidy everything up. I lay down the sleeping roll I brought and take a deep breath.

Blood has been pounding through my veins, and there is an urge to claim and comfort, one that strains against my pants with surprising insistence. But what the cock wants and what the mind needs can sometimes be two different things.

As I head out of the cave and trek back to the camp, I see her from several dozen paces away. Estela is indeed checking a woman's arm, as is Ulla.

The women watch her with that same unsettling silence as she bandages wounds and Ulla sings them closed. She must sense my coming because she turns and smiles at me with the same shy, weary sadness that has been pasted on her face since we first saw each other.

A lump rises in my throat.

"*Amor*[1]," I say in the human tongue. "I need you to help me with something."

Estela's finely arched brows draw together, and a few of the others exchange knowing looks behind her back.

234

I ignore them.

They are allowed to think whatever they will about me, what is most important to me is a moment alone.

"Here," she says, handing a few things off to one of the women with dark hair who they call Melisa. I'm surprised she got away from Niht and Ra'Salore so quickly.

Melisa smirks at me as I hold out an arm and wrap it around my mate.

My hand grazes her cloak and cold flesh. The Fuegorra keeps her warm and safe from frostbite, but the itchy white fabric underneath is... bothersome.

"You should change," I say conversationally.

She shakes her head. "Between you and the cloak, I am warm enough. Any spare clothing needs to be used for them and their wounds."

I purse my lips, but I don't say anything more. We have had this conversation more than once, and it has never ended positively.

We make it a few more paces toward the cave when she gives me a sidelong gaze.

"What did you need help with again?"

I take a deep breath and run a hand over her now-braided hair. I can't stop touching her, reminding myself that she is real and we are going home. Everything is not fixed, but it's... gentler now that she is near.

"I didn't say."

She stops at the entrance, her face draining of color.

"Teo, I have to—they need me—" She's breathless, but we're almost there.

I can't let her run off again. Not yet.

"They will still be there in an hour or two," I say, finally reaching the cave and pulling her inside.

She takes a deep breath and leans into my arm.

I immediately feel her discomfort. It's highlighted in every part of her face and punctuated with the sad song that plays in the air.

I prod her mind and find it carefully closed. Doubt enters my heart.

"Do you still want to leave?" I ask.

She shakes her head.

After a few moments, I guide her over to the bedroll on the ground and sit down across from her. The silence between us is almost as thick as mud, only eased by the low mating song flowing from our Fuegorras. I look at how she nervously glances at the warm spring, confused.

"Are you... all right?" I ask after a few moments.

She looks at me with large eyes, and I realize she's trying not to cry. "I am fine. I just want to help those who are coming with us."

She feels so far away from me, but I resist pulling her in. We've done this many times already; I know she will bury her face in my chest, but her thoughts remain far. She must say the words.

"What happened?" I ask gently.

Her lips begin to tighten as if trying to hide a quiver.

"I—" She takes a deep breath. "They tortured me."

I watch the column of her throat contract, and I hear the roar of blood rushing in my ears. Then, a tear falls down her cheek.

"They didn't whip me, and Rholker never raped me. I told him that the Fuegorra would kill him if he tried, and it burned him every time he touched me."

Only a fool would know such abuse is the only way for a man to hurt a woman.

"But?"

"But he brought in these women. The Six. They are human,

and they have magic. I never thought I'd see something like that." Each word is slightly staccatoed and she closes off her emotions.

I don't push. I just listen.

I do, however, wonder why her Fuegorra was burning people. It is a magic I do not know.

"They ruined some of my memories to turn me against you. They shattered them like glass on a jagged rock. Rholker wanted me to be his, so they tried to erase you." A flood of tears finally spills down. "But they didn't, they couldn't. I tried to be strong. Oh gods. Teo, I am so sorry. For everything I've ever done—I was pathetic and scared. I'll never be that person again. Please. *Please* forgive me," she sobs, reaching forward to take my hands.

My heart cracks apart.

"Estela, my star. Stop. I forgave you long ago." I pull her into my lap. "You helped save all those women. I saw you kill the giant. You are strong."

She melts into me, but I catch her chin before she can hide again and tilt it up. Her face is puffy, red, wet, and perfect. She nearly knocks me over when she is the one to kiss me.

It's a ferocious action, one borne from our weeks apart.

It doesn't stop with the pressing of our lips together. Eventually, she grazes the seam of my mouth with her tongue. I can't help but groan. It's been too long since I tasted her. If this would bring her pleasure, then I would give her anything. Anything to take away the pain and make her smile once more.

I know enough for now.

It's not until her hand slips under my shirt that I pause and pull back.

"Are you ready for this?" I ask.

She nods.

"Please. I need a new memory of you."

I swallow. "Tell me if it becomes too much at any point."

She nods, her chest rising and falling.

It's only then that I reach forward toward her breast band filled with the Enduar diamonds. One quick tug, and it's torn away from her flesh. There's a little build-up of dirt, and whatever cosmetics they put on her have smudged and smeared, but the sight of her breasts with small, lovely rosebud nipples is one I would savor for the rest of my life.

She sucks in a sharp breath at being exposed to the air, so I bring my mouth to each peak, working to warm them so that she doesn't feel the cold. The song crescendos into the room as her pulse quickens at my nearness. There's no shocked pause, only a pleased groan when I relish as much attention upon her as possible.

I put my hand on the strange skirt and tear it off too.

"I'm going to rip out Rholker's eyes the next time I see him for looking upon you like this," I growl.

Her scent fills the air, and it turns on something that has long since been dormant.

My blood pumps harder, and my mouth waters. I lean her back, taking in those large, sad brown eyes.

"You want a new memory? I'll give you one you've never had," I say, my voice low.

Then I lay her back and lower myself between her legs.

"Teo, *oh gods,* wait," she says.

I pause, looking back up at her.

"We've been traveling."

"Yes."

"I've only had time to clean with a washcloth and herbs," she says.

"Perfect. Can I continue?"

Another second passes while I look at her large eyes. "You don't have to do this. What if... what if you don't like it."

I stroke her thigh. "Estela, this is instinct. *I will like it.*"

"But I—all right."

"Thank you." I growl and then tear the remains of her ridiculous costume apart with my teeth. She yelps and then gasps when my tongue makes contact with her skin.

She's sweet, and wet, and I languish both her cries and the way she squirms and grips my hair. I work slowly, memorizing the way her belly muscles tighten and twitch. Her need is directly tied to my own, and when her release comes, my senses are overwhelmed completely.

"My star," I growl, coming up for air while she pants. "You are the most perfect creature who ever has and ever will walk the face of the earth."

Her eyes are glassy and contented, and the worry lines that have marred her skin are now smoothed over. The pain forgotten, if just for a moment.

But I'm not done. I want to seal this fire between us, to plunge into her softness and feel her next release shoot me into the heavens. It isn't until she nods that I realize I accidentally sent that thought directly to her mind.

Her expression softens impossibly further, and it's as if a part of her is mended at seeing what I saw when we came together for the first time.

My clothes are discarded in a matter of moments, and she wraps her legs around me as I lift her up to take her to the water and wash away any trace of Zlosa.

After two steps, she freezes and breaks our kiss. She looks down at the water and holds her breath.

I feel the panic rising up inside of her, and it almost shocks me. It's equal parts exhilarating and heartbreaking to be so close to her emotions once more.

"What's wrong?" I ask as she stands there, frozen in terror.

Then she starts to shake.

"They... they used water to hurt me. It felt like I was

drowning every day." Her breath grows increasingly shallow, and the moment retreats as the passion is doused.

"Sh, sh," I coax, cradling my naked mate to my chest. "All is well. We don't need to go near the water. Not now."

Her silent trembling continues for a few more moments as I try to relax her with the rhythmic rise and fall of my chest.

"Would you like to go back to camp?" I ask.

She pulls back.

"But you—" she reaches down to grasp my cock, but I bat her hand away.

"Later, *amor*[2]."

"Later," she whispers the word as if it were the sweetest promise I'd ever made.

I nod my head again, and then set her down. I put on my pants and boots, but then dress her with the rest of my gear. When she protests, I silence her with a finger pressed to her lips.

"No. We will leave this here. You should never wear anything like that again. That's another promise."

She closes her eyes as if she wants to protest but instead thinks better.

"I'll be better tomorrow. I promise, thank you, and I'm so—"

"Stop. I've already told you to stop apologizing for everything. I am here now, and I forgive you for everything you can think of."

She doesn't speak. Her wide eyes look at me like I am something impossible, and I see what my heart has known from the moment the song started in my chest.

We belong to each other.

I dwell on every inch of her face, hollow as it now seems. I wish to know everything about her, from what brings her joy, what startles her laughter, to what soothes her wounds.

These were questions held back from us. Our pain used to be

our points of connection, but now I see such a vast sea of possibilities in the distance.

I see her belly swollen with my child, our tending to her gardens, cooking in the kitchens. I hear her voice scolding soldiers and blessing marriages. She holds my head in her lap, stroking my skin and singing her tunes. There is peace.

Goodness.

She is brilliant, shining, life incarnate. A life given back to me and made whole.

"My sweet wife, like the little minx you are, you have snuck in and stolen all my sadness. Please, never give it back." I reach out, brushing a curl behind her ear, and then we head out of the cave.

The memory of this place will be my first gift.

I shall spend every waking second thinking of more.

CHAPTER 22
EUCLASE
ESTELA

After the night in the cave, it takes one more full day of walking to reach the base of the mountains. The great, frozen sea with its massive floes is quiet, much like our exhausted group. Aside from the humming from Ulla and the daily checkups with the women, most of the noise comes from the crystals and the rhythmic slap of saltwater against enormous slabs of floating ice.

It's disorienting to come back this way after so much in my life has changed. Five months ago, I came here to escape. Now...

I look at our large group as we trudge on. The elves are fearsome women with strong features.

Assassins, Teo reminds me through our bond. He shows me scenes from the enclave. He glosses over what he had to do to get the elves' support, but I can't fault him.

I haven't shown him everything either.

There is time to compare scars.

Luckily, despite the waning health of a few, no one has died on the trek. They have no carts to pull. There's no blood on the ground or whip-wielding monsters itching for an excuse to make themselves feel powerful at a human's expense.

Memories flash before my eyes faster than I can view them all. Everything isn't perfect. It won't be until Mikal is home— but it is *right*.

I nestle back into Teo's bare chest, luxuriating in his suede skin's soft, silky warmth. They offered me the other *glacialmara*, since Liana had already taught me to ride during our training, but Niht has the four pregnant women mounted atop the creature, and he guides it along with a rope.

Melisa walks close by Niht. A few grouse flit between them. Hers is the sole laugh that rises above us all, sometimes joined by the elvish twins, Farryn and Elanila.

We're so close to home, I can almost smell the inside of the cave. My eyes burn when I think of Arlet or Liana. I ache to know of Svanna and Iryth. I've kept them far from my mind to protect myself, but now, I am free to anticipate our reuniting.

When we get back inside the cave, will you stay in my room?

Teo asks through my mind, and I bawk at his question.

Of course. Why wouldn't I?

He's silent. It isn't until the cloudy passage where I'd tried to escape five months ago comes into view that he responds.

It's been long since I've killed like that. You weren't there the night of our wedding when the giants invaded. I could barely see straight. I worried I scared you.

I twist around to look up at him.

I spent years hearing spewed lies about who you and your people were and weren't—and I once called you a monster. I was wrong. I don't, and will never, fear you again.

His eyes look down at me, burning with emotion.

I can hardly help myself from pushing up and pressing a kiss to his soft, warm lips. The deliciousness of him makes my whole body warm.

One of the elvish women, Glyni, gags.

"To the great Nicnevin, I long for the day when I will no longer be subjected to your constant, annoying... *adoration*."

Another grunts in agreement.

"No, please continue. It's been so long since I've experienced a kiss where the male was well-groomed. I'll settle just for the opportunity to watch," Abi calls.

That makes the elves break out into uncharacteristic laughter.

I don't miss that it's the first time one of them has made a joke, but my joviality is staunched by a fierce raging protectiveness that stirs in my gut when I think of the Enduar men. All two hundred, give or take, will want to know these women.

Just as I turn around, Teo's hand slides over my left buttock, which is delectably close to his thigh on the *glacialmara*. It's a gentle reminder to be careful.

"There will be plenty of men who will do far more than clean their teeth for the chance to spend five minutes alone with you," I shoot back.

It's met with a mix of awkward interest.

As I've spent time healing these women, almost all of them want to meet the Enduares. A part of me worries that they hear about mates, see Teo and me, and then think that such a coupling is *required* of them.

Many want partners. They want freedom, to learn to read, to paint, and to sew, to be something more than breeding chattel.

Many of them, though not all, seek a family.

While I feel confident that all those who live in Enduvida will be respectful, my little home is about to proliferate—more people, and more opportunities for problems. It will be up to me to help Teo and the council find solutions.

It's hard to trust myself enough to handle such a burden.

As we approach the clouded underpass, I look up at Teo.

"When I first came here, I was planning my escape through a passageway in the ice. It spits out into the forest that I tried to escape through later."

He frowns at the memories.

"Was there really a passage?" he asks.

I nod. "There was, but Arlet was stuck. And then we ran out of time."

Suddenly, the full force of the memory hits me as I picture Mikal receiving ten strikes for each lash on my back. For the tears. The anger.

Teo's mind nudges my own, and I let him in. He holds me closer as we move through the narrow channels of ice.

Mist billows around us. His presence calms the raging torment. It's something to be marveled at, truly, that I could know him for such little time and still feel entirely owned by his soul. We belong to each other.

I love him.

As soon as we clear the glacial ice, we hear the clash of swords and an ugly hiss in the distance.

I look back at our group and see the leader of the elves, Ayla, and her alce crane to look beyond us.

Teo curses, and we hurry forward to see several of the Enduar hunters fighting off three of the cold creatures that attacked us before.

My stomach drops. Not again.

"Did they make it into the cave?" I ask my mate.

He shakes his head. "I do not know. We've not been here in weeks."

Behind us, one of the elves lets out their wild, yelping cries. Ayla, Farryn, and Elanila rush forward barely squeezing past us as we clear the ice.

"Hold!" Teo calls to the Enduar hunters. I don't recognize either of them, but I am sure he does.

They wait, watching the elves as the heads of the cold ones are lobbed off in clean strikes, followed by a thorough slicing of the bodies. It takes no time for the creatures to be steaming bodies on the chilly snow.

We fly over on the *glacialmaras* and stop just in front of the group. The Enduares point their weapons at the elves, who bare their teeth in turn. It's a lot of growling and snarling, which is understandable, given the altercation after my wedding.

"Is everything all right inside?" I ask the hunters as soon as we are close enough to be heard.

One of the hunters looks up at me, and it turns out I do know him.

Joso, with his enormous body, thick arms, and cave-cub happy smile. His face lights up at the sound of my voice.

"My King and Queen," he bows deeply, showcasing his armored tail. "All is well. We have just been on watch, attentive to your return home."

Something in my chest squeezes.

"Tell your little guards to stand down," Ayla says down at the men. Her alce raises one enormous foot and stamps it in the snow. Particles of ice float up around its massive legs and cling to its thick fur.

"The elves are friends," Teo says, affirming her words.

Weapons are sheathed, and the hunters turn to the gilded door. The red veins swirling out of the entrance no longer appear like blood to me.

They *sing*.

"You did not tell us that you had a problem with these creatures," Ayla says as mechanisms on the door begin to click and twist.

Teo draws closer. "You know what they are?"

Ayla nods once.

"In our legends, we have a monster called the *baobhan sith*, but that honor is only given to women wronged by men. I think." Her green eyes trail back to the black stains of blood in the snow. "These are called the *vaimpír*, which are the children of the demon Abhartach and the goddess Nicnevin."

I pause.

"Who is Nicnevin?" My mind swims as I remember the witches who tortured me spoke of her.

"Our goddess. Doro's indifferent consort," Ayla says simply.

"I have read of Abhartach—he is a god bound long ago," Teo nods.

"Yes. He was to be bound for ten thousand years," Ayla confirms.

"How long ago was that?" Ra'Salore asks.

Ayla chuckles. "Who knows? And to be honest, I have enough to worry about with mortals. Let the gods sort out their problems."

With that, the door to Enduvida swings open, and a chill passes over my skin as Rahda is nudged toward the entrance.

It's the air that hits me first. The smell of sulfur and Enduar cooking.

It's spicy, hearty, and, oh gods, *warm*. In the distance, the pumps that keep the temperature even work methodically. No sweeter sound has ever reached my ears, I swear it.

The rest of the cave is quiet. Everyone should be sleeping safely and soundly. My awareness shifts back to the humans, and I can almost hear some of the women's breathing change as they walk in.

I slide off Rahda, and Teo follows. He follows alongside me anyway, not minding my deviation from leading the group.

"Welcome to Enduvida," I say repeatedly as they pass by.

Teo nods and holds onto the crystal wraith's reins.

"Ladies, please follow Niht. He will take you to a place where we can eat. Then we will work on distributing supplies and beds," My husband calls as we push into the cave so the bear can pass.

Niht heads to the front of the line, walking with Glyni, and he grins at everyone he passes. He's such a joyful, kind man.

The reactions are as varied as the women's. Some look around fearfully, while others are caught up in every beautiful detail and carving. I smile.

Just wait until they see the crystals. The Ardorflame.

Just wait until you see them again, my star.

Teo speaks in my mind, and I look at him with the most vulnerable smile I've given anyone in a very long time.

Ulla passes by us and shares a smile, as well.

I reach out and take her hand.

"Welcome home," she says in Enduar.

I grin as I choke up. It's been good to hear her and listen to her gentle, kind humming once more. She's been so helpful in tending to the women as we traveled.

"I'm going to the clock tower," she says. "Everyone will want to be awake for this."

"Do you think it will be too much for them?" I ask, jerking my head in the direction of the women.

Ulla considers it for a second.

"I don't anticipate any wild events, and it will be good to have the extra hands to help them get settled into places to sleep."

"Very well," Teo says, and she heads out.

Finally, the line of thirty women, flanked by Joso and the other hunter I don't recognize, ends. Chiding myself for not knowing everyone's name yet, I nod at them.

Joso comes over, his eyes wide.

"This is... incredible." He breathes, while his companion follows the women all the way down the tunnels and into the cave. The one male slave who we brought back comes in as well.

"They aren't just here to be mates," I say quickly, protectively.

He nods. "Of course not. But we've never freed so many slaves, not even on our best stealing raids from the giants' trading caravans."

Mention of the giants suppresses my mood like putting a wet cloth over a candle flame. The gnawing feeling in my gut reminds me that not all is finished, and we are not free. There is still a war brewing. Perhaps the fighting in the feasting hall has slowed things down and forged enemies between those who were seeking alliances, but maybe...

I remember King Arion's words about Arlet and killing every last person in the tunnel. My heart picks up into a gallop, and I take Teo's hand, pulling him into the cave with me. As soon as we exit the tunnel, the full grandiosity of Enduvida rams into me and steals my breath.

Weeks away had altered my memories, and I had a difficult time clinging to what was real, but seeing this is... indescribable. The lights hanging above, the forges in the distance, the mushrooms. The houses.

I curse when I see one of them still in the midst of being rebuilt. It must've been destroyed when the giants captured me. *My fault.* Then I turn to look at the palace's golden walls. I take a deep breath while I look at the focusing crystal and the way it carries the red pulsing light of the Ardorflame.

How could I have forgotten so much?

A new voice enters my mind, one that belongs to neither Teo nor myself.

You've returned, the old feminine voice intones. It reverberates through my bones with a melodic rumble, like the distant echo of mountains shifting.

I suck in a deep breath. *And who are you?*

I am the one who lies beneath. Drathorinna, *as you call me.*

My skin pebbles and a shock sparks across my spine. Each word is packed with the weight of eons of time spent in observation. When Liana brought me to the heart of the mountain to meet her, I was terrified and awestruck by the mother of *glacialmaras*. She was easily the size of three houses, and her dozens of scales looked like reflective prisms. Liana had explained that she would only choose fuegorra readers to ride her.

Sucking in a sharp breath, I think, *Why do you speak to me now? Do you wish me to visit you?*

Your absense has caused a disturbance in my harmony. I am pleased you returned, though I feel the footsteps of many newcomers. Care for them.

But—

Peace, human. I will call you when it is time.

The human women are already crossing the bridge, with Ra'Salore leading them to Hammerhead Hall. They gaze at the lava far below the bridge and step carefully. Sadly, the enormous crystal wraith doesn't respond to my further attempts at communication.

I jump when the clock sounds. It plays a different tune than it usually does at the changing of the early morning hours. It's ringing and insistent, and it only takes a few minutes for some people to start stumbling out of their houses.

Thoughts of the crystal dragon fade quickly while my vision is filled with a blur of faces and surprised chatter that melds with nervous whispers.

I spot Luiz and Neela as they hurry out, the Enduar woman towering over her human mate, but they soon disappear in a sea of blue bodies. Verl, the metal bender approaches, then Siya, mate to the crystal singer. Dozens of others come, and I search through my broken mind for each name.

I remember more than I think. Faol, Keoi, Iryth, and then, my smile stretches wide when I see Svanna.

She parts through the group, throwing her arms around Teo in a bone-crushing hug.

"My King," she says, clearly holding back her misty eyes, and then she looks down at me with her bright grin. "My Queen." She dips her head. "I am fucking delighted to see you both."

My smile practically cracks my face in half as I pull her into a hug. Each action says something different.

Forgive me for trying to escape.

Forgive me for trying to poison your king.

I'm so sorry I couldn't have done more to save Dyrn.

I wish the giants had never come to take me.

Then I see Iryth and their child, Sama. I promise to help rebuild the damaged houses. Soon, they edge away from me, making room for more of the crowd.

I hug and kiss all I see.

Well wishes for everyone are shared, and questioning glances are cast at the new women, but no one wants to scare the humans. Blessings and whispered prayers are offered up around us as someone starts to sing.

The sound tingles my skin. I hold the melody close to my heart, hoping that they can hear the words that beat out of my skin.

Forgive me, please.

It's too much.

It isn't enough.

A large, shadowing person makes his way through the crowd, pushing another short red head.

"Arlet!" I practically squeak. She throws her arms around me.

How can a heart hold this much joy when tomorrow is not guaranteed?

DANIELA A. MERA

She pulls back and gives me an inquisitive, serious look. I know what she means. She wants to know about Mikal. I swallow hard and shake my head.

Her eyes grow wide, and her face slackens.

"But he's alive?"

I nod.

"Por los dioses, Este. Lo lamento mucho,[1]" she says against my cheek as she hugs me tighter.

Things between her and me had been so strange before I'd left. She and I used to be the closest of friends, and now... a divide between us lingers.

Perhaps, in my mission to prove myself as a queen, I can also repair the relationship between us.

"What have you been doing while I've been gone?" I ask, glancing up at Vann as he tries very hard not to look down at us.

I remember the tension between them.

"Weaving. Weaving a lot, which now I see will be very useful. There's an excess of furs that will need to be sewn and stitched for all the newcomers." She eyes all the women with disbelief. "Gods, there are so many. How did you do it?"

I let out a breath.

"I didn't. Not really. There was a slave who attended to me. I would tell her about Enduvida, and she would tell the women. Rholker had just sent more than usual to the breeding pens because..." I trail off—because he wants his army to slaughter Enduvida so he can bring in more slaves. He won't stop until he's hacked away every valuable mineral and metal from our mountain home.

My heart starts to pound once again, but Arlet doesn't seem to notice.

"All thirty come from the breeding pens?" she asks, breathless.

I nod. "There are four who are pregnant."

252

Her eyebrows raise again, and she looks at the Enduares.

"We can trust the Enduares. I know it... but the women will need extra care."

I look to the side, studying one of the humans as they walk past.

"Not all of them. Some are quite eager to run right away from Zlosa and into the arms of an adoring Enduar, but I don't know if they all intend to stay once they are healed. The elves have already promised to take some back to the Sisterhood's Enclave."

Arlet nods, not at all appearing confused. "Yes, I overhead Vann and some of the others talking about where King Teo was heading."

The mention of Vann has me glancing up once again.

"Have you found a mate while I was gone?" It has been her greatest desire since we arrived here.

She smiles, somewhat sadly. "I have found someone, but we are not mated."

I look up at Vann once more, more suspicious than ever, except when her arms go wide, it's not him who steps in.

It's Joso.

I blink.

"*Oh.*"

Joso looks at her with pure adoration, and Vann looks at the Enduar like he'd enjoy peeling off his fingernails.

"I'm happy for you," I say, feeling strangely disappointed as Vann turns back to Teo.

"I will gather the rest of the Council," Vann mutters before he walks off.

I continue to talk to Arlet and Joso, learning that he started to bring her small gifts that he would find while hunting in the caves. He was, after all, famous for taking down the cave bears.

"Isn't that just adorable?" Arlet says, looking at me expectantly, but all I can do is smile.

How can I tell her that I wanted her to settle in with Vann while I was gone? My mouth opens just as a new figure comes up. One whom I could hear long before I could see.

"Estela, the wise woman in training. You have been neglecting your lessons," Mother Liana says with a mock stern voice.

If I thought that my heart couldn't take any more pure felicity, I was wrong.

"It is hard to practice when my teacher and I only had a few lessons before a madman kidnapped me." She smiles and something in me eases. With no one else, I could make such a morbid joke. I hold up my hand where Teo's ring sits. "Besides, I only had these tiny gems on my jewelry."

Teo reenters the moment. "I would hardly call any of those gems tiny."

Liana raises a pierced eyebrow. "Well, I would hardly call them large. You'll have to do better next time. Wise women need large stones with extra power."

Then she pulls me into a hug. She hasn't ever been the most physically affectionate, but there is a distinct maternal grasp to her as she leans in to whisper, "Welcome home, my child."

Tears come once more. And they are welcome as I survey her sleeping gown, which she came out in unashamedly. It's positively covered in glowing stones, and her long white hair is unbound. She notices me looking.

"I'm old. I'm allowed to be scandalous."

Teo barks out a laugh. "*Gods.* Come, *mi amor*[2]. Arlet and Neela can help care for the humans for a few hours. We must discuss everything that has happened."

My breath hitches, but I oblige my mate, and we start to walk away toward the palace. I continue to turn around until I can no longer see the crowd once more. The rest of the climb up the steps starts to feel uncomfortable as my still-damaged memories are prodded at.

Everything is perfect.

Almost.

When I think of Mikal in the caves, the only memories I have are of him holed up in a storage room with a dozen other humans while Keksej and I met with the Enduares about diamonds. He had just been whipped, and he was covered in bandages. Then... he was taken away and I was left here.

When I was in Zlosa, I really believed I'd be able to find him and bring him back. I wanted him to see Enduvida like this. Full of people helping each other, mushrooms glowing, and crystals glinting.

He deserves to see how wonderful it is.

I beg myself not to let a few small imperfections spoil everything else that can happen today, and I squeeze Teo's hand. It is warm and grounding, and it makes the curling acid in my belly abate—if not for a few moments.

I find the other council members waiting in the expanse with the large, bioluminescent fountain and the glowing mushrooms. I see Svanna, Ulla, Vann, Ra'Salore, Lothar, and Fira. Fira greets me with a nod, and Vann passes Teo a shirt.

"I thought you'd appreciate this," he murmurs as my gaze returns to Lothar.

He looks ill, but at least he is alive. A memory flickers of him outside my door the night they took me.

I thank Endu and Grutabela that he wasn't killed.

"Why haven't you gone in?" Teo asks, eyeing the still-closed door to the throne room.

Ulla and Fira furrow their brows, and Vann says, "We were waiting for you. The throne room hasn't been used since you left."

Teo places a hand over his heart, conveying that this action meant more than I understood in their customs. I follow close behind as Teo presses the button that causes the stone to rumble as it slides away.

He gestures for me to enter first, but I quickly realize that the space isn't empty. Atop the crumbling stone throne is an elf with short, wavy hair. His piercing green eyes find mine from across the room as one foot is kicked over the armrest.

There is no movement to stand when he sees us.

"Who the hell are you?" I demand.

He smiles.

"You must be the human Enduar queen. A pleasure to meet you."

Ulla pushes to my side and gasps.

The sound makes his electric eyes pass over to her, and his smile curves upward a little more.

"Hello, my dear. Glad to see you haven't gotten yourself killed by standing in front of any sharp objects."

"This is Thorne," Teo says almost irritatedly to me. "He's the most trusted assassin of Mrath, leader of the Sisterhood of Bhaldraithe. She's Arion's sister." Teo crosses over to him, and Thorne watches with an almost bored expression.

"Get off my wife's throne," he growls.

Velvety butterfly wings brush against my ribcage and heart.

My throne?

Yes.

I smile nervously, wondering if this display is a good idea—if I even deserve it—as Thorne begrudgingly gets up.

"Very well. But allow me to pay respects to the most lovely queen I've ever seen."

He brushes across the room as I narrow my eyes. "I'm likely one of the only queens you know."

Laughter, like the rustle of trees through branches, fills the room.

"Perceptive." He drops to one knee before me and takes my hand. "It is still an honor to finally meet one. May your reign inspire a new wave of equality throughout the land. I tire of kingdoms and their boring, megalomaniac, power-hungry ways. I've been beseeching the gods and goddesses to give me a vengeful female to soak the land with blood for a change."

"Ignore him," Ulla says decidedly, despite how excited she had looked upon first entering the room.

He stands and places a hand over his heart.

"I'm wounded. Come now, don't tell me you haven't thought of a hundred more creative ways to slice up a man than whatever High Lord Cleaver has decided to do." He jerks a thumb toward Vann, who scowls in return.

Ulla cocks her head to the side, and Thorne bites his lip.

"Tell me, how would you kill me?" he asks, pushing her further.

Her eyes narrow. "Are you... flirting with me?"

Thorne grins just as Teo says, "Enough. We have more important matters to discuss."

The elf frowns and turns around, flourishing his hands. "Very well. I suppose we should get started."

CHAPTER 23
ANATASE
TEO

I t isn't until after Thorne is off the throne that I take my beautiful wife by the hand and guide her to her rightful place.

It is a sight to see.

She's dirty from the trek, still wearing her filthy cloak and my shirt, but looking as strong and resilient as she did glaring up at me when she tried to escape the mountain.

"The last three weeks have been eventful, to say the least," I say, crossing beside the throne to lean against it. "Let us start with the greatest threat first." I look down at Estela. "I believe my queen has good information about that."

Her soft, brown eyes look up at me, full of determination. I heard what she said to Arlet—that she didn't singlehandedly save all those women. While she didn't do it alone, none of them would be here without her. Her power continues to prove that every instinct I had about her was right.

"I spent three weeks in the giant court and observed dozens of people. There are three solid issues and one that could be concerning—but I simply didn't learn enough. First, Rholker's kinghood. There is a staggering division between the monarchy and its royal court, as many thought Rholker a weak, sniveling pawn in someone else's plan."

"He was only able to ascend to the throne officially because he married Lord Fektir's daughter. This lord assured him that he would only continue to support Rholker's ascension if he completed several tasks. He wants our mines, so naturally, one of those agreements was that..." Estela pauses, taking a deep breath before blinking rapidly and continuing, "Rholker destroy Enduvida and kill every last Enduar."

The room is utterly silent as each person processes the words.

"Did he touch you?" Fira asks.

Estela takes a deep breath.

"For an entire week, I was tortured by a group of human women. I now know they are *Brujas*, or witches, but they go by the name of The Six. Sometimes the Cursed Six, or even Memory Slicers. I didn't know they were human until the night of the coronation, and one of their hoods was pulled back by a drunk giant. A massive fight broke out when King Arion was hurt. Most giant lords were generally outraged over the fact that the new giant king had trusted humans for something other than chopping wood, reproducing, or polishing their cocks."

The bitterness in her words leaks out, and Thorne watches with resolute approval. He nods as if to say *"Well put."*

"So there's a chance that other humans have power like you?" Liana says.

"I am finding a new part of my power. There is the ability to read the Fuegorra, which we found out after I came to the cave, but while I was in Zlosa I could... glow. When someone tried to touch me that I didn't want to, it would burn that person. Neither power is anything like theirs."

"Interesting," Liana hums.

"To be honest," Estela continues, "both of my powers feel more Enduar than anything—crystals, harmonies, and light. The power that leaks out of the Six is cold, dead smelling, and intent on destruction and accumulation of strength."

"Does Lord Fektir still support Rholker then?" Ra'Salore asks.

Estela shakes her head. "I do not know. In addition to the witches and the giant court, they have forged an official alliance with King Arion. He is the third threat—he wants Arlet."

"I'll tear out his throat if he ever gets anywhere near this cave again," Vann growls.

Thorne appears amused. "Will you? With your big cleaver?"

"Quiet," Liana snaps before turning to look at me. "Is there a reason Mrath's pet is still here?"

Thorne's eyes turn black as they fade into something feral.

"Neither you nor anyone else has permission to call me *that*."

Liana slowly flicks her eyes up at him. "Keep your comments to yourself, and I won't be so ready to give you a thorough tongue-lashing, *pet*."

Thorne's glare is hot enough to burn through Liana's head, and I see our one alliance crumbling.

"I think it is best we all keep our quips to ourselves for the sake of this meeting. Estela mentioned that there still might be another potential threat."

Estela nods. "Yes. It seems that the giants have started bringing swamp ogres back to their ranks. I wouldn't call it an alliance because I saw Rholker refuse an audience with them more than once."

Thorne folds his arms. "You should ask Ayla about that. She—"

"Killed the Shaman Ogre King," Ulla finishes. "She told us when she introduced herself."

Thorne snorts.

I turn to a mostly-healed Lothar, who is in the corner, furiously taking notes. He hasn't asked about Turalyon, but I'm sure he's noticed his absence. Seeing that he doesn't need any extra encouragement to document this meeting, I continue.

"While on our trip, we were attacked two times, in similar spots, by the cold ones. Taeryn mentioned that they are likely called vaimpír, the undead children of a demon. One killed Turalyon," I say, sadly.

At this, Lothar looks up, his lips slightly parted. His brows draw together. "My apprentice?"

The room is silent as I nod. "I am so sorry, friend."

Thorne purses his lips and steps forward. "Vaimpír are little more than pests—they are undead creatures that are easy to kill and have little to no mental capacity. I wouldn't worry too much if you know how to dispose of them."

I raise an eyebrow, tearing my apologetic gaze away from my advisor. "Your fellow assassin mentioned that Abhartach controls them from his bindings."

Thorne shrugs. "She also believes that the gods listen to prayers. I suspect they are not quite as omniscient as we would like to think."

Enduares are nothing if not a deeply ritualistic people with kind gods. The comment rubs me the wrong way, but now is not the time for a theological debate. Especially not with a child of Doros.

"From my perspective, as we went to the Sisterhood's Enclave, we were initiated by killing one of her targets to prove our worthiness. This secured us a temporary arrangement to help rescue my lovely mate. To continue this agreement, I must return an artifact. Only then will they assist us in retrieving Mikal and killing the giant king."

Thorne makes a tutting sound with his tongue. "And you will help Mrath with killing her brother."

I look at Liana who is studying the room like a hunting bird.

"Tell everyone what we know of *Cumhacht na Cruinne*," I say.

Thorne's eyebrows rise as she nods her head. I can almost hear the comment begging to slide off his tongue, but he behaves.

Liana nods.

"My old mentor, another wise woman, assisted with its removal from Arion's father." She looks at Svanna and Vann, who have both been quiet as they listen to everyone's reports. "Would you like me to tell them?"

Svanna shrugs. "You did all the work researching. Vann mostly scowled at hunters from the cave. All I did was... literally everything else. The hunting schedules, the cooking, the training, the—"

"While you were gone," Liana interrupts, "I spent time revising the old archives of the wise women. Don't worry Ma'Teo, they aren't stored in your precious library." Her gaze lands on Estela, who has been listening attentively the entire time. "There is much I have neglected to teach you, Lady Estela. I will rectify that soon, but for now, everyone else should know that it is clear that Teo'Lihk kept it in one of his great stone vaults in Iravida. I believe it is still there."

My thoughts about the battalions protecting the artifact were correct.

"At the bottom of the ocean?" I ask.

She nods. "Yes, but it is not so worrisome. Our people traversed the seas once before."

I remember. "But there was equipment that no one in this cave knows how to forge. Things like crystals and magicked air bubbles that no longer exist."

She shakes her head. "I found some preliminary plans. Crystals fall under the wise women's talents. We don't need the same things as stone benders or metal benders. Have a little faith in my foremothers."

I nod, considering her words as one of the spell lights bobs down over Vann's scowling face.

"Can you build one of these suits?" I ask, amazed.

She nods her head. "I have already begun. I need Estela to help me... when she is ready."

I look at my mate. Her eyebrows are raised. She nods, and I return my attention to the others.

Thorne seems enraptured for the first time since he came under the cave, not a hint of sarcasm or defensive wit is present in his hopeful face.

"This is good news," he says. "I will tell Mrath."

"Yes, why don't you run along right now," Liana says mockingly.

He lifts an eyebrow. "I will leave this room when I wish to. Besides, you haven't even heard what I wanted to say."

I see Estela trying to keep a smile off of her face when I look down.

"And what do you have to tell us, Lord Thorne?" Estela asks.

An awkward silence follows. No half-elf would ever receive such a title. Perhaps that's why his perfectly straight back straightens a bit more, and he preens under her respect.

Interesting.

"Mrath had every intention of killing you all the night that you came to the enclave. She's still not totally convinced that she shouldn't, and I doubt she will be convinced until the greater artifact is returned to its rightful owner. She has sent me as insurance that you don't forget about your deal—and she wants the Faefurt assassins to stay with me until the mission is completed," Thorne reports.

I nod at the very open, presumably honest information he shares. But I can't say I am pleased to have a man who is looking to kill us in my caves, even if he seems friendly toward Estela. "And what do you know of Arion's alliance with the giants? If my time in your enclave taught me anything, it's that you all are swimming in subterfuge and espionage," I say.

"We've heard rumors. He wants access to the humans, not just this... *Arlet* you spoke of. It seems that humans are indeed able to be mated to elves. Before you congratulate yourself for giving him that idea, know that he has been experimenting for some time. Some strays showed up in his city—though, I suppose that could be counted as your fault." Thorne smiles.

My tail flicks out irritatedly as he uncovers the first lie I was told by Mrath. The slaves we freed did indeed make it to Shvathemar.

"I had no other options. If we hadn't sent Lothar to speak with him, we wouldn't have known your group existed. Give us time to right our mistake," I say.

Thorne purses his lips, and Lothar nods approvingly.

"I believe we already are being generous with our forgiveness," Thorne says.

"Onto the subject of the humans," Fira interrupts, after quietly observing. "How many are there?"

Estela doesn't hesitate. "Thirty-three."

The lady of weaving, Fira, nods approvingly. "Well done. I hope they are grateful."

Estela has a strange look on her face. "They don't owe me anything. Freedom is their right, not a gift."

Liana smiles. "Spoken like a true queen. Are they all staying in the under mountain?"

Estela considers the question, and I absentmindedly stroke her hair.

"I believe about twenty-six want to stay. Three want to risk the winter wilds after they finish healing, and Ayla promised a few more that they could go with her to become assassins." Estela speaks with pride. "Ulla and I took care of most of their infections, cuts, and bruises, but four are with child."

Fira nods. "Arlet had a feeling that you might return with some friends. We are prepared with cloth."

Estela's smile is mixed with something that conveys just how touched she is.

"In the morning, we will offer the twenty-six a chance to perform the *dual'moraan*," Liana says with finality. "I will prepare the hammers."

The First Cut is the rite of passage all Enduares take to receive their Fuegorra. It symbolizes their time before and after receiving the light of their gods. At that point, each person will choose their path in the court.

"Excellent plan," I say. "Is there anything more that should be discussed?" I meet each eye, from Ra'Salore to Lothar. They all shake their heads, and I nod wearily.

"Then our meeting is finished."

Everyone bows.

Ra'Salore begins to head out first. "I will check on the humans."

Thorne saunters over behind him.

"I'd love to join. Ulla, will you come too? Perhaps we could continue our conversation from earlier?" he practically purrs.

She frowns. "Later. I have a few things to discuss with the queen."

He exits, though I could've sworn that his smile is just a touch dimmer.

Soon, Ulla, Estela, Vann, and I are the only ones left in the room. I look at my blood brother and best friend, still standing paces away from Ulla.

The last time we saw each other, I was in a much different

attitude. It's written over Vann's face as his gaze passes from me to Estela, and he attempts a smile.

"I am glad you and your mate have made it home safely," he says, fracturing the quiet.

I nod. "Is there anything more that you wished to speak of? Do you not desire to present yourself to the women and see if your crystal sings?"

He shakes his head. "It won't."

I hum at that response. It is the same generic thing he has told me time and time again. A new thought dawns.

"Won't? Or can't?"

My suspicion is confirmed when his eyes widen. Dread curls low in my stomach. *What has my brother done to himself?*

"*Firelocks* is looking well. I saw her with Joso while she spoke to Estela," I say slowly.

A stone wall builds itself up across his face. "Yes. They are... sharing their time."

His tail knocks a pebble across the room, causing the women to glance at us with confused expressions.

I frown. "I am sorry."

Vann shakes his head. "I should help the others. Go, sleep if you can."

As soon as he is gone, I turn back to Estela. All of the air is sucked out of the room as I look at her, acutely aware that we are nearly alone.

Ulla stiffens, as if sensing the change. I know she can't hear the beats of our hearts and the way they synchronize to the mating song, but she quickly excuses herself and hurries out.

Then it truly is just the two of us in the room.

Human and Enduar.

Husband and wife.

King and queen.

Mates.

We draw together like the moon and the tide.

It is not enough to simply hold her hand. I scoop her up into my arms, and she gasps. Every movement, from the way that her lips part to the way that she instinctively curls into my chest, is perfect. I lock it away like precious gold for a time when we might be parted again.

"Let us go to bed," I say gently and whisk her out of the room.

CHAPTER 24

RICHTERITE

TEO

A s I sweep my mate away from the rest of the world, the walls blur before us, and we make our way into the king's suite. *Our room,* as she called it while we were traveling. My blood is thrumming through my ears, and my cock strains against my breeches, waiting to be reunited in all ways with my woman.

Sleep is the furthest thing from my mind.

No sooner than my door opens and closes, her small hands push against my chest. She's breathless, too.

"I need to bathe," she pants.

I nod, thinking of what happened in the spring, and walk to the bathroom. She sucks in a sharp breath when she sees the tub in the corner.

"Can I... take you near the water?" I ask.

She nods, though tears well up in her eyes.

I stand there, frozen as I don't want to make everything worse.

She bites her lip. "Please. Just—don't put me inside."

I nod and take a few more steps.

Tears slip down her cheeks. The hot water warms a few smooth stones, and she fits neatly atop one.

"Don't worry, my star." I brush away her tears.

There is a towel nearby. I pick it up and dip it in the pool. Then I take one of her hands, pushing up the long cloth of my dirty shirt, and expose her wrist. I brush the water over one finger and she trembles.

"What else have they done to you?" I ask, not allowing the rage under my skin to boil up for fear of scaring her.

"First, they would come into my room. They left it cold and half-freezing most of the time. One of their snakes would bite me." She takes a slow breath and pulls up her cloak to reveal healing bites all over her ankles and calves.

I count the pairs. There are eleven.

"They did this more than once some days?" I ask.

She nods with glistening cheeks. "The bite had some sort of paralytic effect. They would lift me off the ground with their magic so that my legs were slightly above my head.

"All the blood would rush to my brain, making it hard to hear and think. It wasn't painful at first, but the sensation of feeling like I would fall was..." She squeezes her eyes, and I take her hand.

As we sit there, connected, she opens her mind to me.

Words no longer serve her, and they need not. I feel her shaking increase as the witches' eyes watch her memories.

I recognize the hollow ghosts of each image.

I see the night we made love in the royal pools, the time we kissed, and when I carried her. The memory of us dancing flits in.

The human witches violated them all with their profane eyes, and then they cut them to ribbons, replacing them with gore and pain.

Then, just as Estela woke, they drowned her. A punishment,

I am sure, that came from Rholker for knowing what we did in the water. I see his cruel face sneering.

My eyes flutter open in time with hers, and I study her hallow, quivering mouth.

"How can you stand to touch me?" I ask.

She presses a hand to the Fuegorra.

"Because we are mates. And because of this magic. Even though those memories are mostly... gone. I know you." She lets out a sob. "I know what you are. I am safe with you."

I shake my head and cup her soft skin, brushing away each tear as it falls.

"I will make sure I continue to be your safety. Would you like to see our memories again?"

Her eyes go wide as if she hadn't considered that.

"Yes," she breathes, grasping my hands and begging me. "Give me them back."

Her eagerness nearly knocks me over.

"Careful," I murmur. "We will start with one. I don't want to hurt you worse than you are."

She takes a deep breath, deflated. "Very well."

The air between us is heavy as I go to the place where all the pain started.

Our wedding night. The first memory that was broken and is possibly the most damaged of them all.

I show her everything I saw. Every scar and reminder of the texture of the skin. I speak the sacred words between us, of love and promised protection. I glide with her through the water as our tongues and teeth clash together over and over. As I explore her body, and then finally, enter. I bind myself to her body and soul.

The feeling is so potent between us that I take a deep breath to keep from spending in my breeches.

Not yet. Not like this.

In real time, she gasps, clearly overwhelmed.

I focus on her flushed face and the rise and fall of her chest. All the tears have burned away in the heat of her skin.

"I—" she breathes. "That was real."

She presses a hand to her feverish skin.

I nod. The closeness between us still feels far away. As our chests heave, almost but not quite brushing, the mellifluous sound fills the room.

"Estela," I say again. "I will wait an eternity for such moments to happen between us. You set the pace. Can I try to clean you once more? Or would you like to?"

Her mouth close.

"No, I want you." Her shaking fingers remove her clothes, and I wait with far more patience than the blood rushing through my veins allots me.

When she is bare, I dip the rag in and rub it over her skin. It is my joy to watch as her flesh pebbles and her nipples bead.

It is pleasure enough.

"Talk to me," she says when water drips down one arm and her eyes squeeze shut.

"Of what, my star?" I murmur.

"You know so much of me, of my pains. Show me your scars," she says, still mostly breathless.

I pause. "You wish to know of..."

"Your time with the giant queen." She hesitates, opens her eyes, and then continues. "I know what your father asked of you —we've spoken of that before. I just want to know more."

The heat between us evaporates. But perhaps, that is for the best if she is not ready to fully submerge in the tub. Perhaps vulnerability is exactly what our moment together calls for.

"I thought of it often as I came for you."

She nods, as I lather soap onto the rag and rub it into the faded powder and grime.

"The woman that Mrath made me kill was Lijasa's sister," I say, trying to fight past the tightness in my throat.

I don't speak of the human she murdered. Not yet.

She looks horrified. "Are you all right?"

I nod. "Lijasa came from a poisoned vine. All those around her were just products of the same world."

Estela watches me. "I don't want to talk about you together... It makes my blood boil. It is hard to hate someone so much when they are dead. I detest abhorring someone I can't strangle."

I raise my eyebrows at her murderous words.

"*Amor*[1], don't worry. I made her pay for every moment. And it was long ago. I had so many years to heal, and I did everything for my people. When you accepted me into your life, you closed any cracks that remained. Don't weep if some of them reopen. I'm sure they will be resealed with you here."

She starts to blink again, and I can see she is going to cry.

"Perhaps that is enough speaking about the past for now."

A part of me wants to ask for more of her stories, ones not tainted by Rholker, but I hold my tongue and stand up.

She looks up at me, her skin still soapy and wet.

I pull off my shirt, and she sucks in a breath.

Her eyes track every movement as I unthread the laces on my breeches.

"I am going to wash your hair," I announce as I tug down the leather, and my length springs forth. Her eyes are wide, and I can almost feel the beat of her heart, the nerves, as she looks at me. "Fear not. There is no pain in this room. Remember?"

Her pace, I remind myself as I step into the warm water of the bath. It feels nice after so many days in the middle of the wilderness.

As soon as I sit down, I gently guide her head toward the water, still leaving her body stretched out over the rocks, and pick up a bowl that once held a bar of soap. I hold my breath, anticipating her to panic at the increased proximity to the steaming liquid.

She shifts and holds her breath until I pour the water over her scalp. Her eyes close but she doesn't protest as I work in soap and untangle every knot. A pleasant melody starts up in my Fuegorra, singing to her as her heartbeat finally slows to a normal rate.

As soon as her locks are clean enough, I section and braid the curls and tie the ends around each other. Brushing a hand over her brow, I lean over and say, "Finished."

Her eyes open, and she makes a frown of protest.

"If you'd like, you can join me," I say, and let a bit of the memory in the pools replay.

It's impossible to miss the way that her legs press together. It has always been this way between us. My invitation, and her initiative.

She will come if she wants or she won't, and I will help to rinse whatever soap remains before carrying her to our bed.

Estela takes a breath and then pushes on the rocks and turns back toward me. She slides into the water and pauses, gathering courage. Just one more movement, and she is submerged up to her hips.

I am frozen as I wait.

She does, and in a burst of courage, she slides down onto my lap so that I am positioned perfectly at her entrance. I gasp.

"For weeks, I couldn't think of this," she murmurs and pushes herself down. I can hardly see straight as she stretches to accommodate me. "They took me from you and forbade me from reaching for you even in my darkest moments."

She pushes more until she is seated to the hilt. The sensation is exquisite, causing my head to tilt back while I groan.

"Thank you for showing me our memories, but I need more

than the past to live on," she says, somehow keeping her breathing even. "I want a future. I want this every night. I don't want to fear the water. Everything you promised me is still clear, and I intend to make good on it."

A dozen meanings pass through her words, but then she starts to move, and every sense of reason flies away in the sensation of her.

She moans, forgetting whatever words she wanted to whisper.

I encourage her as I move my hips in time to meet her rhythm, to make it better and sweeter.

She takes her time, though the time apart blurs my sense of reality. I have no idea how long we spend together, only that we are joined.

When I slip my fingers between us to rub at that sensitive little nub, the release starts. She freezes, hanging on the edge of the precipice.

Then her muscles flutter around me, and I let myself go as our movements turn more frantic. Each thrust is a promise.

And when it's over, my need fades into satisfied exhaustion.

I pull at her braid playfully, and she makes a sound that I feel in the bond between us. Instead of taking the action further, I ease her off me, acutely aware that we absolutely must rest.

She only barely protests, yet I feel the loss of her around me as I dry her skin.

Then I hold her tighter and sling a towel over my hips before taking us from the room.

"I can walk," she says up to me.

I shake my head. "You've already done so much today. I like carrying you—you're very small."

She doesn't protest. When I set her on the bed, she looks around. "Do you have something I could wear to sleep?"

A part of me is sad that she won't sleep next to me, skin to skin. But I open my drawer and pull out a long brown shirt. She smiles and takes it from me then brings it to her nose and inhales deeply.

I opt to sleep without clothes and dry off quickly before sitting next to her.

"I missed the way you smell, too," I murmur and draw my mouth close to her mating mark, licking the now-healed scars.

She shivers.

Then she slips the garment on and lays down.

I pull the covers around us and watch as she tucks her hands under her cheek. She looks so tired.

Twice, the gods gave me you, I say through the bond. *You will never be taken again.*

This ache inside of me is almost healed, but not quite. It is one thing to have her back here in my arms, but another to not know what looms on the horizon.

I know the sound she makes when she comes around me, the way she laughs, and her fiery glances. Her power is the song that leads me forward, and her scars are a map of my world.

Yet... there is so much to her that remains a mystery.

"Tell me a story," I say aloud.

Her form stills under my heavy hand. "About what?"

I drag my fingertips over her arms. "Anything. Whatever you tell me is a treasure, and I am a greedy drake, hungry for more gold."

I feel her laugh through the points of contact in our bodies. She rolls over and looks up at me.

"After Mikal was born, and my mother passed, we were brought before the king. He meant to kill us both."

Fear still pierces my heart for an event long past. I hold her closer. The rational parts of my brain know that all is well, and the story ends in a positive way, but still, this was not what I expected.

"My mother appeared, as a woman cloaked in light, and she stayed the king's hand. He... feared her."

"As he should. You are a terrifying creature, and your mother must have been nothing less."

She smiles. "Mikal cried the whole time there, but after we left, he was calm. Contented. Like he only needed to know his mother once, and that was enough for him."

My finger trails up her arm, over her clothed shoulder, and to her cheek.

"A mother's love is a powerful thing."

Estela blinks. "After that, he was the easiest child to raise. He hardly cried, and he was tidy. He made me feel loved and strong, even though it was my working hard to provide for both of us."

She pauses for a few moments.

"I told him I would always take care of him. I am... inadequate in many ways."

I realize that this isn't quite a story, but these words seem to press on my beloved's heart. In the end, it doesn't matter.

Every word is a precious gem, and a drake doesn't distinguish between gold or jewel. It all glitters.

Her eyes finally flick to my face, and the contact gives me a window into her heart.

It is a beautiful, vulnerable, lonely place. My heart recognizes her from the deepest part of me.

"You are enough," I say slowly.

Those lonely, broken eyes watch me carefully.

"Sometimes, when I'm with you, I almost believe it."

My being fractures into a million pieces.

"Tell me a story every night we are together. I wish to know you in a way different from the bond. Gift me every moment with you and your brother, every memory of your mother, everything that has ever made you laugh. The beautiful and the terrible, I want it all."

A tear slips down her cheek. "I am not that interesting or noble. Not like you."

My lips brush over hers.

"Perhaps I should share more of my mind. We are more than lust and attraction; we are eternal. We are bonded through something greater than grief—you will be mine until we grow old and our bodies leave these mortal forms. Entrust yourself to me. I will cherish you and keep you safe."

"You can't promise that," she says after a minute.

I shake my head. "I am doing it, the gods as my witnesses."

Her weariness mars her features. "But I—"

"I love you, Estela."

She looks up at me with wide eyes. There wasn't time to say the words before, but there is now.

"I—I love you, too."

Something more intimate than everything we have shared passes between us. My heart breaks, but this time, not to shatter on the ground. It breaks and molds itself into something new.

It rises from the rubble and soars far away from this plane.

"Sleep, my love. I look forward to more tales of your life tomorrow," I say, brushing my hand over her eyes.

Several minutes pass, and I wait for her to say something else.

"My star?" I whisper at last.

Her mouth curves up into a sleepy smile, but I can tell that the dreams claim her before she can respond.

I place a hand on her hip drawing her near, inhaling her clean scent, and let that drag me into dreamland.

CHAPTER 25
TOURMALINE
ESTELA

Before I was taken from Enduvida, my favorite part of the day was the clock tower's songs. I can tell we've slept late when I hear the bright tune of early afternoon.

I push myself up, and the world tilts sideways as I drag my head from the pillow.

The hand grasping my hip tightens at the movement.

As does the tail wrapped around my leg.

My heart starts to race at the sight of the blatant possessiveness, and for one of the first times since being tortured, it doesn't fill me with panic.

Teo lets out a long growl that turns into a purr as I place my hand atop his and lean down to press a kiss to his forehead.

Only then can I slide off the bed and run to the bathroom.

This room was always beautiful, but its opulence feels exaggerated as I compare it to the bleak cottage in Zlosa. The Enduar plumbing system is a luxury that only can be fully appreciated after weeks of being stuck in a cage with a bucket.

When I'm finished, I look at the mirror for the first time since the night of the coronation.

The reddish scars on my throat from the metal collar and Teo's teeth are the most prominent things I notice, along with the frizzy curls that puff out of the top part of my braid and curve around my face.

Another damaged memory surfaces, the first night that I gave in to Teo. After he died.

No. Not dead.

A logical part of me wars with the conflicting memories that tell me he didn't die, but I see him bleeding out on the bed, and everything goes hazy with tears.

It's easy to picture how his eyes went back into his head, and his skin turned cold—grey. And then he was a monster who wanted to kill me.

I push away from the sink and slam into the wall. Then the dry heaving starts.

My whole body shudders just as the door opens and warm, soft skin wraps me up.

"Estela, my love," Teo says in my ear. "Was it another memory?"

I nod weakly, letting myself sink into his warmth as we sit on the ground.

It's like a bath, one before all the torture. My aching joints and pounding skull ease in his presence.

My mind opens.

He rubs my back, taking every awful thought. It isn't until every trace of panic is gone that I realize he is still naked.

Thick, muscled thighs cradle my hips.

Tears dry. Heat scalds me.

There's so much I crave with him that has been left unexplored.

Without speaking, Teo shows me his version of the ruined memory from the night he nearly died.

He wakes up sore, though his heart pounds like a drum. I see the door open and watch myself come out of the bathroom. I feel the smell burrow into his senses and the feral need it awakes.

As the memory progresses, we get closer and closer to my climax. My skin gets over sensitive as I watch. He shocks me when he puts his hand between my inner thighs in real-time.

His hand strokes the sensitive skin there. I watch the memory for as long as I can, gasping in his arms as he works the space at the apex of my thighs.

My slickness makes each stroke soft and silky, and just...

"Perfect," he growls.

And the memory fades.

Everything moves from desolate, clammy panic to warm passion. Everything is low, sultry, moving to the rock of my hips against his hand.

When I come, it hits me by surprise given our slow pace.

I slam against his chest and think about how it felt to lower onto him the night before. It was... powerful.

There were few times I was so in control of what I wanted.

His mouth moves forward to kiss my throat from behind. Kisses slowly trail up the column of my neck until he reaches my ear.

"Do you love me?"

I nod.

"Then whatever you want, my star, is yours. When you are tired, rest your head on my lap. I will give you my strength when you feel weak, my courage when you are afraid, but most of all —I give you every piece of my body and soul. *Use me.*"

My whole body quivers at the lush sound of his deep voice. It is fine that he enjoys speaking to me through our minds, but there's something about the vibrations of his throat against my tender skin that is... home.

I feel it from the tip of my scalp to my toes.

It's natural to turn around once more, to wrap my legs around his hips for a change and press onto him. It isn't the same as the water, but I like seeing him pushed against the cold stone wall. It makes my frantic movements against his hips feel like peace.

His eyes flutter closed as we rock together again and again.

I take his hands, interlocking our fingers and pushing them against the wall to gain more traction.

He presses his hips up to meet mine with every stroke until the heightened awareness comes, and he breaks free from my hands to wrap his arms around me. Each contraction, every jerk, every explosion of warmth is amplified by the tight clasp of his arms.

We fall so hard and so utterly together that the crash has us slumping back against the wall. He doesn't speak, but his hand is almost reverent as it rubs absentminded circles along my back.

When I look up, I find his hair sticking out around his head. It's wild and untamed, like the first wildflowers that blossom in spring. I've never seen the silver locks so messy before. Reaching out, I try to smooth down one of the strands, only for it to pop back up. I laugh.

He looks down at me, his strong jaw tipping toward that glowing mark on his neck as he mocks anger.

"Don't you know that a man doesn't like to be laughed at after lovemaking," he growls.

One hand lightly smacks my bare ass, and I shiver.

"I'm laughing at your hair," I say, reaching up to twist one of the tangled silver strands around my fingers.

He purses his lips.

"I like it like this," he says. I pause, grinning, all the pain from earlier washed away in the fire between us. "I think I will wear it like this every day. Let the others look at their king, thoroughly ravaged by his queen. Let them be jealous."

My eyes go wide, and my cheeks turn red. "Absolutely not. Let me braid it."

His hand stops tracing lazy, branding circles over the scars on my back, and he looks down at me.

"You would braid my hair?" he asks softly, trying not to reveal just how much he enjoys the idea.

I nod.

He grins. "Very well, my queen. As you command."

He pushes up.

I marvel at the way we feel together. Time apart hasn't ruined the way we fit. My mind doesn't show me a ruined memory. Instead I see his eyes as he listened to me ramble about my dream, how he promised me safety.

Gods, I'm trying so hard to make sure that I don't fuck things up again. I don't want the giants destroying any more houses. I can't be careless like I was after Mikal was first taken. During those weeks, loneliness was a cruel thing, and it made me cruel in turn.

When Teo returns, he holds a rag to clean the sticky seed between my legs before leading me back into the room. He hands me the stone comb he used the night before, sets me on the bed, and then sits in front of me.

The naked intimacy between the two of us is enough to fill an eternity of spaces.

I feel anything but small in this moment, if not a little nervous. I bite my lip. His braids are always precise and long-lasting.

"What if I don't do a good job?"

He doesn't speak, just lets my fingers clumsily comb

through every knot and kink. When the hair is mostly smooth, I section and begin to fold each silky strand over the other.

Enduar hair is soft, much softer than human hair. While I might use the texture of my curly hair to maintain the structure of a style, the pin-straight silk slides out of its bindings at every chance.

Exasperated, I try again. Then once more.

When I am finished, the result is a loose plait with a leather binding that is doing far too much work.

I throw my hands over my head.

"I give up! You do it." I push off the bed, heading toward the tunnel in our rooms so I can finally find some of my own clothing.

He follows me. "Absolutely not. You've honored me with your efforts, and I want the world to see."

I look up at him and his loose hair that's already falling out. My eyes drop lower to the beautiful, long cock that fills up the emptiness in my soul. Heat spreads over my neck.

"Go, dress yourself. Or we will never leave this room," I choke out.

He laughs but turns.

I should go into my room—*I really should*—but the muscled cheeks of his buttocks ripple with every step, and I realize just how beautiful every part of him is, from the lean, long torso to the muscled tail.

So many ideas flood my mind. Ideas I don't even recognize.

It felt wrong to be so consumed by him when we had other things to do.

But... being together gives me strength. Gods know we will need a lot more of that before we leave.

Don't mess this up again.

I push the cold words away.

Teo dresses first and comes into my room to help me with

the fastenings at the back of the dress I've put on. It's simple and leather, but my inner thighs are sore. I don't want to slide anything over them just yet.

He fastens the buttons at my back, smooths down my hair, and takes me out of the room.

When we are out of our chambers, the wonder returns. It's hard to believe such a beautiful place exists in the world.

As I study the mushrooms we pass, I look up. "Can we check on my garden?"

He looks down at me and grins.

"Of course, my star."

As we walk out of the palace, we start to see other Enduares. The air is full of anxious excitement.

I hear the Enduar word for *human* more than once as we cross the path and greet person after person. They welcome us back and bless us with their kindness as we make our way to the greenhouse.

When I walk in, the musty, damp smell of mushrooms hits me. I see the tall, beautiful Enduar woman tending to them with water and songs.

Ulla turns to look at me and grins.

"Estela, I'm glad to see I'm not the only one worried about our little leafy plants and fungi," she says. Her apron is already covered in dirt.

I smile and step forward, taking in another deep breath of damp earth.

"The humans brought more herbs and plants with them. I'm hoping we can cultivate a whole new row."

We make it to the small patch at the end with crystal lights. I stop as I look down at the leaves that have started to nearly overgrow. Even for two months of growth, they are flourishing.

"*Por los dioses*[1]," I breathe.

Ulla grins. "I think it's time you show me how to use some of these for the kitchen."

I smile. "Yes, absolutely."

As I kneel down, I brush my fingers against the lavender. I look up at Teo.

"We can use this one to soothe any rashes or raw skin. We should cook some with animal fat to make salves."

He nods and then reaches into the pocket of his leathers and withdraws a small bit of stone paper and his spectacles. A peculiar sort of joy bubbles up when he starts to write down what I say.

I point to a few other herbs that are for flavor, and some that help with coughs. He scribbles as I work. I look at the scroll and think of the books in the giant court.

"You know, the doctor I trained with used to have a book with pages of paper. He called it an herbal, and he would write down each recipe with great care. It helps others learn the art of healing."

The mention of a book reaches back into my recent memories.

My eyes widen.

Melisa. She has my things, including the books. I need to ask her for them.

My racing thoughts are staunched when Ulla's tail brushes my feet.

She smiles as she sniffs some of the basil leaves she rubs between her fingers.

"Hm, I would very much be interested in a written log. We could use a scroll to practice your writing as well."

I pause.

"We could. Scrolls are nice. I just... there is something about flipping through pages." Then I shake my head. "Nevermind. We can get a scroll some other time. We should go work on cooking.

We have much to discuss with the humans today, especially if we are going to offer some of them a Fuegorra."

Ulla nods, and we continue to gather what she had come for to take back to the hall.

Everything is so familiar in this place, and yet it holds every inch of magic for me that it once did.

Teo doesn't leave my side for a second, though I am sure there are other places that he needs to be.

As Luiz fills pots with water, Teo retrieves a scale to measure ingredients, and I cut the roots, herbs, and mushrooms. Then we prepare the meat, and there is an easy peace between my husband and me.

He is precise with each cut, and his cubed vegetables are much nicer than mine.

Once everything starts to stew, I take a deep breath. *Sopa de carne* [2]is a slave dish, but it smells a thousand times richer with the *ruh'glumdlor* meat over whatever we could scavenge from field mice and squirrels.

When it is nearly finished, two familiar faces join us.

"Luiz!" Ulla calls out, giving him a one-armed hug as he arrives to help.

He greets her and then turns to me.

"Estela, it's so good that you are back," he grins. Then he pulls on an apron. "Apologies for my late arrival. Neela was sick again."

My eyebrows furrow.

"Is it the coughing sickness?" I ask, suddenly worried. After being kept in the mountain, the herbs that the giants had traded diamonds for were used to cure this sickness, one that seems to persist even with the curing properties of the Fuegorra.

He looks at me with a bemused expression. "No, it's our child."

I freeze.

"Neela is pregnant?"

He grins and nods. "She's nearly two months along now."

My mind starts racing. It makes sense, they discovered their matehood around the same time as Teo and me. The only difference was they performed the *Grutaliah Bondyr* mating ceremony almost instantly. I spent nearly four months under the mountain with them...

"Congratulations. I wish health for the mother, the child, and you," I say, repeating well wishes from the camps.

He smiles when Ulla looks over at me.

"How many moons do human women bear their younglings for?" she asks.

I think of Arlet, especially when she first came into my hut after she had lost her baby.

"Nine turns of the moon. Sometimes it can be less, but the baby doesn't always survive."

Ulla frowns. "Enduares only carry for six."

I stop cleaning. "Six?" Typically, in the forests, large animals carry their young for more time. For some reason I had imagined that it would be the same with the Enduares. Six months is much less time, particularly for certain ailments like morning sickness or backaches.

It also means that a mother could meet her babe much sooner. That causes a small pinprick of excitement to burst in my chest.

Teo continues to scrub a pot, a strange sight for a king, but I can tell by the rigid set of his shoulders that he is trying not to listen in too closely. He's a predictable man. He wants children like fish want water, and I...

I want a family.

I think of what I said to the human slaves: that having a child in Enduvida was adding, not subtracting.

Except, we still have much to do. We need to kill Rholker. I won't have a child until Rholker is gone.

But, perhaps, some things can't be prevented.

My eyes widen when I think of what Teo and I did the night before. I might not know the arts of pleasure, but I know that if a man comes inside a woman without protection, a baby tends to follow.

I look up at the man who can both slice through a giant and wash my hair with the same hands.

"I wonder what that means for the human women carrying Enduar children," I say.

Teo freezes.

"*Are* there any women carrying Enduar children?" he asks, causing Ulla and Luiz to pause awkwardly.

Normally, I would freeze too, but, *oh gods.* The sound of his voice is so beautiful. The tentative hope there is enough to split my heart clear in half. His emotions flow freely through our bond, causing little sparks of light to flutter against my heart.

I stand there, doing the calculations to figure out the last time I bled. My heart plummets when I realize there were a few days after I arrived in the cage. It makes sense—having sex twice after taking something to prevent pregnancy wasn't exactly a recipe for making a baby.

I take a deep breath. "No, there aren't."

Teo's face relaxes. Not relieved, but... disappointed. He pushes the emotion to the side quickly, but I can't unsee it.

All I can think of is watching him hold Sama in the tunnels months ago, and feeling like he was made for that. It would be easy to give into that and run back to our rooms right now. But babies are helpless, as Nandi found out when Rholker tore her child from her arms and beheaded her.

If he could, Rholker would kill mine and Teo's child—that is for sure.

It's... not the time.

The rest of the preparations pass quickly, and then the food is finished.

Just as we start to prepare every dish in the place, several more Enduares poke in and out, asking for what we need. I hear the human language filter through the space as the women begin to arrive to eat.

Along with them, Enduares hang back to the edges and corners throughout the space, watching.

Only one approaches me as I serve bowl after bowl of the soup.

It's a young Enduar girl. I know her—she interrupted Ulla more than once. Velen's daughter.

I wish I could remember her name, but smile down at her as she approaches me.

"Queen," she starts in her broken common tongue. "Missed you."

Then her mouth splits into a grin, and she holds out something for me.

It's a gem the size of her palm. I recognize the deep shades of purple and the almost chalky raw edges.

It's amethyst, one of my favorite stones.

"For you. Happy," she tries to form sentences with her eyebrows drawing together.

My heart expands in my chest. Amethysts do reflect happy songs, ones that bring joy to anyone who hears them.

I take the stone and hold it close to my chest.

Ulla, who's been watching the exchange, sings a few notes and causes the crystal to glow in my hands.

My eyes grow wide. Even though I knew it would happen, it still amazes me to see the crystal in action so quickly and feel both its song and the joy that melody amplifies. My surprise must still be evident because the little girl starts to laugh.

I also laugh and look down at her. When I repeat the notes with my limited singing ability, the gem barely glows for me.

"That was very kind of you, Rila," Ulla says affectionately.

Rila! That was her name.

The girl in question grins once more.

"Good! I help?" she looks pointedly at the empty bowl still in my other hand.

I nod and hand her the empty dish. She seems capable enough. When I ladle in the hot soup, her brows scrunch together as she turns and heads back out to the group of women, looking for an empty set of hands that still need a bowl.

As I watch her, I find nearly every slave watching me.

Each eye pierces the exchange with mixed expressions. A few look like they're about to cry, some are almost amazed, and others almost appear mistrustful.

Each different emotion has been one I've witnessed or felt. But I hope our display cements their thoughts about Enduvida.

They should know that we are willing to give anything to ensure this life doesn't disappear under Rholker's rule.

By the time every bowl is given out, Liana has joined us.

"We should talk to them about what happens next," the wise woman says to me. "Arlet should be here soon."

I nod, washing my hands and standing in front of all of them.

Teo hangs back.

"*¿Todos tienen comida?*"[3] I say in the human tongue.

Everyone nods slowly, and I take time to look them all in the face.

The one male slave they brought back peers at me, a frown on his gaunt face, but I smile at him. Pressure settles in my chest as the rest watch me, and I catch Melisa's eye.

She gives me a reassuring nod.

I make another mental note to ask her about the jewels and the books.

It's a strange space to be in—to know just what they must be thinking and be so aware that my words can either frighten or soothe these people. I'm not that good with words; I have no silver tongue. Even my crystal singing pales in comparison to the rest of the city.

"As you all can imagine, living in a cave is not ideal for humans," I start feeling my heart in my throat. "The lack of sunlight will do cruel things to your mind, skin, and soul. While leaving the cave is an option, we have had problems with attacks. Add in the state of our relationships with the giants, and the wisest place to be is here. Luckily, we have a way for you to get sunlight."

I reach to the neckline of my dress and pull it down as far as I can to show the Fuegorra.

There is a ripple of reactions through the group of women, but the leather is too tight to showcase everything fully.

Luiz steps forward and pulls up his shirt, allowing the lines and contours of the crystal to be easily studied.

"*¿Qué demonios es eso?*"[4] one of the women with a swollen belly says, holding her midsection as if she could shield her unborn child's eyes.

"It's called a Fuegorra, and it is our most sacred stone," Mother Liana says. "Enduares have used these gems since the dawn of time. They extend your life, help your body heal when you are ill, and signal your mate. The insertion is not painful, I can assure you—especially since we already have several humans who wear them in their chests."

At this point, over fifty people, both human and Enduar, are crammed into the hall, and the humans are looking unsure at best.

One woman raises her hand but begins to speak as soon as I look over at her.

"That child has no stone in her chest. Will we need to place one in our babies when they are born?" She points to Rila, who's still dutifully carrying bowls to be refilled with soup. Under the attention, she smiles and gives a little wave of her tail.

I look at Liana, completely unsure of what kind of answer to give her.

Liana steps forward, picking up Rila. "Enduares are already adapted to living in the mountain and do not need sunlight. As for the children who will be born in this cave, I know not. Enduares complete the ritual as a rite of passage when they become adults, and I think that may change as our peoples intermingle."

The last line hangs heavy in the air.

I remind myself that they were excited by this idea. The Enduares are dying out, and the humans need liberation. Mating is inevitable.

Still, I step in and say, "I have spoken to all of you at length about the realities of life in Enduvida. If you do not wish to stay, I would remind you all that there are other options."

Ayla comes forward, "I will also remind you all that we will take whoever wishes to go with us to the Enclave with us when our business in this place has been completed. However, like Enduvida, the Sisterhood de Bhaldraithe has rules. You will not be free to roam. The elven lands are too dangerous."

Another human woman raises her hands, "But there are stories among our people of humans finding refuge among the elves."

My stomach drops, but Ayla continues.

"Stories are not always fact. The current Elvish King has made a deal with the giants. You will not be welcomed there as anything other than what you were in Zlosa."

The room goes quiet.

I study the faces of all those who watch us, looking for a solution to the problems.

"I want to stay—put that rock in my chest. A choice to live is more of a choice than I've had before," one woman says. Then she turns to the Enduares in the corners of the meeting place. "I choose love. I choose a future."

A few other women nod and stand with her, resolute.

The men come to look at the women and are practically jumping off the walls to scoop up each eager human, but I raise my hands.

"Quiet! We will go slowly. The first step is the ritual. Those who want it will come to the grotto behind the palace tomorrow, and we will speak with our allies to send the rest out soon after."

There are nods all around, and I can see some of the women coming to approach me. I catch Arlet on the side of the crowd.

When I turn around, I find Teo suspiciously missing, as are many of the men who were itching to pounce.

A part of me understands their desperation. I remember what it was like to see Teo with all the hope in the world when he first met me.

Liana stands at my side. "This will not be easy. But, if no one tells you thank you, let me be the first." She bites a piercing in her lip and says, "This is not the ideal time to save our population, but fate waits for no one."

I nod.

"I worry about the men approaching them too quickly."

Liana's eyes glitter. "Do you not think their mothers raised them with honor, dignity, and patience?"

I shake my head. "Who's to say they even know their mothers? We all do ugly things when we are pushed against the wall."

Liana wraps her arms around my shoulders. "Queen Estela, these Enduares are not pushed against the wall. They are seeing the light at the end of the tunnel. Our people are not cruel—we praise women. Each one of those slaves will be a queen in her own right."

I swallow.

She's right. I just... don't know how to tell them that and let them believe me. Perhaps I can't. Perhaps that falls to the Enduares themselves.

"Do you know where Teo is?" I ask.

Liana chuckles. "He has gone to speak to the hunters."

I bite my lip.

"Teo is very good at making his men obey."

CHAPTER 26

SODALITE

TEO

Last night, I had to corral nearly every male in Enduvida and effectively send them home before dark. Tensions are running high—not in a malicious way, but the curiosity gnaws on them.

This morning, we will perform the *dual'moraan* for each human who wishes to receive their Fuegorra and stay under the mountain.

I should be with my wife, but instead, Vann came to my room to escort me here. The men, it seems, wanted permission to join our trek to the cavern. That led to a hearty discussion about rules.

It's been nearly an hour, and I'm still looking at the hunters, stone benders, and craftsmen who have congregated in front of the armory.

"I said it last night, and I'll say it again. You won't speak to them until they have stones in their chest. Even then, I expect you all to behave."

"But there are so many of them. I can count at least eight houses that must be repaired if we hope to expand with so many families," one of the hunters, Faol, says, his tail swishing thoughtfully behind him.

A feminine voice enters the conversation.

"If you think that a house will be enough to sway a woman into your bed, you might be right."

I turn and see the raven-haired human dressed in red.

"Melisa, I do not know if it is wise for you to be here."

She looks at me unimpressed. "I wanted to know what you were scheming about. And, believe me, I've handled worse than all of you."

A part of me believes her and has the good sense to be equal parts impressed and worried. "I am trying to explain why the women should be unbothered for a while."

She raises an eyebrow. "Do you know where they have been?"

"My queen told me they all came from the breeding pens," I say.

"That's right. They were tied to a table, treated like chattel, and still walk among us. These women are not fragile flowers who will crumble at any man's attention. We knew what we signed up for when we met Estela outside the Zlosian Palace."

I look at her skeptically. "Not everyone seemed happy in that room with Estela."

She shrugs. "They just finally have a voice. Don't fault them for wanting to use it. But that doesn't mean they don't want to be here."

Every Enduar watches her with almost painful intensity, and she takes every inch of attention with practiced grace.

"Estela is a wonderful woman, but she was never in the breeding pens." She looks at each man there with her black-brown eyes. "They consisted of a large expanse of rooms. Women were kept in close quarters, unable to work or leave for a period of four months while their cycles, temperatures, and bodies were monitored closely for signs that it was time for them to be placed in a room with a man.

"Then, they are left there for three days. Once the man is spent, the women are returned to their beds. If they are pregnant, they are gifted a hut. Some men go along with it, while others beat their women. Some forced them into any manner of painful positions."

She speaks slowly, and I fist my hands, doing my best to hold back the mounting rage.

It hurts to think of anyone being treated in such a way. Each of the men looks up, utterly silent. They all hold similar expressions of disgust.

"So *that* is where all of these women come from—four small walls. Sure, they are wounded, some already carry children, and they all are tired, but don't think for a second they aren't strong. They want what Estela has promised—homes, mates, families —lives where they work for what they eat and nothing more," she says.

Keio steps forward. "I will gladly care for a woman with a child. I spent all of last night arranging my things, and there is space."

I step forward. "You do not even know if you will be mated to one."

He shakes his head.

"I do not care."

I raise my hands. "No one will claim any of the humans without a mating song that the woman has accepted. No men will touch the women unless they ask for it."

Niht looks offended. "My King, this is already known. We don't need your lectures."

I shake my head. "Has Melisa not just explained the hell they have spent days living through? My Estela was a furious creature when she came to the mountain. I do not know how these women will react, but you must move slowly. And if I hear of even one single misstep, you will be banished from this court."

There is silence all around.

"May we attend the ceremony tomorrow?" Faol asks.

I know their meaning. They wish to know if their crystals will sing.

I purse my lips.

"No. Undoubtedly, some of you will have mates in this group—but I have no way of knowing how many. Give it time." I am pleased when even Melisa nods at this.

There is anxious shuffling all around, but I put it aside.

"Anything else?"

Vann, who has been tight-lipped since we walked to the training area, nods. It's a short movement, almost imperceptible. It tells me he has something that he does not wish to speak of in front of others.

"You all may go back to your duties. We need extra meat for our newcomers," I say.

"And soon, new sources of food because the *ruh'glumdlor* population won't keep up, and the humans don't like bats or spiders," Keio grumbles.

Annoyed, I swat at him. "That is true. You should solve that while skinning the next cave rat and tell Ra'Salore."

There are a few laughs, and I hear the word *Ra'Sa* leave the mouth of another. I don't have time to dwell on that before Vann takes me by the arm and pulls me away.

"What is it?" I ask, noting that Faol follows us as we walk.

"There is something you must see," he says.

I look back at Melisa who is smiling up at Keio. I don't hear what they say, but Vann is already leaving, so continue across the walkways, up the tunnels, and out of the large golden door leading out of Enduvida. Ra'Salore joins me at my side, and I notice he's retrieved a sword.

Whatever I was expecting, it isn't the stain of red spread around the mostly mangled body of a human man. His arms are stretched wide and there is a message carved into his chest.

THIS ISN'T OVER

My blood runs cold.

I look around, trying to see any sign of the giant scum that would've brought this to our door to deal with. There is none.

"Trouble in paradise?" Melisa asks from behind us.

I startle and turn around.

"You followed us," Ra'Salore spits out.

I think of how Estela did the same thing when we first met, and step forward. "Shouldn't you be preparing for the *dual'-moraan* ceremony?"

"I was when I spotted you hurrying out of the cave. Your wife told me I was welcome anywhere," she says, batting her lashes.

I grit my teeth. "You must tell no one that this has happened."

She drops her sweet mask and narrows her eyes.

"You wish me to lie?" Her tone is haughty, but there's a look in her eyes of almost disappointment.

She doesn't like that I'm keeping secrets.

I don't either— it makes my insides squirm.

"No. I am asking you to help maintain the peace. We are still at war with the giants. I can promise we will protect everyone inside, but right now, our actions need to be calculated. A story like this would cause unnecessary panic."

She bites her lip. "And what if I tell your wife?"

"I will tell her myself," I say firmly. Though, I don't know if it will be necessary. Estela has been through so much—protecting her is just as important.

Melisa accepts my answer, then turns back to the body. "This is from the giants, yes?"

I nod.

"If they wish to fight you, why don't they bring an army right away?"

I take a deep breath, but it's Vann that speaks.

"Estela reported a nasty skirmish on the night of the coronation. That has likely strained lots of relationships. Rholker has been cut a lot of slack. It's hard to tell how much more they will spare."

Melisa nods. "I used to be the whore of Foreman Eneko. He's one of the few giant supervisors in the slave fields and he has lots of information on Rholker."

I grit my teeth.

"I... am so sorry."

She looks up at me. "Don't be. I do what needs to be done. Which begs the question, how do you solve a problem like this?"

I drag a hand over my face. "Information and allies, so that we might make a solid plan. We have already made great strides toward resolving issues with the information Estela brought back."

She looks dubious. "What information?"

I adjust my shoulders. "She learned the names of several lords and some of Rholker's inner workings, and it has already helped us begin to make a plan. Of course, the fight she started has caused complications. We need to know what those are."

She scoffs and pulls out two books from her dress. "I bet she has barely scratched the surface. She gave these to me before we left. She'll be wanting them back."

"Thank you. I will give them to her." Melisa's words give me pause. "What do you mean 'scratched the surface'?"

Ra'Salore looks at her as she swishes her body into a demure pose.

"As a comfort woman, I know many men. My master... loves to talk." Every word is innuendo-laced.

"Would you share that information?" I ask.

She smiles. "I would do more than that. I would go back as your spy."

I shake my head just as Vann and Ra'Salore start to protest.

"Absolutely not," I say.

She frowns.

"If you love women so much, you must trust us to know what is best. I can do this—if it worries you, then let me bring one of your men." She points a lazy finger at Ra'Salore. "Ra'Sa would make a handsome human."

Ra'sa? She doesn't know how to create a proper nickname, but Ra'Salore makes no move to correct her. I find it strange, but I push the thoughts to the side.

"Lord Ra'Salore detests the overworld. We will find someone else," I begin to point to Vann or Keio when Ra'Salore turns to me with narrowed eyes.

"No need to search. I would do it, My King."

My hand stills, then drops back down to my side. "You would volunteer to leave again? The last time you left, you hated every second of it."

Ra'Salore scoffs.

"Give me one reason why you should go," I say.

"I understand I was unpleasant, but now I have experience walking the land above. Besides, she pointed at me when she asked."

Melisa smirks. "That I did. He seems good with his magic."

I drag a hand over my face. "I suppose now we should figure out how we are going to hide a seven foot Enduar with a tail."

As if on cue, Thorne steps forward from the shadows. I grit

my teeth seeing Mrath's assassin so close to me. "Pardon the intrusion."

My lips press into a tight seam. "Anyone else hiding?" I call into the tunnel, frustrated.

"No need to get heated. Mrath sent me here to keep an eye on you. It seems like this delicious little human has an in with the giant lords. She's even recruited a big blue bodyguard." He grins, looking at a scowling Ra'Salore. "Glyni can glamour him into a human without any problem, but it would only last a few days at most. He'd need to bring some of the magic with him, and the mission should be short."

We need every advantage and ally we can muster. And Melisa was wise with what she said earlier—my need to protect can't snuff out her talent.

"Very well. You will leave as soon as you are ready," I take another step forward. "But you will not be able to get the Fuegorra. Not yet."

Melisa nods. "Something to look forward to then."

I look back down at the grotesque message, feeling the regret pile up in my insides.

"What shall we do with his body?"

"Bury it. Burn it. Cast it in the sea," Melisa says over her shoulder before she walks back into the entrance of Enduvida. "Humans are not quite so sentimental about their mortal vessels. We spent too much time being treated as beasts."

CHAPTER 27

OBSIDIAN

ESTELA

T he *dual'moraan* is scheduled to start in an hour. I head down to the scrying grotto alone, only to find ten women are already waiting for us.

I haven't had a chance to visit the wise woman's crystal cave, and I was hoping for a few minutes alone with Liana, but I change my disappointment for a smile. Melisa, Abi, and Paoli aren't unwelcome sights.

With the exception of Melisa and her red dress, they all are wearing simple leather tunics, with well-fitted leggings that reach down to their ankles. I recognize a few of the other women whose infected cuts I had tended to—Carolina, Salma, and Isaraya.

"You look nice with your hair piled atop your head," I say.

Melisa reaches up to pat the tightly wound style. "Arlet helped me," she says simply. "That redhead could tame an ox's locks."

I smile, peering over Melisa's shoulder and wondering where the redhead in question is. When she doesn't appear, I frown. I'd hoped she would help me direct the women, especially since she had actually been through this ceremony before.

My attention turns back to Melisa.

"Arlet taught me everything I know." Which, admittedly, isn't a lot.

While we chat, more arrive, and I realize that almost every woman has decided to stay. The human man who was brought back, Kade, nods at me but stays silent at the back of the group.

"Today, you travel deep into our city to hunt for your Fuegorra," I call to the group. "It will be placed in your chest, and once you put it in, it cannot be removed. You will be counted among the Enduar people."

Many nod, but it's the pregnant woman from yesterday who lets out a whoop.

"More than ready. I've eaten better during the last two days than in the last five years," she calls.

Another agrees. "And the bed they've given me is so soft, I almost slept right through the morning."

Laughter twinkles through the group.

"I saw one of the men playing with a child yesterday, and I swear, my legs were practically falling open."

I sputter as more of them laugh.

Melisa claps a hand on my back. "Chin up. You know, I never knew either of my parents. Here's to children knowing where they come from!"

Several of the women raise their water glasses into the air, as if they were fine goblets of mead and take a long drink.

Melisa looks like she'd like to say something else, but Liana's head emerges from her sunken crystal cave. I cross over, trying to get a few glimpses of the scrying grotto where Liana and I spent weeks training my Fuegorra reading skills and learning the names of crystals. I can already hear some of the songs pouring out and see the sharp rods of pointed beryl and citrine formations.

Liana is clad in so many gems that I wonder how she walks. I hold out my hand to help her up, and she gladly accepts, squeezing it once before returning her grip to the solid gold bauble she holds under her other arm.

It looks like a portable lantern hanging on the end of a long rod.

"What's all this?"

She smiles and jerks her head to the side. "We call this a thurible. Everyone not receiving their Fuegorra today carries crystals, but, as leader of the procession, I get to light a bit of mushroom incense and guide you all down to the cavern."

I study its shape more closely, noting the geometric patterns present everywhere else in Enduvida. There is a lot that looks like gold down here, making up door frames and armor. They call it Enduar metal, but this...

"It's beautiful. It looks like real gold."

Liana nods. "It is." She turns her gaze to the small container. "I don't work with metal much as a wise woman, but there are a few ceremonial pieces I managed to keep from before the war. Here, hold this."

She passes me the rod and pulls a handful of dried green mushrooms from her pocket. She places them in my other hand, and I marvel while they leave behind a faint, glowing residue.

I wait patiently while she opens the container and motions for me to place them inside. She follows my actions by striking a rough black flint.

Sparks rain over the mushrooms, and a small tendril of green smoke curls in the air. The wise woman looks up at me and smiles. A strange anxiousness blossoms in my belly.

"Is it time?" I ask.

Liana nods, then faces the humans.

"Human women," her eyes land on Kade, the old elven spy that came back with Teo, "and man. Are you ready to hunt for your crystal?"

"Yes!" they call out.

It is then that the singers, Velen and Ulla, step forward, carefully cradling bubbling rods of iridescent black goethite. Their clothes look like something straight out of Liana's closet.

They sing a song that feels like the first dawn of a new life—it is deep, haunting, and stirs my soul with inspiration. The music that pours out of them is not unlike the beauty of a stream flowing along or the crash of waves against the beach. They use deep breaths and the backs of their throats to make low guttural sounds, beats, and clicks. It sounds as if they were unleashing the spirits of a million Enduares, clawing their way through rock, silt, and ash just to join us in this moment.

They walk through the women who watch with unfettered awe and form a line.

Liana swings her golden thurible back and forth, creating decorative patterns with the cloyingly sweet smoke that leaks through the holes.

Only then, with the wise woman at the lead, do we start our walk to the caverns deeper in the mountain.

I flank the group, with Arlet and Melisa walking just a few paces ahead. Svanna, Iryth, and many other Enduar women come next.

It's notable that none of the unmated men are in sight. I'm not surprised. A part of me is pleased when the elves come to join our procession. They have offered to help with combat training tomorrow, and I must admit that I'm eager to join them.

As we walk out from behind the palace, Teo joins us, and then Vann.

I look at my mate as he draws closer to my side. His braid is neater today, but there is so much to appreciate about his physical appearance. For one, he is devastating in dark colors. From the black earrings to the black circlet upon his head, he's something entirely too beautiful to belong to this world.

He catches me staring up at him and shows me a mental image of me tangled up in his sheets. It causes me to stumble.

His warm hand wraps protectively around my waist, and the butterflies flutter frantically in my stomach.

He leans down the two foot difference between our heights and kisses me. "Wishing you a good morning and bringing you this."

My eyes drop to the two quartz towers he holds in his free hand. He gives me one of the columns, and it starts to glow in my hand. My eyes are glued to the glowing stone as we begin to move through the city.

More join in behind us. Even the youngest children trail along to the ethereal chants that light up the entire cave. As we pass the Adorflame, it seems to pulse to the beat of the words.

When Thorne finds his way to my other side, I look up at his well-styled white-blond hair.

"Care to become an honorary Enduar, Thorne?" I ask playfully.

He smiles with ease. He's watched every movement within Enduvida with careful precision and while I don't trust him completely, I do like him.

His smile curves up partially. "It is a... primitive display. But I suppose it's charming. Especially, I imagine, for humans whose rituals were stolen from them."

I don't know how to respond, but sadness chokes my throat.

I think of what my mother said to me about a goddess and look back around the vast cave. It's a thing of dreams. A mystical land that should only belong to the gods, not mere mortals.

When we continue past the forges and toward one of the gates that leads deeper into the mountain, the stone and metal benders pause their work and track our movements with careful precision. Some of them have gathered near the tall, shining metal bars, uninvited but eager to join along. They hand out hammers and hold their fists to the unseen sky and shout once for each woman.

We descend, and the air changes. The temperature grows colder, and a pulse of magic penetrates under my skin. As we move, I become more sensation than person.

"What can I expect when we get to wherever it is we're going, Your Highnesses?" Thorne asks, striking up a quiet conversation despite it really just not being the time.

My eyes continue to drink in every detail, trying to memorize and experience what I never got. "I was given a Fuegorra when I was half-dead. I never performed a ritual."

He appears confused. "Aren't there some vague instructions about each crystal choosing its owner? Who chose yours?"

My brows furrow. "I don't actually know. I guess I had assumed it was Mother Liana. Is that right, Teo?"

Teo looks over at us. "I knew that Estela was my mate from the moment I saw her. Liana and I chose the stone."

"And how did you feel about that?" Thorne asks me.

"Sad, honestly. But I would be dead if they hadn't done it. Maybe I wish I could've come down here, but I spend lots of time with the crystals. I'm a Fuegorra reader—still mostly untrained, but one day, I will take Liana's place."

Thorne looks back at Liana who is still chanting and swinging the thurible. He almost smiles.

"I can see it."

We walk a few more paces over a bridge when I lean toward Teo. "What happens first?"

He holds my hand and whispers. "Well, as you saw,

everyone received their hammers from the crafters before we started down this path. When we reach the Fuegorra Cavern, Liana will explain to everyone how to look for their gems. From there, one by one, she'll use her magic to place the stones in everyone's chest."

"And what does everyone else do?"

"We watch," he says, clearly amused by my curiosity.

Whatever he says next is swallowed up by gasps and exclamations coming from the head of the line. I push away from the line, trying to see the front. I only take a few steps when a small set of hands reach around my thigh, and I nearly jump.

When I look down, I squint, waiting for my eyes to adjust to the dim room. As soon as they do, I clearly see Rila.

I'm so shocked, but Teo laughs.

"It seems you have a fan."

Siya, Rila's mother, comes hurrying up. Her braid is a much darker grey than most Enduares, and she has a round face that radiates kindness. I'm told that she's a weaver with Arlet.

"My Queen," she says with a bow. "My deepest apologies—I took my eyes off her for one second."

The little girl hugs me tighter, and I give the mother a wave.

"It is fine. Walk with your mate. Teo and I will keep her out of trouble."

Rila grins at her mother who smiles and thanks us tenfold before walking up to the head of the line to find Velen. Rila's small hand slips into mine, and it reminds me of the younger years with Mikal.

There's something about children that can heal bits of the soul. Their trust isn't to be taken lightly.

It doesn't take much longer for us to reach the glowing chamber at the end of the tunnel. The walls are as black as the moonless night, and flaming orange and red chunks of crystal are scattered throughout. None are as big as the column inside of the Scrying Grotto. Each one calls out a few notes before falling silent.

Once every person has piled into the dark room, the singing stops.

The stones aren't silent, but I have this itch under my skin as if they aren't talking to me.

"Listen for your match," Liana's powerful voice fills the room. "It will sing a melody that you will recognize instantly, just as clearly as I speak to you now. Be mindful of your hammer strikes, though. The crystal you break out now will be sported on your chest till the day you die—no one wants a lopsided oval like the one Velen cut twenty years ago."

I look up at Teo, who is grinning. He winks at me and makes a crude shape with his hand, confirming that Velen did indeed have a phallic-shaped stone embedded in his skin.

The stone-faced singer. How... delightfully funny.

When Liana stops speaking, the same silence returns, only now accompanied by the unsure steps of humans who lack any kind of night vision.

Teo once told me that the Fuegorra would heighten my senses, and I suppose a part of that is true, but most of the space around me is still a mystery.

I pull on Teo's arm, bringing him down to my level. "How does the gem attach to the skin?"

His lips brush my ears, and I shiver. "There is a magic that binds it there. It is almost like a fire that melds the gem with flesh, but as mentioned, it is painless."

Rila looks up at me. "Mama says I can get one when I'm older."

I stroke her silky hair. "Yes, you will."

She gives me a toothy grin, and I realize both her pointed canines are missing. It makes my heart squeeze.

Many more minutes pass before the first sound of a hammer against rock sounds, followed by a triumphant laugh.

Liana's voice breaks through the clash of hammers.

"Queen Estela? Would you join me?"

I freeze, and Rila looks up at me. Handing her off to Teo, I move across the cavern and stand next to Liana. The expression on her face is hidden in shadow, but she leans over to explain.

"I know that you didn't get to experience this before, but I thought it would be a good test of your magic."

My chest fills with a surprised sort of gratitude. There are two powers within me—the one that attunes me to the crystals and the light that burns. I've used the heat often over the last few months, but I'm still warming up to the ways of the Enduares.

"Just tell me what to do."

The reddish light gilds Liana's hands as she moves them out to either side of her body. "Abi, daughter of the humans, approach."

The woman walks forward, and a strange buzzing energy builds in the air. She holds out her stone, which Liana takes.

"Bare your chest, my child," Liana says.

Abi reaches up and undoes the ties around the neck of her tunic. She pulls down the garment low enough so that the valley between her breasts is on clear display.

"Estela, take this and hold it in place," Liana gently instructs.

I reach forward, placing the stone on her chest. Abi's sharp breath vibrates through the stone, and it warms against her skin.

"Follow my lead," Liana murmurs. Then she places her hand over mine and hums a monotone note. I match her pitch, and my Fuegorra lights up, as does Liana's and Abi's. For a second, I fear the heat that comes after the light, but it doesn't come.

The glow isn't bright white. It's orange. The glimmer pulses in time with an ancient song, like the composition of a heartbeat, as the stone heats. For a second, I glimpse the world through different eyes. Instead of seeing Abi, I see myself standing next to Liana. We become two souls tangled up in energy and song.

Then our Fuegorras dim, and Abi steps back panting. Her hand flutters to her chest, probing at the stone before tightening her tunic neckline.

"It—it's done?"

"Yes," Liana replies.

While the wise woman calls to another, I look down at my hand in wonder. How can this palm have the ability to both burn and bless?

I ponder this question as the next twenty-seven humans approach. Liana seals the gems while I hold them in place, enjoying the out-of-body experience of seeing through another's eyes. The faces and perspectives begin to blur together, and I swear that I can feel a tangible link between each person in the room.

Taking this stone wasn't just a ceremony, nor was it solely about extending lives or hearing crystal songs. It was a joining of a people for a lifetime.

As we leave the chamber, I see the tear-streaked faces of each woman, most of them smiling widely. Melisa catches my eye.

I never saw her approach to receive her gem.

"What happened?" I demand.

She takes a deep breath and rolls her eyes. "I didn't want to do the ritual. All right?"

"Why not?"

She pins me with a long, hard stare.

"Why don't you ask your husband?" She increases her speed and pushes away from me, looking for someone else to talk to.

I stand there awkwardly at the side of the cave.

It stings.

When Arlet and I first made it to the caves, I was, admittedly, a poor friend. I felt like she left me behind. But Melisa and I had a connection—an understanding.

But now, seeing her clamber away wounds me.

When Teo appears at my side, he's carrying a sleeping Rila. He looks uncomfortable at seeing my disappointment.

"Did she say something unkind?"

I shake my head. "No. She told me to ask you why she wasn't getting a Fuegorra."

He sucks in a sharp breath and looks at Rila's tiny form against his shoulder.

"We should speak of this later."

Most of the group was already halfway up the tunnel, but I pin him with a strict stare.

"Why? I think you should tell me now."

Without thinking, I press into the bond that connects our minds, trying to find the answer he's so reluctant to share.

He appears surprised, and I stumble back, my hands flying to my mouth.

"I—I'm so sorry. I didn't mean to push like that."

He takes my hand.

It's okay. It's common with bonds. You just need to be careful, my love.

Melisa volunteered to go back to the giants to help us get information about Rholker's plans. It will take time for us to launch a counterattack against him—we need to make sure we are prepared.

I feel anger rise deep in my belly. First, for my outburst.

Then because he didn't tell me, and lastly, she finally escaped them and would be going back.

"No," I say firmly.

He shakes his head. "*Mi amor*[1], it was her idea. You can't tell her what she can and can't do."

"Like hell, I can't," I grumble and start walking up the tunnel alone.

It isn't long before my mate catches up with me, but I don't want to look at him just yet. I need to find a way to convince Melisa to stay.

CHAPTER 28

APATITE

TEO

The next three days pass in the blink of an eye. With the new humans adjusting to under mountain life, I have little time for much else between meetings. More and more scrolls pile on my desk as we plan to first retrieve the artifact and then march on Zlosa to kill Rholker.

Some days, the pending future doesn't feel real. It's just calculations, crystals, and endless hours of talk.

Estela has been subdued. When I presented her with the books that Melisa had given me, she revealed that one contained Rholker's writings, and the other was something truly awful: a book bound in human skin.

After that, we went back to work.

She has fallen into a quick rhythm—actually, a back-breaking speed. She scrubs pots, holds children, and listens to these humans until her eyes can hardly stay open.

Today, we both rose early. She went to train with the elves, humans, and Svanna, while I came to oversee the progress of the crystal suits that Liana and Flova have been working on in order to retrieve the artifact. Reports indicate that they have a unique feature that I would enjoy seeing.

Thorne has requested to join this particular journey, as he has made it extremely clear he will dive with the rest of us. When someone shoots him a mistrustful glance, he looks unfazed and observant, the same expression that he has had the entire time he's been in the caves.

There's something about him—I can't quite put my finger on it, but I do not trust him. Despite the fact that several seem to appreciate him, including Estela and Ulla.

His quiet, silent presence fades away as my mind swims with things I could do for Estela to help ease the hurt of Melisa leaving. She wears the jewels I've given her every day, but there must be something more.

The day that she helped me put on my armor is still fresh in my mind, and I think of her wearing a matching set. Golden plates to protect her soft human flesh. It would be wise.

The idea sticks, and I decide to discuss it with Flova after we've inspected the suit.

Thorne takes a deep breath, still walking in silence next to me, and I look at the knives gleaming on his belt.

Curiosity loosens my tongue.

"You are friends with Mrath—did you ever know Arion?"

Thorne stiffens. "I am Thorne the *Peredhel*—the *halfing*. Why would I have any dealings with the Elf King?"

"You tell me," I say.

No one has been unkind to Thorne or the other members of the sisterhood, but there is discontentment in the air. The crystals can only amplify what others are feeling, so when we look upon this snowy-haired man, sneaking through hallways, I know a few Enduares are reminded of Arion.

He doesn't respond, and all too soon, blistering heat from the forges greets us before any of my people do.

TO IGNITE A FLAME

I spot the back of Liana's crystal-covered tunic and the familiar bend of Flova's spine. They stand in front of a table, concealing the suits from my view.

"Ho!" I call out, and Liana looks up.

She nods in my direction and then scowls at Thorne.

At least I have one ally against him.

"Your Majesty," she says, and I feel proud of her for snuffing our guest.

Thorne grins at her and gives a short bow.

"Mother Liana, a pleasure as always. I love the blue gems you've used for your brow jewelry today." One of his gloved hands reaches up to tap the space on his eyebrow to demonstrate.

Liana purses her lips. "They are my least favorite pieces."

I stifle a laugh, but she turns to me.

"Estela has not met with me. I've reminded her twice, and I had hoped she'd help with this project," she says.

I frown. "She is... occupied with the humans."

Liana quirks up her eyebrows. "So I've seen. I would appreciate it if you would remind her to come. I'd like to make the final suit with her."

"Very well. Where are these grand creations?" I ask as Flova turns, giving us a view of the table.

Before me are three suits that glow blue in the forge light, despite looking like they are made of glass. Unlike typical armor that I've worn into battle, they aren't separated into many pieces, and there are no gaps between sections.

In fact, they look more like statues—inflexible and solid.

"There are three. One for you, one for Lord Vann, and one for Master Thorne."

I look up at Flova who is wearing a look of supreme pride.

"May I touch them?"

Flova dips out of the way with his hands behind his back

and the wrinkles on his face deepening. "Of course, My King. I think you'll like what you find."

The closer I get to the suit, the louder a dull note pierces my ears. I wince.

"That is... unpleasant."

Liana nods. "Yes, but it is the best we can do. Perhaps with many more months to explore frequencies, we could find something more palatable. But we are on a strict timeline."

When I reach down and pick up one of the crystal gloves melded into a sleeve, it flexes in my hands, as soft as the finest leather. My surprise must be obvious because Thorne comes over and picks up a piece of a different suit.

"Impossible," he breathes.

Flova tuts.

"Not so, blood cousin. My benders have spent weeks perfecting this design. The magic is thanks to Mother Liana, and you will find that they are extremely durable against the pressures of the ocean."

I nod. "It will not crack when we dive deep."

"Precisely," Liana says.

Thorne looks up at her. "How does it provide air for us?"

Her lips flatten, but she answers him far more graciously than I would have.

"You will put this on, and you will spend time where there is an abundance of air." She gestures around her exaggeratedly. "It will create a bubble that will go with you into the water. Similar to the gills of a fish, it will filter the breathable elements from the sea. I don't think you should spend more than a few days in the water, but it will have to be enough to explore the ruins."

My mind wanders to Iravida. It was a massive city, far beyond the capacity of Enduvida.

"Are you sure? The capital was once one of the largest cities known to mankind. I can't imagine that a few days will be enough—"

"Not much is left. I have seen the ruins through my Fuegorra —Estela is coming by later to see what she can scry. I may know where the artifact is but it is clouded from my vision. I am preparing a map for you to look at." She eyes Thorne once more as he squeezes the glass-like crystal.

It makes a high-pitched noise as it flexes.

"When can we test this?" Thorne asks.

Liana looks at Flova, who crosses his arms and surveys the three suits.

"I need to make a few minor adjustments, but I think that you could do it as early as tomorrow. In fact, I think we must insist. The sooner..."

"Eager to be rid of me?" Thorne asks, interpreting the silence.

"Yes," Liana says without hesitation.

A part of me wants to deny that, to say that everything isn't so bad, but the desire to laugh wins out.

Thorne doesn't find it quite as humorous.

"Tomorrow it is then." I turn to Flova, "And while we are here, there is another matter I'd like to discuss. I will need another set of metal armor for the queen, one that matches mine."

It's Thorne's turn to chortle.

"Armor? How romantic."

I cast a single glance at him.

"Yes, Lady Estela will surely love it, especially since she came asking for one not too long ago." Flova nods approvingly.

My eyebrows rise. "She did?"

Flova nods. "Perhaps not in so many words, but she liked to see how it is made. She asked questions about how it is to be worn, what it protects, and things of the like. She's a delightful woman."

I am utterly at a loss for words. I didn't realize that my little mate had such a hunger for things of war. Of course, Enduar women are hearty. Many have joined us in the pursuit of blood and vengeance, but it makes my pulse raise to think of my soft, broken love swinging a sword to lob off the head of Rholker or one of his minions.

My father took vengeance to a new level, but I have no disillusions that we aren't heading toward another Great War.

I wince.

Thorne misinterprets my expression. "Come now, you can't tell me you haven't thought of a woman fighting before."

I whip around to look at him, and he almost staggers back in surprise.

"You don't know anything, *Elf*," I sneer. Flova has already gone back to work, and Liana is ignoring both of us. "You've seen Enduar women."

"Ulla lacked basic training. She could barely point a short sword at me, but she's much improved now," he smirks.

I glower.

"You are teaching Ulla how to fight?"

"Why would it matter if I was?" he asks.

"She already knows how to fight!" I insist.

He shakes his head and makes a tsking sound.

I step closer. "Leave my people alone."

He throws his hands up. "Yes, yes, I will be going now."

I stare at him for a long hard minute before he does just that. A bit too slowly for my liking.

As soon as his pristine white head is out of sight, Liana comes to my side. She gazes in the direction of Thorne with thinly veiling mistrust.

"He's hiding something. I smell it all over him, and the crystals whisper it into the air," she says in a low voice.

I look at her.

"I agree, but he is still an ally."

"For now," she adds forcefully. Then she looks at me. "If you are thinking of Estela fighting, then she should be working on her Fuegorra training as well. She did very well at the ceremony. I'll be the first to admit my displeasure that she has met with Flova and not me. Is she... healed?"

Drawing one lip between my teeth, I consider her words.

"She is strong and ready to take on the world."

Liana goes still, the jewels on her face flashing. "I heard what she said, but was there more to the story?"

I take a deep breath. "Yes and no. They tried to break her mind. It's hard to know exactly what saved her, but I believe it was a combination of the Fuegorra and the mating bond."

Liana places one finger on her temple, gently nudging the piercing above her eye.

"You would be right. As you know, the bond you share is powerful magic—it goes a long way in healing."

For a moment, I am lost to memories of her in my bathroom, legs parted, eyes closed, but mind open. We turned pain into such sweet ecstasy, and it makes my blood race with an unsuspecting surge of lust. It's the wrong time, but the insatiable nights we spend wrapped up together have done nothing to quench the thirst I have for her body.

Drawing myself up to my full height to erase the images while I speak with gods-damned Mother Liana, I open my mouth to respond but find all I can manage is a firm nod.

Her white eyebrow curves up, almost concerned.

"Is everything all right?"

"Yes."

She gives me a confused look, and then reaches into her

pocket and pulls out a few shards of obsidian about the size of her palm. They've been carefully flint-knapped into thin rectangular sheets, sharp enough to cut leather. Handling them requires extreme care. Expert stone cutting aside, my eyes catch on their paintings.

I recognize the vibrant blue and green pigments from several precious stones: lime azurite, melachite, lapis lazuli... And something that smells of a beast. Bone, I realize, as my eyes study the contours.

There are figures painted on each of the cards. Enduares, but the light paintings of brown human bodies now accompany our azure forms.

"Cards, of a sort," she says. "We used to use these to maintain our connection to the stars and stones—to help us read the Fuegorra."

I nod as she hands one to me. The sharp edge passes along my skin, not quite cutting but almost uncomfortable.

"I don't think I ever saw these used."

She shrugs. "It was more popular with the women in Enduvida."

I purse my lips. "You mentioned that you had found dozens of traditions lost to time while you were looking for answers in the royal library. Is this one of them?"

She nods, but I see the question in her eyes.

"Do you wish to teach these things to Estela?" I ask. The wrinkles in her face deepen. "You are her mentor; it is your choice what she learns and when."

Her mouth twists down as if she were tasting something bitter.

"Obviously. I merely want to ensure that she is well enough to handle physical training and learning magic. I know that woman. She'd lie to me if the task looked interesting enough."

Nodding along with her assessment, I cross my arms and gaze back at the impressive suits.

"Anything that you can teach her might be to our advantage when it comes time to face the giants," I say simply.

I've seen the bloodlust in Estela's eyes. The fear.

She needs every inch of power that she can—whether it be learned or gifted.

Liana is pleased by the answer. Then she takes back the stone card, stacks it atop the others, and carefully wraps them in a stretch of leather.

"Tell her to seek me out in the morning. And make sure she isn't too tired to work hard."

I grin and push away from the workstation.

Liana picks up her small bundle and tells me goodbye. I wave back to her and head toward the palace. I need to find my mate and make her stop frowning.

After, I'd like to work on translating Rholker's book.

CHAPTER 29

RUTILE QUARTZ

ESTELA

F or the last few days, I've spent my time harvesting
seeds from flowers, cradling Sama in my arms, and
tending to the few women whose infections still hold
strong.

When Teo told me that Liana wanted to work on our magic
again, I was worried. There is much I need to discuss with her,
but a part of me is... worried.

I haven't had a chance to tell her about my visions, the *Bruja*
witches, my burning light magic, the human-bound book, or
Melisa.

It was confirmation to stop avoiding her.

It's not until I leave the palace that I realize just how early it
is, noting that the houses throughout the city are quiet. The
song that comes from the clock tower is gentle—like a lullaby
meant to encourage the restful slumber of every ear it touches.

The lights above me are dim, but I don't need to go far.

I walk past the throne room, through the back hallways that
pass several meeting rooms, and the Royal Library, and then I
find myself in the mushroom garden. Their faint light illumi-

nates the massive statues of Enduares long since passed. As I cross, awareness prickles at the back of my neck. I stop immediately.

Slowly, I turn toward one of the statues, almost instantly recognizing the likeness of my husband. As I look up, I see Teo's sharp cheekbones, broad shoulders, and veined arms—only the expression and turn of his eyes are different.

I suck in a breath.

"They say that Endu is more stone than god. Like a man carved out of bedrock," Liana's voice says behind me.

I startle, squeaking as I turn around to look at the wise woman.

Today, her hair is wrapped tightly around her head in elaborate designs.

Pressing a hand to my head, I gasp for breath, "Gods on their stony throne."

A smile streaks across her face. "It's heartening to see how well you are adapting."

Her hands are clasped behind her back, and she sweeps her eyes up to the towering statue before gazing across in the opposite direction to look at the others.

I swallow. "My curiosity for your gods is endless. I believe that, seeing how regal these men look. Is that Endu?"

She takes a pause.,

"That is Teo'Likh, Teo's father. The rest are also old kings of the Enduares. Teo's family line. I suppose it is as much your line now that you are our proper queen."

I blink and nod my head once.

"Was he always as cruel as they say?" I ask conversationally, trying to ease into such a hushed topic and avoid the subject of my magic.

Teo fears and hates his father. I know he questions whether the old king planted seeds of darkness in his heart. He's spoken of what it was like to be raised to kill for the throne, and my heart aches each time.

But now, I look at Teo'Lihk with burning curiosity, wanting to know what he once was.

Was he once like the kind man who sings me to sleep and strokes the nightmares away with sweet words?

"He was always hard. Cruel. Don't you remember? We have spoken of this before," she says, a little concerned.

My eyebrows draw together, alarmed. "Have we?"

She looks confused. "Yes."

I search through my memories for the lost moments.

"I remember your telling me that his father sent him to kill the queen, but I remember little else."

She nods. "You told me that the witches ravaged your memories. Has this faded?"

I scan the ground. "Most... most have come back. Teo helps me."

She places a hand on my shoulder. "Teo was not present for this conversation. It makes sense that some things might be gone—I cannot show you the memories the same way, but I can tell you. Please let me know if this happens again so I can restore the records."

There's a deeply unsettled feeling in my gut, one that distresses me far more than I would like. I have to force myself to take a deep breath, smile, and thank her for her generosity.

"Have you tried writing your memories? In case there are any other stray bits of damage?" Liana asks suddenly.

I look up at her and then quickly close my mouth.

"No."

"Why not?" Those silver eyes prod at my defenses.

I swallow.

"I can't write well enough." It's only a partial truth, but it broaches the subject of something far too tender to speak about.

She gives me an incredulous look. "You can, and there are those who could help you if needed."

"Didn't you call me here to discuss my magic?" I say.

She flexes her jaw. "This is pertinent."

I let out a long breath. "I haven't used my magic since we came back to the caves. It's... unpleasant to think of the power inside of me. Of what it can do."

Liana's face softens. "There it is. You feel guilty."

"Guilty doesn't even begin to describe it," I mutter.

"So then describe it to me," she counters.

I ball my fists. "When I was trying to help heal Dyrn, I ended up speeding up his death—"

"You were easing him into a less painful death. There's a difference."

I shake my head, insistent.

"It's not just the Fuegorra. While I was in Zlosa, I found this tight, glowing thread inside of me. When I pulled on it, I shined like a star. When Rholker touched me, he was burned. That's never happened before. What if I do that to someone here? Teo? Or Arlet? What if I hurt little Rila?" My voice wobbles. "I've caused enough pain."

Liana purses her lips. "Now I see."

"See what?" I ask.

She cocks her head to the side. "You believe that you deserve the pain you've been put through."

I stiffen.

"Yes, that's it, isn't it?"

I say nothing.

"It's hard to make mistakes, even grave ones at times, and then have to learn how to overcome them."

I finally meet her gaze. "It's easy when someone is all good or all bad. I am... both."

She smiles. "Things are rarely black and white, even in regards to our enemies."

I take a deep breath. "I fear what I can do with my body."

She nods and places her hand back on my shoulder. "Even with my visions of the future, there is much I don't know. One thing I can tell you with absolute certainty is that if you don't train, you will always fear your magic. It will make you dangerous later down this path."

I grit my teeth.

"I don't want to hurt anyone else." Then I amend with, "Except Rholker."

She pats my cheek. "Understandable. But you won't ever truly have the freedom to promise yourself that if you don't learn control. Do you understand?"

I nod despite my burning eyes.

"It's good that you train with Svanna and the elves. They will teach you how to fight as a woman should. Now, you must train with me as a *wise* woman should."

I nod my head. "You are right."

"Of course I am. Lesson one, forgive yourself for the mistakes you made and, most importantly, change," she says firmly.

I manage a soft yes through the moisture gathering in my eyes.

"Come now, my child. Don't let the shadows swallow you up now, not before we have a chance to start. Follow," she commands, letting me go and walking down the steps toward the scrying grotto.

I do as she asks, focusing on keeping my breath even, so that I might not spiral into the unknown abyss that still lurks in the back of my mind.

Passing into the grotto is difficult, as it is on an incline that descends into a chamber. I have to use my arms to lower me down and then crouch to reach the right spot, avoiding sharp crystals.

Once inside, however, it calms me down. The harmony in this space is intoxicating and peaceful all at once. The ebbing pulse of mineral music and magic massages my skin, making my scalp tingle and my fingers itch to touch each surface, smooth or jagged.

I stop my perusal of the area when I spot a figure. Liana wasn't alone, apparently.

"Lord Vann?" I say, surprised to find him sitting, legs crossed on the ground.

I wipe under my eyes quickly, drying any evidence of my high emotions outside.

Around him are dozens of small pots filled with shimmering liquids. With a small brush, he paints on rectangular pieces of black obsidian.

He looks up at me with a stiff expression.

"My Queen, good morning. I was helping Liana paint her cards," he says simply.

"What cards?" I ask.

Vann hands Liana a card and a brush, and she begins to paint, too.

I knew that she had been wanting to speak with me, but I knew nothing about cosmic pictures of humans and stars on the cards.

She jerks her head to the side, gesturing for me to sit between Vann and a sharp spike of pale yellow citrine.

"Come, gaze upon the *hlumscri.*"

I let myself smile despite my mind being weighed down with Liana's words and thoughts of Melisa and her choice to leave.

"Hu-loom," I fumble. "That means *glow* in Enduar."

She smiles. "Glowing cards, in the common tongue. Very

good. Sit, sit. Vann won't be rude. See if you can tell me what kind of stones I've crushed to make the paint."

I blink and then gingerly reach forward to collect one of the cards. As I pick it up, I let it shimmer in the light emanating from flecks of dozens of different gems. It takes practice to open not only my ears, but my heart. There's a beating song that seems to latch onto the negative thoughts in my mind and steal them away. The movement of the sound reminds me of the *ruc'rad* scavenger rats that steal food.

"I hear the obsidian for certain," I say.

She huffs a laugh as the card itself is clearly razor-sharp obsidian. "Do you, now? How about anything else?

I press my lips together, glancing at Vann as he holds a shard close to his face with expert precision. Listening carefully, I also notice the evergreen song of malachite.

"Malachite?" My voice has an uncertain wobble to it that I know causes the frown on her face.

"You aren't wrong, but I'm sad you can't hear more." She picks up her own card. "This is a tradition amongst wise women. It is an exercise akin to tuning an instrument. It should, in theory, open up your soul." She reaches up and taps my forehead. "It should also open your mind. Perhaps you will have another vision."

My brow crinkles under her strong, warm fingertips as I look back down at the cards. A few are still drying from their fresh paint.

"Can I touch the others?"

She nods. "Yes, but mind the edges. Why don't you pick the three that you feel the most called to?"

"I don't—"

"You want to get better at magic?"

I sigh. "Yes."

"Learn to connect to your greater self. As mortals, we call to the stars above. We ourselves are made up of ancient spheres long since crushed to dust that traveled to our planet and created all that we are. If we are merely another configuration of dust, then why not speak to our kin?"

He's going to be in the room while I pull on my lyre string and release my magic?

I look at Vann once more, and she sighs. "Kor'Vann, leave us be."

He looks down at the half-painted card in one hand and his paintbrush in the other. "But I'm not—"

My power has been an important tool, but I would be lying if I said I wasn't afraid of it. Having him watching, even if that observing is good-natured, blocks off my desire to pluck my mystical lyre string and make the gem glow to life once more.

"Please. This is difficult for me."

He takes a deep breath, and I dislike the hardness I find there. He is such good friends with Teo, but we have little interaction outside of that.

But his large, silver-blue eyes soften as they watch me. "Very well, My Queen."

Relief flashes across my body.

"Thank you." I smile as he carefully sets down what he was working on and leaves the cavern with a friendly wave.

Satisfaction blossoms in my chest as I watch him go, but Liana is insistent.

"We are alone now."

Watching the wise woman trail her fingers across a line of beryl and quartz is mesmerizing as each stone flickers for a second, like a light bug, and then fades back to their glimmering darkness.

I swallow hard.

Liana frowns while she watches my reaction. "Enough. Turn off your worries for a second—listen."

My eyes return to the sparkling ground and scan the different images, taking particular note of the image of the human woman and Enduar entangled together like two swirls of water rising up from the ocean. They crash together in a mess of browns and blues. It's a beautiful sight.

Slowly, I pick up the card and bring it closer to my face.

Liana is silent, but I can hear her pleased expression through the stones around us.

How strange..

It is as if each crystal is fine-tuned to her and all her needs. Even I can admit that kind of skill is appealing.

Shifting the stone in my hands, a jagged edge nicks the side of my finger.

I hiss and place the injured digit in my mouth as I look at the others. It's no great harm, and the bleeding stops in a few moments, thanks to the Fuegorra.

As it does, the enormous piece of Fuegorra crystal in the middle of the room flickers to life.

My pulse races as I look at it.

Something presses at the back of my mind, seeking entrance. I furrow my brow.

"Focus. You can play with the gems after," Liana snaps.

My gaze lowers back to the ground, and I look at the other images, some of the starry nights with glowing jewels and a variety of chalices. One such *card*, as Liana called it, catches my attention, and I lean forward. The stars are written with six chalices of glowing silver and gold paint. Four remain upright and organized while two spill their cosmic contents upon the land.

I pick this one up, too, and place it next to the image of the passionate lovers.

As I wait, looking around, there's an image of a skeleton reclining on a throne, dressed up and regal like a king. It taunts me with its haughty smirk, bony chin resting atop its fist.

Rholker's face flashes in my mind, and I think of revenge. Of the pretty dresses and the expectation that I would be his. I pick up this *hlumscri* and place it below the others.

Liana watches my choices carefully, and then her eyes return to mine. There's a new type of harmony in front of me.

Each card has the most subtle differences. The tune comes to me easily, showing me the right cards. It's almost like plucking different strings of a single instrument.

"Do you feel you've chosen correctly?" she asks.

I look down at them. "I don't really know what I was meant to look for."

"A wise woman acts from deep in here." She places a hand on my belly.

I recoil, and all echoes of another being in my mind slide away.

"I'm using my magic right now. I don't want to burn you," I say, panicked.

"Then don't." She replaces her hand, and there is no smell of sizzling flesh. "You worry about many things. That is felt in here." Her other hand comes to my breastbone where tension bunches under her fingers.

Her strong touch reassures me, and it is... empowering. The twisted knots inside of me start to melt away.

"Let the crystals focus you. They'll naturally bring out your power."

I can do this.

"You have a gift. It cannot be taught to someone who does not possess it; it can merely be nurtured, respected, and strengthened over time. Do you understand?" Her voice is low, and her tongue is much less sharp than it often is when we discuss such matters.

I close my eyes, giving way to my body. Liana's hand pulls away, but the humming and sparking against my skin doesn't. It continues to skitter across my skin with pulses of fire.

"Estela," Liana's voice comes again. Louder, but not sharper. "Are these the ones you wish to select?"

Liana wasn't lying when she said this would focus my magic. The Fuegorra blazes to life on my chest, then flows through me. It covers my arms and legs, extending past my fingertips, beyond the grotto, filling the cave. The crystals around me wish to hold it, amplify it, but it's too much power. The brightness burns my retinas through my eyelids.

"Pull back, Estela," Liana insists.

The lyre string inside of me vibrates back and forth, but doesn't still.

"I can't," I grit out. "The string inside of me moves too fast."

"You *can*. You control yourself. Reach out and grab it. Don't worry about getting hurt."

Gathering every ounce of strength in my body, use my mind to reach toward the magic. When I grasp on, I wobble, and a pain splits through my head. But then... the light starts to fade.

Relief spreads across my skin, cooling the heat from before.

As a child, I would've thought that magic was mostly wielded through one's hands and body. I never knew how I would have to protect my mind. First, I learned to keep unwanted thoughts away from Teo. Then I had to push past destroyed memories and regain the truth.

Now... I learn to control myself.

"Do you think you chose the right cards?" Liana asks, breaking through my thoughts.

My eyes snap open, and I take a deep breath.

"Yes," I say.

Liana shifts, crystals gently hitting together as the fabric rustles.

"The second of the crystal cards you've selected symbolizes loss and hope. Some of the chalices are pouring out their contents, lost to time and the vast space around us. You cannot get them back, but look at those who are still full. You must accept what you've lost, and rejoice in what you have."

The interpretation confuses me, especially since the first name that comes to me is my brother's.

"Mikal is not lost," I say, my voice low and icy as I glare at the woman across from me.

She shakes her head.

"It doesn't need to be a person. Estela, you have just spent a month tortured and humiliated every day. Perhaps you have... lost something."

I press my lips together.

She picks up the next card. "You are in love with your mate. Your future will be blessed with every wish that either of you desires. It is a strong union—one strong enough to take on new challenges."

I swallow. Teo has always been the better half of my soul. It truly was a gift from the gods that I was given him when I wasn't prepared to be anything other than bitter.

Liana's fingers trail over to the last card, pausing.

"The last card speaks of death. Of rotting riches and decomposing power."

"Is that one foretelling Rholker's fall?" I ask, unease curling in my stomach.

Yes. Death suits you, a dark voice whispers from somewhere deep within.

Liana tilts her head to the side.

"It could be..." she trails off, and a new feeling builds in my stomach.

"Could be what?" Sweat is gathering on the insides of my palms.

She takes a deep breath.

"I do not mean to speak doom, but we are planning to do many dangerous things in the next few months. Traversing the sea is not simple—neither is taking down one king, let alone two. The death could be someone else."

I think of the worries that weigh down on me in the moments alone, the crass, bloody words spoken about my people. I think of Melisa's sacrifice and her willingness to return.

What if it is she that will die?

Or you.

Taking a deep breath, my heart races in my chest.

"Melisa will go back to Zlosa to look for ways to free more humans and find out what Rholker is doing. I wish to give her something to part with."

Liana listens intently, then nods, looking around the room at the reds, blues, and greens that twinkle. "What do you think would make an acceptable parting gift?"

I look around me, trying to recognize the names I'd learned before. Citrine, Fuegorra, topaz. Each has its own song. My eyes snag on a few stout pieces of beryl, the crystals that used to be in my bathing pool in my room.

I stand up and walk to the red stone, one that matched the dresses she wore when I first met her and stroke a finger along its surface.

All other songs fade, and deep in my gut, there's the feeling of supreme rightness.

Turning back to Liana, I say, "This. I'd like to give her this."

Liana nods thoughtfully. "Beryl is a beautiful stone. It heals, but it also promotes love. Giving her such a thing could be a mistake when she travels back to her master."

I purse my lips. "But she is wounded deep inside. I feel it the same way I did for my mother. I want her to be safe—I trust that she will not be carried away down incorrect rivers."

Liana smiles. "You have grown so poetic. What a very Enduar way to speak."

I grin, feeling lighter around her for the first time in weeks.

"Yes." It only takes a gentle press of my fingers to loosen the crystal and pull it out of the wall. While rubbing away bits of dirt and debris, my mind wanders back to the blessings that Teo mentioned Liana gave him before he left the caves. The *hlums'dor*.

The wise woman is crouched over, picking up each of the cards that had been laid out for my convenience, I realize. She was waiting for me.

Bless her patience.

"It is time for you to approach the Fuegorra," she says, gesturing to the enormous crystal jutting up from the ground that matches the one in my chest.

I take a deep breath. The last time I did, it gave me a vision of my future—of power. I place the crystal in my pocket and walk over to the small step in front of the gem.

Flickers of red and orange spark as I draw close.

"Hold your hands up as if you were about to touch it," Liana says. "Loosen your shoulders."

I obey each command and wait. Before, it had been instant, and while there is activity, it is not as potent as I once felt. The life force of the Enduares is... complex.

The seconds drag on, and I glance over my shoulder at her.

"Am I doing something wrong?" I ask.

She shakes her head. "No. Your connection is strong, but unpredictable. I need you to look into the ruins of the under-water city to see if you can spot the artifact."

I purse my lips. "I've never done anything like that."

She sighs. "The cards were supposed to help you, but it seems they have just added to the weight on your shoulders."

I can't deny it.

"Try touching the gem again. It shouldn't work, but maybe you just need contact," she says.

I nod and reach out.

As my finger grazes the smooth face of the stone, my own gem glows to life. "This keeps happening. Do you know why it's so bright?"

"Sadly, I do not. Put your other hand on and think of Iravida."

As soon as my other palm connects with Fuegorra, my vision swims with billowing black and silver glimmers. When the cloud of confusion clears, I see a massive city stretching out in all directions at the bottom of a sea. Lights glow and bob through the water, with large glowing apexes positioned in the middle of buildings.

I gasp.

"What do you see?" Liana demands.

It's unnerving to be speaking with her while I see the ruins of an ancient world.

"Iravida—it's beautiful, but why is it so bright?"

No answer, and then, "Push outside of the city—past the castle."

Without moving a single muscle, I picture myself moving forward and shoot ahead like a spear. A part of me knows that I'm underwater, but since I don't feel wetness against my skin, my usual panic doesn't ignite.

When I reach the outskirts of the massive walls, I see black. Not just darkness, but utter blackness.

"I can't see anything—it's too dark," I say. "It feels like there's something down there."

"Something? Like the artifact?" Liana asks.

I wait in the ebbing darkness. The longer I stare into it, it almost feels like it's staring back at me.

"No, just... *something*. Something vast and unknowable."

"Are you all right?"

I nod.

"Good. Then maybe it's best if you release your hold. Just do it carefully."

I nod and then begin to peel my hands away.

The vision fades, and I press a hand to cover the new blinding light that burns my eyes.

"Did I do it right?" I ask.

She smiles and steps forward to put her hand on my shoulder.

"You did it exactly right. Well done." Then she squints. "Gods, why is it so bright?"

I laugh. "The witches—*Brujas*, as slave legend says—called me the Daughter of the Light Weaver."

The wise woman cocks her head to the side and bites her lip piercing. "What does that mean? Is it a title among your people?"

I frown, a little deflated. "No, it isn't. I've never heard of it before. I had hoped you would know."

She looks thoughtful. "We shall study it after we bring your brother home."

A weak smile spreads across my lips, eager to change the subject.

"How do you give a *hlums'dor* blessing?" My gaze travels around the room, and I take a moment to practice pinpointing each crystal's song. My mind clears as the citrine sweeps through my mind, clearing all the thoughts that have been compounding. Beryl seeks to heal the aches in my joints, while amethyst gives me a light feeling.

It is easy to understand why Liana would want to be here

when every inch of the room loves whatever sparks of magic we carry.

"Ah. Excellent question. Is this about the one called Melisa again?"

"Yes," I say.

She smiles. "A blessing isn't nearly so formal as a rite. Tell her what you hope she will find on her journey—safety, peace, rest. Then let your Fuegorra speak to hers. You felt the connection we have with the others during the ceremony."

"She doesn't have one," I say sadly.

"Hmm. You are correct. Then you will need to listen to your Fuegorra to see into her soul."

My eyes grow wide. "How do I do that?"

She looks back at me. "You know how to do it with Teo."

"Yes, but he is my mate," I respond.

She smiles. "Part of being a wise woman is being a seer. There's a good chance that your mother had this gift—perhaps that is what the witches meant when they said she was a light weaver—it's possible she saw that which many simply ignored. Your gifts will let you look into someone's soul, sealing whatever hopes you have upon them. It helps to touch their head."

It doesn't sound exactly right, but my curiosity is piqued, so I turn toward her.

"I would like to practice."

She draws back, looking at me through slitted eyes. "I need no blessings. I care for the Enduar Court."

"How can I practice?"

She waves a hand. "Find Teo."

I shake my head, stepping toward her. "No, I'd like to practice here, with the wise woman who is experienced in such things."

She lets out a long breath. "Very well."

Then she turns to face me with her tall, lanky frame. Every inch of her weathered grace is beautiful against the backdrop of the crystals. She holds out her hands on either side and then lets them fall to the side.

"Give me a blessing, Lady Estela."

I smile and then feel embarrassed. Reaching forward, I touch her shoulder.

"I bless you with..."

My words dry up. Scanning through every hope I'd have for this woman who, in so many ways, has cared for me with a depth I can't ever adequately thank her for.

"With—" I try again, "With rest. With joy. That you will feel the depth of love those around you have."

Her eyes are impenetrable as I look into them, trying to find some sort of confirmation that I was doing this right.

Then I place a hand on her forehead, and a glowing crack appears in her well-protected emotional barrier.

She blinks as I feel the weight of age, duty, and time seep into my soul. No one would look at her and think that she was anything other than fiery and well-lived, but there's a heaviness that sags against me as the connection between us grows. Her eyes see the past and the future with a clarity I don't possess. Even the fragments and pictures the Fuegorra gives her are so... perspicuous.

An air of ancient, sacred weight presses down, lightly accompanied by the screams of a dying people. One of the wraith mother's vast crystal wings unfurls before me. Liana's unbound hair scandalously billows behind her as she holds onto a saddle attached to *drathorinna's* back. Her eyes glow like moonstones as she chants. Then the scales beneath her light up with the same power.

I can't look away—can hardly pull back.

341

When I do, her eyes meet mine, fully aware of everything I felt. She looks down at me, waiting for me to speak.

But the words have run dry.

Every time we train, there is something new that I learn. A miraculous, hidden world revealed to my eyes.

"You rode *drathorinna*. You are... powerful," I say dumbly. An ache starts up in my chest as I think of approaching the wraith. The crystal beast draws me in with her power, and yet she has not asked me to return to her cavern.

Liana smiles.

"Of course I am, child. If you think you are ready to take on my soul, perhaps I have underestimated your powers. We should return to *drathorinna* soon. As you saw, it's been too long since she's ridden into battle."

I suck in a breath. "Really? I should tell you that she called to me when I returned."

Liana cocks her head to the side. "That is a marvelous sign. What did she say?"

"She told me to wait."

Liana smiles and brushes a strand of hair from my face. "Hmm. Then, sadly, you must wait. I apologize for promising a visit I cannot guarantee. Go, run along, and meet me here after. I still need help with the final crystal suit."

"But I have more questions," I protest.

My hand goes to the book in my pocket, and I prepare to pull it out, but she shakes her head, and her white bun glistens in the light.

"Later. I have more to work on."

I let out a disappointed sigh. "Thank you, Mother Liana."

She smiles and waves me off.

I take one more moment to luxuriate in the warm joy inside the cave of crystals, all perfectly attuned to those like me, and then slip out.

The sword training will start soon. The energy flowing through me needs some kind of release. Hopefully, Ulla will be glad to see me.

CHAPTER 30

SHATTUCKITE

TEO

S crolls are sprawled across my desk, along with measuring instruments and the two books that Estela brought from Zlosa. She gave them to me to translate. Currently, Vann sits at my side while I work.

"Fektir is an old man full of demands. First, he wants me to make Aska a queen. Then, we must destroy the Enduares to gain access to their caves and wealth, and finally I shall make my reign the richest dynasty the giants have seen in years. Fektir sees us as the most powerful people in the land and sees me as a vessel for his immortal honor. I don't trust him, but he's the only way I can sustain my crown," I read off.

Vann shakes his head. "He's a fool."

"A dangerous fool who plots for our annihilation," I say darkly.

"I look forward to his death, and I hope it is a fitting end to such an awful beast," Vann says.

I look up from the book and push my glasses further up the bridge of my nose. "Are you still displeased that I didn't bring you with me to see the elves?"

He snorts.

"I don't think my memory is that long." He brushes a scroll filled with my calculations of Iravida's ruins. "However, since you've brought it up, you plan to take me with you to the ocean?"

I grunt.

"And after? Will you be taking me to march on the giants after we find the artifact?"

I narrow my eyes in mock irritation.

"Svanna already spoke with me. She thinks that she and Lothar would be better at protecting the cave for the stretches of time where we will be gone. Not that she didn't enjoy working with you, but she thinks I need the extra support. I tend to agree."

The words are blunt, but Vann smiles.

"I like tending to the cave, but there's something about the possibility of death that puts me more at ease at your side. I don't know if you should be going on this mission."

"If I didn't know better, I'd think you were worried about me while I was gone," I say, nudging his shoulder.

"Immensely," he says without humor. But then I see the tell-tale curl of the corner of his lip. "You and I have fought together since we were children. I half expected you to lose all your instincts without your good luck charm."

"Is that supposed to be you?"

He nods.

"I was there the day that Qa'Velo decided to challenge you at the academy, and at the battle of kings, not to mention the day the volcano spilled over land and swallowed our home whole..." He trails off, remembering such bitter days, but the sadness quickly flashes away. "I was also there the day you found Estela and stole her away."

"Perhaps you do have a certain penchant for saving my life and witnessing my pivotal moments," I say with a laugh.

He raises an eyebrow. "Is that an apology for leaving me behind to visit the elves?"

I scowl at him.

"No. I stand by choosing those companions, and I am glad that you stayed home with... the others." I lean back in my seat, studying Vann's face. He has purple bruises under his eyes that I haven't noticed before. Asking him about Arlet outright has proved fruitless, so I try a different approach. "Did you at least spend time with the court while I was gone?"

He grunts. "Yes. Though, I came here to talk to you about Turalyon's brother. He held a private service without inviting... anyway."

It's clear that I won't get any more about his time in Enduvida while I was absent, so I open up about myself instead.

"It was... difficult to speak to them. It was an accident as he wandered far from the protection of our camp. I shouldn't have brought him, but our choices were limited. He was essential in finding the sisterhood. Lothar was still unconscious from the attack."

Vann nods slowly. "Perhaps you're right. I only wish that I hadn't been confined here without anyone to speak to."

There it is. He kept to himself. While I genuinely believe he was the best defense to keep in the cave, another part of me wanted him to go to Arlet. Perhaps without my watching him, he would seek comfort in her.

Glad to see I was damned wrong.

A few of Estela's thoughts filter over the bond, but I close them off when I realize she wasn't speaking to me, but a small child.

"I saw Arlet and Joso volunteering in the school. She's been teaching the little Enduares the human tongue," I say carefully.

He meets my gaze.

"I know what you're doing. When I say I didn't have anyone to speak with, I didn't mean about *Firelocks*."

"I think you are denying the feelings you have for her, and it is hurting both of you," I say with finality.

He looks at me for a long time, but I can tell that his focus isn't really on my face. He's far in the past.

"Arlet is a good person. She's sweet and kind to every single person in the caves, humans and Enduares alike... Joso is blessed to share his time with her," he says.

I pause.

"I like both of them, but I don't know if I like them together. She was interested in you before he swept her up." A part of me is glad that he is finally sharing with me, so I choose my words carefully.

Vann opens his mouth, and then closes it.

"You are still too angry to admit how you feel about her, aren't you?" I ask.

His eyes darken. "I'm not—"

"Angry? You are. It comes out in everything that you do related to her. Do you not think that your late betrothed would want you to be happy?" I ask.

Vann could easily be a statue. "I came to you to help run your calculations about Iravida, not talk about women."

I let out a mirthless laugh. "I am your brother. Can you fault me for worrying about you?"

"Yes," he says bluntly.

A true laugh flows from my gut to my mouth. When his easy grin fades, a new question pops into my mind.

"What if you are her mate, denying both of you happiness? Is that not selfish?"

He looks thoughtful again, and I'm glad he isn't snarling at me over the insinuation.

"Even if we were, I would never know. My heart..."

Tilting my head to the side, I wait for him to continue.

When he doesn't, I say, "Come now. Your heart is fine."

He gives me a strange look. Something stirs deep in my gut —the same premonition I had before when I was leaving to visit the elves.

"What have you done?"

Vann stands up abruptly.

"Nothing recently," he says with a smirk. "Now, I'm off to work on the hunting schedule with Lothar."

"Vann—" I start, but he brushes out of the library.

I let out a frustrated sigh, only to see Arlet standing in the doorway.

She looks at me with wide eyes.

I push out of my seat.

"Arlet. Hello. Is everything all right?"

She blinks.

"Why were you speaking about me?" she demands.

My tail swishes behind me.

"I—You'd have to ask Vann," I say.

Her mouth tightens. "No, I don't think I will. He wouldn't tell me even if I did."

"How much did you hear?"

"I heard you say that he has been denying his feelings for me," she grits out, her red hair stark against her pale, freckled face.

I press my lips together. "I'm really not the one to speak about this with."

She takes a deep breath and steps further into the light, revealing her intricately woven outfit. One she made, no doubt.

"I came to tell you that Estela was looking for you. But then I heard... Vann." She wrings her hands. "Vann hates me."

I give her a sad smile. "Vann hates many things, but you are not one of them."

Her eyes grow wider, then she turns on her heel and rushes away.

I sit there for a minute, hoping that Vann won't come to pound in my skull.

CHAPTER 31

BOLEITE

TEO

E stela collapses on the bed next to me.

"Fine, I forgive you for not telling me about Melisa sooner," she pants.

The evidence of our lovemaking fills me with pride.

I stroke her cheek. "I'm a simple man. I see my mate sweating with a blade in her hands, and it's time to steal her away. *Again.*"

She lays on her back, her cheeks flushed and her chest heaving, and casts me a long, appreciative glance.

"I was trying to train."

I smile. "You can train with me."

She raises an eyebrow.

"I doubt that, sincerely. You are not a woman—how can you teach me to fight as Svanna or Ayla? Not to mention how much... larger you are than me." She props herself onto one of her pretty forearms, and her breasts glisten the color of polished bronze in the low light as her dark curls stick to her face.

I shamelessly let my eyes pass over her again and again, wanting so desperately to take in every sweet detail of her.

TO IGNITE A FLAME

We haven't been together long enough for such a feeling to end. We belong to each other, and we need to never forget that.

As I stand, her small, brown hand goes to my calf. "Wait."

Every inch of my body freezes at her command.

"Where are you going?" she asks, sheepishly, as if she were shy about her utter power over me.

"The suits are ready. We need to test them soon, so that we might look for the artifact for the elves. I need to check on them again and meet with Thorne. Then we need to glamour Ra'Salore and prepare for his and Melisa's departure."

She worries her lower lip. "Liana and I spent all afternoon together. I have something to tell you."

I sit down again. "What?"

"I made a suit with her and Flova. I had a lot of extra energy after our training. And... it's for me. I want you to take me with you."

"Into the deep sea or the meeting?" I ask.

She takes a deep breath. "Both. I don't want you to leave without me."

"Estela, my star, come with me wherever you wish, but the mission will be dangerous. The sea is... vast. Terrifying. I have never been there before, and we will be seeking out the cursed and ruined city of my people. Even I am a little fearful."

She gives me a look that reminds me of just how stubborn a woman she is. Her eyes are deep flames as she glares straight at me. The Fuegorra in my chest begins to warm in a way that is unrelated to the mating bond as she looks at me and *sees* every part of soul. This is the power of a wise woman.

"I have already seen the underwater city in my vision. I'm ready for this." She doesn't flinch at the danger—she hasn't in a long time.

Her power skims across my skin, causing me to shiver.

Seeing her laying before me, unapologetic, powerful, and rested from our twisting and turning makes my cock stir.

"What exactly did Liana teach you?" My voice comes out much lower than I intend.

She juts out her chin, looking at me with her burning eyes.

"I have been planting with Ulla in the afternoons, and now I'm meeting with Liana in the mornings. Not to mention my time sword fighting in the evenings. I am not weak. You have shown me I am not broken. Take me with you," her voice pours into the room.

The song between us is a rumble of heat and passion and promise. I could no sooner deny her than cut off my left hand.

I draw my knees onto the bed with me, crawling toward her. "Very well, my love."

Her hand travels to my thigh as a smile spreads across her lips, and her eyes drop to the evidence of my stirring blood.

"Very good. Now stay still, and then we will go to look at the suits together."

Slowly, she draws up, crawling into my lap.

"I dream of this feeling," she whispers as she pulls her hands around the back of my neck.

There are no barriers to unwrap and pull apart so I feel the slide of her skin against mine with an acute intensity.

Her mouth goes to the mating mark on my neck.

She kisses once, then bites.

I let out a groan, and she smiles against my skin. "Thank you for letting me go to the sea with you."

Then she pushes onto me with one thrust.

She doesn't wince as I stretch and fill every inch of her. She *moans*. When she pushes back from me, her pupils are dilated enough to darken her entire eyes. Our movements synchronize as she bites her lip and bares her neck to me. I can't help leaning forward and biting her mating mark.

There is no hesitation, not even when I pierce skin once again. The metallic tang of her blood fills my mouth as her fingernails trail down my back, scraping with such sweet intensity.

Her hips tilt forward with more fervor, seeking out her pleasure in a way that I can hardly stand. She doesn't wait for my permission. She uses me as she wishes.

"Take it, my star," I whisper to her ear as she rocks back and forward to a frantic pace.

The Fuegorra's song vibrates her whole body, heightening every sensation as her mouth parts and her head falls back.

I drag my tongue along her collarbone.

"Teo," she pants, breathless.

"Yes," I growl.

"Lay back," she demands, pushing me over.

I obey, and then hitch my hips upwards as she gasps, eyes rolling closed. I impale her as deeply as our bodies can allow, and she welcomes every hard inch with such unbridled passion.

It doesn't take long to finish, and she collapses against me with a sweaty slap.

Instinctively, my hand comes up to brush away the hair from her overheated skin.

"You are so beautiful," I murmur, brushing my knuckles over her shoulders. "I stole you away as a kicking, biting creature, desperately looking to escape. To *kill* me, even, and protect your brother. Your mind was consumed with one thing... and now?"

She looks up at me with her tired eyes. "Now what?"

"Now you are a queen. Rescuing humans, training your magic, strong. Decisive. You come to me without a stitch of shame to take your pleasure which I will happily give. It is... magical."

She blushes hard. "I—"

"No," I cup the sides of her face. "You are mine. You are

powerful—take what you need. I live in awe of every appetite of yours. We will make a marvelous pair... forever."

She swallows. "Forever. You don't fear the future?"

I shake my head. "Fate gave me you. I once feared that you would never be able to stand to look at me... but now, look at you. Our hearts beat in time. We can fell any enemy—rebuild any kingdom. I have you."

Her breath hitches.

"I know. Now get cleaned up. It is time to meet with Thorne and Flova."

She smiles at me, a sight as bright as the sun on my skin, and pushes off.

I watch every curve flex and wobble as she saunters to the bathing room, but I lay back on the bed, looking up at the metal ceiling. My words still ring in my chest and heart, resounding just how truthful they were.

Anything is possible with this woman of mine.

AS WE WALK INTO THE FORGES, FLOVA AND THORNE ARE ALREADY conversing.

Thorne has a sleek rapport with the smith, as he waves his hands all around him. I imagine some story coming to life.

I see his smirk follow his punchline as Flova tips his old head back and laughs. I grimace. I dislike how easily Thorne has charmed so many in our court.

A few of the Faefurt assassins are scattered about as well, inspecting the suits and poking at their flexible crystal surfaces.

They whisper at each other as we approach.

Estela hangs on my arm and says, "Lord Thorne, how nice to see you again."

The white-haired elf pauses and turns to look at us.

TO IGNITE A FLAME

I get half a glance before a warm smile fills his face, and he gives me a deep bow.

"Dear queen," he says to her shoes. "What a delight to see you again, as well." He nods in my direction. "Your Highness."

Estela's warmth leaves my side as she breezes over to the suits.

"Flova, why didn't you show me the others?" she asks in my people's tongue.

His face melts into a smile.

"Melting crystal is hard work, milady. We were busy," he replies conspiratorially, and they start to comb through the details.

Liana and Vann arrive moments later. They both wear frowns as they look at the elves in the group. A part of me wishes to commiserate with them, but I stand my ground in an offering of peace.

"Is everything completed?" Liana asks.

Flova, who was wholly wrapped up in the kind words of my mate, looks up.

He nods. "I am happy to say yes."

Liana smiles. "Very well. When will we test one of these out?"

I cough. "We will be taking Estela with us."

Vann frowns. "We will?"

Liana gives him a withering glance. "Of course they will. Teo, Estela, and... Thorne. Travelers of the sea!"

Vann steps forward, scowling. "I'm hurt you forgot me in your list. The *four* of us will go—who knows what creatures lurk in the ruins of Iravida."

Liana agrees.

"What indeed." Then she clasps her hands behind her back. "My apologies, Lord Vann."

I look at Flova, then back at the suits. "You really have worked miracles with this.

He nods at me, pleased with himself.

Estela smiles. "When will we go?"

Vann shrugs. "Tonight?"

"Tomorrow, after Ra'Sa and Melisa leave for Zlosa. Thorne can perform the test."

The white-haired male laughs and says mockingly,

"Yes, send the enemy so you don't have to peel my body off of some giant urchin." Then Thorne straightens and points to Vann. "I think not. What about that hulking mountain?"

Vann glares but says, "I will do it."

"Don't act like this is deep sea diving. Meet me in the royal pools—it will be easier to test in shallow waters."

Everyone relaxes, but I look back at Estela and feel anything but calm.

I will be fine, she says back to me, with a smile. My heart warms.

Very well, my queen.

CHAPTER 32
ELIAT STONE
ESTELA

Another day passes, and then it's the morning that Melisa is supposed to leave. She and I sit together at one of the larger stone tables in Hammerhead Hall, eating the food I helped prepare. Abi and Paoli are here as well, as are Iryth and Sama. They sit across from Melisa and I while Abi strokes Sama's head.

"He's so... big," Abi says.

Iryth feeds Sama on her breast as she smiles at Abi. She's the only Enduar currently sitting with us, and I appreciate her knowledge.

"He is nearly six months old—it's normal for him to be so large. Fear not for your small body if you are mated to one of our men," she says with a laugh.

Sama punches out his fist, and Paoli picks up the crystal toy that tumbled to the ground. When the silent girl with a hollow face hands it back to Iryth, the Enduar woman glances at Abi.

"This means thank you," Abi says as she puts a flat hand on her lips and moves it forward and slightly down.

Iryth repeats the action, and then asks, "And how would you say it in the human tongue?"

Then the Enduar adjusts Sama's head as he grunts and punches another strong fist. Their conversation is interrupted when Arlet joins us and sits next to Iryth. Then she puts her finger inside Sama's hand.

"*Buenos dias, mi amorcito,*[1]" she coos at the enormous blue babe.

I smile, thinking about the conversations she and I have had about children. Thoughts of having my own family surface, especially after the cards that Liana showed me. There must've been a dream I had last night... Most of the pictures are obscured, but I swear, if I focus, blurry images of a baby flicker behind my eyes.

I crave that life the more time I spend in Teo's arms.

Iryth turns back to Melisa and me, but her eyes stop on the raven-haired beauty next to me, who has put on the red dress she wore when we first arrived.

"We are grateful for you, you know. To choose to leave and return to the giants is something we respect deeply." Iryth's accent is stronger than her mate's, but it is warm and rich with kindness.

Melisa stares at Iryth, visibly uncomfortable. "Thank you," she says. Her shyness is unlike the front she's put up previously.

I wrap my arm around her shoulders and squeeze. "You are very courageous."

"Ra'Sa will take care of you," Arlet says with a smile. My brows furrow as I think of the Enduar once called Salo. At first, Teo told me that he had reverted to his full Enduar name. And now... I glance up at Melisa, knowing that she gave him such a nickname.

From what I can tell, she is pleased with its use, though she flirts with every Enduar the same amount. Everyone in the cave adores her.

It isn't until I hear purposeful steps behind me that we turn and see Thorne, Teo, and Ra'Sa.

I blink at just how good the elves' glamour is.

He looks completely human.

A very tall human, to be sure, but his blue skin is now a rich, umber brown, like the fading golden light that filters through the trees just before sunset. His tail has been hidden in the loose pants cinched around his hips. His long hair is now black, and it hangs in a thick braid.

I frown at such length.

"That's too long. No male would have gone so long without having to cut his hair for tree lice," I say, swinging my legs over the bench.

He narrows his eyes at me. He's never been particularly friendly or open, particularly since his brother died, but he's looking at me like a forest fowl glares at a fox prowling in the bushes, preparing to steal her eggs.

"I am sorry. You need to cut it off," I clarify, and he growls.

"Absolutely not," he replies simply. Firmly.

Melisa stands at my side. "Come now, I think you'd look handsome with short hair."

His blazing eyes land on her.

She smiles and flutters her long, curly lashes at him.

Without another word, he grabs a knife from his waistband, takes his long black rope braid in his hand, and slices off the strands at the base. A blunt sheath of black hair falls to his chin, but it doesn't look unpleasant. It adds to the general ruggedness of his appearance.

Everyone around me stills as they stare at the braid hanging limply in his hand. My throat tightens, and a sad silence tracks the movements with deep intensity. Then the black hair fades back to silver.

While I know that hair has great significance, I don't understand the emotion. I make a note to speak to Teo about it later.

"Once again, I'm sorry, Ra'Sa," I say after a moment.

He straightens his back. "I am already conspicuous because of my height. You were right—it is best to blend in."

"You should place your hair in your home, friend," my mate says, appearing at my side.

Ra'Sa nods and leaves the hall, but Melisa tracks his movements far longer than a casual interest would dictate.

"Men are so easy to bend," she says after a few moments.

I look at her. "You'll behave as the two of you travel together?"

She looks at me. "Me? I have no idea what you mean."

I smirk. "I wouldn't touch him if I were you; you'd eat him alive."

She bites her lip. "No. I won't touch him—he'd never let me anyway. Good men don't want someone like me."

Frowning, I take her by the hand. "First, you must be delirious. Of course they would."

She avoids my gaze and gives me a noncommittal hmm.

I squeeze her hand. "Second, do you have everything you need?"

She blinks as if exiting a daydream. "I—I think so."

I reach into my pocket with my other hand and pull out the red beryl I took from the scrying grotto. Pulling back her fingers, I place it in her palm. "I know you don't feel the songs as strongly yet, as you still don't have your Fuegorra, but this will help you. Sing to it—think of us. Come back soon."

For the first time, I see fear flicker in her eyes. There is a worry there that she hasn't seen before.

"I—" she trails off. I squeeze her hand tighter. "Eneko is going to be furious."

"You'll come home with Ra'Sa. And I'll take you down to the caves to perform the *dual 'moraan*. You'll come home and have a family," I say as if I were invoking the ear of every god in the universe. She would be a fool to think a good man wouldn't want her. She's brave, beautiful, and kind.

Her eyes glisten. I touch my hand to her forehead, begin to murmur the words of safety that I know. She has no Fuegorra to speak to, but she has a friendship that cracks open a window to her deepest soul.

She presses her forehead to me as I see her cry for the first time.

"You know, you don't have to go," I say as Iryth and Arlet come to join the hug.

She shakes her head. "You have your family—I have..." she trails off. "I have my things."

Her answer is strange and guarded, but I hug her anyway.

Iryth's warmth radiates around our circle. "You are brave, Meli. We thank you for what you are willing to do."

Melisa looks up at her, and then her eyes drop to the baby tied to Iryth's chest, squirming as Abi and Paoli wrap their arms around Melisa and squeeze. "You all are too good to be true."

Arlet smiles. "You get used to it."

Looking at the redhead, I say, "You adjusted better than most."

She smiles and squeezes my shoulder as she pulls back. When we turn around, Mother Liana waits for us.

The time has come. I grab Melisa's hand, and I pull her along with the wise women. Simple conversation is made as we walk up to the tunnels.

When we reach the gate leading out of Enduvida, Liana also

offers Melisa a few words of encouragement while we wait for the men to return.

When the very human-looking Ra'Salore walks back up, Melisa tenses.

"These are speaking stones, I have prepared as many as you could take," Liana says, holding out a pouch. "Try to only send the most important information."

Ra'Salore takes the bag and stuffs it into his pack. They won't take any *glacialmaras* because of the risk of discovery.

As we say one last goodbye, my heart hangs heavy. I savor Melisa's wide eyes as she looks back at me.

The giant golden doors shut tight just as Teo's large hand slips into mine. I suck in a breath and look up at him.

"You look like you could use a drink," he says.

I let out a long breath and nod. I don't drink often, but I think this moment calls for it.

He pulls me along, past the golden carvings and faint pump and press of metal in the distance. It is calming and familiar.

When we reach the palace, he grabs something from one of the tables in the royal library. Saying goodbye to Melisa still hangs heavily on my heart as we continue walking in utter silence.

It isn't until I see the faint glow of spongy fungi that I freeze. The royal bathing pools. Their familiar, muggy warmth assaults me as the air around me goes cold.

"Wait," I say just as Teo uncorks the bottle to my left.

"Tomorrow, we will leave in those crystal suits. You, my queen, have insisted on coming. Hell, you even made your own damned suit," he starts, gesturing to the other side of the cavern. I see them, laid out carefully on the other side of the cavern. "I have just finished trying them with Thorne and Vann, and there were no problems. You need to practice, too, but I thought you would appreciate some privacy."

I purse my lips, still hardly breathing as I pick up the clothing-shaped crystal.

"*Mi amor*[2], you wanted to come. Tomorrow, we will be diving underwater for who knows how long—ideally less than three days. I won't take you if you don't feel ready. There is still time to back out."

The thought of water all around me, with just the thickness of the enchanted crystal keeping it out of my mouth and lungs, makes my chest tighten.

Strong arms draw me in, and a tail wraps around my hips, pushing our bodies flush. The instantaneous calming effect is almost unnerving. My heartbeat slows, and my breath comes back.

"Oh, my star, how can we continue like this if you are still having difficulty near a few pools of water?"

I push off of him. "I can do it."

He releases my body and hands me the bottle. "Prove it."

"Do I need to put on one of the suits?" I ask.

He shakes his head. "Not yet. I'll settle for you getting in the water first."

I grab the bottle and take a swig. Wiping the excess mead from my lips, I hand it back, and then clutch at the hem of my tunic. In one swift motion, I pull it over my head. His eyes darken as I push off my pants, leaving nothing more than the silken undergarments around my hips.

There's a moment of power as I look at him, knowing that my almost nudity continues to entrance him whenever he looks upon me.

I kick away the clothes and step into the water before he has a chance to say anything. I make it to my knees and then midthighs before I remember how deep the water is.

You're in control, I remind myself, and then push further until the fabric clings to my hips. It's then that the memory of our wedding night resurfaces—it's not quite ruined, as Teo has shown me what passed between us in these caves time and time again, but it scalds the space behind my eyes.

When the glowing water coats my hands, my memory flickers and repairs itself.

I remember... wonder—delight—in these pools.

I take one of my hands out to see the sparkles moments before I close my eyes and dunk my entire head underwater.

A second later after reemerging, there's a splash that crashes over me, dislodging me from my footing and pushing me deeper.

Teo's tail wraps around me, hugging me close to his chest. I slap against his wet leathers, blinking away glowing sparkles. We are so close.

Glued together. My breath escapes me, and the outside world fades.

"I—"

He cuts me off with a gentle muzzle.

"It's not so bad," I say, realizing that my breath isn't as restricted as before. It fills me with pride.

Then his hand trails down my body, cupping my buttocks, as he holds me impossibly closer.

I gasp.

"I'm sorry—forgive the instinct to pull you out of every dangerous situation," he murmurs.

Sighing, I lean forward to kiss the mating mark on his neck. The rumble that buzzes between us wakes up something I thought I'd never feel in the water again.

The wet tip of his tail trails across my skin—slow, silky, and tantalizing. It isn't until it brushes down the cleft of my ass that I gasp.

It moves lower.

"What are you doing?" I demand, grabbing the length in my hand.

He looks down at me with half-moon eyes and hooks his thumbs into either side of the silky fabric at my hips. "I'm helping you relax." Then he pushes it down off of me. I let the undergarment float down around my ankles and then kick it away.

The thick weight of his tail is pleasant. It's spent hours caressing me, comforting me, and holding me. Its feather-light touch has been delightful, but it isn't until I have it in my hand that I realize I've never really touched it.

Curious, I slowly slide my hand up its suede length. Teo lets out a deep guttural noise in his throat.

It's his turn to inquire.

"What are you doing?" as he places his hand over mine.

His grip loosens as my hand slides back down, and he shudders as I reach its tip. The tuft of fur at the end is covered in glittering water, and the hairs part to reveal a thick, blunt end.

Nothing like the pointed armor tip he wears. This tail has killed and comforted. All for me. I rub a finger over it, and he watches, unamused.

"See something you like?"

Clinging to the warmth spreading through my veins, I rub my finger through the hair. "Is the hair necessary?" I ask.

He furrows his brow. "What?"

I think of how easily Ra'Sa cut off his braid. I would never ask Teo to do something similar... but some fur on a tail...

I reach for his belt, where I know a knife is. "Do you trust me?" I ask.

He watches me with blatant intensity but nods.

Slowly, I shave the hair from the end. His jaw tightens, and I can see words pressing against his lips, waiting to be spoken.

Gathering up my courage and maintaining eye contact, I move the length under the water and brush it between my legs.

"Do Enduares play with their tails when they mate?" I ask.

He is utterly frozen. I rub the now bald end over the sensitive spot at the apex of my thighs and let the frictionless sensation of the water smooth its journey across my skin.

I moan once, enjoying each moment. His hands grip onto my hips bringing me flush against his chest as ragged breaths pump out of him. Then I position the tail at my entrance.

"Do your women even do this?" I ask, breathless.

He doesn't respond. Slowly, I inch the tip of the tail further in. It's not as wide as him, but it still sparks sensations that I feel from my scalp to my toes. He watches me, hungry and enraptured, as I move the tail in and out, letting my head fall back.

"Estela," he growls as he watches me use his tail for exactly what I need. It's torture for him, but it's sweet. He watches with a frustrated awe unmatched by any other emotion.

The next time I thrust him deep, he pushes with me, and the tip curls forward. The acute movement shocks me, and a new type of pressure builds with alarming swiftness.

Stars glow in the cavern as I gasp, and the pressure of his muscles release only to curve right back.

"Teo," I choke as the wave of pressure passes over me with the swiftness of a building crumbling to the ground.

For a second, I black out completely, only roused by my sweet Enduar, holding me close in the water.

"My love," he pants.

Love.

"I love you... That was..."

He growls in my ear. "It was beautiful. You are like a puzzle, one that I wish to spend all my time solving. I will keep my tail shaved from this moment forward if it would bring you such sweet release." He looks down at me, his eyes full of desire. "I only wonder what other marvelous things your sweet body can do."

My heart continues to race in my chest as I nod, boneless. Hopeless.

I open my mouth, but no words come out.

"Shh, sweetness."

I shake my head, swallowing against the pounding of my heart. "No, please. I feel like that was just..."

Slipping my fingers into the waistband of his trousers, I pull them down just enough to graze his cock with the tips of my fingers.

"Don't ask for me out of obligation," he growls, even though he grabs his shirt and pulls it off.

I shake my head. "Believe me—I want this." I guide the head to the pounding between my legs, sighing in relief as he grabs both my wrists and pins them above my head.

My heartbeat thrums through my body as his other hand comes down and circles around my throat.

"You are mine," he growls, pushing in. I feel so filled. Stretched. Impaled. Cared for, and powerful.

Whole.

The world blossoms with new colors with each stroke. Such beautiful pleasure curls my toes and slides over my skin, until finally, he joins me in the bliss. The hunger fades.

The fear is gone.

"I am ready to go to the ocean with you."

He squeezes my backside again. "And we will come back here once we return."

Then he pulls me closer. "Sometimes I wonder if our children will have your beautiful, delicate features or if they will look as I do."

It's so unexpected, and yet... not. The more I see just how much love heals both of us and makes everything as it should be, the more I realize that our future continues in one unstoppable round.

What if the power between us fades? Can we plan for the future with two behemoths of missions looming in the distance?

I study my mate's face.

Later.

He grins down at me. It's such a beautiful sight, and I feel terribly inadequate. He is perfect, without any scars while my body is imperfect with every scar. Not even just scars from lashings and punishments, but the growing marks around my thighs and breasts.

He interrupts my thought. "Are you ready to practice for tomorrow?"

I take a deep breath and look over at the crystal suits that have been left on the side of the pool. "Yes."

Together we walk out of the water, still entirely naked. As he brings up my suit, I look for my clothes.

He strokes my skin. "You don't need them right now. This is just a trial before tomorrow."

As he helps me slide the flexible, clear material onto my skin, I'm happy to find out that it fits like a glove. But then the sound hits.

It's high-pitched and slightly unpleasant. Not so much as to be annoying, but I think it will be a problem.

"You get used to it," he says as he finishes closing the magical clasps.

Then he holds me out and I resist the urge to cover myself. I am fully clothed, and yet fully naked and on display.

He assesses me, pleased, but when I meet his eyes, I see the heat there. I smile weakly at him, and he bends down to get my helmet.

As soon as it is placed firmly on my head, I let out a breath, expecting to feel restricted, but it is not. The sound improves once the ensemble is complete, and I walk stiffly over to the deepest pool.

I step off the edge, sinking down into the glowing water.

As soon as I do, my vision is filled with glimmering particles and the luminescent algae that accumulates at the bottom of the dark pool. I swim down to it, feeling... calm.

I can breathe like normal. I am comfortable.

The water doesn't invade my suit. It doesn't even touch my skin.

I let out a laugh, and somehow a bubble passes through the material. Pushing water through my closed hands, I spin in a circle.

It feels good.

Delighted, I kick back up to the top and burst out of the water. My laugh lights up the area, and Teo, who is now sitting on the edge of the pool, grins at me. He reaches out and takes my hand.

"You seem pleased. Was there any discomfort?"

I shake my head, smiling. "No."

He nods once. "Good. We leave tomorrow."

My stomach knots up at the thought. A warm pool with pretty, glittering things is one adventure, but the cold dark ocean...

You can do this.

CHAPTER 33
YUGAWARALITE
TEO

The parting caves are a sacred place in Enduvida. They create a direct channel between our city and the open ocean. After the Great War five decades ago, we started coming here to send the Enduares to be home with their family members.

There is a set of stone doors left wide open, letting out the sound of a massive waterfall crashing down on stone, drenching the air in a humid mist. This mist is neither dark nor cold like the vaimpír's mist, but it still reminds me of death. Carvings from our ancestors line the walls, illuminated by both spell lights and glowing crystals along the wall.

After an endless day of planning this trip, I could deduce that they would lead us to the deeper ocean, despite no living Enduar knowing their exact course into open water.

While the unknown is uncomfortable, I'm confident everything will work out. It is fortunate that we have a lower entry point to the sea than the beaches outside the mountain—it will save us time.

"Iravida was destroyed, sunken, and moved in the eruption.

It used to be much further out, but the volcano made the plates shift when it destroyed our old home," Liana explains to Thorne as Flova makes final adjustments to his suit's fit. The wise woman then bites the crystal piercing in her lip and smooths her hands over the clear material, tuning the harmony of the suit.

Unlike our fun in the pools, we are all given leather clothing to put under our protective gear. The ocean can be dangerously cold and we need to have a layer of insulation.

Vann is already completely suited up and ready to leave. Estela stands at my side, quiet, but just as fascinated as I am. She continues to talk to Flova, and I walk to the tall companion in the corner.

"Are you ready?" I ask.

Vann nods. "It has to be today?"

The question surprises me; Vann isn't typically one to be so upfront about his reservations or fears. I nod firmly. His eyes travel back to the crashing waters.

The roar fills my ears with such force that it resembles the rhythmic pulse and beat of war drums.

"The test yesterday was perfectly fine. You came back in perfect health. We will be fine—I trust Flova."

"I do too, but I have never spent much time in the water. They told us that we would only have four days under the ocean, but we don't know if that will truly be enough."

"I've spent time calculating—" I start.

"Damn your calculations. Perhaps you shouldn't even go with us. Sending the king and queen into some dark, cavernous hole? Where is the sense in this?"

I frown, remembering what he said to me about going on all these dangerous missions. "There was time to bring up these concerns."

He shakes his head, bitter. "No, there wasn't. We didn't

discuss bringing Estela. You told me just yesterday. Dissuading anyone of this plan was impossible, which is why I volunteered. Someone needs to protect you from yourself, and I am officially extending such a vow to your mate."

My heart contracts. "And I appreciate it."

He shakes me off. "Show me by finding this artifact."

He walks back, away from the channel that spits out into the ocean and follows me to my mate. Liana helps Estela to open and seal each part of the suit, perfectly encapsulating every part of her.

The helmet was designed so that the magic would let her breathe underwater for an extended time. It's shaped like a bell, but the crystal itself slightly exaggerates her features.

I smile at the sweetness of her. Her eyes snap onto me, furious—which only makes me smile wider. As if her beauty could be diminished by a bit of silliness.

Besides, I saw her in the outfit yesterday, free of clothes. I have nothing but fondness for the creation.

"Put your suit on," she chides. The rose quartz placed around the helmet amplifies the sound of her voice, filling the entire cavern.

It takes a few mere moments to reach past her, pick up the hefty thing, and start to assemble it on my person. Thorne slings the pack over his shoulder, uncharacteristically quiet.

"Will anyone come to see us off?"

Vann grunts. "No."

"No? Why not? You people celebrate everything, from a babe eating its first solid food to miners bringing back a new crystal," he rants.

I shrug. "They will celebrate our return. If we are successful, it won't be long before we march on Rholker. Removing him from the throne is still our number one concern, after returning what my father stole. I told them it was better to stay underground, either training or preparing supplies."

He lets out a long breath but says nothing more.

"Remember, you can only open the bell to eat and drink for a handful of moments. The magic isn't strong enough without a seal from the crystals, and you could lose air," Flova says gruffly.

Vann and I pick up another pack. The only person who will carry nothing is my mate—as is only right. She should be able to focus solely on following her visions to the artifact's location.

We walk through the Cave of Sorrows, and it brings back memories of every member of my court who has passed on to the next life. I walk, head high, full of purpose.

It isn't until we reach the crashing waterfall that will lead us down that I pause.

Liana nods to us, raising her hand high and speaking the oldest tongue. The Fuegorras on our chest light up, turning the clear crystal red, save Thorne. He curses again and says, "I'll go first."

Then he reaches the spot and lets himself go. His form disappears in a few seconds, and Vann follows. Holding the hand of my mate, I guide her forward and let her go next. As I step into the water, it eagerly embraces me, pulling me under with a powerful surge that propels me into a collision with the rocky edge. Swirls of bubbles, shimmering lights, and intricate cracks whiz by in a mesmerizing dance too swift for my eyes to capture fully. The underwater world reveals itself not as a realm of darkness but as one filled with a profound sense of weightlessness and an unseen presence that nudges my consciousness.

The intense pressure suddenly dissipates as I am forcefully expelled into the vast expanse of open water. A soft radiance emanates from the crystal suit adorning my body, casting a gentle glow around me. In this luminous space, I realize that I am not alone in emitting light. A symphony of bioluminescent creatures flickers and dances around me in a breathtaking display of underwater magic.

"Estela," I call to the smallest glowing suit, one that I swear is a little brighter than all the rest. The sound shoots through the water, and she swims over to me, close enough that I can watch her take in the beauty around us.

Beneath us, the ocean floor is strewn with fragments of ancient stone abodes, scattered like forgotten dreams on the seabed. I had anticipated that the relentless currents would have shifted Iravida's resting place, a deduction that now unfolds before my eyes in silent confirmation. The underwater world is a mesmerizing display of vibrant life—iridescent fish darting through swaying seaweed forests, delicate algae painting the rocks in hues unseen by daylight, and ethereal anemones dancing to an unseen melody. The sheer brilliance of this hidden realm overwhelms my senses, each detail more enchanting than I could have ever imagined.

Estela's gaze mirrors my own astonishment as she hungrily absorbs every facet of this submerged landscape. I can't help but ponder what this underwater paradise might have looked like in its prime, devoid of the haunting remnants of the Enduares' shattered dwellings that once echoed with laughter and love.

It's one thing to calculate, and another to see it with my own eyes.

"It is... beautiful," she breathes, her voice distorted with the ocean. The quartz not only inhances the volume, but it seemingly absorbs each word. They buzz along with the uncomfortable high-pitched noise of the suit. "Just as I saw in my vision."

I bite my tongue as a long ago memory haunting me for the last month flickers.

The skin of my hands tears on the stone, and I pant as I look at Iravida. It's a sea of red and orange, and the mountain we had existed

peacefully next to has rivulets of lava flowing down at an eerily fast
pace. The ash-filled air whips around me while sparks of lightning
glimmer over the mouth of the mount.

I feel fear, pain, and grief. So much loss. So much heat.

Hands extended, I rush forward, ready to push.

I blink away the memories again, sweating inside the crystal. It's been so long since I thought of that moment... it feels like it's been locked away.

This underwater city is a mass grave.

But ghosts need not haunt Estela, too. I take her hand and pull her forward.

"What are we looking for?" Thorne says.

"The royal palace." My father must've kept the stone somewhere near his chambers. I never went into one of his vaults; he was the only one allowed in.

"And is that ungodly large building with glowing red fire the palace?" Thorne continues, breath lightly fogging his helmet.

I follow his direction, and see the pulsing red. I blink.

That's not a palace.

"I saw that, too. Isn't that an Ardorflame?" Estela asks.

"It looks like it, my lady," Vann says, his arms slicing the water with precision as he powered through each stroke. The red magic emits contorted streaks that don't match the water.

The cold seeps into my suit, and I shiver. I can only imagine what my little wife must feel. Tugging her hand, we push on, slicing through the water as fast as it will allow us. As soon as we draw close, something darts in front of us, causing thick bubbles to form and push us out of the way. The force of the movement takes Estela away from me.

"Estela!" I call. Immediately, I dive toward her as she propels away. Her scream breaks through the water as she grasps at her neck, kicking out her legs. Before I have a chance to reach her, she kicks backward, and whatever is holding her captive quickly releases her.

I swim past her, prepared to slice whatever creature dares to come near my queen, only to stop in my tracks as I see a blue tail flick to the side, propelling them further.

A steely black crystal suit comes clearer into view. Shock reverberates through my soul. I push toward Estela, now having a clearer view of the body. Two arms, two legs, and old Enduar armor.

"Stop!" I call out.

In response, a sea-worn sword riddled with holes slices through the water. I recognize the style of the blade and the tarnished golden hilt. *This is one of my people.*

"We are Enduares!" I call out in my language, careful to enunciate each word with painstaking clarity.

The sword's sharp edge freezes mid-swing, a glint of bioluminescent light bouncing off its jagged, holey surface as the Enduar approaches. His towering figure looms closer. The intricate details of his armor catch the eye, each piece crafted with a level of sophistication surpassing our own suits.

The crystal is more clouded than ours, just barely hinting at his ragged, muscled physique and deteriorating clothes. My mind races as I gaze out at a lost member of my people. Is he alone? How has he survived down here this long?

"You are Enduar?" he repeats, his helmeted head turning toward Estela and then returning to me. "You speak my tongue, yet I do not recognize this figure."

He releases Estela, and I grab her crystal suit, pulling her closer. "I am King Ma'Teo, son of Teo'Likh and your former crown prince."

The Enduar continues to point his sword toward me but doesn't move much further than that. I hold out my hands, but Vann and Thorne flank my sides, weapons drawn.

"You are a troll?" Vann calls out.

The Enduar nods his helmet, tail moving behind him to help him tread in one place.

"Where do you come from?" the Enduar calls.

As I look at him, I feel the tension fill the water.

"We come from Enduvida in search of the palace ruins," I respond. "Are their others with you?"

The man ignores me.

"You travel with many different... creatures," he says, pointing the tip of his blade at Thorne and Estela.

The attitude is old—as old as the civilization we once lived in. The mistrust of others is familiar, like my father's backhand.

"You even bring an enemy into our midst," he says.

"That elf is no enemy," I say, though I am not sure I fully believe it. It would take too much to explain, so I try a new question. "Do you live down here?"

The Enduar pulls back gracefully in the water as a large fish with a body as wide as a bear comes before him. It glows insistently in the inky water with brilliant blue and green dots of light that highlight the pattern of its body and fins.

"Come," the Enduar commands.

I can hardly believe what I see, but the fish carries him quickly. I grab onto a fin and hold Estela in my arm.

As we cut through the water, my mind races with more questions than there will be time to answer.

He brings us to the red light with surprising speed, and then he dips toward what I now recognize as a large bubble.

He stops the enormous creature and then leads us forward. We head to the floor, and then he pulls us in.

Air and gravity resume as water slides off our frosted suits. I peel back the helmet, walking forward with purpose, only to see not one, not two—but dozens of Enduares around us. All men. They look at us with hateful glares, and I keep my mate tucked close to my shoulder when their cruel silver eyes trail to her.

What the hell is happening? Estela asks in her mind. *How did all these men get here?*

I don't know, I say, following behind the warrior. The man before us is no hunter. His eyes speak of war—of domination and bloodthirst.

Of shameless conquest.

It is like stepping into the past and twisting it to the tune of death.

He doesn't turn to look at us as he guides me past all the sets of judgmental eyes. We walk in silence until we approach the Ardorflame. It is smaller than the temple in Enduvida, but it pulses with the same gods-gifted magic.

Standing before the rich, pulsing light, is another Enduar with a missing ear. His hair is cut short, like Thorne's, and his shoulders are broader than any Enduar I've ever seen. The rugged cuts of him remind me of my father's legacy as he turns to glare up.

I freeze in place when his eyes meet mine. One of his eyeballs is replaced with a crystal orb that studies us with the same intensity as his good eye.

I know him.

Our guide salutes his leader who doesn't acknowledge him in return.

"Tir'Suel," the Enduar who brought us calls out. "I have found some of our kind in the open waters. They request an audience."

The leader's name brings forth dozens of memories from my old life.

This is the head of one of my father's private battalions. There were ten in total, each containing a thousand highly trained soldiers. Most were men, but women fought for him as well. As I glance around the room, I see no sign of female Enduares.

"Fuck me. Prince Ma'Teo," Tir'Suel sneers in our native tongue.

I can practically hear Vann's teeth grinding, and I wonder if he has made the same connection I have.

"Tir'Suel. Leader of the ninth royal battalion," I say, refusing to lower my chin in his presence.

"I thought you were dead," he says flatly, seconds before his eyes drop to my side. Tir'Suel's gaze lingers on Estela, his eyes narrowing as he takes in her radiant form encased in the shimmering crystal suit. A flicker of anger passes through his steely facade, quickly masked by a veil of indifference.

It was a mistake to bring her. I place my hand on my hip, where the sword is attached with a special sheath.

"I didn't know that anyone else was spared after the eruption. I have been living in what's left of Enduvida with the other survivors," I say, my voice tinged with trepidation and lingering sorrow. "I would've come sooner if I had known that it was even possible to survive this long down here."

Tir'Suel's sharp features are etched in a permanent scowl, his eyes betraying a deep-rooted bitterness.

"So you live in the summer city?" he asks, his tone dripping with disdain that stirs a pang of defensiveness within me.

"Yes. It was the only place we had left," I respond, frustrated by his callous judgment.

His lip curls contemptuously, and his words cut like knives, "Cowards. All of you. You should be dead on the ocean floor, like those that surround us now."

"Enough! I do not wish to fight." I take a deep breath to steady myself and try again, determination fueling my words. "We seek passage to the royal palace," I declare firmly, my voice echoing with unwavering resolve through the damp bubble that encases us.

"The palace is no longer a sanctuary for you," Tir'Suel proclaims with venom dripping from each syllable, sending shivers down my spine and igniting a spark of defiance within me.

Vann steps closer toward me, his hand instinctively tightening around his weapon as tension crackles in the air between us. Tir'Suel has the audacity to laugh—a chilling sound that echoes through the desolate ruins around us, stirring up a whirlwind of conflicting emotions within me.

"What do you intend to do with that? You both are no better than pups sucking on your mother's teat. Do you think, prince, that I don't see the marking on your neck? I see the female cowering at your shoulder. You have mated outside of your people, refused to die with honor, and now, after all this time, you come here. Why, sniveling little rat?" He spews his words like poison.

My blood begins to pump hotter and heavier. "I will not be spoken to this way."

"No? Well, where have you been for the last five decades while we rotted away down here—protecting your legacy and watching over our people's graves?" he bites back.

I stand up. "I didn't ask you to do this. In fact, I've come—"

"You wouldn't have made such a great sacrifice! Look at you, you are weak, crawling around in a castle gifted to you while we die and wither down here."

His words reverberate through my mind like a haunting melody, reminiscent of my father's stern voice that has lingered with me for an eternity—a voice I have struggled to silence. The sacrifices I've made, trading my time, health, and even the very vessel of my being for the Enduares, now weigh heavy on me.

"What if I agreed to take you to the surface?" I try one last time.

He shakes his head. "I would rather die down here with my people than go to that disgusting city."

Help me undo the straps, I say through the bond to Estela. It takes mere moments for us to peel off the crystal.

"You romanticize death as if it's the only noble path. But you're oblivious to the anguish of enduring life," I call out to him, grasping my blade tightly, its familiar weight a comfort from days long past when I trained alongside the soldiers in my father's regiment. The air crackles with tension as I raise the sword, a silent challenge hanging between us. Engaging in combat, a brutal dance where respect is earned through bloodshed—this is the only language Tir'Suel understands.

"If you insist on speaking in the language of violence, then draw your weapon," I say, my voice low and threatening.

He looks at me and laughs. "I will look forward to seeing you fall on your ass."

"I will not fall. But you might," I say.

Teo, Estela protests. *Be careful.*

I must do this.

That response is met with silence, though her fear is potent. It's bitter on my tongue.

The water surges relentlessly against the shimmering protective shield enveloping the compound. Through the translucent barrier, colorful fish dart past. The echoes of imaginary screams reverberate in my mind, refusing to fade as I locked eyes with Tir'Suel, his presence, unfortunately, real.

In one swift motion, Tir'Suel dons a ragged tunic over his bare chest and seizes the weapon lying at his feet. His gaze hardens as he swiftly aims it towards me, his stance poised and ready for combat. With legs planted firmly apart and arms extended in a commanding gesture, he braces himself for the impending confrontation. Reacting instinctively, I shove Estela behind me, stealing a glimpse of Thorne ushering her to safety amidst the escalating tension.

I begrudgingly make a note to thank the half-elf.

"You have made a mistake coming here," he threatens before lunging at me. I narrowly jump out of the way. "You will do your duty to your people and die a noble death at my hand."

His blade slices towards me again, but this time, I parry. The force of the impact throws his weapon back. He growls and readjusts his position.

"You. Will. Die." He swings around, dealing me three sweeping blows with staggering precision. I am forced back across the slick ground, and my feet slide. "When you see your father in the afterlife, tell him of the warrior who killed you. That it was I, Tir'Suel, captain of his one thousand mightiest soldiers who avenged him by massacring his frail, sniveling son."

I block another of his blows, and the smell of fish and deep salt water fills my nose, mixing with the spark of metal. "Even if you were to kill me, I doubt I will ever see him again—tyrants are not beloved by our gods."

He scoffs, and I use the opportunity to thrust at his unguarded stomach, using the weight of my tail and arms to give power to my swiping blow.

It clips into his skin, but he jumps back before I can cut deep. A small red stain spreads on the salt-stained fabric.

"Perhaps not," he grits out as the blade comes down against me again and again. "But they will condemn someone for diluting their royal blood."

He launches at me again, a flurry of calculated strikes aiming to break my defenses. Despite my efforts to shield myself, one blow breaches my guard, slicing into my shoulder with a sickening sound.

"Shit," I curse, summoning a surge of determination to push him back. "You are blinded by your narrow beliefs if you think the gods concern themselves with such trivial matters. Your ignorance will be your downfall."

Echoes of my father's disapproving voice taunt me, questioning my resolve and foresight. Defiantly, I rebuke his words, asserting my commitment to safeguarding my family and securing a future for my people rather than heedlessly endangering them.

With renewed vigor, each strike I deliver carries a weighty purpose.

"Seems like you retained some lessons from the academy," he remarks between gasps for breath as I deflect his blade with precision. Seizing an opening, I swiftly pivot and swipe my tail toward his feet, disrupting his balance.

As he stumbles and hits the ground, wasting no time, I drive the sword into his heart.

"Fuck..." A wet gurgle punctuates his final moments.

Exhaling heavily, I glance back at Thorne and Estela. Her expression betrays shock as she gazes upon the lifeless figure before her. My Fuegorra has already begun healing the wound, but I shift my shoulders as the prickling, hot discomfort sears the open cut.

"What was he saying?" she inquires, despite her familiarity with Enduar language nuances. The ancient dialect may not pose significant barriers, yet I choose not to repeat his derogatory remarks about her heritage.

"It is of no consequence; he lies silenced now." Lifting my sword overhead, I pivot around the watching Enduares who observe me intently like vigilant hawks. As I look back at the men waiting for me to address the group, I try to memorize each face.

There are so many of them. I feel a thick emotion coil in my chest wrapping itself up like a rope. Two hundred and seventy-nine Enduares exist in Enduvida. There are nearly a hundred standing before me with a few more trickling in.

More of my people live. A peculiar kind of hope is starting to bubble up.

Many more, mi vida[1]. *Though, they don't look as friendly as those who live with us now,* Estela whispers.

The Enduar who brought us here from the ocean emerges from the sidelines, his presence commanding attention.

"Tir'Suel lies dead by your hand," he declares in a voice that resonates with authority, casting a regretful gaze at the crimson pool seeping from the fallen general.

Without hesitation, I raise my sword defiantly. "So he is! He chose death over freedom from this underwater prison."

I look around at the Enduares who have started to congregate. Without their crystal suits, all that is left is haggard clothing.

"Will any of you challenge me for the ability to lead you?" Anticipating a clash of steel and wills, I brace myself for opposition, but to my surprise, no one steps forward. Instead, the leader of our escort drops to one knee before me, offering up his sword in a symbolic gesture of allegiance.

"You plan to take us to the surface?" one says.

Something stirs in my gut as I think of Tir'Suel's hateful words. Any of these men could believe just as he did, and there isn't much time to craft an answer. "Tell me, if returning to the surface is what you long for, why have you not left yet?"

"What the fuck is going on?" a voice growls. A tall Enduar emerges from one of the huts, leaning heavily on a gnarled cane. He is the same age as me, but his scarred face tells tales of battle, and his limp speaks volumes of sacrifices made in service to his cause.

He isn't familiar to me, but the power pulsing in his exposed

Fuegorra tells me all I need to know. Not quite what a wise woman is, but a... stone bender of significant power. Moreso even than Ra'Salore. I watch the stones shift beneath him to make his way more manageable.

As soon as he looks at me, he stills. "You've got to be shitting me. Gods, you look so much like him."

"My name is Ma'Teo, King of the Trolls. I have just bested your leader in a fight to the death, and now I would claim control of this battalion."

The man stands there, eyes flicking between our motley group and the bloody body on the ground.

My whole body tenses when he doesn't respond. I feel Estela return my side. "I have just asked your people why you don't return to the surface."

He grimaces and jerks his head to Tir'Suel's lifeless form. "We all swore a blood oath to Teo'Likh that we would guard his secrets to the death. Some of us have tried to leave." He waves a scarred hand. "If Suel caught someone trying to leave, he'd feed them to the sharks. If they tried to leave by themselves... Well, long story short—they're all dead."

He takes two more steps forward. "How did you get here?"

I swallow. "We live in old Enduvida. It is not far from here—there is a channel in the ground that put us directly over the ruins."

The crippled Enduar's mouth falls open. "That close?"

I nod. "What is your name, Soldier?"

He chews on his cheek. "I am called Si'Kirin, the animator of stone."

The men around the enclosure are quiet, hanging on every word.

"Si'Kirin, would you accept my leadership?" I press.

"You intend to relieve us of our blood oath to your father and let us return to the surface?"

"I do," I start. "But it comes at a price."

Angry words break out all around us.

"What kind of price?" the Enduar who brought us in out of the water demands.

"Same question as Ner'Feon," Si'Kirin calls.

Ner'Feon steps forward.

I draw in a deep breath. "There are less than three hundred Enduares left. We are at the beginning of a new war. We have come to retrieve an artifact my father stole from the elves to secure their allyship. If we were to bring you to the surface, you would be expected to fight."

The men look around, murmuring. Another stands next to Si'Kirin and Ner'Feon.

"My name is Ka'Prinn. As you may have guessed, no women live with us. Tell me of your strange consort."

I grit my teeth, and a surge of protectiveness bubbles inside me. "This woman is my wife and your queen—she is not strange."

"How did you come to mate with a human?" someone calls.

"We are dying out."

"Would we be able to mate with humans as well?" Ka'Prinn asks.

"It is no different than before. Yes, but there must be a mating song."

Ner'Feon strides forward, stopping a few paces before Estela and me. Vann also draws near, the blade glinting in hand, but the Enduar pays him no heed.

I stare at the Ner'Feon with an icy look, waiting for him to speak.

"You have bested our leader," he says. "You are the rightful heir to the throne, and you have offered us a way out if we help you retrieve some treasure from the ruins and fight in a battle we know nothing about."

"That is correct," I say with a nod.

"It is a hefty fee."

"You don't seem to have much choice," Vann chimes in.

Ner'Feon doesn't even bother to look at him. "Will you swear a new blood oath to us, promising all that?"

I search his deep blue eyes and take a moment to ponder his question. The gravity of the situation weighs heavily on my shoulders.

I think it is a good choice, mi amor.[2]

What if they hurt the humans?

A phantom hand brushes over my mind. *We can keep them separate for a time—you yourself have asked them to fight for us. You aren't the kind of man to leave your people down here to rot.*

She's right, for better or worse. It isn't like they would immediately integrate into our people. They would need to survive yet another battle to kill the giant king.

With the decision made, another spark of warmth lights up in my chest. Our city will grow yet again. A part of me hopes it will continue to multiply until we fill the city once meant for a hundred thousand people.

"I will swear the oath," I say at last.

Ner'Feon looks pleased and bends his knee, placing his hand over his heart in sign of fealty. "Then I accept you as our king."

All the others follow suit, some with more reservation than others. Si'Kirin eases himself down with the power of his stone bending and gives me an approving nod.

Vann appears at my side, pressing a knife into my hand. I look up at him, and he gives me a nod.

"I support your choice," he murmurs as I hold the blade in my handle. He knows better than most the value of good soldiers.

I drag the sharp edge over my hand with every eye on me. I ignore the sting and let the blood pool before the Fuegorra can heal the wound. Then I hold my hand out, drawing on my powers.

The ground rumbles, and a column of stone appears before me. I let the drops of blood spill atop it.

"With Grutabela and Endu as my witnesses, I swear that I will bring you all out of the water and return you to our people's caves. In return, you will all be loyal to me and your queen. You will take us to find the artifact and fight alongside my army."

Ner'Feon watches the blood seal our contract with a strange ferocity, then hits his chest once and starts to chant in the old language. The Fuegorra on their chests light up as the others join in, hitting their chests and bowing their heads in time with the beat.

The sound grows louder and louder. Estela slips her hand into mine, gazing upon the men as they swear their fealty. When the volume reaches its highest point, the chanting cuts off.

An eerie silence follows.

I feel a mix of relief and anticipation. The Fuegorras glow brighter in the dim light, illuminating the faces of my newfound allies.

"Our time draws short. Tell me, does anyone know of the Elvish Artifact?" I call out.

The ground shifts, and Si'Kirin stands. He flashes me a smile. "Do you mean the *Cumhacht na Cruinne*?"

Thorne, who has been a silent onlooker, steps forward. "Yes. That is what we seek."

He smirks. "It was my job to tend to the artifact from time to time. I haven't checked on it in months. Not since this." He gestures to his twisted leg.

"Were you attacked?" I ask.

"As I am sure you've seen, there are a great many creatures in the sea. Not all love us trolls."

"But, how far away is this artifact?" Vann interjects, concern etching his usually stoic features.

He purses his lips. "Come, My King, it is nearly what you might consider nighttime. I am sure you are all tired. Rest—eat —while I explain."

We are guided back to a set of tables, where filets of fish and small squids are roasting over a bubbling pocket of lava near the temple. It is nothing short of miraculous to see something so hot exist in a place deep into the world's hidden places.

"Sit," the man says as he hobbles over to tend to the food. I try not to look back at the group of men who have followed us. Among them is Ka'Prinn, who watches Estela with eyeballs so wide that they look as though they might fall right out of his face.

I growl at him when he gets close to her. "Touch her, and I'll slice your tail right off," I threaten in Enduar. "Get out of here."

He turns back to me, bows, and then leaves.

"Why do you want the artifact?" Si'Kirin asks.

"I will give it back to the elves," I say without hesitation.

The man purses his lips, considering my words. "Are you sure that is a good idea?"

"Perhaps it wasn't so wise to steal it from its owners in the first place," Thorne hisses, no longer silent.

Si'Kirin fixes him with a hard stare penetrative enough to cut through crystal. "It wasn't stolen entirely—it was given. And your king hungered for power just as much as Teo'Lihk. You would be a fool to think otherwise."

Thorne doesn't respond, which I find odd, considering he has consistently corrected others about his affiliation to the elven throne. The degrees of separation between the sisterhood and the royal court aren't wide, but they are significant—to him, at least.

"Something tells me it was destroyed in that damned

volcano. Is that why you feed us stinking fish and pacify us with your old words?" Thorne spits.

Si'Kirin tilts his head to the side. "The artifact wasn't destroyed in the eruption, thank the gods, but it did... sink. It is beyond the city, in the depths of the cavern. It used to take me nearly a day to check on its evergreen glow. It has been a few years since I have gone to look at it."

Thorne looks like he'd slice the man's throat open. "Then how do you know it is still there?"

He looks unamused. "This ocean is large and hard to navigate. There is more water than land in this world. If someone had come to claim it, I would know. It has a way of making its presence known. "

Thorne insists. "When you say you tended to it, that means... what?"

"After the eruption, the underground vault where it was stored was cracked. We found it had sunken deep into a crevasse. It was nearly impossible to get close to it, but, like I said, you can feel it. You will know for yourself when you go for it," Si'Kirin says.

Estela lets out a scared little yelp from my side, and I turn to find one of the Enduares dropping her braid.

The braid that I wove this morning.

I see red, grabbing another Enduar's hand and slamming it into one of the stones above his head. "What the hell do you think you are doing?"

His eyes are wide, more shocked than in pain. "Her hair... It is not like an Enduar's. I wanted to see if it was soft like our females, if this is what we are meant to mate with."

I grit my teeth. "Don't ever touch my queen again. And if you speak like that in front of the humans, I doubt even your mate would want to touch you."

The man nods once, fear in his eyes. I soften. I detect no

malice inside of him, merely a curiosity that might be explained by fifty years separated from any female. Duty can do much to warm one's soul, but the inhabitants of this bubble don't seem particularly friendly toward each other.

I can see it in how they walk as individuals, hardly speaking. After the war, everyone in Enduvida was quiet and distant. I can extend an inch of grace to them as they see Estela for the first time.

"This is your last warning: don't touch my wife," I command again, punctuating each word with as much power as I possibly can. Her hand finds mine, and I bring it to my mouth to plant a soft kiss.

He watches the movement and then nods, rubbing his wrist as I step back. I turn to Si'Kirin. "One of you will take us to this spot after we are finished resting."

Si'Kirin, who has been watching the exchange closely, nods. "It will be done. You can stay in Tir'Suel's old room."

I nod and then return to Estela. "Are you well?"

She looks at me with her deep brown eyes and smiles. "Yes. Thank you—*te amo*.[3]"

Those words change everything. They remind me that we can do this.

CHAPTER 34
OSMIUM
ESTELA

The morning isn't kind to me. My arms and legs burn with weariness from swimming, and my head still rings with the dull screech of my suit. It did not take us long to be brought to this bubble, but water is heavy in a way that is hard to describe.

When Teo shook me awake, I didn't want to open my eyes. I wished to stay in the embrace of dreams a little longer.

It was a good dream, the kind that makes one cry a little when they open their eyes and realize it wasn't true.

It was of...

I bolt upright, blinking furiously. My hand flattens against my stomach.

It was of me, belly swollen with Teo's child.

Disoriented, I look around the hut devoid of color and all furniture save a bed. Then I see my mate watching me with an alarmed expression. To see the tenderness in his eyes pierces straight through my heart.

I think of when I caught him holding Sama, speaking sweet nothings to Iryth's adopted son. My heart clenches.

His large hands reach forward to cup my cheeks, and they dwarf my skin.

"Estela, my heart, what is wrong?"

I open my mouth, but no sound comes out. My eyes trail to the damp hut around us, and I inhale a deep breath of salty air. How can I tell him I dreamed of our child when we are in the middle of the ocean?

Closing my mouth, I lean into his hand, and put on a weak smile. "Nothing. I was merely surprised to wake up here."

He smirks, clearly amused. "It is not a place I would return to."

We share a laugh, and then he helps me dress and fix my hair. With weary resignation, we pull back on our crystal suits. Teo's was broken in the fight, so they gave him Tir'Suel's old suit. It is dark and menacing, but it fits him well.

As we leave the small dwelling, I take in the sights of this place once again. Everything is water-stained and damp, and the inky world outside of this is hard to make out, save the glowing speckles of light floating through the water. A few fish swim close enough to show off their glowing scales, but the rest of the light and depth is no more than a blur. Enduares can see in the dark quite well, but my eyesight is still painfully human in comparison.

To me, it looks as though we are stationed in the middle of a sea of stars.

We meet back up with Si'Kirin, and everyone is silent as they watch us approach the edge of the magical bubble. While the others talk, I raise my hand and put it against the thin barrier between dome and sea.

My arm passes through with little resistance, and I wonder what magic could sustain such a way of living for so long.

"What do you make of this place?" Thorne asks, coming to my side.

I look up at him. "I think it is a miracle."

He huffs a laugh. "I am sure that it is a relief to know that there are more than three hundred of your people left, but I don't know if I would like to invite these men into my home."

I bite my lower lip. "Looking into an ancient society is hard enough to fathom, but these people are only fifty years separated from the Enduares I love so dearly."

He huffs a laugh. "You really do love the trolls, don't you?"

I look at him. "Before I met them, all I knew were stories of ruthlessness. The giants told us slaves that the Enduares ate humans—that they would violate us and throw us into their enormous fires. All of that stemmed from lies that started after the Great War. Their old king destroyed the continent, but I think they have proven that that false version of themselves doesn't exist."

His eyebrows rise. "Perhaps in Enduvida. But does that mean you will take these other... Enduar soldiers into your city? They don't even call themselves by such a name, they keep referring to themselves as trolls. They are direct and loyal to violent displays."

I look at the men speaking with Teo. Bits of the people I know in Enduvida peer back at me—their strength and ingenuity. Not to mention their intense neatness and organization. A part of me also knows that this solitary bubble at the bottom of the ocean has preserved some of their cruel, bigoted old ways.

"I trust them... I think," I say at last. My eyes flick back up to Thorne. Logically, I know that he is here with Mrath, but there's something about him that makes me feel at ease. I don't see him as a threat like some of the others. "When I came to Enduvida, I tried to poison Teo. I believed the things I was told, and I changed."

"So you believe that they will adjust as well?" He gives me a skeptical look. "These men aren't harmless."

"I wasn't either."

Thorne accepts my answer and is silent as I join my husband. Teo senses me without turning, his arm drawing me close as soon as I approach.

"*Mi amor*,[1] these men will take us to the spot Si'Kirin spoke of," Teo says.

I nod as Ner'Feon and Ka'Prinn come into view. "Thank you for helping us."

The men bow deeply, and the taller one says, "We are ready to leave when you are."

It turns out we are ready to leave quite soon after that question is asked. We walk back to the edge of the bubble that I was playing with, and one by one, we push into the water.

Swimming away from the Ardorflame, a sense of unease creeps through me, seeping into the depths of my soul. The underwater world around us is aglow with ethereal plants and creatures that dart past in a mesmerizing display.

Dozens of pillowy creatures radiating a soft pink hue ascend to our left, their movements fluid and hypnotic. Sadly, their luminescence offers little guidance in the dark expanse.

Jellyfish, Teo supplies. *Careful. Sometimes their tentacles are poisonous.*

My head snaps forward, inching closer to the fish that guides us along. The curiosity fades as other small lights blink around us. They no longer mystify me, they represent potential dangers.

Time drifts by slowly in the hushed aquatic realm. It's impossible to discern how many hours have slipped away since we departed from the temple towards this vast, cavernous ruin; it could have easily consumed most of the day. Midway through our journey, an enormous fish illuminated in green-yellow hues glides near us. It's similar to the creature that took us from the ruins to the temple yesterday, and Ner'Feon turns back to us.

"This is a *hlum'cranok*. Grab on when it gets close!" he exclaims.

My eyes fix on the fish as it moves closer. Then, with one last push, I seize the opportunity and cling to its fins.

My heart pounds like a drum, each beat synchronized with the rush of adrenaline. The crystal-clear water flows smoothly over my sleek suit, its gentle caress heightening my senses. My familiar panic doesn't claw at my insides, but I feel something call out from the distance. It's not so much a sound as a presence. I focus on the rhythm of my breaths.

In and out.

In and out.

Teo adjusts his position in front of me.

Is the water upsetting you?

No, I respond quickly. *I just... do you feel that?*

He confirms, but we both grow quiet as we ride along the majestic form as far as it will carry us.

With each passing hour, fatigue begins to weigh down my limbs. Despite my prior preparations for this expedition, I yearn for the comfort of a soft pillow upon which to rest my weary head. Exhaustion settles over me like a dense stone tethered to my legs, dragging me down and chilling me to the core. I honestly am amazed at the physical distance we've covered.

A profound sense of depth unfurls beneath me as my muscles protest with each stroke through the water. The darkness below seems to yawn wide like a hungry abyss eager to engulf me. This realization pumps more adrenaline, dispelling any traces of drowsiness and sharpening my senses for what lies ahead.

When I make the mistake of looking down, it is a deeper black than I have ever seen. It coils with possibility and power. That blackness is something that would prefer to be left unknown for the rest of time. I swallow, physically struggling to look away.

"Teo," I gasp as the creature guiding us along continues to rush through the water.

My husband's hand, covered in the crystal material, reaches out for me. When we touch, the barrier between us sets my teeth on edge, and I mourn the loss of his skin. It would ground me.

The water feels more viscous as the darkness encroaches. It swallows the light from the fish and our suits. Our creature starts to move more frantically, resisting how the two Enduares at the lead try to guide it through.

The black waters seem endless. As I glance down again, I still can't see further than my feet. My Fuegorra sparks and sputters in my chest.

I panic, but Teo's grip tightens on my hand as I start to thrash and kick my legs. This sets off the creature carrying us along.

The fish dodges and jolts, disturbed by our movements. I cling desperately to its smooth scales, trying to steady myself as it darts through the murky depths. The darkness seems to press in on us from all sides, suffocating me. This is what eternal torment feels like. Not fire, but the silent terror of falling forever into the mercy of an enormous, starving creature slinking in the shadows.

Ka'Prinn shouts something in Enduar that I don't quite catch as fear claws at my mind.

Then Teo pulls me away from the thrashing creature. It speeds away from us, the deep shadow quickly swallowing up its glow. I feel the horrible, unsettling sensation of plummeting.

I grasp at the water as fast as my body would allow. In my mind, I had known that we would need to go somewhere perilous to complete this mission. It was worth it to get the help of Mrath's sisterhood. But that knowledge means nothing to my body as I am frozen in the frigid water above the utter darkness.

Teo pulls me into his chest. "My love, it's okay. Just breath."

"There's something down there," I gasp.

He nods. "It is likely the artifact."

I shake my head, still trying to breathe. "No. Not a magical object... there's something. It watches us."

He furrows his brows. "Estela, stop. We're going to be all right. I won't swim down until your heart slows."

I suck in a gasping breath just as Ner'Feon swims up.

"It is time to descend."

I shake my head, my heart still racing. "No. We need to leave." I try to push out of Teo's grip and turn back. "Thorne, please. Let's leave."

Thorne's face is only partially illuminated. He's taking too long to answer me.

Then, a disturbance in the water hits Teo and me, blowing us apart.

GO.

I thrash through the water. New arms grab onto me, and I find Vann holding me as he tries to swim away. It's useless when the water changes. Slowly, at first, we begin to move in a circle. Then it speeds, a whirlpool dragging us down toward whatever thing watches us beneath all light—beneath all civilization.

Helpless, I cling to Teo as Thorne clings to me, and Vann clings to him.

In my heart, a string of prayers starts up to my mother. To the woman of light, wishing for anything. For my powers to strike up at once. For Teo to split open the world and simply replace the mind-squeezing black with scorching reds.

The whirlpool finally stops as we hit stone—hard. My breath is rammed out of my body, and the crystal covering my body—so well crafted, so strong and flexible—cracks. Water seeps into my back, wetting the leather clothes I wore underneath.

All of our suits stop glowing, wholly robbing us of our sight.

I look up. Despite my blindness, my senses feel the blackness moving.

"Teo?" I call.

"I'm here," he says from a spot nearby. "Everything is fine."

"Are you all right, Vann? Ner'Feon? Ka'Prinn?"

I try to move and more water leaks into my suit. The fear clawing at my nerves crawls to my throat and tightens. "My suit is cracked," I say.

The relentless dampness creeps further, a chilling embrace threatening to drench me head to toe. Each icy droplet feels like a cruel hand tightening around my throat, stealing the warmth from my body. It's almost as if I were back in Zlosa. Without the shield of the crystal suit, I am left vulnerable, my very survival hanging by a fragile crack that threatens to spread at any moment.

"Estela," Teo says frantically. "Keep talking. I'll find you."

I can't breathe.

"Estela!" he shouts.

My mouth opens and closes, only for a sob to break free. My mind races, grasping for answers in my memories. When I helped Liana make this suit, we combined heat and magic to break down and reform the crystal. I relied heavily on her ability. It might be possible to use the heat from my light magic, but I can't remember how to draw in air.

My love, I can't find you.

Teo, my suit—

399

The dark rises above us, all sensation and shadow. Unbidden, my Fuegorra starts to glow brighter and brighter. An undercurrent wraps around me, pulling me physically off the stoney ocean floor. I scream, and the water stops seeping in.

Teo's voice shoots through the water.

"Estela!"

The crimson glow of the stone casts a red sheen to the swirling flecks of sea waste as they dance before me. My voice is frozen in my throat, fear gripping me tight as my husband's question fades into the background. The water ripples ominously once more, and a massive object passes over me. Despite my inability to move, my magic thrums with an intensity that terrifies me, its power feeling alien and uncontrollable.

The power sings directly to my Fuegorra, causing the crystal magic to intensify. Images start to pass before my eyes. Some are memories, and some could be visions of the future, but they pass too quickly to pluck one out and examine it.

I tug against my restraints, feeling the pulse of crystal and stone all around me. The magic pushes deeper into another magic connected to the stone in my chest. It slides past the gem and onto the glowing thread running from my head to my toes.

All it takes is one pluck, a spark, and I catch fire. My red glow transforms to white heat.

The light continues to expand, brightening the tremendous dark hole surrounding us. Then a colossal stony hand stretches back out, controlling the currents that hold me in place. The graceful, powerful arc of masculine fingers reaches toward me until, at last, glowing blue eyes snap open.

I am close enough to look directly into the vast circles. They appear to be made of two smoldering sapphires. Long locks of pure white marble float around a grey head as it gazes at me.

My heart skips a beat, but exclamations come from beneath

me. I can hardly hear them. When I try to twist down and see Teo, the magic tightens.

"Daughter of the Light Weaver," a voice as old as the world rumbles through the water. It snakes through the liquid and salt until it radiates through my whole soul. It is somehow quiet and booming.

"Who are you?" I choke out, feeling those penetrative eyes bear into my flesh, searching my heart. Seeing every selfish choice, every drop of blood I've spilled. Every evil thing that hid inside me.

"You do not know me?" the enormous stone man says to me. "I am the father of the trolls, King of Stone and Crystal. Lover of the Goddess of Stars. My children call me Endu."

The word makes everything around us rumble that much harder. I remain frozen, lost to his words. Helpless to his power.

"You are... a god," I breathe. It's so quiet I wonder if he can truly hear it.

He nods slowly. "I am."

The statement feels more profound than it sounds as if his existence stretches far beyond the confines of my mortal understanding.

I twist away and look down at Teo. All of the men have been bound in a similar fashion, and each tugs against their restraints. The space separating us is substantial, as they linger far closer to the ocean floor than me. My bound arm reaches toward Teo.

I can just barely make out how his eyes are widened in disbelief, and a mix of shock and wonder dancing across his features. After a moment of stunned silence, his voice trembles with awe as he calls out, "My god, Endu, is that really you?"

Endu's gaze shifts from me to Teo, a small smile spreading across his stony features. "Yes. It is I," he rumbles, the sound resonating through the water.

The other men remain silent, but not Teo. "I had not thought this place an appropriate dwelling place for a god. Do you not reside in the center of the earth?"

"Is this not the earth? I came a time ago after the screams of my children woke me from a thousand-year slumber. When I arrived, I found them all dead, so here I stayed, guarding their bodies and sending them off to life to come. Some decided to linger, and I felt I couldn't leave them. It is... pleasant here, surrounded by stone. My home is wherever I can best care for my offspring." He exhales, sending spiraling eddies full of sparkling particles all around us. "The question is... why are you here?"

I look at him, his eyeball larger than my entire being. I watch him with a furious beating heart. "We seek an artifact from the elvish god. One that was taken by the old king of your people."

He tilts his great head to the side, hair flowing out around his face. "The orb of the universe? I have been keeping it safe for Doros."

My eyebrows furrow as Teo calls up. "Why not give it back to him?"

Endu scoffs, and the ground beneath us quivers. "Why should I unless he calls upon me? Surely you know of the cracks between our peoples."

He extends his hand again, lighting up the water with ancient symbols I cannot quite read.

As the words begin to travel through the water, one approaches me. Both my Fuegorra and my lyre string begin to heat up in my chest, and I gasp at the pain.

"His child searches for it now," I say, jerking my head to the spot where Thorne treads water.

Endu pauses, the light channeled through me white hot. He searches my soul for something. It is pure, too pure for my mortal vessel.

I let out a groan.

"Do I hurt you, Estela of the Humans?" he asks in a voice that is surprisingly gentle.

"I would appreciate not being used as a lantern."

Though, in truth, if it means not dying at the bottom of the ocean from a suit crack, I will endure it.

He barks a laugh. The sound pushes me back against my powerful tethers holding me in place. "You have spirit. Grutabela gave your mate a gift when she chose you and bestowed upon you a drop of power."

He flicks his finger, and the pain from the light lessens. I suck in a deep breath, relaxing against the sensation.

After, his eyes lock onto mine. I should bring up the orb. Instead, I ask, "Is this drop of power why you call me the Daughter of the Light Weaver?"

He tilts his head to the side. "No. Your powers of light are divine, but they do not come from Grutabela or me. Your mother is known amongst the gods—touched by the goddess of humans."

I furrow my brow. "In the eyes of the world, humans are seen as godless."

He pauses for a long moment. "Is that truly what you think?"

The weight of his full attention is unsettling. I open my mouth, prepared to say I don't know, but instead choose honesty. "No, it isn't."

"Very good. The gods weave their influence in ways seen and unseen, known and unknown. Your mother was a vessel for the divine light. She's passed that gift to you, as my queen bequeathed a drop in your soul the night your Fuegorra was placed in your chest to show you the ways of our people." Endu's voice is calm, almost soothing in its depth, as he regards me with those shimmering sapphire eyes. "The two powers working together... well, that is something I've never seen."

His hand comes to his mouth, and he taps his stone lips. "You have piqued my curiosity. It is not often that we see one of your kind. I will make you a deal: answer one question with truth, woman, and I will give you the artifact." His voice booms through the space.

I take a deep breath. "Merely one question? Should you not bargain for more?"

He smiles. "Consider it a test of your character. Two goddesses have seen great potential in you. I am still making my decision. Truth is precious and oftentimes hard to find in mortals."

I nod, feeling the weight of his words settle on my shoulders. "I accept."

He smiles. "As God of Stone and Crystal, I would ask you what you fear most?"

For some reason, I had anticipated him to ask about my powers or Teo. This is something deeper and more intimate. My life flashes before me. Loneliness is the first emotion I feel, but I don't fear it. Hell, I have wallowed in it. I was such a wretched, spitting thing, trying to survive while stained with the blood of my mother and the weight of slavery.

Next, I think of Rholker. He terrifies me, but he is not my greatest fear.

Two faces pop into my mind. Teo and Mikal, and then a ruined memory follows. The memory slicers made me fear water one night of torture at a time. Even touching such thoughts causes a shudder to run down my spine, but still, that is not my ultimate fear.

No, what I fear most is my weakness.

Slowly, I open my mouth. "Love has not come easily for me. I loved my brother the best way I knew how, and I fell in love with Teo like one might fall over a cliff. Letting them in has caused me to be vulnerable. The thought of being powerless to prevent harm from befalling those I love, of being unable to stop the darkness from spreading—that is what truly terrifies me."

I gaze into the depths of Endu's sapphire eyes.

Endu's eyes gleam, as if he understands the depths of that fear. "That is a noble fear rooted in the vulnerability of your heart."

The god is pleased; I can feel it in my bones. "Your human goddess seeks to free herself, child. Just as you were bound, so is she. She has guided your steps and made you a catalyst. When I give you the artifact, make friends with my rival's offspring. Fell the giant king. Free your people in the name of your goddess— Ashra."

The name lights up my entire body, and the magic holding me in place eases.

"What binds a god?" Teo demands. His face flickers in and out, as do the other men as my eyes open and close.

"A dark magic hidden since the beginning of time. I cannot say more."

"She isn't the only one bound. What of Abhartach, god of these cold creatures that attack us?" Teo asks. "Is he some vengeful lover?"

Endu looks down at him, but shakes his head. "That thing should have nothing to do with the humans. Do not confuse a goddess with a demon, child."

Teo is silent, but Endu flits his gaze between Teo and me. "Your mate is strong, much like you, Light Weaver. It makes me miss my sweet Grutabela. It will be long before she sings to me from the heavens." He dips his chin to Teo. "Forgive my harsh tone. The one whose name you invoke is still bound; there is little reason to worry over that demon."

"So he is indeed a demon and not a god?" Teo calls.

Endu nods. "Yes."

I tread in the water, my restraints now gone. "I have spoken truth to you. Release me, and give us the orb," I say, with bravery that doesn't reach my heart.

He smiles. "I am a god of my word." Then he reaches into his chest, scraping and opening up his holy body to withdraw a small orb hanging from a chain.

Thorne gasps.

"That is it?" the elf asks.

Endu lets it drop. "Yes, Child of Doros. Take it back to your people, and be allies with my children again. Before you leave, I will give you one last gift."

The god raises his own hands, and the song in my chest bursts forth, resonating through the walls of the crevasse. The echoes of the melody fill the space, blending with the light that radiates from Endu. I feel a surge of power coursing through me, connecting me to the very essence of the gods. It's a moment of pure magic, where time seems to stand still and the world narrows down to just me and the divine presence before me.

When the song ends, I feel different.

More.

"What have you done to her?" my mate demands as I sink into his arms.

Endu's glowing eyes take him in. "I have touched her heart and purified it. It is an offering to Ashra for letting her children mate with mine and salvage your futures. A token of gratitude."

The water around us vibrates in time with immense energy, one that I have never felt so acutely before. My suit finishes cracking down the middle, and I scream, clawing at Teo's chest.

"I will send you back to your home, Daughter of the Light Weaver. These waters are too deep for your small mortal form."

The light in my chest flashes. A strong burst of energy drops us off in the Parting Cave. I cough, spitting up seawater, and find my suit completely gone. My fingers tighten around a hot orb.

The *Cumhacht na Cruinne.*

It is solid yet pliable. Its pulsing energy is the only sound that accompanies it.

Someone slips it out of my hand as everything fades to black.

CHAPTER 35

NUUMMITE

TEO

My dreams are pure light. The god-touched shine of Estela as a statue suspended in time and space. A vessel of radiance that warmed my entire soul to see her soar. Speaking with a god.

My god.

The memory is as intricate as the veins of metal that form between slabs of rock and the channels of lava that flow through the earth beneath my feet. When I try to touch her light in my dreams, it dims a little compared to letting it just... exist.

Then, a scene fades back into my thoughts. More ghosts locked away in the back of my consciousness.

My eyes open slowly, but the light above blinds me as the heat from beneath scorches me. I feel the mountains roll and the channels of magma carefully left unseen by the overworld pulse. They are drawn upward toward the same magic that keeps me from seeing.

The light shifts into something molten and hot, boiling my blood and cooking me from the inside out.

I scream.

The pain momentarily subsides enough for me to see my father

408

standing atop the castle, arms outstretched toward the volcano he created.

"Orfka ir asuso, hlumgla estra..."

My stomach drops, and I move to grab him, only to find myself bound as I thrash back and forth. The chains bite into my wrists. I growl, but my father doesn't move from his spot. I pull with all my strength, searching for my power as the earth roils beneath us, causing the palace to quake. With one last roar, I pull apart the chains. They are raw against the hot air, but I grasp onto him first.

"What are you doing?" I scream.

His trance breaks, and his black eyes focus on me.

"Do you have any idea what you just did?" he demands, his face filled with ugly black swirls. I hold tight onto his arms, bringing them down to his sides. He makes a guttural noise. "Stop! I'm doing this for the world. If we don't destroy it now, one day it will destroy us!"

I shake his shoulders, "What are you talking about? The threat to the world isn't the giants or elves—it's you."

He looks as if I had slapped him.

"You are my son!" he screeches. "You will obey!"

I shake my head. "No. Not anymore," I growl.

Then, he shoves me. Hard. I stumble and fall toward one of the rails. My hands rip on the stone, and I pant as I look at Iravida. It's a sea of red and orange, and the mountain we had existed peacefully next to has rivulets of lava flowing down at an eerily fast pace. The ash-filled air whips around me while sparks of lightning glimmer over the mouth of the mount.

I have to do something.

The land has already begun to collapse. Screams somehow rise above the sound of the earth shifting and rending beneath us.

Vann is below, and there are hundreds of others trying to flee.

Without questioning myself, I whip around and grab my father by the shoulders.

"Stop!" I cry. I'd turned a blind eye to all the wrongs in the past, but this was too far.

My father was revered as one of the most powerful men in the land. How could he be reduced to such insanity?

He shoves me hard. "I'm doing this for our people!"

The words fracture my heart, and each piece breaks off and sinks into the destruction. He has to be stopped.

I look around.

It's just us.

The answer comes, clear as crystal: it's my job to end this.

"Please," I beg. "I won't ask you again—stop this!"

He turns to me, eyes glowing with hands raised. "I will not."

Panic takes hold. I rush forward and push with all my might. He sways and then falls to the depths of lava below, and I don't even look.

A father who had used me all my life, hungry for power, gets no more of my care. Instead, as my hands burn, I look down to find light sinking into them. It seals the bloody scrapes and makes them ignite with fire.

I turn back to the heat of the volcano and hold my hands up. A power that was not there before stirs.

I had always been strong—my family was blessed with a vast well of magic, but this is something... more.

The force of the eruption threatens to draw me out and swallow us whole.

I demand it to stop.

Hundreds of thousands were already dead.

Maybe millions.

But I could stop it from taking everyone.

Slowly, the lava comes to an end, and the ground quiets. Then, the ground beneath my feet begins to crumble.

Screams pierce my skull. There are flashes of red, ochre, and *yellow. They slosh with a vibrant heat that scorches to the core. It crashes over our home as we stand, helpless.*

Everything sinks into the sea.

A sensation of being terrifyingly weightless comes as the stones of our tallest tower fold to the ground. A rock lands over my leg, and I call out in pain. For the first time in months, after all the killing and the seduction, I think myself ready to welcome death.

Instead, a large blue hand is thrust into the rubble. "Teo!" Vann yells. "Grab on!"

A light to my left draws me out of slumber.

Slowly, my eyes blink open. The hunter assigned to wait for us in the Parting Cave must've brought us back to the king's suite because that is where I returned to consciousness.

Every part of my body is sore from the endless swimming. Though the royal pools had made swimming feel like something out of a dream, actual hours spent traversing through the deep is more challenging than running through sand. My skin is sore from chafing against the crystal suit and sticky with sweat.

Estela's weight rests heavily on my arm, and I lean down to kiss the top of her head as she continues to sleep.

She... glows.

Faintly. Even now. The aura of her soul never fully turned off.

In this silent moment, I allow myself the luxury of watching this creature in my arms while pain churns in my soul over the memory. It is a small pleasure to know how much we have grown since she's returned. Each piece of her is my treasure, from the stories of her raising her brother to the way that she laughs so carefreely around her fellow humans.

How can I tell her of my deepest shame?

We've spent the month working through each of her memories, and mine have been buried under grief, Lijasa, and the aftermath of the war.

411

I've tried so hard to erase every inch of my father from my mind, and yet... a part of him has clawed its way back out.

She stirs, arching her back into the movement for a second before letting out a groan.

She likely is as sore as I am.

A problem deeply needing to be fixed.

Later.

Another flash lights up the crystal near my bed that my councilors use to communicate with me, and I extricate my arm from under her head as gently as I can. Though she stirs again, she never fully comes awake, not even as I wash away grime and sweat, change my clothes, and fix my hair. It has been long since my own fingers wove my braid. I wish to stay in this room, to tell her of what I have seen, but instead, I open the door.

As I quietly close the door behind me and hurry out, I find Lothar waiting for me with a grim expression.

"Lord Lothar," I say, almost surprised to see him after so long healing.

He dips into a bow. "My King, I hope you are well. There has been a problem with two of the new Enduares."

I groan, memories of yesterday rushing back.

They led us to the chasm where we found the artifact. Endu must've sent them back with us. "What now?"

Lothar shifts his weight to his good leg. "They awoke an hour ago, and they have already scared the children and some of the humans by running naked through the tunnel to... hunt."

"Gods-damn them all. Where are they?" I demand.

He nods and leads me through the halls toward the throne room.

I sweep in, tail swishing, and my eyes narrow as I look at them, seated on stone chairs, wearing nothing. They seem unaffected even though seven hunters point their weapons at their throats.

Vann is there, bearing his familiar cleaver and scowling.

"What the hell were you thinking?" I shout at them.

Ka'Prin looks up at me. "You knew that our clothes were mostly destroyed underwater. You saw our stained camps..."

"There are plenty of clothes in Enduvida; you could've asked someone."

Ner'Feon frowns. "We tried to ask the human women you told us of, but they did not understand our words even though we spoke in the common tongue."

I press my palm to my forehead. We had no time to discuss the same measures I've been careful to implement with the others in my court, but I can already imagine what a woman would think with a tall blue creature skulking around with glinting knives and ball sacks hanging low.

"I am sure there were clothes in the house you were taken to," I insist.

The two of them glance at each other.

"We wanted to catch a kill for our first meal—to show our usefulness to the court. Perhaps to catch the eye of one of these women you say we can mate with. They are... small. Like your bride," Ka'Prinn says.

I groan, but he isn't finished.

The Enduar curls his lip. "Humans are ugly in many ways. Strange."

"Not strange," I growl.

Ka'Prinn continues, "Then soft. They will bear us small younglings, and their... overabundance will soon dilute our race. It is disappointing to spend my life serving your father's orders only to be rewarded with a half-meal."

They want strength and power. Dominance.

I walk forward, slam my fist into his face, and use the same aching fist to grab his braid and yank it back.

His eyes flash.

"First. Keep your poison inside your body where it can only hurt you. You don't speak to the humans, nor will you ever breathe those words in any inch of Enduvida. Those humans have been treated poorly by the hands of men—giants and humans alike. They have become our people, and I'll die before we add Enduares to that list."

Then I switch back and forth between Ka'Prin and Ner'Feon.

"Second, you will be clothed at all times that you are in a shared public space. Third, no hunting unless you coordinate with Lord Lothar." I jerk my head to the man at the side.

Lothar steps forward. "I lead the hunters."

I point a finger. "If you wish to join us, you will listen to everything he says."

They watch us with mistrustful, deadly eyes as I release Ka'Prinn.

"I understand that you are eager to rejoin your people. But much has changed in fifty years. We have new traditions, a new life. This life is gentle and structured, but kind. Humans are our salvation. Learn to soften your edges, or we will banish you to the water."

The weight of the words sinks in as I bark the orders at them, much like their general.

Ner'Feon looks at me and stands. "And if one of us decides that we would challenge you after all?"

Anger singes at my spine and makes the tips of my ears grow hot. "Do it. It will not be a hard challenge for me to ram a sword through your naked chest."

He huffs out said chest, and every hunter in the room tenses.

Vann laughs. "You are a fucking simple-minded fool, Ner'Feon. Really, you didn't seem this thick in your camp."

I raise my eyebrows at Ner'Feon's challenge. "Do you think

any of my men would obey you if you killed me? You want to lead this group, but we don't function in such ways. They would kill you within the very minute my heart stopped beating."

The hunters around the room nod in agreement.

Ner'Feon slides back into submission. "You made a blood oath that you would bring the rest of us home to fight in your battle."

I take a deep breath. These men already have their Fuegorras. They will be powerful, and we have over a hundred more to bring back to this city.

"I will send a team after Mrath meets with us," I say with finality.

"And how long will that take?" Ka'Prinn demands..

"I do not know. The others have waited since the Great War. An extra week or two will not be the end of everything," I say evenly.

He glowers at me with a look that could cut through steel. Let him be angry if he uses the fury to change.

"We will go back to our dwellings," he says, standing. I nod to Lothar, who takes his hunters with him as they follow the men out.

"Your food will be brought to your home. Speak with your new leader, so that he may put you to work," I say as they stomp out.

As soon as they are gone, I relax once more and look at Vann. He glares at the exit, fuming.

"How dare they say those things," he grumbles.

I raise my eyebrows. "Not too long ago, you were as angry as they are about the humans."

Vann turns back to me. "That was then. I have since learned they have their value."

I narrow my eyes and assess him. "They most certainly do."

He jerks his head around, and I see the faintest glimmer of light on his neck.

My eyes widen. "Have you found a mate among the humans?"

It all makes sense, the softening, the gentleness. The longing looks at Arlet and the threats of death against Joso.

His expression looks shocked, and his hand flies to his neck.

"What do you mean?" he demands.

I grab his hand and tear it from the spot on his neck that now looks dull. I frown, so assured of what I had seen moments before. "Hmm. Your neck is dark, brother."

He steps back. "Of course it is. My heart belonged to my betrothed Adra and none other. Recognizing the value in allies means absolutely nothing else."

I nod. "Rightly so." I straighten. "I am sorry that we have not had enough time to speak in depth of your time here while I was gone."

He waves me off. "There will be time once this all is finished."

The solemnity twists my features downward. "But what if there isn't—"

"We will make it through. There will be time," he says firmly. "Also, the artifact was removed from Estela and placed in the viewing room."

"Thank you." I think about going into the deep.

It had seemed simple, right on the scrolls. In the library, I could plan every aspect, as I did with the elves. But the magnitude of life sometimes cannot be contained to words on a page. It demands to be lived in every ugly, awful way.

Some of us will die when we kill Rholker. Several of us already have. It is a lot to ask for the promise of a healed future when we cannot guarantee that.

But hope is sometimes enough payment for great risk.

"I have been meaning to ask you about your tail. Were you injured?" he says, pointing to the bald tip. The one that was shaved.

I clear my throat as new images flood into my mind, then smile. "No. It was for Estela," I say proudly. Even mentioning her name now reminds me that I wish to go to her and speak of my nightmare, but Vann's face keeps me here for a few moments longer.

His brows furrow.

"What could she have possibly needed that for?" he asks seconds before his eyes widen.

I give him a look full of meaning. "Her pleasure is my commandment."

He sputters. "What in the gods' grey caves could the humans do with—" Vann abruptly cuts off and stiffens, and the song in my chest that swirls around me day and night, never truly leaving me alone in silence when she is in the city with me, starts up.

He bows and clears his throat as he sees Estela enter the room.

"My Queen. I was just leaving." Estela nods at him, and he hurries away.

I look at the luminosity casting away shadows within the throne room.

My mate. *The Daughter of the Light Weaver.*

"*Mi amor,*[1]" I say slowly. "I was about to come find you."

She moves with an unsure grace and smiles. "*Mi vida*[2]," she murmurs as she glides into my arms. "What troubles you?"

I brush my fingers over her hair. "My father."

She stills. "Did something happen?" I see the way her eyes harden, ready to fight every one of my demons. Her loyalty touches me.

417

"No, just memories from the past. I dreamt of... the day my father wielded the volcano to destroy my home," I say softly.

Her eyes study my face. "You can tell me all about it, if you'd like."

Such kind words strike a chord in my chest. When I first woke up, I just wanted to unload every word upon her, to deal with my shame. It has been long since I have faced the reality of what I'd done—killing my father to save those who were left.

I worry what she will think of me. Would she compare me to him? Or, perhaps Rholker, the one who also killed his father to keep her captive?

She waits patiently, and the words she spoke to me after we arrived in Enduvida return.

I know what you are. I am safe with you.

I take her hand in mine. "Grief... addles the mind, I suppose. I have thought of the volcano and the endless days that came after so many times. But last night, I was forced to remember that it was I that ended the explosion. I pushed him into the lava. I *killed* him."

Her hand reaches up and cups my face. "You *saved* hundreds."

My eyes burn as I place my hand over hers. I feel fragile, like I might crumble under the slightest tremor. "What kind of man kills his father?"

"A man who puts goodness above blood. The best kind of man." She holds me tightly. "Sometimes it frightens me how similar we are. In all this time, you have been so gentle with me about my memories, now it is my turn to care for you. I need you to know that my heart aches for everything you have lived through. I hope you know that I see you and know who you are. I love that person. Please don't be unkind to him. What he did was heroic."

My heart fills with so much love I could burst. The road to

this point was not easy, but to let someone see you so fully, and not run? That is what I imagine Vidalena is like. Warm. Perfect.

When I press my hand into the tender muscles of her lower body, she whimpers. "What is wrong?" I demand, still filled with protectiveness after her display of unconditional love.

She shakes her head. "I am well. It's just... every inch of my body hurts."

I look down at her. "Would you like me to rub your aching muscles?"

She leans her weight more fully against me, and I instinctively sweep her off her feet and walk to the throne. As we sit down, she looks up at me.

"Do I... look different?" she asks.

I smile. "You look like the sunrise and a sun-soaked sky." I brush some of her hair from her face.

She smiles and leans into the touch.

"Do you know, when I left the cave after you'd been taken, I felt the sun on my skin in a way I hadn't for a long time. It made me feel... alive. All while I was dead after you'd gone. How fitting that your god-touched gift made you glow like my own personal sunshine."

She shakes her head. "You speak like a poet, sometimes."

I stroke her cheeks. "I do love the poets of my past."

"One day, I will read them all. I've been learning so much with Ulla," she says.

I nod, marveling. Yesterday we were at the depths of the cave, conversing with a deity.

And now... we are as we're meant to be. Together. Peaceful.

We luxuriate in the calm before the storm.

I cast such sad things from my mind and study every inch of her. The first time I held her, she was a hissing, wounded creature covered in dirt and rage. She is still hard, but it is beautiful how quickly love changes a person. The magic of my people let me see her for who she was before she changed.

"I am sure you will read them all. You are a spectacular woman—In the time I've known you, you've learned to read and speak much of my language, and you brought thirty-three women to their freedom. You introduced plants to a sunless cave. You escaped from the giant king. Spoke to a god. Swam the depths of the sea. You are the next wise woman."

Her eyes line with silver. "But there is so much I haven't done. My brother... the others..."

"You will do it all in time," I say, utterly sure.

"Liana showed me a few cards. One spoke about death. I worry..." her brow furrows. I place my hand on it.

"No more worrying. I don't doubt our future, and neither should you."

"I don't deserve you," she whimpers.

"Yes, you do," I respond, drawing her into a kiss. Her arms slide around my neck, and her legs shift until they straddle my hips. She rocks forward once, and the sore pain in my body is soon replaced with want. It flushes out everything else except the woman in my arms. My hands fall to her soft bottom and squeeze.

She moans at my mouth. "Perhaps we should go back to our room," she says with a smile.

I pin her with a stare. "I think I prefer to stay right here. On our throne."

Her eyes go wide. "But what if—"

"If you do not wish someone to see, then I suggest you take your pleasure quickly," I say firmly.

Her cheeks flush as she reaches for the laces of my breeches. The moments are not soft and gentle; they are quick and full of need. When we are both spent, she falls against me.

A queen delighted upon her throne.
A good omen.

CHAPTER 36
DUMORTIERITE
ESTELA

E very part of my body is still sore when I drag myself to the royal library, away from my mate and the obscene way he plays my body like I play my magic.

I can't believe he made love to me on our throne.

My mind swims as I walk through the palace.

When I looked at myself in the mirror this morning, there was something unrecognizable looking back at me. I feel different, much like I did when they first put the gem in my chest. But now, a faint glow glitters across my skin. It doesn't fade with time or washing.

I am stronger. Lighter. The darkness that once lurked in my soul feels more like a bubble swelling in my mid-section waiting to be popped. For the power to spill out of my fingertips and into the world.

I find I crave such things.

Teo went off to check on the new Enduares, and I've come to the royal library. Something Teo said about reading has me thinking—letters have been so important to our love. He has spent so much time pouring over these words. What could I learn from them?

Voices filter out from the library as I draw near, and I hang back, listening as Thorne's voice comes into full volume.

"Mrath and I have known each other our whole lives. She is... trustworthy. When she wants to be," he says.

"And does she want to be?"

"Yes, my sweet little bleeding heart."

It surprises me to hear Ulla scoff. "You already spoke to her, yes?"

Silence, that I take to mean a nod.

"In fact, she has been quite curious about every second I've spent with you all. She will come to retrieve the artifact within the week."

I inch closer to the open door, grateful for all the time I've spent slinking in the shadows. However, I do wonder how the glow hasn't alerted them.

I should interrupt them and break this off, but Thorne has been kind to me. Not quite a friend. A part of me is confused that I didn't see his fascination with Ulla before.

Ulla is seated in an intricately carved stone seat, while he is sitting on the table, a glass of wine in his hand. He swirls the crystal as he talks and looks at a severed leather band in his other hand.

Theatrical, calculating. And yet... utterly absorbed by Ulla.

"I was on my way to tell your king when I saw your pretty little head bent over a few scrolls. I couldn't help but pop in."

Ulla leans back, and it's only then that I see her long hair flowing off her shoulders.

He cut off her hair tie.

I blink, even more enthralled by this pairing.

"Well then, if you are finished taunting me, you should find King Teo," she says, grabbing at the tie.

He jerks his hand away. A true smile spreads across his face as his teasing smirk fades. "What will you give me?"

She pauses. "For a ruined strip of leather?"

"You seem quite eager not to walk out of this room without it," he counters.

She stands, grabs his shirt, and pulls his face close to hers. They are about the same height, and her strength is well-honed.

"Give. It. To. Me," she grits out.

"Why did you step in front of my blade, *mo chuisle?*[1]" His voice is soft as silk but loud enough to fill the space.

The moment has taken a turn I wasn't expecting, far too intimate for me to behold.

I start to move, ready to scurry away silently and let them... finish whatever that was. I barely make it two seconds when Ulla says, "My queen?"

I freeze, and heat spreads throughout my body as I'm caught in the act. Slowly, I turn and walk back to the library's door.

"Hello, I was just..." my mouth runs dry.

Thorne lifts an eyebrow. "You glow now? What the hell is this place?"

I frown, but Ulla glares at Thorne.

"It happened after traveling through the deep," I say, aware he was there when it happened.

Thorne laughs. "Marvelous. We saw some very excellent... fish down there."

Ulla doesn't yet know about Endu, and I'm not quite sure I want to talk about it right now. Thorne, however, was there. In a way, it feels like he is extending me a branch of friendship.

I purse my lips and try to process this new information as he slides off the table, lands on his feet, soft as a cat, and saunters by.

"I'll leave you to your boring scrolls and ink," he says, parading out the door while drinking the rest of his drink.

When he passes me, he pauses, gives me an exaggerated bow, and says, "My leader, Mrath, is delighted by our successful mission. She will be here within a few turns of the sun." And then, he leaves.

At last, I step into the room and cross to Ulla, who is trying and failing to rebind her hair.

"Stop fussing," I say gently, pulling the tie off my braid. She looks up as if to protest, but I shake my head. "My room is much closer than yours. Is it all right if I help you?"

When I had first come to Enduvida, Arlet and Liana styled my hair, but that was before I learned about the custom of braiding. Ulla looks up at me and smiles.

"Only if you don't mind touching another's hair."

I pause. "Humans don't all follow those rituals. Would it be strange for you?"

She shakes her head. "I would consider it a gesture of our friendship."

I grin and take her silky hair in both hands, nearly shocked at its sheer volume. Her hair is similar to Teo's, and a strange feeling twinges in my gut when I think of my nonexistent child having long, soft hair like this instead of the wild curls that my mother gave me.

"We weren't being indecent," Ulla says after a few moments.

I smile, as I twist the hair atop her head. "An Enduar concerned about being seen ravishing another's mouth? You wouldn't need to be ashamed if you were. Gods know I have seen my fair share of indecency in Enduvida."

She brushes her hand over the scroll. "I wouldn't say that if he were an Enduar. But he's not one of us. He's an elf," she says.

"One of us? Ulla, I'm a human," I say, laughing almost. My heart almost can't take the excess of friends I've acquired lately.

She waves her hand, "Humans are one of us. You've proven that well enough."

I quirk an eyebrow as I finish wrapping her hair. "Isn't Thorne half-human?"

She freezes. "What are you saying?"

I shrug. "Nothing, but he doesn't seem to be the enemy."

With one final tug, I finish securing the bundle of hair at the top of her head. It's not my best work, but it seems secure enough.

"Why did you come here again?" She asks, clearly not wanting to continue discussing Thorne.

I slide next to her. "I wanted to find some paper to write down my memories."

She smiles. "You've been practicing your writing. I think that would be excellent. You should write down the plants as well. We have a whole bush of the one you call lavender now—not to mention some of the other herbs we use almost daily." As she speaks, it's almost as if she is eager to cast off thoughts of all else.

I smile. "That is a good idea."

She stands. "I'll get the things." Then she bustles off down an aisle. I look around the library, a place mostly unknown to me. The rows of tall triangular shelves, mostly scrolls, but a few tomes, are stunning.

Calculations from sleepless nights spent Teo spent here after leaving our bed are still scattered over several tables. There's a contradiction of messy, wild studying that meets meticulous organization and reminds me of my husband's mind.

He's very neat... but just below the surface, there's a bit of chaos.

TO IGNITE A FLAME

I like this room very much.

When I look at one of the walls, I see a scroll that has been unraveled and tacked up for all to see. Stepping closer, the text seems familiar. Not for the words, but the drawing at the bottom.

It... my marriage contract. My signature is the universal hand gesture for *¡vete a la mierda!*[2] There's an undeniable crassness, especially in contrast with Teo's tidy script. Ulla comes up behind me and laughs.

"I've never told you this, but it was very creative of you," she says, laying out an ink well, a sharpened crystal, and a scroll.

I frown. "I think... I should redo it."

She shakes her head. "You can't. That's a binding contract. Be proud, you certainly will be remembered for all those who come after."

Her words revive the anxiety pulsing in my chest. All of the fears of our extinction and death return with a vengeance, demanding to be let out and shared with all. It's as if I am standing over the vast, black expanse in the sea once more. Just waiting to be swallowed up.

A hand rests on my shoulder. I look up to see Liana. "My child, breathe."

Ulla looks at me, clearly alarmed. "I don't know what I said."

I shake my head and sit down. "You did nothing. I am fine. Thank you for getting this for me."

The women position themselves on either side of me. "Do you need help spelling the words?" Ulla asks, still clearly concerned.

I shake my head. "I want to try for myself."

"Writing will do you good. If you want to be free from pain, you must be willing to do what needs to be done to cure the wound," Liana says, pleased.

I nod. Teo has been helping me so much, with our memories

together. He calms me through each moment, but I am slowly realizing that a court is not just a king or his advisors.

I put my pen down and think about what I should write. My eyes slide closed as image after image passes through my mind. Not the tender intimacy between my husband and me, but Dyrn. The funerals. Tirin's sacrifice.

Putting my pen to paper, I take a deep breath.

> *A hunter, barely older than a boy, gave his life for humans to live in the tunnel. His name was Ra'Tirin. They took his head back to the giant court and placed it all on a wall. I stole it and burned it to give him a proper burial away from the true monsters.*

Each letter is almost painful to write, and tears spring to my eyes. This happened while I was at the giant court, but the memory is already blurry, caught up in dozens of others.

Liana touches my shoulder. "You really honored him that way?"

I nod.

Then I put my pen down again.

> *When I was nine years old, my mother had my younger brother, Mikal. The bastard of the Giant King Erdaraj. He was large, and my mother was small. I was the only one around to assist with the birth, though I knew little of the act. She screamed so loud it hurt my ears. I was scared.*
>
> *Mikal was born, and the blood never stopped.*

The king had many children with the wives in his court, many of the sons sank into obscurity over time, and every daughter was swiftly murdered. These men—Terksat—the giants called them. They hated my brother.

As did the giant princes.

A teardrop falls onto the paper. I press my hands to my face. "I don't know why I'm writing this. It wasn't one of the memories attacked. But I can't forget those moments, too," I say, sadness ripping apart my insides.

Thinking of Mikal reminds me of the giant woman beheaded in the court, and I cry harder. She had no mother to save her.

"Get Arlet," I hear Liana say as she rubs my back.

My friend's name is bittersweet. We've grown so far apart. It hurts to think of what was lost between the two of us.

"The king wanted to kill Mikal and me after our mother died. And when I was in the court... they chained me by my throat, and they brought a woman to be beheaded. They had killed her child," I sob, finally looking up at Liana. "I wish you'd never showed me those cards. What if we are the ones who die? What if we doom the future to a life of the giants and not the... peace in Enduvida?"

"Of what do you speak?" Ulla demands, but Liana purses her lips, her eyes growing glassy as she continues to stroke my back.

"Estela, the cards weren't supposed to frighten you so. They were meant to help you practice crystal reading."

I sniffle, "I—There's so much I don't know about reading the future. About this magic."

Liana nods. "And now you are god-touched. Daughter of the

Light Weaver. You have more magic than you know what to do with."

I nod. "Yes, I feel it."

Liana wipes one of the tears off my cheeks. "You are a fast learner. Why don't we go riding tomorrow? Perhaps the proximity to *drathorinna* will inspire her to call you."

My heart stutters at the thought of the giant mother of wraiths. I long to join her at her side, and pluck out new notes of power, but I must be patient.

"Or pick some of your flowers?" Ulla offers.

Shaking my head, I say, "No. Mrath is coming. It will have to be after."

Behind us, I hear Arlet's voice. "Estela, are you all right?"

She says it seconds before her arms wrap around me. It's a level of kindness I'm unsure I deserve, but I accept it anyway. I nod against her.

"I'm sorry, I was watching over the new women. Some of them have been learning to weave."

Liana watches this. "How did you two become friends?"

It's an awkward question for me to answer, considering the cavern between us. One that Arlet doesn't seem to notice.

When I continue to be silent, Arlet clears her throat. "She saved me and took me in after the man who'd gotten me pregnant cast me out."

Ulla's eyes grow wide. "You were in the breeding pens?"

It's strange how much they know about those places now. To be honest, it's more than I do.

Arlet nodded. "They put me with a boy I'd admired my whole life. I was praised when it appeared I became pregnant. But then... soon after we were given a space so that he could help me with the pregnancy and prepare a space for our child, I lost the baby."

430

I blink, reliving her pain. The air is too heavy. Everyone is quiet.

I look up at her. "Daniel deserves to die a slow death."

She shakes her head, sad. "No, he doesn't. He's an ass, but... we were all in pain."

Liana furrows her brow. "He cast you out after such a loss? And you defend him?"

Anger crawls up my arms. Arlet tends to be like this— malleable.

"Daniel watched when the first prince cut off one of Arlet's fingers so she would tell him where the baby was." My words are so hot, they burn my throat.

More silence. Then Ulla says, "Let me see."

Arlet reluctantly holds up her hand, showcasing the sloppy stitches I made and its skewed placement.

"I sewed it back on after they branded me in front of the entire pit."

Liana nods. "Vann has a few missing fingers. Has he shown you?"

Arlet stiffens. "No. But Joso has told me of them—says that it makes his grip on his cleaver more impressive."

Liana nods.

"I think it would be good for you two to write together. Estela is losing some of her memories, and you have been with her for so long. You also are an excellent reader," Liana says affectionately.

Arlet's pale skin goes pink, and I furrow my brows. "You've been reading scrolls?"

Arlet nods. "Some are... love stories."

For some reason, that makes me laugh.

"Saucy love stories?" I ask.

Her red face is more than enough of an answer.

I laugh. "Do they have pictures?"

Everyone around us laughs, but it's Liana who says, "Some do. Let me know if you need recommendations." She steps back. "Hurry with your writings. We have to plan for the elves' second visit if what Thorne says is true."

Ulla follows her out, leaving me alone with my friend.

Arlet shakes her head. "It's so strange to see how different they are from the Enduares from the ocean. I think the stories we heard fit them more, though the flesh-eating still sounds excessive."

I nod, feeling uneasy again. Spreading a hand over the scroll, I think of what to say.

"Do I get to know why you glow now?" Arlet says.

I take a deep breath. "There was a god at the bottom of the ocean. *Endu.*"

Her eyes grow wide. "No. Really?"

I nod. "He spoke of many things, but especially of our goddess. He said he was helping her by touching my soul. Her name is... Ashra."

Arlet tilts her head to the side. "Ashra."

I nod. "I'll be honest, I still feel very little about it. I think she had a connection with my mother, but I feel much more in tune with the Enduar gods. Especially..."

Arlet nods and tucks a piece of hair out of my face. "I agree. But it is interesting to think about."

I nod, and the silence stretches between us again.

"Estela, I know you have been busy—I have been, too. Gods know you do so much... but it's almost time to get Mikal. Are you ready?"

I look at her, and my chest swells. Months apart. Would he be proud of everything I've done?

Nodding my head, I swallow and say, "Yes. More ready than you can imagine."

It's then that Liana returns to the room.

"Liana. Back so—" I start, but she stumbles forward, grabbing a piece of paper and a pen. A stone falls from her hand and crashes against the ground.

I bend to retrieve it.

"My queen," she gasps. Her eyes are wide, and she blinks in rapid procession while her Fuegorra lights up like a dazzling beam of magic. "This is a message from Melisa and Ra'Salore."

"What does it say?" I ask as Arlet guides her to the chair.

Liana starts to write as her breathing slows.

"Rholker..." she spits, looking right at me. For the first time since she barreled back into the room, her eyes are clear. "He's killed off thousands of slaves."

Blood rushes to my ears, causing a dull roar.

"What?" Arlet says through the shock, and my hands go numb.

My redheaded friend picks up the stone with the message and the paper that Liana had been writing on.

"Pens are burnt, men are rounded up and whipped, thousands are dead. Rholker is still here, and he has definitely secured a relationship with Arion," she finishes.

I sit there, frozen.

All because a few dared to escape. I had thought that he would've been weakened by the fight, and everything would be all right.

I was wrong.

I push away from the table and go find my husband.

CHAPTER 37

TROLLEITE

TEO

Mrath's return feels like déjà vu. Gods only know how Thorne had been communicating with her while under the mountain, but I don't press the white-haired assassin.

Estela and I wait for the elven leader outside of Enduvida, flanked by twenty hunters, the mounted Faefurt Assassins, and Thorne himself.

My wife is anxious. Since we've started to get word from Ra'Salore and Melisa, the news is dire. Rholker is eradicating humans at an exponential rate, and I just feel...

Helpless.

Mrath rides atop an alce, much like Layla's, and she wears a crown of thorny twigs that wrap around her temples and elongate her already narrow face. She wears dark green armor, the kind that blends into the fray of the forest but is stark against the snowy mountains.

Behind her, a hundred women come bearing glinting weapons and hungry faces. Some ride bears or wolves, but a great many *run*. Their elven bodies are strong, used to running for incredibly long distances.

No sooner than they draw a hundred paces, the Faefurt assassins at our sides rear their beasts, thrust their weapons in the air, and let out a series of high pitched calls. It stirs the bones.

They certainly don't inspire immediate trust, but they are much more lively than their men—I'll give them that, Estela says in my mind.

I smile down at her glow and press my hand against the small of her back. She leans into the gesture, and a warmth as powerful as the sun itself thaws my insides.

In the moments before our guests approach the entrance, I let myself linger on my dulcet woman. Memories of her whispered late night stories caress my skin. The intimate familiarity between us is as heavenly as any conversation with a god.

It is a taste of all that is good in this life.

"Butcher of the Giants!" Mrath calls out, now close enough to be heard. "I heard you killed thirty giants in under a quarter hour when you retrieved your mate. Well done."

The name shocks me, for I have been long removed from it. It is not the name cried out in my bedchamber.

Estela steps closer to me, and I raise my head to meet the leader of the Sisterhood's gaze straight on. "Mrath, it's a pleasure to see you again."

The clops of her alce come to a halt, and the massive creature lets out a discontented huff of air. Ayla's own steed lets out a high pitched noise before it kneels before Mrath, bowing.

She sits tall, shoulders perfectly straight and graceful.

"I'm sure it is. I must admit, I am also... contented to know that our meeting this day will not be one of bloodshed. I commend you and your people for making good on our deal." Her eyes glitter.

There is an undercurrent to our simple words, one that speaks of pain and exacting payment if we had come up wanting.

But we didn't. Therefore...

"This is my wife, Queen Estela, of the humans and Enduares," I say.

Estela dips before the assassin, still glowing. Mrath watches her with fascination.

"You look like some heavenly messenger sent to heal us all from our pains. How quaint," the elf says.

I angle both me and my wife to the side, gesturing to the entrance into our city. Lothar and Vann part for the elven princess to pass. As she slides off of the alce, I watch her feline grace.

We push through the tunnels. Estela and I lead the way, Mrath just after, and all the others following closely behind. A welcoming song has been arranged, and the first notes touch my ears about halfway into the tunnel.

Mrath listens, curious, but does not say anything as she follows past the singers and to one of the bridges—the one that leads to the palace.

I stop before we cross, and turn back to her. "Would you like a tour of our caves, Lady Mrath?"

She surveys the massive cave housing our thriving city. Her green eyes almost glow as she stands near a mushroom that towers over her and bathes her in a bluish, green light.

Her mouth curls at the corners. She turns back to me with precise swiftness. "You honor me with your generosity. I will see the caves once you have shown proof of your mission's completion."

I nod and lead her across. We walk up the palace steps, past the fountains, mushrooms, crystals, and statues, and into the viewing room. It feels like it has been so long since I've been in this place.

The last time I came here, I met my bride.

I cast a glance up at the mirrors, enjoying the all around view of Estela. Her healthy glow has filled out every part of her, smoothing over the sharp edges and forming her body into something strong and beautiful.

It is my duty to cross to the side room where we keep the diamonds that were once traded with the giants. The light from within pours into the room as the orb gently floats out.

Mrath gasps. She looks like a woman possessed as she is drawn to the godly object. Thorne is close behind her, as are Ayla and the few others who are able to fit into the room.

She grabs something from the small bag at her side and reaches out, murmuring words too low and ancient to understand. In her hands, she holds a necklace made of curved, polished bones. The necklace's cage gapes open, and the *Cumhacht na Cruinne* is drawn into it.

Once the light is tucked inside, the light dims, and she snaps the contraption shut. It's then that I realize it's a crude version of a skull on the end of a chain. She slips the new pendant over her head, and every one of her subjects watch in rapture.

Her eyes flutter closed as she takes a deep breath, as if she could suck up every molecule of power from the air.

"This is most excellent. You have secured yourself a long, profitable ally in me, King Teo," she says. "As long as you help me take down my brother."

I smile. Her pledge fills me with trepidation.

I reach out my hand, which she takes.

"Let us draw up a more official contract then," I say.

She laughs. "I would be more than delighted after you show me how you all live."

That is all it takes for the tension between our peoples to ease. I haven't forgotten what she is or what she's capable of, but I don't hate the way it feels to bring her to the forges, or the weaving looms, or the crystal caverns. She is polite and smiles at Estela's lush plants.

She asks questions, greets human and Enduar alike, and even uses her magic to grow a little thorny flower for Niht when she sees him. That hunter is well-liked by the elves.

Our contract is easy to draw up, as most of the terms have already been discussed multiple times. It isn't until she asks about our plans to fell her brother and Rholker that I pause. We have spent so much time working on reaching the artifact, and it is hard to accept that we must now plan not one, but two invasions.

"Rholker must die first," Estela says. Her hand is steady as she points at the battle map before us, and her voice is resolute.

"One could make the case that dethroning my brother would give us even more of an advantage in a battle," Mrath counters.

I study her unhurried position. "What do you know of Rholker's court?"

She cocks her head to the side. "I know that the new king faces deep reservations from his court and barely acquired his official title. He has signed a treaty with my brother and it is rumored that he's tried repeatedly to have the swamp ogres train with his ranks."

I draw in a deep breath. "Do you know anything of his exact location?"

She purses her lips. "Getting someone that close has been... challenging since the night of the coronation."

Estela almost looks pleased. "We have sent our own people to infiltrate the ranks. We have not heard from them, but I am confident that targeting Rholker first, while he is still weak, will be a good plan."

Mrath frowns. "I want my throne."

Thorne, who sits at her side, utterly still compared to the time he spends away from her, snaps his head over to stare at her.

I don't know what that action means, but I say, "And you shall have it with my help. But bringing back more humans is of the utmost importance."

Her eyes trail away from me and to Estela. Then she cocks her head to the side.

"Don't you have a brother in captivity?"

Estela doesn't try to hide it. "Yes, but it is not only about that. Rholker will continue to destroy the land we tend. He seeks power, and he is motivated to possess things he shouldn't want. He needs to be killed before he becomes a tyrant."

Mrath flicks her wrist. "Kill one tyrant, and another pops up a few centuries later. What's the point?"

It's Estela's turn to look at the woman.

"Then we keep taking them down, for years of peace are worth the pain. And who's to say if such patterns won't end?"

Mrath considers this for a long moment. "Well spoken, Human Queen. We will proceed to kill Rholker first, but we will need to know where he is. It's likely that he is in Zlosa, but acting without assurance is death."

"Upon that we all agree," I interject.

The finer details of our plan continue to be ironed out. We will wait for Ra'Salore's and Melisa's word, and then we will march. Mrath has offered us one thousand soldiers, but she expects at least two hundred Enduares to fight.

Ner'Feon and Ka'Prinn will be pleased when I tell them of our plans tomorrow.

Once everything is signed and squared away, we move on from the scrolls and memories of war. This night, there is to be a feast, and we all leave to find ourselves in the thralls of revelry.

I sit on the edge of the bed as Estela slides a close-fitting purple gown over the curves and contours of her body. There are a series of buttons on the back, which she tries and fails to fasten.

"Come," I say, my voice rumbling as she perches her pretty, round bottom on my lap. My fingers tease the skin of her spine as I do up each button, but my hands linger on her ass as she stands.

She turns around, somehow shy once again, and then slips into the comfortable slippers she often wears. Her skin glows, as do the lights overhead, and all of them glimmer over the shimmery material of her dress, giving the effect of her being covered in water.

I stand, grabbing the jewels I selected for her off the dresser. I slide rings on her fingers while kissing each of her knuckles, then fasten a necklace around her slender throat, and set a crown with a ruby the size of my thumb upon her head. Its fiery energy reminds me of her, intensifying the brightness of her smile.

She is stunning, and when she smiles, I feel like I would die to keep that look on her face.

"Shall we?" I ask.

The smile grows brighter, and my heart stutters when she slips her hand into my arm.

We walk to Hammerhead Hall, past our bustling city. For the first time in a long time, it is bursting with people.

Flames tall enough to extend over the buildings fly into the air. The pleasing crackle of the fire joins in with the pleasing tunes that pour out of the singers.

When we arrive, the festivities have already begun.

We are greeted warmly, and we go to stand near Mrath. She

lounges in one of the chairs, watching as Niht dances rather poorly with Glyni, the elf.

As Estela and I both take the seats at the end of the table, she looks at us and laughs.

"My, aren't you two a proper couple," she says, smirking.

Estela smiles, but I see the flicker of uncertainty in her eyes.

"How are you this evening?" she says, conversationally. Politely. All the manners that she has learned with Liana come to the surface in this moment.

Mrath swirls the wine in her cup. I watch it, knowing that it is not something we had under the mountain before her arrival.

"Well enough. Your people are heartier than I remember from my youth." She takes a long drink. "They wouldn't let me visit with your kind. My father kept me hidden to ensure that I wouldn't fall in love with one of you and bring his kingdom to its knees."

Her eyes go to Estela. "Imagine thinking that one girl's love could destroy a whole kingdom."

Estela swallows. "I think love is rather powerful."

Mrath smirks. "Oh?"

Estela traces the plate that was set out in front of her.

"I've seen obsession change an entire court in a matter of months. And I've seen love…" she glances at me revealing a bit of her changed heart, however briefly, and it sets my soul on fire. "…change a heart—the stoniest of hearts—in half the time."

Mrath makes a disgusted sound. "Gods. If this is how the trolls always were, I'm glad I was sequestered in my room."

I cross my hands, smiling. "Do you not wish to dance? Your women seem to enjoy it immensely."

All of our gazes turn back to the drunken joviality around the fire. The women have linked arms, kicking out their legs and chanting in time with the singers.

The elf twins, Farryn and Elanila, grab a cloak from one of

their sisters. They've been with us since we retrieved Estela and have proved to be valuable trainers.

Everyone watches as they theatrically wave the fabric in the air in front of Niht, a true friend of the elves it seems. Seconds later, when they drop the cloak he runs behind one of the beams as if they had performed some great magic.

Younglings, whom I can't remember allowing at this party, scream with delight, and all of the elvish women howl with palpable mirth.

Estela huffs out a disbelieving laugh. Thorne, who has taken a seat next to Mrath, looks over at my wife, immensely amused. The joke is too simple, ridiculous, and not something I would expect from a group of murderess women. I can't help but laugh as well.

"Yes, well, women are peculiar, marvelous creatures," Mrath starts, as if needing to explain her sisters.

Whatever she was going to say next is cut off by the sound of slow clapping.

It precedes the thick, black mist that curls across the ground.

Mrath and I bolt to our feet, turning to the source of the sound as the music stops, and the laughing is silenced.

Three women stand in the entrance to the open hall wearing black cloaks and gowns. Their hoods are down, revealing painted faces, dark hair, pale skin, and black eyes.

Estela stands, pushing away from the table despite the way I reach for her.

"Dahlia?" she says loudly.

The women turn to look at her.

The one who leads the small group has a snake that curls around her throat, licking at the side of her face. I see the rounded, human ears and realize that these must be the witches who tortured my mate.

"Essstela," the snake hisses.

"Daughter of the Light Weaver," the woman says. "I am not Dahlia, she is still at the Giant King's side. My name is Syra."

"What are you doing here?" Estela demands, back straight. The glow emanating off her grows brighter in warning.

If the women notice, they don't show it.

"When we met in the giant's home, we offered to let you come with us if you would leave these Enduares behind," she says slowly with that haunting voice.

"I refused you," Estela says. I feel her pained rage through our bond. When I was faced with the memories of Lijasa, I was a mess, but her? She stands strong.

"It was the wrong choice. Dahlia has decided to extend an invitation once more. This time in exchange for your brother's life," she says.

Estela stands there, frozen. Everyone watches the exchange, but I see the parents discreetly hiding their children behind them.

Good.

When they mention the giant court, I deeply regret that we haven't heard from Melisa and Ra'Salore. Their information would be very useful in talking about Rholker.

"What do you want from me now?" Estela says.

"What we have always wanted," the woman says. "We came to King Erdaraj to have your mother. When he would not release her, despite his promises, we thought all hope was lost. That is, until you came here, and your magic was... awoken. We seek your light."

This time, it is me who interjects.

"Why?"

The women turn to us. "Our master demands it."

"And just who is your master?" Mrath calls at my side, her hand already sliding some hidden weapon out of her trousers.

"We will not share that. Our time grows short. My sisters help Rholker even as we speak, but what is done can yet be reversed. Give yourself over to us, and we will end this all." The cavern seems to darken. "We will spare this cave, your king, even the children. Rholker will die where he stands. The war will be over. Stop the bloodshed, king. Save your meager court."

Another, not Syra, sniffs the air.

A fraction of my mate's mind opens, and I watch her consider it.

No, I tell her. *Don't give in to their lies.*

Teo, it's a chance to end everything.

"One of you has made an agreement with us before. May they come forward, and vouch for our honesty!"

I wait for someone to approach. None do. I write it off, focusing my attention back on my mate.

Estela, I plead. *They only want to use you. If you go with them, they'll break your mind and abuse your power. Don't give in.*

She takes a step forward, and I prepare to run to her. Then, she turns and looks at me. I see the grief written across her face, and how her eyes are filled with tears.

I don't want anyone else to die. I can stop it. I have spent the last sixteen years of my life planning for one thing—saving Mikal. I haven't looked beyond that point... until I met you. You forced me to think of life past ensuring his escape. I love you both. You are my world. If saving both of you means going with them, I will do it.

No. You might save us today, and then kill us tomorrow.

"Take another step toward my fucking wife, and I'll slice your head off your shoulders, witch!" I shout.

It works to get her attention off her. I only need a moment.

"Be careful how you speak to us, troll," Syra snarls. She holds out her hand, and a ball of dark energy swirls in her palm.

Please, my love. Think of all the things waiting for us. If you go, you will never come back. If you stay, then we can fight to have every wish our heart desires. You'll be free, you'll see Mikal again. We'll have children, and a life after pain.

"Well, Essstela? We grow impatient."

My words latch onto her mind, so I keep feeding her images from the past. I show her how I've pictured how our family will look.

I can feel her will swinging back toward me.

But she says, *Love is selfless.*

Please, you are allowed to be a little selfish, I say. *Stay with me, my star. Don't let yourself become something evil.*

"I—I will not go."

Relief floods my senses, a gentle wave of calm amidst the silent gazes of the women. Wisps of mist unfurl from the earth, carrying with them a whispered utterance from Mrath—*vaimpír.*

The cold ones. A shiver dances down my spine as I clasp my beloved closer, their words lingering in the air like an ominous premonition.

As the mist retreats, a haunting sight emerges before us—a horde of chilling undead materialize into view. Their pallid forms mostly bare, adorned only by midnight-black locks and eyes that gleam like polished onyx. Without hesitation, the Enduar men and elvish women spring into action, brandishing otherworldly blades with fluid grace. Some engage the creatures head-on while others shield the defenseless in a frantic bid for safety.

In a moment of urgency, I reach for a weapon nearly forgotten, just as Vann appears by my side. The ground beneath us trembles with my resolve echoing through it like thunder. Never again will they steal my love away. And so it is that my fury summons forth molten rage from below, the lava answering my call.

Vann's cleaver strikes true against one of the vaimpírs

lunging towards me, its impact resounding with grim finality. As its head rolls free from its shoulders with a sickening thud, Thorne and Mrath swiftly dispatch another assailant that dares to encroach upon us. Soon enough, the air is thick with the acrid stench of ebon blood.

Embracing my wife protectively, she pushes me away before seizing a blade meant for food rather than foe. With practiced precision born from Svanna's tutelage, she drives the knife deep into the vaimpír's heart. A cascade of viscous black ichor spills out as her treacherous deed unfolds before wide-eyed witnesses.

"Traitor," gasps the fallen witch before dissolving into wisps of smoke at Estela's handiwork. As others attempt to aid her, Estela's radiance intensifies to searing brilliance. Those who dare draw near recoil in agony as charred remnants mingle with tainted blood.

The Fuegorra blazes incandescently across our battle-ground, banishing shadows and confusion alike. Its fiery touch weakens our frigid adversaries' defenses, rendering them vulnerable to our blades' merciless onslaughts. With unwavering determination, Estela wrenches the knife free from one fallen foe and pivots to meet another's advance with lethal precision.

My bride screams. It's an awful, tortured sound. I yank the snake off of her leg and slice it in half as it tries to curl around her calf. It hisses and steams as it falls to the ground in pieces.

Estela quivers. The magic in her chest flickers and dims.

"What's wrong?" I demand, drawing her into my arms.

She looks up at me.

"I—I..." Her speech is broken by her panting.

Her eyes squeeze shut against the paralysis.

"My star," I say, panicked as the light flickers.

But then, just as swiftly as the light disappeared, it glows back to life.

It isn't the gradual dawn, sneaking over the mountains. It is lightning slicing through the sky. All at once, it blows me back. It smashes the tables and chairs and cracks the walls. It is not the Enduares or elves that suffer the effects of the blow; it is the undead creatures.

Under this burst of power, they *dissolve*.

Like lightning, the brilliant light fades, and Estela lies on the ground several paces away from me.

As I approach, I look down and see a pattern around her body, etched in the stone beneath our feet.

Like rays of sunlight.

I suck in a breath, and her eyes drag open.

"My Queen!" a voice calls, followed closely by the sound of stirring all around the room. In a second, Arlet is at her side.

"Estela," she cries, shaking her shoulder.

I move in protectively, not wanting any part of her body jostled. "Arlet," I say with a demanding tone.

Others circle around us, and I can scarcely bear to reach out and check for a pulse. Her chest doesn't rise or fall.

She doesn't move.

My sunlight...

Tears slip down my face. I put my hand on her cheek.

And her eyes snap open.

A collective sigh burns through everyone in the room. I look over to see the elves gazing in wonder.

My mate pushes up and winces.

"Is everyone all right?"

Her eyes find me first, and the glow returns to her body.

It is a primal pleasure to see that it is my face that heals her, that she is moved by my presence.

"Yes," Vann says to the side. Others agree.

447

I slide my hand around her, helping her to stand.

Everyone gazes on her in wonder.

"We are safe now," I say to her. "You saved us."

She looks around the room, surprised. I grin.

It's Mrath who steps forward, her face reverent and thoughtful.

"This morning, I promised you one thousand of my finest women." Her eyes take in my mate, clearly in awe. "Make it two."

CHAPTER 38

HAUYNE

ESTELA

Two Weeks After The Feast

I'm tired of training. It takes from sun up to sun down.

The terrifying, unsettling thing about feeling the power thrum under my skin is my inexperience. No matter how much I learn, there seems to be more. I could dedicate a lifetime to playing the enchanted lyre of my music and still find new chords. Some of my attempts at melodies prove weak, others too strong.

Tonight, it wakes me up from my nightmares. Screams plague my sleep like almost visions. That is why I rose earlier than any Enduar—even Liana.

Normally, after nightmares, I wake up nauseous, and Teo rubs my back until I drift back into sleep. Tonight, there was a voice that whispered in my waning consciousness.

Drathorinna.

I eased out of my mate's arms, and replaced my body with a pillow and placed a chunk of amethyst next to his head to prevent him from waking. Then I'd placed some moonstoon on our nightstand, just to be sure he'd sleep soundly after a long day of endless work.

Now, I follow the tunnel down to the *glacialmara* stables where my mentor had brought me a handful of times. When I find the right spot, Rahda bangs against her stall, insisting to be set free.

She is restless, as if she, too, heard the whispered word that gives me purpose.

Once atop her smooth back, I don't need to guide her through the tunnels as she carries me along to that sacred place deep in Enduvida.

The air turns stale and ancient, and then streaks of light cut through the pitch-black cave.

I hold my breath and see her form in the distance, filling the space. Her crystal scales gleam in the low light, and her long tail stretches out behind her, curling around her body as she rests.

She is a mountain of luminous beauty. I dismount Rahda who has already started to shift and squirm beneath me.

Waves of power radiate through the room, each hitting me in the chest.

This time, I anticipate my Fuegorra's pulsing heat. It accompanies my god-touched glow, in recognition of her power. I let the song fill the space, hitting every enormous crystal that juts out toward me. Step after step, I cross the space toward her. Her eyeless head swivels toward me, and I stand under her scrutiny.

Fearless.

With Rholker killing slaves, we need to march on Zlosa soon. Liana will be joining us in battle against the giants in Zlosa, but *drathorinna* has been slotted to stay home so as not to cause too much damage.

Something about that doesn't feel right.

Perhaps that's why the voice called me here. Now I'm

standing before her, actively pushing away every thought that tells me to wait for Liana.

There isn't any time left.

The weavers have made under armor for everyone, and the armor that existed before has been mended or remade. Twenty of the underwater Enduares have been brought back to Enduvida, and Teo spends his days training them with Lothar and Vann.

Training is long. Tensions are high.

Everyone is spread thin, and we need to leave within the next two weeks.

I take a deep breath and step forward in my nightgown, feet bare against the stone. My unbound hair hangs down my back, and I wait.

You heard my call, the old creature's voice slides along my mind.

"I did," I call back.

Then approach, wise woman.

At last, I move forward. It feels like it takes a small eternity to cross the way.

When I arrive, I reach up to touch one scale.

I feel the mother of crystal wraith's continue to take in my power, my elastic strength flexing and bowing as the vibrations around me pick up in speed.

When my fingers connect with her crystal, light blasts out of my arms. Energy dances across the walls of jagged rock and lightless moss, lighting up the entire cave. My back muscles tense as I arch with the sheer force of power.

Even *drathorinna* lets out a long symphony of twisting melodies and harmonies, waking up the entire cave. Crystals glint, and small *ruc'rades* scurry away.

Gathering every inch of my courage, I reach up, grabbing onto one scale. And then another.

I climb, slowly at first, until I reach her back. I pause, still standing and waiting for her to react. The dizzying height makes me sway as I peer at the stony ground.

If I fall, I might die. It would take them a long time to find me since I hadn't told anyone I was coming.

Sweat beads along my skin, but I take a few fortifying breaths before stepping forward toward the junction of her shoulders and neck. It's far too wide to straddle properly, but she is unearthly still as I sink to my legs and take up my best approximation of a riding position.

I look around, trying to find something to hold onto.

As I do, the twinkling sound floats over crystal, and a small handle forms over one scale.

I let out a long breath and reach for it.

As my hand connects with the solid material, the mother of all *glacialmaras* starts to move. It feels like the earth quakes beneath my feet as she stands.

Gods only know how long she has laid dormant, but I can feel every quiver and groan of rock as she stretches her legs. It takes ages for her to take her first step.

Then, slowly, scratching chords drown out the beauty of her musicality as wings peel away from her sides.

I try to adjust my position to accommodate her movements as solid crystal expands. The sheer size of the being beneath me inspires terror and joy all at once. It is mesmerizing.

The cavern deep in the mountain looked like it was plenty spacious, but now, with her entirely unfurled, she looks like some celestial steed of a divine being, swallowing every inch of the space.

Just as I think I've got a hold on her movements, she takes a step forward, and I slide across the sharp scales. My grip on the crystal handle slips. My inner thighs slip and chafes against the surface, and I cry out at the stinging, sharp pain.

It hurts like hell.

"*Hostia*[1]," I scream as another movement thrusts me forward, nearly vaulting me off the creature.

My arm pulls out of my socket, and I hear a pop that produces more awful pain.

I scream again.

"*Por los dioses*[2], this was a mistake," I huff.

Reaching with all my might, I manage to swing myself up and latch onto the handle with both hands. With a firm grip I pull myself up, despite my screaming shoulder. When I am back on the neck of the creature, I feel the sickening power beat against me.

Blood drips down my legs, and my arm throbs, but my Fuegorra heats up, knitting my skin and bones back together.

What happens next is what steals my breath.

My magic has always felt erratic and dangerous, but with *drathorinna*, the lyre string running from the tip of my head to my toes finesses its perfect tune. It's not merely a harmony in the air, but a rightness in my body that makes me want to soar.

I let out a yelp, now anticipating her movements as she brambles through the space. I hear the *ruc'rades* and *ruc'cieles* squeak to light as she squeezes herself through the hole. The space is not nearly big enough. I duck as close to her body as possible as she pulverizes everything in search of the open air.

Stones stumble down, sharp and deadly heavy, but none touch my body.

Fear pierces my heart when I think of the humans and Enduares above. I am helpless to the movements of the creature beneath me.

Keep them safe.

I pray at the same time I curse my idiocy.

Why did I come here alone?

As we clear the space, we crawl out onto some hidden

plateau along the black Enduar mountain range. Relief floods my body, all the way to the tips of my fingers.

I let out a whoop as her wings stretch once again, this time reaching their full, vast glory. The first beat is followed by a joyous cry from her tongue-less body. The air stirs in a relentless torrent, blowing back my clothes and hair.

Once again, I hold on for dear life, waiting for her to move. She doesn't—just sits. I kick my bare feet gently into her sides, and she continues to stretch in the moonlight.

For the first time, I fully realize that I have let this monster out of the mountain with no real way to control her or get her back in.

Acid slips through my veins. This was supposed to help our problems, not make them worse.

Respira.

Gasping breaths come in, and I close my eyes. I think of everything Liana told me, of the cards with the magic futures, of the Fuegorra, and reading crystals, and visions, and giving blessings.

I begin to count; not mindless steps; but the good things in my life.

Teo, Mikal, my home, Arlet, Meli, Svanna...

Soon, I am filled with light.

It's then that my eyes reopen.

My magic can connect with other crystals. I lift a shaking hand off the handle and lean forward to press my palm into her stones. It takes a moment for me to focus my concentration properly, but when I do, the light begins to burn.

For a minute, my awareness slips away, and I no longer see. The world is black and white and perfectly clear.

All around me, there is sound and frequency, like strings of light that can be followed in every direction. It is a miracle to achieve such perfect clarity while sinking into such utter darkness.

Drathorinna listens to my command, and when I point her towards the lines that lead to the sky, she follows.

My human body feels the rush of air, and the bite of frigid temperatures, but my other senses discard such discomforts as we fly under the moon itself.

When we draw high enough for the wind to scream against the melodies we create and the air to grow thin. Only then do I aim to return to the ground.

I realize my mistake when she begins to spiral downwards. I pull her back up, and we gently lean into each other, sensing the right way to go. We avoid the mountain peaks and the other creatures that roam the night sky.

High in the misted clouds, the lyre string in my chest is pulled back, and then, a beam of light shoots out of *drathorinna's* mouth.

It draws me out of her mind in shock, and when I return to myself, a voice hits my head almost instantly.

Estela, my star.

I gasp when I see the world around me. We cut through clouds. Ice whips at my face, and when the creature veers to the left, I look down. There is... nothing keeping me from plummeting to my death. From this high above the trees, my stomach lurches. The snow glistens, fires burn in the distance, and the stars twinkle.

The world is so much bigger than Zlosa or a cottage. It is bigger than the enormous city under the mountain.

For a second, I don't respond to my mate, I savor the sensation of being brought to my knees before that which I had never known.

My star, Teo says again, this time more insistently, *how you shoot across the sky. I see you atop the glacialmara. Please, come back down.*

Worry returns. What if *drathorinna* hurts him?

As if reading my thoughts, *drathorinna* sends me something akin to, *"I will only attack when you say."*

Warmth spreads throughout my chest, and I look down to see the entrance to Enduvida. I am too far up to see anything more than a few meager glimmers of what I assume to be spell light below.

Tapping back into my enormous mount, I push her back to the ground.

My stomach lurches as we draw near to the hard ground. We pull up with not a second to spare, and our landing is still a hard crash. I scream as I am yanked around once again, this time jolting off the creature.

The terrifying moment of weightlessness is ended in a second when a claw reaches around me, holding me safely before lying me on the ground.

My chest heaves, and I sense others draw near.

Teo and Liana are the two who approach, but I can barely move my neck. My body is weak from clutching onto scales for dear life.

I experience the sensation of still being in the middle of the air, burrowing through time and space.

Teo and Liana kneel beside my body, and my mate brushes away the snow from my face.

Liana's eyes are full of wonder and pride, but Teo looks half mad.

"Well done," the wise woman says. "You have proven your-self a formidable asset to our court. I never told you that she acts like a focusing crystal."

"Hah!" I smile weakly, my eyelids drooping again. "I saw it when we were practicing the parting blessings.

"Enough," my mate's voice booms. I still as Teo's hand passes over my face and body. "Are you hurt?"

"I feel fine."

A muscle in his jaw feathers. "You look like you're about to pass out." He pulls a chunk of citrine and puts it to my brow before he starts to sing. It doesn't take long for the weariness to fade.

I reach up and grab his hand. "Teo, I am fine."

He sucks in a sharp breath. "I woke up and you were gone. I feared..."

My stomach drops, like a stone plunking down in the middle of a pond. "*Mi amor,*[3] I wasn't trying to run away. I thought you knew I would never want to leave you again."

He slides his arms under my knees and around my back. I lean into him as he picks me up.

Instead of continuing our conversation, he says, "We have received word from Melisa again."

My eyes snap back open. The last update was so awful.

"And?" I choke out, throat dry. I fear the horrors her words could contain, especially after the last message.

Teo looks down at me with such wonder and tenderness, and it makes me restless. "The giant lords are planning to launch an attack on Rholker. They want him dead."

I stare at him, letting the words seep into my skin. If there is a mine... there are more slaves suffering under Rholker's hand. "Is he already dead?"

Teo shakes his head. "Not yet, we must ride soon."

Everything in my soul and the world around me stills. "What of Mikal?" I ask. "With Rholker dead, we will be able to find him easily."

Tears slip out of my eyes. So close to reuniting with Mikal.

But... Revenge is closer.

When my head muzzles into Teo's neck, both of our Fuegorras begin to light.

It's not the simple mating light both Teo and I have experienced before. This time, as we touch, I am sucked into his soul. My magic is a lyre string, and he is a deep, burning cavern into the depths of the known world.

I reach out into the cavern, spiraling down into all. That. Power.

The ground beneath us quivers.

Teo halts, eyes wide as he gazes down at me.

"What was that?" He demands.

Liana comes over, grinning. "It seems your visions are coming true."

I blink rapidly. "I think... I just accessed your power through our bond."

Teo's hold on me tightens. His pace picks up, and he takes me back into Enduvida faster than even Liana can walk, all the while the spell light bobbing around us.

The magic from earlier has left me depleted, and I feel weary in his arms. I don't question him, though I do send a few stray thoughts of surprise when we walk past the palace.

"Patience. We have come to see something new," he murmurs.

He takes us along the moving pathways, over the caverns of lava, past the pumps which control the air, and over to the forges.

When he sets me down, I sag against him and clutch onto his arm. He guides me forward, past tools, and the fire which is now merely a scattering of glimmery rocks.

He walks to a stone chest and removes the lid. Slowly, he pulls out a set of golden armor. In his hands, it looks as though it would be for an Enduar youngling.

I look closer at the breastplate, finding it was clearly made for a woman and see some of the strange crystal glass from the underwater Enduar suits between the breasts.

Slowly, I approach.

My hands slide over the material, but the tune of this creation isn't sharp. It feels like a star beam.

I bask in the excellence of the piece. The way the metal looks from the elbow caps and gauntlets, to the greaves and shoe coverings.

When I pick up a piece, I feel just how weightless it is.

My eyes find my mate. "Did you make this?"

He shakes his head with a smile. "I can do many things, but I leave metal and fine stone work to the benders."

My hand slides over the smooth metal. "Will you help me put it on?"

He grins and comes over, picking up one piece at a time. Slowly, he fits them over my thin nightgown, fingers languorously trailing across patches of thin stone silk and bare skin. I shiver as he covers my torso, my arms, and then finally, my legs.

"Wait, I remember this," I say, delighted to find a memory mostly untouched.

He looks up at me from his kneeling position and smiles. "Yes?"

My hands go to his head, which nearly comes up to my chest as he kneels, and my fingers slide through his silky locks.

"I helped you put on your armor before you left," I say, luxuriating in testing my movements in the light coverings.

Teo hums.

Once on, I find each piece has more substance than I thought, but it is not so much to make my muscles groan. Perhaps after many hours of wear, it would be worse. I'll bring it to show Svanna and Ayla tomorrow.

"Thank you," I say quietly.

459

Teo beams at me. "So you like it?"

I nod. "Yes. I love it very much."

His eyes grow heated as he reaches up and unclips my breastplate. He removes both of my arm coverings, and then he pauses to set aside the fine pieces and to trail his hands over my arms, across my back, and then around my belly.

"When I awoke and saw you gone, fear returned to me with a cruel vengeance."

I place my hand atop his, marveling at the size difference between them, and soak in every inch of warmth that radiates from his skin.

"The crystal wraith's call took me out of our room. She told me to come alone—I hadn't thought to tell you."

He leans forward and presses a kiss to my Fuegorra, and heat stirs between my legs. I press my hand down on his chest.

"It brings me joy to see you flourish in Enduvida. In this life as a queen," he says. Then his teeth brush over the sensitive skin of my collar bone

"I never wish to leave. You should know that." My voice is breathless.

He bites on the side of my throat, but retreats far too quickly.

Everyone still sleeps, and the forges are empty, but dear gods, what if someone walks in and sees us?

Then I think of the passionate kissing I saw at one of my first parties under the mountain, and I feel better—but only slightly.

I expect Teo to calm my thoughts or pick me up and whisk me away. Instead he says, "Relax," and works to remove the armor he strapped onto my legs.

I shudder as his fingers dance around my calves and inner thighs. His hands slip up under my gown, reaching toward the strip of cloth around my hips and pelvis.

He grins at me, and pulls it to the side. I gasp, and he claims the sound with his lips as he strokes momentarily before thrusting a finger inside.

"I live for such noises. They are nearly sweeter than any song," he murmurs against my mouth.

Each sound is swallowed by his excellent kisses, and I lean into the sensation. Every inch of exhaustion is shoved backward as my hands go to his laces to, release him.

He groans.

I fist him, but he has other plans. He wraps his still-bald tail around my back and pulls me forward. Time has taught him just how to angle the puzzle of our bodies and I sink right onto his cock.

It's such a sweet pain.

I let out another sound, and he grins as he works out every delicious sensation that I've grown to acknowledge as love.

No sooner than my eyes had fluttered closed, they reopen as he puts his hand on the side of my face.

I grip at his forearms, and his eyes meet mine. At first, it is a passing heat, but then he doesn't release me. My chest contracts as we move.

Pressure builds in my lower belly, but it's nothing compared to the way I am laid bare before him looking endlessly into those eyes. Vulnerability as I've never known it.

Tenderness as every person deserves to experience at least once.

A new connection forms between us, one that lasts past the time of release.

When our moment finishes, a tear slips down my cheek. Not from pain or sadness, but from gratitude.

The urge to apologize comes up once more. I swallow it down and throw my arms around his neck, kissing him as he slides out of me.

This is intimacy as I have never known it.

"I love you," I whisper against him.

His arms tighten.

"*I love you, te amo, mihk daourn,*" I sob into his hair as he clutches me, saying the phrase in every language I know.

He pulls me back, and his eyes crinkle. "I've never said that to you before. Not in my language."

"Thank you, my mate, for giving me wings to fly." I pull back, placing my hands on either side of his face. "I will protect you with my power, my influence, and if necessary, my own body."

The memory of our wedding vows pours out of me. His large, blue eyes glisten.

"*When* we have a family, I will also protect them. I am yours, body and soul." The small change of the wording, from 'if' to 'when' seems to break what little resolve he has. He presses kisses against my cheeks and murmurs sweetness through our bond.

We stay like that for far longer than we should, but I can't bear to bring myself away from that spot. From his eyes... filled with quiet love.

PART THREE

CHAPTER 39
RHOLKER

Two Weeks After Melisa's Last Message to the Enduares

The smell of smoke draws High King Rholker to the throne room. He hurries because it is an unexpected scent. The consort statues were not meant to be lit until tomorrow.

Just as he clears the room, he sees Lord Fektir bring his spear down with a meaty thunk. A dozen giants surround him, four holding torches between the ceremonial pews.

Rholker rushes forward to see them staring down at several bloody corpses. Rholker gags, holding his sleeve over his mouth, and pushes forward.

"What's this?" Rholker demands, looking at the black cloaks stained with putrid blood the color of tar.

One of the soldier's spears nudges a severed head to the side, revealing a pale strip of flesh with black tattoos.

Another warrior holds a torch and a bottle of flame oil.

Rholker's skin grows cold. "You slaughtered the Six?" he asks, visibly panicking.

Lord Fektir raises his chin. "Two of them. I caught them snooping around the royal decorations."

"Bullshit. They called me here to meet." Rholker withdraws a sword from his belt, but his hand shakes, causing the light to dance across the blade. The giant king hasn't shown this level of weakness in a long time... not since his brother was alive.

"Did you at least kill their leader Dahlia?"

Fektir purses his lips. "She wasn't here when we arrived."

"Fuck!" Rholker roars. "You have no idea what you've done. They'll come for me, for you—*they'll burn our city to the ground.*"

The guards stare at him, torches flickering and glinting on the drenched floor. The smell continues to permeate the king's nose.

"You are thinking like a small man. We'll kill her when she arrives. If they are *all* dead, they won't hurt a single giant in Zlosa," Fektir says, drawing his hands behind his back.

Rholker shakes his head, still staring at the mangled bodies on the ground. "Damn you Fektir. The terms of our agreement were being met. We signed the treaty with Arion. The witches were helping me—I promised them protection while they were here."

"What a foolish thing to do for an enemy," Fektir snarls. "You think that just because the results are pleasing that I can turn a blind eye to your methods? I won't have your weak spirit taint who we are."

The lord's spear tip is pointed toward Rholker, who then withdraws his own weapon.

"You know you can't kill me," he says darkly. "And I don't give a shit if Aska is primed for breeding. You will never force me to sire a child with your bitch daughter."

Fektir smiles darkly. "I was right about you. You're riddled with weakness and indecision. That's why you didn't finish killing off the slaves like I told you."

"Thousands are dead, and you are complaining we didn't finish the whole stock? We can't grow without workers." Rholker holds the blade higher, leveling it with Fektir's throat. "If you have something to say, spit it out, old man."

Fektir grins. "Nandi's son. You told us all that you had gotten rid of him, and let us all assume the worst."

Rholker's shock is as palpable as the falling snow outside the windows. He had sent the boy far away, to be murdered when he was a man old enough to hold his own blade. It had been a show of weakness, but there was something fundamentally wrong to the king about killing a child. He'd felt it ever since Erdaraj had brought Mikal to be executed at barely a week out of the womb.

"You don't know what you speak of," Rholker says.

Fektir steps forward, the disgusting squelch of blood underneath his boot breaking the silence.

"I didn't realize just how much progress you'd made on the mines, Rholker. I will say, you surprised me with the idea of keeping a child locked away in a manor. No one would've ever found him."

Sweat beads on Rholker's brow, decidedly signaling that he'd heard enough. Drawing back his blade, he lets it crash into Fektir's spear. The wooden shaft of the spear splits in half.

Fektir laughs while throwing the pieces of wood into the pews and grabbing an ax from a fallen warrior.

"There we are. I've always wanted to witness your battle capability!" he bellows. The force behind his first swing sings in the air.

Rholker ducks, then snarls, "I'm going to kill you. *Guards!*"

Not a single warrior moves.

"Do as you wish to me, but I've already told the other lords. They're preparing to retrieve Nandi's son, the true heir, as we speak," Fektir says, grinning.

Rholker yells and tries to charge. The guards who ignored the king's call shove Rholker back, hard. He slides through the fetid blood, leaving a foul streak across the ground. And his head crashes into one of the benches with a loud crack.

His eyes cloud over, and black edges his vision.

Screams of grown men fill his ears.

Seconds later, his vision clears, and a small tattooed hand reaches out toward him, pulling him to his feet with dark magic.

Dahlia stands there, murderous and alone.

Behind her, Fektir is nothing more than pulp, blood, and silver fabric. The guards are slightly better off. Most of their body parts can at least be identified.

"My sssisters are dead," Dahlia says, her snake swirling around her neck.

It pauses, looking at Rholker, and bares its teeth.

Rholker swallows. The demonstration of power laying on the ground behind the womens' forms is warning enough. He holds up his hand.

"It was not by me, I—"

"You have broken your deal, Giant King," she continues.

Rholker swallows, panting.

"*They broke your deal,* and I'm trying to help you get revenge," he says, desperate. "They are going to the mines, where my brother's son is being raised. If they find him, then I will no longer have a right to the throne."

Dahlia looks down at him, hood down with her black pupils swallowing every inch of white. She looks at him like this information was worth less than dirt.

"If you want my armies and the souls of my slaves, then you have to prevent him from becoming king," Rholker says. "If you kill me, you will not find a willing participant among the other lords in my court."

Dahlia stares for a few more moments and then says, "Very well. This is your last chance."

CHAPTER 40

EUCLASE

ESTELA

War is fast... until it isn't fast enough.

I sit atop *drathorinna*, this time with a proper saddle and full golden armor, protecting my body from the few rays of sunlight passing through the grey clouds and the icy chill. Teo is seated behind me, both of us tied to the crystal handles on her scales. Below us, troops march and ride every manner of creature. Enduar and elf alike race forward, armor glinting, beasts bounding.

Last night, after traveling for three days, we were camped out near the Giant capital when we received a plethora of information through the speaking stones—maps, warnings, and words. The first part played through my mind:

Rholker is leaving Zlosa as we speak. Deep in the forest, near to where the swamp ogres live, there is a mine. He has gone to secure his throne against a bid by Lord Fektir. He travels with one remaining Bruja, *and we expect they will arrive within the week. We tried to slow his departure, but the information we were given was about the three Warriors sent to chase him. Beware of them.*

I was furious upon hearing the message.

We were so close.

This morning, we took our provisions and left for the Giant City with bear, wolf, *glacialmara,* and in my case, crystal dragon. We travel at a swift momentum, and it isn't fast enough. It will take us four more days at least to reach the location.

Battle drums play below us, dictating the rhythm and step of two thousand and two hundred soldiers. It pounds through the air. The road is tiresome, but our army is strong.

Given what I saw in the giant court, Fektir's plotting wasn't surprising. He is the kind of man who can smell weakness and exploit it. Rholker is a scheming creature, a powerful one at that, but it seems that his brashness is finally paying off.

Both of them are ends of the same venomous snake.

I feel the eyes of those below watch us as we fly ahead. My goal is to be the first to make it to our campsite so that the elves and I can cover *drathorinna's* shine. Then Ulla and I can help those sick or mildly injured from long travel. This trip has also already forced me to heal animals, which is surprisingly enjoyable.

When we settle down for the night, everyone does their best to be light of spirit and vibrance. Elves talk animatedly around the fire while the Enduares sing songs of each other's people and show off their different brands of magic.

Stone shards fly through the air, birds flap in formation, and Thorne makes himself disappear and reappear. Apparently, the assassin is also quite the singer. He joins Ulla more than once in a tune intricate enough to bind even the most monstrous beast.

A hundred of the ocean-dwelling Enduares came along with a hundred of the Enduvida dwellers. Ka'Prinn and Ner'Feon were happy to retrieve them under the condition that they swear a blood oath to Teo and me. Their fealty is not something they take lightly, even if I feel uneasy about them occupying space next to the others. Sometimes they spend hours blowing hot breath over campfires with harrowing tales of the creatures that live in dark water.

Tonight, everyone finds ways to entertain themselves, but for me, the act of setting up camp again is... somber. I feel slow, knowing that every second spent resting is a second Rholker gets further ahead.

Long after the dancing and the songs end, my anxieties still mount. Teo holds me close in our tent and speaks peace to my mind, but I can feel the same nerves fluttering under his skin. We curse ourselves by sharing emotions too heavy to speak aloud.

When we are one day away from the mine's location, the joviality is reduced to quiet focus. It is as if we are a group of skeletons.

As planned, we break into four groups, one for each side of the mine.

I worry over Dahlia. Her magic is powerful, as are the cold ones her sisters controlled in Enduvida. When we left home, I had wondered if they would attack us along the way or spy as her eyes, but there have been no attacks.

In fact, it might be the longest we've gone without seeing one while traveling.

In the center of the main camp, we have set up an elaborate battle map in my and Teo's tent. We lay on cushions perched on top of rock beds, surrounded by stone silk and pillows.

After the elves and I cover *drathorinna* in trees and supplies to hide her glow, I return to Teo's side and sit on seats pulled up from the ground by my husband. Vann sits next to us, as does Mrath, Thorne, Ayla, Liana, and Ner'Feon. There are a handful of other leaders in the elvish armies, and they all listen with their sharp ears and glinting eyes.

Mrath watches Teo intently. "I still believe that attacking at nightfall is the opportune choice."

Teo frowns. "I still feel that daybreak would be wiser. They will still be fresh and unassuming. Though, I know how you enjoy killing under the cloak of night."

Mrath grins, but it is Ayla who says, "Darkness is an assassin's greatest friend."

I swallow and look down to the mapping of the giants' mine. It shows two towers connecting to a wall that holds a large area of slave pens. There is one structure inside the compound, presumably where Rholker is, and then there is the entrance to the mine.

The wooden manor built for higher officials' visits is not so big that it would take more than an hour to explore all of it, but Rholker is a scheming creature. The witches he harbors even more so. There are many ways that this could end poorly.

Since I already know the plan like the back of my hand, my thoughts race as the others go through the strategy once more, moving pieces across the hastily drawn battle map.

Vann has an excellent strategic mind, and it's his hand that dances across the table.

"So, the first leg includes our stone benders. We'll tear down the towers, and then throw everything to the elves and remaining Enduares to ambush the sides of the mine. Once the towers come down, the wooden walls will fall, too." He knocks over the pillars made from crudely carved stone. "Then, we'll lure as many of the giant warriors out as possible."

The figures for giants look more like rounded blobs than towering warriors, and my heart sputters at the thought of seeing them in battle.

"We have to slaughter them all," I say, reaching out on impulse and knocking over the figures.

Mrath stands, leaning over the figures. "Agreed. There should be no survivors. I want my involvement in this to be kept quiet, at least for now."

"Someone always escapes," Ner'Feon says, with his gruff voice.

Mrath grins at him. "Not with my sisters."

Vann clears his throat, "With the giants occupied on the ground, the remaining assassins will be settled on top of the mountain."

I watch his hands point to the entrance to the mine, and wonder just how long this mine has been functioning. The giants know to be that close to stone is a mistake with the threat of the Enduares.

Mrath says, "Give me the bender who can animate stone armies."

Ner'Feon frowns. "Si'Kirin should be one of the benders helping with the towers."

"Yes," Teo says. "He is too valuable not to have against all that brutish force."

Mrath sighs, "Very well, but you will send at least one of the stone benders with us. Having someone create a smoother passage would be invaluable."

Vann, who has been watching quietly, nods. "I will speak with the men."

Ka'Prinn glares at him, but doesn't press further.

I splay my hands across the cool stone beneath me, growing anxious with the endless planning.

"To continue, along with the stone bender, the rest of your assassins will then attack from the top of the mine. This will leave the entrance unguarded," Vann says.

Everyone nods, and I realize we've reached my part.

"Two hundred elven soldiers will approach the entrance, with my flying above on *drathorinna's* back with Teo. The giants have catapults, which could be problematic, but they should be too distracted to launch any."

The image of massive boulders being hurled at me while soaring through the air makes my stomach twist.

Teo watches me as I think through the plan, then he shares.

"There are two options with Rholker: either he rides into the battle like his father did, or he is holed up in the house with his witches protecting him. They command the vaimpírs, so we must be prepared for anything. If he is indeed inside the manor, we will fly straight there and land. Most of the compound should be cleared from humans and giants by this point."

"If we see Rholker on the battlefield, should we kill him?" Ka'Prinn asks, eyes glittering in the low lights.

"Yes," Teo says without hesitation.

I bristle.

A part of me understands the bloodthirst in my mate's eyes, and yet I don't want anyone else to lay a finger on Rholker. It should be me to kill the man who made my life a living hell.

Endu's words ring in my ears:

Fell the giant king. Free your people in the name of your goddess —*Ashra.*

With him gone, the giant government will collapse. My people will be free.

"The question remains: daybreak or midnight? King Teo, you can't honestly expect us to leave this evening," Ner'Feon says.

"I have already said I prefer the moment the sun cracks over the horizon," Teo reiterates, clearly frustrated. Mrath is an efficient woman. She's been reasonable, professional, and wise. But... she brought the majority of the troops. She gets final say.

Her response is interrupted by a commotion outside the

tent. I stand up just as a few hunters pull back the flaps and in walks three great ogres. Their heads tilt to the side, and they crouch to avoid ruining the fabric roof. Though they aren't as large as giants, they clearly are much taller than the elves.

Sounds of shock manifest behind me as the elves and Enduares congregate in front of the map, blocking the strategy from view.

Chirping crickets, gurgling water, and the smell of humid bog take over the tent, and I stare at the armor of moss and branches that cover their lumpy skin.

I recognize the man in the middle almost instantly.

"Shaman Ogre King Braareg," I say breathlessly, giving him a slight bow.

His green eyes snap onto mine, and he frowns. He looks less out of place than he did in Rholker's library, with the spell lights casting sharp shadows over the planes of his face.

"It is you again," he says gently. Though his expression was soft as it landed on me, he casts a glare at the elves.

"Trolls, elves, you have come to our lands without permission," he says.

Maldita sea.[1] The border between their land was unclear when we scoped out a place to rest. The tension in the meeting reaches a new high. Teo steps forward, about to speak, when Braareg holds up his hands.

"Save your words, king. I am the shaman of my people, and as such, my connection to the astral plane is greater even than your human light weaver. Yde has whispered your intentions in the wind. You have come to kill Rholker."

Mrath looks at the ogres with visible disgust.

"You are correct." Her voice is deep, and her words come out slowly.

Braareg doesn't move. "There is a darkness in the mines. Show me your plans."

Mrath laughs. "You can't be serious. Didn't your backwater magic already show them to you or are you baiting us?"

"Mrath," Teo says in warning. Then he takes a deep breath, studying the Ogre King. It's a thing to watch as the Enduares and elves, save Mrath, lean in, waiting on his next words. They are drawn to his magnetic ability to lead. His quiet confidence strikes me as it has a million times, and his self-assurance brings peace in a way that nothing other than a capable leader can provide.

"Shaman or not, you are blood kin to the giants," he says at last. "Surely you must understand why we would be cautious about your coming into our meeting and demanding our strategy."

The Ogre King stares at Teo for a long moment. "We do share blood with the giants, but we no longer consider them our kin."

Mrath laughs. "No? Really? I suppose now would be the time to announce that I have also stepped down as leader of the sisterhood." Her chortle cuts off as she thrusts a finger into the air. "Come now, you sound like petulant children. You live because the giants decided to let you live over the last millenia. You wouldn't turn your back on them."

Braareg glares at her. "Do children not break free from their parents? Or is parricide only acceptable for the elves?"

"That's quite a large word—"

"If I still held the status of bloodkin as legitimate, I would've alerted Rholker of your arrival half a day ago, and you would already be waging war," Braareg says with finality, cutting off Mrath's insult.

I consider this, thinking once again about how the giants disrespected him.

The giants believe in themselves and their future, and they think that the rest of the world is conditioned to believe they are beneath them because they say so. It isn't far-fetched to me to believe that the ogres have had enough. *Humans* have had enough. As have the Enduares.

After casting my thoughts to my husband, Teo nods slowly. "Why are you here then?"

Braareg straightens his great green shoulders. "To see if you would speak to me face-to-face, as king of my own right."

I take a deep breath, showing Teo all the times I'd seen the ogres just behind corners, in dark hallways, and shadowy rooms. It takes courage to step forward and draw the gaze of their glowing eyes. My shoulders straighten, just like Liana showed me.

"Rholker did not respect your rule. I saw evidence enough of that during my time there," I say firmly.

Braareg looks at me and says, "I keep wondering where your collar is."

I glare up at him, letting the anger seep out of my pores.

"I broke it and cast it into some heap of rubbish." Then I nod. "As a Fuegorra reader of my own people, I believe I understand what you do quite well. I recognize you as both shaman and king."

Braareg's eyes gleam. The wind blows around our tent, causing the fabric to billow and flap. The hunters who had led them inside rush to hold down all parts of fabric. He turns to Teo.

"Do you share your queen's sentiment?"

Teo nods. "Yes."

Braareg's eyes are cast to Mrath, then land on Ayla. The curves of his lips turn down.

She killed the old Ogre King, no? I ask through the bond.

Yes, but she also inadvertently made Braareg king. Ogres don't use a familial royal system, so his power would've awoken at the

TO IGNITE A FLAME

death of the old shaman. I think he would've attacked her if he wasn't begrudgingly indebted to her actions, he says back.

"What a thing it is to be ignored and humiliated by those who share your distant blood, no?" Mrath says, pushing past the battle map. "I will accept to share our plan if you swear your blade to our battle. Will you join us in our fight?"

The ogre looks down at her, and the wind dies down. "We will not join a fight we were not originally invited to."

"I would invite you now," Teo says firmly.

Braareg considers this, and the men he brought appear intrigued. One of them stands dangerously close to Thorne, who has stealthily left Mrath's side and appeared at the outskirts of the tent.

Teo tries again. "One king to another, I ask you to join our fight. Rholker's family has poisoned the giants for long enough —let us usher in a new era together."

My mate holds out his hand as if he were to shake Braareg's.

"Neither of you have involved yourselves in swamp business before. In fact, you have purposefully left us out of the council of three. Trolls, Elves, and Giants have had enough power for too long," the king says at last.

"I am not of the elvish kingdom," Mrath says decidedly.

Braareg pauses to think again, as if still considering each word deeply. "If you have come to kill Rholker, then finish your business. It will be the first kindness between our peoples. And the next time you have an inter-kingdom summit, I expect an invite."

"So that's it? You come to tell us we are on your land, that you have some spiritual sight from your goddess, demand to know our plans, and then leave?" Teo asks. Through our bond, I feel the tension knotting through him. His frustration is hidden under reason, but he grows impatient.

Finally, the Ogre King opens his mouth.

"I came to see if you would share with someone your people once considered lesser—to see if Yde's blessing would follow you in your battle plans. You sought to make a deal, as your people always have. It is not the time for us to join the fight. The enemy of my enemy is my friend, but a friend is not an ally. Not yet."

Teo looks at him for a long, hard minute, and I can't help but feel like we lost something.

It sets every nerve on fire. We could've used the extra help.

But then, Teo surprises me by asking, *What does your Fuegorra tell you?*

When I catch Liana's eye, I find her watching me. She presses her lips together, and my mind wanders back to the scrying grotto.

I suck in a deep breath and close my eyes, trying to ignore the pressing silence. I press my hand to my belly as I look inward, prodding at both forms of magic in my chest, both bestowed by goddesses. An answer comes quietly.

Let it be. It is not time for the ogres, but they will be of use in the future.

My eyes snap open, and I let the answer flow to my mate. Then he says, "Very well. We appreciate that you are hosting us."

Braareg looks pleased at the compliment, and then, with all his swampy glory, he turns and leaves out of the tent.

Mrath huffs out an incredulous breath. "That's it? You're just going to let him go?"

Teo turns back to her. "He's right. I have never heard of an allyship between the trolls and ogres. In fact, we have indeed left them out of most of the major events in the last recorded millennia. Diplomacy is long. Surely you know that, Mrath."

He's careful not to mention my vision, for some reason.

Mrath glowers but doesn't say anything more.

I am mostly glad that we didn't have to deal with a premature fight. The ogres seem formidable.

"You seem very confident of that answer," she seethes.

Then Teo says bluntly, "You should be, too, as someone who hopes to enlist as much help as possible in marching upon your brother."

Mrath rolls her eyes. "I grow tired of this conversation and the endless debate. I have decided we will march at midnight."

Ka'Prinn and Ner'Feon open their mouths in tandem, but Liana shakes her head as Thorne reaches for his blade in threat.

"Very well. We will march at night. It is not so late yet. Sleep for an hour or two, and we will ready ourselves," Teo says. The two water dwellers scowl, but say nothing else.

With an agreement finally in place, the meeting finishes, the others leave, and then it is just us and the silence. My mind races with the meeting—the ogres, the elves, the inevitable blood that will be spilled soon. A part of me fights against the encroaching moment with denial.

Teo breaks me out of my thoughts by stroking my cheek. "Are you well?"

I nod, slowly. "My nerves threaten to eat me alive. There was a moment when Braareg walked in that I was truly frightened."

He nods. "I trust what you saw. His arrival was a front. You should feel peace. I think seeing him was the beginning sign of healing our land through united peoples. Now, we should try to rest before..."

The midnight battle.

I take a deep breath and let him lead me over to our makeshift bed. My heart continues to race, and my stomach churns, but I let him remove my armor. He rubs my muscles and kisses me sweetly.

"Tell me another story," he says gently. "That usually seems to settle your stormy thoughts."

I look up at the leather tent above us, seeing the image of Mikal nearly dying, before diving deeper into the memory. Why he was in the fields in the first place.

"When Mikal was ten years old, I was meant to go to the breeding pens. He didn't want me to leave. It was a natural thing for a young boy to do; he felt so protective of me." I blink away the burning sensation in my eyes. "He saw how Rholker treated me, though I tried to protect him from the worst parts of the prince's attentions. I think he felt it was his job as a boy who would one day be a man."

Teo tucks one of the hairs behind my head. "As was right. He was very brave."

I look at my husband. "No, I was older. I was protecting him. Going to the breeding pens could've given me the chance to have a child and bring one of the human men into our hut. He would've had someone else watching him, instead of a seventeen-year-old mess."

Speaking of such things feels fundamentally wrong while laying in bed with my mate, but Teo doesn't look upset. He places his spectacles on his nose, which kindles a warm attraction.

I take his hand as he continues to listen. "Anyway, he thought that if he got hurt I would have to stay and heal him. He knew that the giant king didn't want him dead, and while he was mostly left alone during work hours, there were certain... *measures* taken to ensure he was well. I think Erdaraj mostly liked seeing the ghost of our mother's face peeking back at him."

Teo's face clouds.

"That's awful. Gods," he drags his hand over his face, "what did he do to himself?"

A part of me knows how deeply Teo has felt the loyalty to his family. That was why he obeyed his father when he sent him to Lijasa. The injustice of it all makes my blood burn.

"His first day in the lumber field, he was careless, and he destroyed one of the lumber carts. They put him on a whipping rack and tore his back apart."

The words are blunt, but the memories slice right through me.

Teo stills at the pain radiating off of me and the glow of my skin pulsating across my arms and hands.

"Then what?"

"Rholker wouldn't let me go to the breeding pens anyway. So, Mikal did it in vain. As a present, I rescued an old fox for him. He loved it for as long as the creature lived, and I think about how sweet he was with that small animal."

Teo smiles.

"We don't have many pets under the mountain. He's sixteen, so I don't know if he would still enjoy such child-like things. If he does, I will happily take him hunting through the tunnels myself. I know some of the elves have a kindness between their domesticated wolves." He offers and then draws away from me to begin to rub my tight leg muscles, after a long day of riding.

Then it's my turn to smile. In many ways, he is a better parent than me with his nurturing spirit. I subconsciously lay my hand over my stomach.

"You will be a good father." I freeze when I realize the words actually slipped past my lips.

His hand stills on my calf muscle as he looks at me with those large silver blue eyes.

"Estela," he murmurs. It is a plea, a prayer. It is *fear* itself. Not for the idea of being a father, but for the fact we are discussing this a handful of hours before we charge into battle.

Looking at him, I realize that I haven't bled in a long while.

When I first returned home, I had assumed it was because of my malnutrition.

My thoughts race, and my grip on the windows in my mind loosens. I had considered getting or making contraceptive potions, but every time I broached the subject... I realized I didn't want to. Some part of me craved such a connection with my mate. It wasn't carelessness, it was a damned glimmer of idyllic thoughts.

My heart rate picks up. "I—I don't know why I said that. I don't know—"

In a blink, he moves from his position, and then he is kneeling on the bed next to me. I wish I didn't think it was so pleasing to see him lean down and place his ear to my belly.

"Teo, I don't think that's how that works. You can't just hear a small babe—"

"I would hear my child," he says firmly.

"No—"

"Yes. I would. I would know our creation," he says again, so sure.

I think of the dream, and I adjust my position on the bed to accommodate his enormous head and the corner of his spectacles pressing into my skin.

After a minute, when he is still silent, I ask, "Well?"

My insides feel like a cacophony of fluttering butterflies.

He slowly removes his head and looks at me.

It's as if a cloud has crossed in front of the sun. His face is so shadowy. My stomach drops, not anticipating this reaction.

"You aren't going tomorrow. We must change our plans."

I suck in a breath.

That's it.

My eyes burn, and surprise, joy and worry run rounds on my heart. "I'm still coming with you."

He shakes his head. "No, it is too dangerous."

I bolt upright, locking my gaze onto him. "Am I carrying our child?" A fierce urgency claws at me, desperate for confirmation. The weight of his words hangs in the air. He had confessed his deepest longing for this moment, believing he would only be unworthy. Every fiber of my being craves to absorb his every reaction, to reach out and trace the contours of his face, to seal this revelation with a kiss. The silence between us crackles with anticipation as his eyes meet mine, revealing a tumultuous mix of dread and fragile optimism.

Cradling his face in my hands, I beg. "Say it."

His lips quiver before parting slowly, tears welling up in his eyes.

"You are carrying our child," he whispers.

All of my love and terror balance precariously within my heart. When I think of how I was treated as a child, whipped and mocked and leered at, a fierce, raging sense of protectiveness flairs to life in my gut. Endu has told us to kill the king to free all humans—that now includes our babe.

If I am to have a child, it can't be in a world where Rholker still breathes.

"Then I must go with you." I declare.

As he begins to shake his head in protest, I tighten my grip on his chin. "Teo, consider my feelings. If your father was still alive, would you want him anywhere near our child?"

Teo's jaw tightens as he processes my words, a storm brewing behind his eyes.

I continue. "I will not be denied my revenge. Bring me to fight alongside you. Stand at my side as we slice the head from his shoulders. Present it to me, as you promised on the night of our wedding."

"Estela, I..."

In an instant, Teo opens the floodgates of his mind, unleashing a torrent of harrowing visions. Death dances before my eyes, screams echo in the darkness, and horrors beyond comprehension unfold before me like a grotesque tapestry. Amidst the chaos, I see his mother's tragic fate on the battlefield —wolves tearing at her flesh as she hangs lifeless.

His paralyzing fear reverberates through me like an earthquake as I bear witness to his anguish and resolve to share in his burden.

I lean back.

With every inch of power nestled in my body, I hold my head high. I think of the first vision the Fuegorra gave me, the one in which, surprisingly, I felt his power rumble in my veins somewhere in the future.

I will not die here.

While I do feel confident about that statement, some dark part of my head remembers the image of the crystal card of death. It looms over me, and I choose to ignore it.

"We both know that visions are imperfect. And things can change, but I choose to believe that we will live on past this night. You will let me ride with you. Today, we will kill the king. Tomorrow, we will find and save my brother. In half a year, when the child in my belly is born, it will be the strongest, bravest half-Enduar creature the world has ever known," I say firmly. Even though, as I speak the words, the images of the cards dance behind my eyelids.

Teo strokes my hand. "I can't lose you, too."

My chest cracks open. "Then keep me at your side."

Tears build in his eyes.

"Very well, *mi amor.*"

I kiss him. It contains every wild emotion. It isn't until our lips part that I realize just how fearful I am, too.

Luckily, just as the words are heavy on my tongue, someone comes to the tent, and Teo pries himself away from my side.

I exhale, grateful for the sensation to fade.

Murmured voices flit through the tent, and I close my eyes tight.

Moments later, Teo returns. He holds me close.

"They confirmed that Rholker is there." The silence is short, but it stretches across time and space. "And so is Mikal."

I suck in a breath, and the world around me slants on its side. I wasn't expecting that.

"The scouts saw him?"

Teo nods. "As have the two slaves the assassins snatched."

Mrath works quickly.

Teo pulls me close but I feel like I'm going to burst out of my skin. "I can't sleep. We should leave now," I say, trying to move. He holds me down.

"No. Sleep, my star. I can't keep you from the battlefield, but I see how tired you are. Rest while you can."

As we lay there, with our mission just on the horizon, Teo's hand wrapped around my midsection, I think of what Endu told me about gods and goddesses.

Ashra. Spare me and my family this day.

I repeat the words begging her, and then begging Grutabela, and Endu. It isn't until I sit on the brink of sleep that a strange, disembodied presence sinks next to me.

One that brings much-needed peace.

CHAPTER 41

SERENDIBITE

TEO

Every nerve in my body feels like it's going to combust. We march in an hour, but I'm lying awake in my bed.

Estela is nestled into my shoulder, sleeping soundly.

I have been here, alternating between watching her rest and reading a scroll titled *A History of Giants* to see if there are any other morsels of information about Rholker or his family I could use if he tries to negotiate. The man has been motivated by being underestimated, and I had felt so confident when I started scanning the words. Now, each sentence floats away from me in the whirlpool of my thoughts.

I remove my crystal spectacles, rubbing my eyes. My mind races harder.

Once, I stood on the precipice of a dark future with too many men, and too few women and children. My people were *dying out*, and I had accepted that was the end of everything. I spent so many years believing and repeating to myself that I just needed to survive until death.

I could pass my crown onto some other person, perhaps

Vann or a mated couple. They could die out or slink off to some elven town and simply... fade away.

We had paid for our sins in extinction. Millions dead, a war that ravaged the lands, not to mention the preference to not mingle outside of our species. Maybe we deserved to end.

And yet, here I am, looking down at my mate. In her womb, my child is growing.

Our child.

A small creature who is neither Enduar nor human carries on my story. Pieces of my very soul.

Have I atoned enough? Am I weak, as my father believed?

The youngling will be another person to witness the moments of my life and remember me, continuing this circle yet again. Will they find me wanting, like I found my father?

The crown is a heavy burden; some may even consider it a curse. I swear I could never ask this child to do the same things my father asked of me. I wouldn't train them to be a weapon of death or ask them to sacrifice their dignity for information.

If I could, I would shield them from bloodshed and subterfuge.

My arm is already tightly wrapped around Estela, and I dare not move for fear of waking her.

Dread and sickness curl in my belly as I think of how she wants to come with me to the battle.

A part of me wishes to leave her here—to slip out and leave the war behind her so that no part of it can touch her already scarred flesh. She is stubborn, but she doesn't know what it is to be dragged into the clash of metal and the stink of blood and gore.

No, she shouldn't be anywhere near any of this. But if I leave her here, even with someone to watch over her, it's also possible that she could be harmed by giants or ogres invading the camp.

Such a thing is just as inconceivable as taking her and watching her be hurt.

This is how I spend the next hour, torn between both outcomes and praying with all my heart that I never see either of them come to pass.

When the first sounds of midnight camp movement begin, fresh waves of terror wash over my skin.

Estela and I will not be with the first leg of warriors and hunters to close in on the fortress. That will consist of our finest benders, whose mission is locked on the stone towers of the mine's fortress that protrude into the clouds, sharp and pointed like the tips of the giants' spears.

It disgusts me. I've spent years paying for my father's sins, but Rholker remains unchanged by his father's legacy. He continues to cause the world so much pain, and he remains unrepentant.

I murmur profane prayers.

May their strength rend such towers to the ground so that the elves may burn down the wood harvested from the carcasses of trees.

May the animals swarm them and pick at their flesh...

When Estela stirs, I look down at her and watch those few sweet moments when she wakes. Her long black lashes brush against the skin on her cheekbones, and her eyebrows scrunch together as her body flexes.

My prayers change.

Please, on the lives of Endu and Grutabela, stay the weapons of the giants. Shield her from any harm. Protect my child.

I take another deep breath, grateful for the way she causes me to soften and pull away from the darkness, when her eyes flutter open. I lean down and kiss her cheeks. The moments between her dream bliss and crushing reality are sweet, and they almost catch me off guard.

When the reality of where we are crashes into her, she bolts upright, curls puffed in every direction. She looks over at my lap and sees the scroll.

"Is everything okay? What is this?" she asks hoarsely.

She slowly pulls the scroll into her lap, and I marvel as she works to read. She's still a novice, and I help her through the more complex words, but she is *reading.*

"*The royal line has been preserved by rigorous repopulation efforts over the last four thousand years,*" she reads in my tongue and then looks up at me. "Why are you reading about this?"

I shrug. "Light reading helps calm my nerves."

My poor attempt at humor fails.

Her hand goes to her belly instinctively, and I watch the movement. She swallows.

"How soon until we leave?" she asks.

"At least a few hours. We must wait for the towers to fall," I say, picking at the blanket which covers us both. Despite the thick fabric, my skin is clammy.

She looks around. "Do you have spare parchment? I need to write before we go,"

I take her hand in mine. "Write what?"

"My memories. My head is too full. I dreamt of Mikal again," she says, taking an unsteady breath. "If something happens today—"

"Nothing will happen. I will be there," I say resolutely, feeling the tears crowd in my eyes once again. It's a weak action, but my emotions are frayed and scattered.

She shakes her head.

"If something happens to my memories or me, I want my story to live on. You should know as much as possible," she says gently. "Please. I do this to help my mind, not hurt you."

The protest sits on the tip of my tongue, but I cannot bring myself to say it as I smooth back some of her wild hair. My throat bobs.

"Let me get a scroll."

As I stand, the chilly air bites into me. I walk to the crate containing writing supplies and select what she has requested. Before I return to her, I walk to the flap in our tent. Slowly, I pull one side open and suck in a sharp breath.

Hundreds of elves are already dressed and ready to leave. Their sharp weapons glint in the starlight, and though I can make out their shapes with my Enduar eyesight, their black clothing and dark-colored beasts blend into the night.

Flicking my eyes up to the sky, I look at the moonless sky. Hoping it will not be a bad omen, even though Liana assured me it wouldn't be.

Marching under a new moon is as good as securing Grutabela's blessing.

Then I see Ayla and a few of the other squadron leaders. They ride their enormous alces, leading the formation lines. There is the soft crunchy press of snow into grass as the predators move, and the rustle of leather and clink of metal.

When I see the stone benders who accompany them, I suck in a sharp breath. I do not know them all yet, as many come from the deep ocean. But I recognize the stone animator Si'Kirin.

Dread coils in my belly.

And thus, it falls upon us like a black cloak and a dagger to the throat.

More poetry flits through my mind as it sinks in with fierce finality.

The Second Great War begins today.

That thought adds kindling to the fire of determination. We will be able to staunch most of the impact with this attack, ideally eliminating the rest of the human witches who tortured

Estela, but King Arion and his elves will be the next battle. Mrath hungers for the blood of her brother.

"Teo," Estela whispers, as if she doesn't want to break the silence around us.

I tear my eyes away from the thousands of elves, beasts, Enduares, and *glacialmaras* moving outside.

"All is well, my star. The first regiment has begun to move," I say, turning back to her. I return to the bed and help her glowing form off the ground. "Let us prepare for battle."

We open the chests housing our blades and armor. I blink back tears as I see her crystal-studded breastplate, and the way it begins to sing to her without even needing to open her mouth.

I draw her hair over her shoulders, untangling knots and braiding her hair into a crown around her head. I help her put on her under armor garments. Each touch is a reminder of my love, a prayer.

I'm lost in my thoughts until her breastplate is clipped on, and her legs and arms are covered. We will ride in on a mythical creature and burn the remaining giants to the ground.

Estela is still hesitant because her magic is not refined, and she doesn't want to kill any of the humans.

When she is fully dressed, she looks like a queen of battle. Capable, but... *gods*. She's not meant for this. Just like my mother wasn't meant for this who should've stayed an instructor at the university, filling young minds with knowledge instead of being sucked into my father's destructive orbit.

Her hands reach up and stroke my unkempt hair. Without words, I turn around and kneel, letting her braid. Then, just as we did the day I fought the creatures in the cave, she helps me with my armor.

Her fingers do not tremble as they did that day. She does not look afraid.

She should.

"Now what?" she asks.

I cup her uncovered cheek. "Now we wait."

It doesn't take much more time after that to feel the ground shake beneath us. The crystals that were silent upon moving now pierce the air, across the distance to our camp.

It is an overwhelming beat, one that sparks movement and action before thought. It hasn't been long enough since the battle song last played.

When the air stills, I know it's time. Only a few moments of quiet are spared before the roar of crumbling stone pierces the air.

Estela's eyes grow wide, and she dashes out, squinting to make out the cloud of dust that shoots up in a long column before billowing out like a mushroom cap. We are easily an hour's walk from the mine, but it looks far closer than I realized.

"Can you see it?" I ask, knowing that while her eyesight has improved, it is not effortless like mine.

She nods, silently.

It is time for the second regiment.

Soon, the third group will go in from behind and invade the camp from the top of the mountain mine.

And then...

Gods, it's happening too fast.

"Teo, Estela," Mrath's voice says from behind. She commands the space, fully dressed in her black armor, covered in razor sharp leaves. "It is time to move." She stands with a group of her dryads and Thorne.

My heart stutters, but Estela turns around, proud. "Let us uncover *drathorinna*."

We follow the elf to the dome that was made from the trees to cover the dragon's crystal glow. Slowly, the twelve of them work their magic, releasing the bindings around the drake.

She stretches her long neck and expands her wings.

If the elves are as awestruck as the rest of us, they do not show us tonight.

I can feel a new battle song start up in camp, an elvish sound. It matches the beat of my heart, the same as Estela's. We walk together, but when she reaches *drathorinna*, she climbs to the top like the tree climber she once was.

Following behind her, I feel the amplification of the war cries. The marvelous creature takes a step and then another.

"Teo," Vann calls out. "Are you ready, brother?"

I jerk around to look at him.

It is a vision from my past to see him in full armor, and his cleaver hanging from his hand. We fought alongside each other through many battles, cutting through our enemies with a frenetic need that once drove the giants to their knees in submission.

He was meant to ride, but that was before I knew about the child Estela carries. There's no one I would trust more at my side to help protect her.

"Come," I call, gesturing him up.

He looks at me, confused.

"What are you saying? I came to wish you luck."

Estela turns, a protest written on her face, but I give her a pleading look and say, "Every butcher needs a fine cleaver. Let him come. We can keep you safe," I say.

She presses her lips together, nods once, then calls, "Lord Vann, your king wants you to fight at his side!"

Drathorinna extends her wing, and Vann studies it, clearly hesitant. Then, he climbs up, and the wing moves, depositing him behind me. A new handle appears on the back of the great beast, and he clutches on.

"Holy shit," he mutters from behind.

"I know the feeling," I reply. Only a Fuegorra reader can control such a beast.

Luckily for us, my wife is one.

We move with the troops, getting into place, and then when the signal comes, we lift off, flying right through the front gates.

CHAPTER 42
TANZANITE
ESTELA

I am not a stranger to death and carnage. I have seen executions, whippings, and fights between slaves and giants.

But nothing—not the training with Svanna or a lifetime of torture—prepared me for battle.

Everywhere I look, blood spurts, and flesh is cleaved.

A thousand miniature battles are fought against the larger massacre, and it's unclear who will come out as victor—even though golden armor is glinting more abundantly than bare giant chests.

The first elf I saw impaled didn't look like she was going to be bested by the giant. Even flinching away from such a gruesome death didn't save me either from seeing a giant torn in three.

When I catch sight of a helpless slave lying in a pool of his own blood, I foolishly look away only to see the severed arm of an Enduar. Blood and gore are everywhere, and yet, none compares to the smell.

Thousands of bodies are strewn on either side of the mines.

It takes effort to keep from leaning over *drathorinna* and vomiting all over her crystal scales.

I think that most of the dead are giants, but that doesn't quell the sickness.

Power thrums under my skin.

The cost... the cost is too high.

I hadn't anticipated my instincts to have such a sway in my plan.

What's wrong? Teo asks through the bond as the wind rushes past us, blasting my skin with icy air.

I have to help.

Estela, we had a plan— he starts, only for my control of the crystal drake to twist us to the side.

Her power doesn't come from breathing fire or ice; it comes through me. While working through her eyes, I realized she can act as a focusing crystal for my light.

The light around me begins to glow stronger, and the shouts that had called to us now intensify. I feel the power of the dragon well up inside of me, and the same fear I've felt before mounts.

I haven't practiced enough. My breath freezes in my throat for a terrifying moment while the power surges through my body.

It overtakes me, aiming at the dozens of giants running toward the group of elves fighting with everything they have.

The power reaches its peak as quickly as a gasp, and then the lyre string inside of me is set free. The magic zings past me, and into the group. In an instant, screams are cut off as a blackened hole tears through flesh, stone, and earth.

I slump back toward Teo, feeling the effects of such a strong burst.

That wasn't wise so early on in this battle. You will tire quickly if you continue this way, Teo expresses with his battle-worn experience through our bond.

I reluctantly agree.

With one last heart-shattering look, I tear myself away and head back into the mining compound. In the corner of my eye, something hurls towards us.

It's Vann who calls out a second before a large boulder crashes into the side of *drathorinna.*

The horrible sound that emanates from us must be heard throughout the mine.

My hand flies to my own side as I feel some of her scales crack. I sense the reassuring weight of the armor shielding my growing child within. Hot tears well up, threatening to spill, while a surge of fierce determination floods through me, fiercely protective of the life blossoming within my womb.

When another rock hurls at us, I am more careful. We evade it with more ease. My blood pumps, and I'm coated in sweat.

The wall is mostly broken, but the stone benders' attack wasn't enough to thwart the use of the catapults.

Another stone nearly hits us as we rise over the compound, looking for a place to land. My senses are heightened as I look at the arrows, spears, and rocks preparing to be launched at us.

How are there still so many?

My question is left unanswered as the hiss and wizz of lethal objects flying past us quickly depletes the energy I thought replenished.

It's then that I notice movement from the mouth of the mines. I had seen humans fleeing, but now hundreds of them begin pouring out of the caves.

Some of the giants who were fixed on us now turn on them, and with swipes of their massive weapons, begin to cut them down.

"No!" I scream.

Teo's mind reaches out to carress my own, and together, he helps me angle *drathorinna* down toward the ground. His hand slips around my midsection.

I suck in a breath.

We'll do this together, I say.

I'll keep both of you safe.

I feel the nudge of my power, but I'm acutely aware of my limitations. I know that I can't both hit the giants and avoid the humans.

The ground gets closer with every second, and I cast my thoughts back to my husband.

We need to jump, I shout down the bond.

Not yet, it's still too high. You'll both get hurt, Teo pleads.

The wind blows back the skin on my face, burning it from the sheer speed and force. Just as the screams of those worrying we are about to crash touch my ears with shattering magnitude, I pull up.

"Now!" I scream, ready to go, only for *drathorinna* to be violently shoved to the side with the impact of another boulder.

The collision throws all three of us from our seated positions. My heart stutters, and I scream at the weightless horror.

Death, death, death, death comes.

The voice that had been quiet for weeks whispers.

I hear, not feel, the ground rumble beneath me. It moves and shifts like a torrential wave, part of it reaching up to cradle me and the men.

The breath is still knocked out of me when I crash into it, but the shifting formations of stone guide my body to the ground unbroken. My hand goes to my midsection.

Nothing feels wrong, so I leap up a second later, surrounded by fallen humans and giants. There are many more still fighting than we had anticipated while we landed.

When I look at the manor, I find it surrounded by black mist.

Damn.

Teo and Vann are faster than me, and I watch them draw to each other like moths to a flame. I've never seen them fight together, but they move in synchrony as they slice through scarred flesh.

A leg is cut away from a body, a stomach stabbed. They plow through the field like the terrors that I have only heard about. *The Butcher and his Cleaver.*

My mouth falls open, stunned, when I see Svanna cut a giant clear in half in the distance. She bangs her sword against her chest, roaring with blood spattered across her armor. This isn't the woman who taught me how to hold a sword. Another Enduar catches my attention just as my hair stands on end.

There are human screams behind me. I turn around, spot three slaves, and charge. When I am face-to-face with a giant warrior, I feel nothing but courage. He grins down at me, hair matted with blood and tattooed chest heaving.

"Run!" I shout at the slaves, and they scramble.

"Yes! Scatter like the insects you are!" he roars.

There is something familiar about him as he laughs and reaches forward, his fingers trying to grasp my armor. The brilliant magical string within me flares, and my glowing skin burns his hold. The sound of sizzling skin and smell of charred flesh fill my senses.

Holding up the sword I've been training with for months, I adjust my stance. My gifted power makes me that much more formidable against him.

"The king's little whore," the giant spits at me.

I don't wait for him to taunt me more. I thrust the sword toward his legs. A downed giant is much easier to stab.

He jumps back from the attack, laughing. "Now I see while Rholker kept a collar on you. The bitch can fight!" Then he swings his spear.

My eyes widen, and I just barely duck out of the way. The force of air coming with his spear causes me to tilt, and I fall on my side. I cry out.

He is bolstered by the sound, and I see the humans flocking behind him.

He's getting close to my child. Too close. I force myself to my feet with a yell and look back to see Vann and Teo fighting off seven giants at once. Adrenaline refuels me as I lift my sword again. Rallying every bit of strength in my human body, I charge the giant.

As I swipe left and right, he finds the attacks pathetic, like a lamb charging a warrior. He laughs again and deflects each one with ease. The force of his block jostles my shoulders.

"Where is Rholker?" I yell back.

He smirks. "Preparing to kill you, should I fail."

Then I lunge forward, slicing across his leg. Somehow, I catch how his eyes go to the manor, the one we planned on Rholker staying in.

Good.

The giant shoves me away. I fall on my ass with a yell, then scramble to my feet.

He hisses at the blood staining the fabric around his thigh, then spits.

"I led you around the night of the coronation," he says, his eyes on fire. "I preferred you with more flesh showing."

He hauls all his weight back and wedges the tip of his spear between my breastplate. The metal strap groans as he tries to pry it off.

I scream at the force. Light from within fills my eyes, and I grasp at a fallen sword. He shields his eyes, but I spot the space under his ribs that would kill him almost instantly. I thrust the blade through, up into his stomach. He roars, and I angle the blade skyward, piercing his lungs and heart. He stumbles and collapses.

I fucking did it.

I sink to the ground, exhaustion wearing on me as I grab my stomach. All the training wasn't enough. It was never going to be enough.

I can't keep doing this.

But the war inside of me is cut short when several more humans run past, grabbing weapons from the fallen giants.

"¡Por la libertad!" they scream, thrusting weapons in the air. Their emaciated forms twist as they thrust themselves into battle, hacking a way to the exit.

When the first falls, I force myself to get back up.

Por la libertad. For freedom.

For my freedom, and theirs. For freedom against the threats on the Enduares. For a better life for my baby.

I must end this.

Weary, I press my hand to my throbbing shoulder, and then I pull my hand away to find it coated in crimson.

Hostia puta[1].

My Fuegorra glows to life, but I push on. I drag my dizzy form toward the manor. Not two steps in, I trip. My gauntlets land in a puddle of blood. I twist around to see the ripped open stomach of a slave.

I gag, trying to drag myself to my feet while avoiding catching my feet on any more lifeless forms.

There are few giants left, and all of them are engaged in battle. It's pure luck that my stumbling is met with no resistance.

When I finally reach the manor, a tendril of cold, black mist extends toward me.

Grey hands reach out and latch onto my arms. I turn

abruptly to come face to face with a vaimpír. I screech, scratching at their limbs with my gloved hands, but the creature is not the same skulking, hunting demon from the caves. It holds me in place as it drags me along—as if it were following orders.

"Estela!" my mate screams across the battle.

Turning toward the sound only makes me stumble. My strength is depleted. There is none left to fight against the gray hands. While my energy is sluggish, they don't seem like they are going to hurt me, and I need their help to get to Rholker. I feel my magic working to save me, but between riding *drathorinna* and fighting that giant, everything is moving in slow motion. This might be a mistake, but...

Seconds later, just as the door comes into view, a vaimpír hisses, and chilled blood sprays over my face.

Then Teo's hands are on me. The smooth surface of a crystal is pressed to my face, and a few coarse notes of song pass through his lips. A wave of energy washes over me as the stones on my armor glow to life. Strength returns to my legs, and I can stand.

Vann appears next to Teo. They hold onto either side of me.

"We need to find Rholker," I pant, even as the mist fills my lungs, and a memory of torture returns.

Teo doesn't speak as he pushes open the door. I step across the wooden threshold and choke. Waving my arm, I inhale deeply and use the heat of my magic to burn away as much of the mist as possible.

A staircase materializes abruptly in front of us, just as the piercing wail of a baby shatters the silence. A forceful gust of wind surges through the room, hurling Teo and Vann back-wards, out of the manor.

"No!" I scream just as the heavy door slams shut with a resounding thud. My anguished cry echoes as I whirl around to pound on the solid wood barrier.

The piercing wail of the newborn reverberates through the room, triggering a surge of primal urgency within me. My imagination conjures thoughts too awful to speak out loud. Babies are so fragile—akin to the life blossoming within me. That fuels my determination to ensure its safety. As I take a step towards the staircase, a chilling creak sounds from the door to my left.

I leap back as Dahlia steps out. And then, towering behind her, Rholker emerges holding a massive baby in his arms, a surreal and primal sight that sends shivers down my spine.

My eyes go wide, and rage coils itself up my spine. I need to get that baby away from him.

"Estela." My name on his tongue sounds like an exhalation. Almost as if he's been holding his breath since I left. Then his voice deepens. "Have you come to kill me?"

Our eyes meet, and I see the red that rings his once-yellow pupils while black veins creep up his neck, like rot.

There is an undercurrent of dark magic in the room.

He's turning into a vaimpír, I cast the words to Teo.

I feel his recognition spark as he pounds against the magically sealed door. When he tries to reply, his message is muffled.

My gut drops, and I take a slow step forward, looking at the child squirming in his arms. He could kill the helpless thing faster than I could blink. Rholker would only keep a baby if it would be of use to him.

Nandi's face flickers in my mind. I remember her screaming at Rholker, dirty and hungry. She called for her son, the true heir to the throne.

Do you see Nandi's son in this court?

He never said the child was *dead.*

That must be her son.

New emotions war inside me. On the one hand, giants are evil and dangerous. On the other... it's a baby.

A baby I can't watch die.

My gaze returns to his face. "I've come to free the humans."

His red eyes search mine, unfeeling. "Humans will never be free."

I remain silent, looking at Dahlia who merely watches, curious and threatening. I killed three of her sisters, where the other two are, I don't know.

"You once offered me a measure of freedom," I say slowly.

His grip tightens on the child, eliciting another sharp cry.

"Because I loved you. I have been far too kind—I spared you once. I spared Fektir's daughter. Even my brother's son... I thought it would be cruel to kill a babe, so I brought him here. He could grow and die as a man with a weapon in his hand, without knowing who he was." He looks down at the child, and memories of Nandi's screams fill my ears.

I thought he had taken the baby to kill it.

He takes a step forward.

"Even after you ran the first time, I loved you. But you ran again. You destroyed my chance at ruling." He takes another step. "I made you a promise that I would kill all you love."

Every muscle tightens.

"I don't love that babe. Spare it, please," I plead.

With almost robotic movements, he continues to approach me. "He was found out by Lord Fektir. Others will come soon to take him home and claim the throne. The time for weakness has passed. I must kill it."

Dahlia looks at me with a curious expression, then says, "Give me the child, Rholker. Be with your love."

My stomach twists as my gaze drops to the woman who tortured me. I don't trust her any more than I trust Rholker.

"You told me I must kill him," Rholker says mechanically.

Dahlia looks up at him. "I will handle it for you. Take the Light Weaver's daughter and show her your gift."

Rholker's glossy gaze changes, softening into something more giant and less undead.

My mate continues to beat on the door behind me, and the ground rumbles again.

"Tell the troll to call off his magic. I have something to show you," his voice rumbles.

I swallow.

"Do it now," he demands.

Teo, stop.

No, his voice growls back. I could cry when I hear him clearly again.

Please, or they'll kill the child.

From the deepest place in my soul, I cannot handle the death of something small and innocent. Not the giant baby, and not my own child. The feirce instinct guts me from the inside out. My breath holds, but the rumbling beneath my feet stops.

Rholker smiles and passes the baby onto Dahlia. It's only then that I hear the slither behind me. Pain quickly blossoms from my thigh as it latches onto my flesh and poison leaks into me.

"Not again," I groan as the familiar paralysis floods my body. I stagger and fold onto the ground, as Rholker's boots walk up next to me.

Please, don't let this hurt my baby. Please!

Then the world goes black.

CHAPTER 43

AQUAMARINE BERYL

ESTELA

D*rip.*
    Drip.
    Drip.

I cringe at the liquid notes that rouse me from sleep. My whole body hurts. But when my eyes peel open, I gasp.

Morning light filters through the dusty window, casting a golden hue on the swirling particles in the air. The manor is quiet, and the black mists have completely retreated. Stacked logs make up the walls and ceiling beams.

As I scan the space, my eyes lock onto the body swaying gently from the ceiling. My arm shifts away from his space around my belly, and for the first time, a small flick of heat sparks deep within. A tangible life force reaches out to me. Time seems to stand still as my heart races with dread, every detail of the room etched into my mind with haunting clarity. And then I see him.

Mikal.

My hand falls.

Chains are wrapped around his shoulders, connecting to

one of the beams overhead. His scraggly dark hair covers his face, and his unnaturally long human limbs stretch out from a bloody, malnourished form.

"Mikal?" I ask, my voice breaking.

He doesn't stir.

Por los dioses[1].

I push myself up, ignoring every protest of my body. I stumble forward at his feet and look up to see the faint rise and fall of his chest. I reach out and touch his filthy, bare foot.

Fear presses down on me with urgency. We're too vulnerable, too much can go wrong.

"I'm going to get you down," I say, tears already spilling over my cheeks. I look around frantically to see something, anything, that would help me get him down.

A sound stirs from the shadowed section of the room.

As my head twists, I see the plush chair in the corner, filled up by the massive, dark presence of Rholker.

I freeze.

He watches me with his crimson eyes.

"I wouldn't do that if I were you. Though, I must admit, it's moving to see you on your knees," he says slowly.

Each unearthly intonation of his voice sends a chill up my spine.

"How long has he been here?"

He doesn't move. "Since the day after you returned home to Zlosa."

The sound of Zlosa being referred to as my home coats my tongue with a bitter taste.

"You've left him chained up for two months?!" Rage heats my skin, causing the glow to expand. I'm going to tear him apart.

He raises an eyebrow. "No. He wasn't always hanging. Sometimes we chained him there." His veiny hand gestures to the other corner of the room, where bloody tools are laying next to a table.

Bile rises in my throat, and I quickly turn back, touching the cold skin of my brother. A part of me is glad that he isn't awake. How can I help undo such pain?

"He's half-giant. He could've survived worse," Rholker says casually.

My chest heaves. I fear touching him and hurting him further by pulling on his body. I just need to get him down.

"The Six tended to him, as well. Kept him alive. Healed the worst of his wounds," he says again.

I grit my teeth. "Why are you telling me this?"

"Because..." he trails off. "I suppose because it pleases you. Despite all you've done to me, I still wish to grant you a kindness."

I push myself to my feet, feeling the glow of my chest increase. I haven't rested, and the magic Teo gave me is fading, but somehow, I still have enough adrenaline to do this.

"Kindness?" I say, my voice unrecognizable. "You aren't even fully mortal, are you? What do you know of kindness?"

He stands, and the shadows bend with him. "I know enough. My father denied the power that the human witches offered him, only conceded to small bits and pieces here and there when it was useful, especially when making you fear the Enduares. I did this to stabilize my kingdom. You gave me no other choice when you ruined everything the night of my coronation."

My fists ball.

"How did I ruin everything? You married Fektir's daughter. They placed the holy crown upon your head. *You were fine.*" I spit the last words.

He cocks his head to the side, and the motion is so unnatural as if he had broken his neck. "Fine? You started a fight at my coronation, turned the ogres against us, and effectively ruined my credibility. You took thirty-three slaves with you and killed twenty warriors. We tried to squash the rebellion—poisoning the men's food, burning slave pens... executions. None of it worked. In the eyes of the court, if I could not keep you in line, then I wasn't fit to rule. You are *the* reason I lost everything."

He lets out a bitter laugh. "And worse yet, I went down this path for you. Because I wanted you."

My mind swims.

Were the hearts of men really so fickle as to burn the world over a woman?

I open my mouth, but he holds up a charred, grey hand.

"Enough talk. Now that you are here, it is time to make good on my promise," he says, withdrawing his spear from the wall.

My eyes look between him and Mikal.

I stretch myself as widely as I can, protecting as much of my brother as possible. My awareness teases the lyre string, prepared to pull hard and release a light hot enough to roast the giant.

"If you want to kill him, you must kill me, too," I say.

And your unborn child, a voice reminds.

I suck in a sharp breath. This is all wrong—I wasn't supposed to do this alone. Even thinking about the death of my baby makes me want to tear out my own heart, but I am running out of options. Rholker must be stopped.

Rholker falters for a second. He looks between the two of us, clearly torn. And then, he tightens his grip on his weapon, black mist billowing behind him.

He holds the spear up and points it at my heart.

I swallow.

"Two birds with one spear then," he murmurs, then he draws the weapon back.

My breath stops.

There was a large part of me that hadn't believed he'd actually do it. Time slows as his arm cocks back fully, and I let out a gasping breath.

This isn't just about me.

This is about my family.

My mother had taught me about love.

A love so ferocious it could tear the clouds from the sky and split the earth in two floods through me. The stone in my chest flares to life with the power of the gods.

I think of the cards, of the visions, the meeting with Endu.

My future has been set for a long time, and it does not involve dying.

"In the name of Endu, Grutabela," I rasp through clenched teeth, feeling the cold metal of the spear pressing into my flesh, "and Ashra," a searing pain pierces my chest as the spear makes contact, "I command you to stop."

The spear drives deeper into me, and suddenly, a radiant light bursts forth from within my being. At the same time, terror courses through me like a raging river. My precious child flashes before my eyes.

I gaze down in horror as I see the weapon drive through my chest, shattering bones and rattling Mikals's chains as it impales him, too. Blood burbles in my throat as I struggle to breathe. Rholker staggers away from me, his form wavering in my failing vision.

Before I can crumble to my knees, Mikal's hanging body stops my path. I tug against his chains.

My sight blurs as an explosion of blinding light emanates from me. I feel and hear its sheer power causing sections of the manor to tremble and fall apart.

An overhead beam splits with a deafening crack.

"Fuck you, Rholker," I spit.

The beam falls and impales Rholker mercilessly through the

chest. His rib cage cracks and folds under the impact, and he instantly collapses with a muffled thud.

"Estela..." he chokes.

His red eyes widen in shock, staring at me as his life force fades away.

As I release a trembling breath, I fixate on the lifeless giant form before me, pain now starting to be replaced with numbness. In that moment of devastation, I can only think about how Teo should have been by my side. We were meant to face this together.

Grief consumes me like a relentless storm raging within my very being. Each tear that falls carries the weight of my shattered dreams, each sob echoing the crack of my bones. The oblivion that envelops me is suffocating.

The baby within me...

I can't feel it.

Oh gods.

I strain to sense any flicker of Mikal's heartbeat behind me. Silence.

My mouth opens as another sob tears apart my chest.

"Teo," I whimper.

Death. Death. More death.

But I'm not fucking dead.

Yet.

The blood is leaking out around the spear and sliding down to my stomach. The heart in my rib cage struggles to beat, its squeezing lopsided and unsettlingly wet.

For a second, I swear, I can hear my mother's dying screams the night Mikal was born. The stuttering breath and the panting words still ring in my ears.

This is for you. Take care of him.

But she came back to stay the king's hand when he wanted

to execute my brother and me. She appeared in a vision to give me a lepidolite stone and escape Rholker.

She died because she said she loved us, but she can't stay away. Perhaps... she exists in the next life with regret. Perhaps she discovered that living for her children was more important than dying for us. What I had imagined as being selfless for Mikal and me was really... selfish for everyone else. Especially Teo.

And then, I understood one thing with stark clarity. It robs the final flickers of stabbing pain from rippling through me.

I don't want to die for my brother or baby or mate.

I crave glowing crystals and intimate moments, luminescent pools and the smell of stone, cries and laughter and *aging*—but darkness is already creeping in, leaving behind the image of the card of death.

CHAPTER 44
RICHTERITE
TEO

"Estela!" I scream as we beat against the door to the great manor.

My wife. My babe.

I take my sword and attempt to dig it into the dark fog-covered wood, but we are blown back. My body rattles as we hit the ground, and a dark figure appears out of another cloud of billowing mist. The smoke stings my face.

"Godsdamnit," Vann grunts, sitting up next to me.

The remains of the slave's rebellion and escape are scattered around us along with the evidence of our long fighting. At first glance, all of our troops have retreated. "King of the Enduares," the cloaked black figure says, holding a baby in her arms.

I charge forward, sword pointed as Vann also gets to his feet. "Take me back to Estela!"

She holds up a hand and a wall of mist wraps around my weapon, tearing it away.

"I will not fight you this time," she says. "Though I have not forgotten what happened to our sssisters."

A snake curls around her neck, flicking its tongue toward the crying baby.

I shouldn't care for that child. It's the enemy...

And yet my heart breaks for it.

My fingers twitch to take it away. I can't watch him die here.

"Teo," Vann says, low voice full of warning.

As if sensing my thoughts, the witch raises the babe.

"The deal that bonded us to the giant king is over. I have no use for this little one, yet. Consider the baby a peace offering since you have been taking care of the Light Weaver's daughter."

I don't wish to move, fearing the trap.

Sound from all around us begins to stir as the woman's fingers begin to twist and contort.

I look around to see a sea of undead rising to their feet, just like the cold ones. Their gaping wounds turn grey as their unseeing eyes snap open, red as blood.

"Gods damn them all," Vann exclaims, diving for his cleaver.

I also curse, watching the ugly creatures take ragged steps forward. Grabbing another weapon, I hold out the blade, ready to cut down each undead with Vann at my side.

"Take him as a gift or we will ensure he joins our army," the witch says.

That causes me to pause.

"I accept," I say, my grip on the sword loosening.

The second I step forward, black mists swirl in a raging vortex. It blows back both of us back onto our asses. Just as soon as it starts, it ends, leaving the baby on the ground.

Be wary of those who approach, troll king. May we not be enemies the next time we see each other.

The black voice rings in the air, leaving an acidic taste on my tongue, but I ignore it in favor of the giant baby wailing on the steps.

"Shit," I say, grabbing the infant as Vann hacks at the impenetrable wood. "We need to get inside before those others arrive. If the women are gone, Rholker is still there."

"Cave rat!" a new voice booms across the distance.

The ground trembles beneath our feet as the voice echoes through the air.

I hold the crying giant baby close to my chest, feeling its tiny heart pounding in fear.

Vann's eyes narrow as he looks towards the source of the voice, his grip tightening on his cleaver.

Four giant lords and half a dozen warriors pour into the empty compound, their towering figures gleam with sweat in the overcast sunlight, highlighting their tattoos and sweaty skin. Their yellow eyes are something out of my nightmares.

"Give us the boy or we will kill you!" one calls out, his voice like thunder in the stormy sky above.

"Enough have died today," I call out. "Do not come closer if you wish to live."

The giant lords exchange glances, a low rumble passing through them as they consider my words. One of the warriors steps forward, his massive hands tightening around his war ax.

"You dare threaten us, cave rat?"

Vann brandishes his cleaver, the metal glinting in the dim light as he stands protectively in front of me and the wailing giant baby.

"Call me that again, tree rutter," he challenges.

One of the giants cocks back his enormous spear.

When he hurls it, I take both Vann and me to the ground. The child wails.

I know we can't let them take the boy, even if it is a giant.

With a deep breath, I focus my mind on the molten core of the earth beneath us.

Lava magic flows through my body, a power as old as time itself. The ground begins to shake violently as fiery cracks split open around us.

With a guttural cry, I unleash my magic, calling upon the power of the lava to rise up and protect us. Streams of molten fire burst forth, enveloping the giant lords in a wall of inferno. The heat is so intense it sears their skin, blistering and melting their tattoos. The giants are caught off guard by the sudden invocation, and their screams fill the air. Fire and lava continue to cover the area, reducing the ground beneath them to a savage, molten pit.

The volatile energy tears against me, overheating every part of my body and promising to inflict scars that will never fully heal.

Vann cries out, as does the boy he now holds.

"*Run*," I pant, struggling to keep the magic at bay.

The lava cools at a rapid pace, and I lose my grip on the magma. The ground beneath us begins to move and shift again, by a force as powerful as my own.

But it's not coming from me.

My skin begins to heat, as Vann races away, sensing his way along the stone and darting across the non-molten ground to one of the fallen walls. I feel helpless to the mounting magic. It's like water running over my skin, leaving my body to be used elsewhere.

Silence descends, and then, seconds later, the walls of the manor explode.

That moment of peace was just as charged as the sound that rips past me, blowing me and everything else back. I land on the ground, hard, feeling my armor crunch against a dead body.

I don't have time to look at the fallen when the light shines out around me, as brilliant as the explosion of the star.

Pain rips open my heart. Not from injury, but my mating bond. I clutch at the gem in my chest.

"Estela!"

I curse every god as I reach for the light.

Waves of sound and some other dimension wash around me. I push against it, even as it rams me backward. Every muscle screams at me as I move.

The white light stays, but the resistance fades. I only make it a short distance on my hands and knees before I slump over, feeling the light pulse around me, wondering if this is what it is like to be in the eye of a storm.

After another moment of rest, I look up and see the collapsed floor with two bodies impaled, connected together with a spear, leaning against each other for support. I would recognize the deep brown curls and small body in the rubble of the end of the world. The form behind her is easy to deduce.

Estela and Mikal.

The wail that rips past my lips is agony entombed in sound.

I hold my chest, and tears burn down my cheeks as a burst of adrenaline has me spinning toward my wife. I kneel in front of her and cup her cheek.

Her eyes flutter open, and her irises go in and out of focus.

"Mi amor[1]. You have... all my stories," she chokes out as a bit of blood drips down from the corner of her lip.

I shake my head, touching the spear through her chest. She winces.

"Teo, bury... the three of us together," she pants.

"No, no, no," I cry, abandoning the weapon in her chest for her face. "I made you a promise. You would never be taken again."

519

She smiles, showing blood-soaked teeth. "I did everything I could to... make amends. Forgive me."

She lets out a breath of pure life and then stills.

"You are gods-touched, Estela," I command. "You will not die."

In her chest, her Fuegorra flickers. It beats in time with my own.

I look up to the sky and scream the name of my goddess.

"Grutabela!" I call with every inch of conviction. I call with the fear of a man who has lost everything and refuses to do it again.

"Endu promised me that my wife would live—that *we* would live on. I let you take my mother, my father, my people, *my home*. I do not accept this!"

My belly and chest shake as a tear falls down my cheek.

The air around me shifts, and a woman emerges from the lingering light. She looks like Estela, save her shorter stature and fuller lips.

The Light Weaver.

She looks down on me, weary.

"Twice, I have intervened for my children. Once after Mikal was born, and then when Estela was kept captive. I... should not do it thrice."

I look up at the woman. "Should not?"

She frowns. "They will be safe in the afterlife. Estela has done what she was meant to do. Rholker is dead, his father is dead, and her people are free."

I sit there, helpless, next to the grotesque scene. "She and Mikal should be safe with me."

The woman studies me. "You have others to care for."

I shake my head.

"I have given my home, my love, *my body*—all for my people.

Allow me to be godsdamned selfish for once," I plead, kneeling before her with my arms stretched out on either side.

The Light Weaver looks down at me, sad, but silent.

"What do you want?" I demand. "You said you shouldn't, not that you couldn't."

She presses her lips together. "You would give me something?"

I stand up, knowing that my wife is already gone. "I would give you anything but those who lay next to me."

The woman studies me. "Your father took something, long ago. The power that flows through you."

I grit my teeth. As if in response, my hands glow like they had after I pushed my father.

Estela's mother Aitana steps forward.

"It is a sorrowful story told in the heavens, that Teo'Likh, with all his power, was not satisfied. He was given a gift, and then demanded more so he could play the part of a misguided savior and destroy the land."

I press my lips together.

She looks at me. "The gods speak through me now. They are fond of you, approving even. Give back the stolen power, and they will return Estela and Mikal from the land of the dead."

"I want our child, too."

Aitana freezes. "Child?"

My heart pounds as I clench my teeth. "Didn't you know Estela was pregnant?"

She blinks, and I swear her eyes are growing watery. "Then my children and the babe it shall be. Prepare to trade."

I take a shaky breath. "Without my power, my people will be helpless."

She shakes her head. "Not helpless. They will have your gods-touched queen. But the volcano... it will be dormant."

"Will you take all my power?" I ask.

She frowns. "You seem to think you can negotiate. Do not mistake your gods' pleasure at your clever spirit for weakness."

It's a hard blow, but love requires faith. And, with Estela, I have a lot to believe in. I nod my head. "Done."

The woman raises her hand. "One last point. If I do this, I will never be able to save her again. I swear it. The gods do not take kindly to resurrection, for that is the realm of the demons."

"You won't have to. We grow stronger daily. I will keep her and her brother safe. I will protect our child," I say resolutely.

Aitana frowns. "Power in exchange for lives."

I take a deep breath. "Lives are taken for power every day, surely you can make the opposite true."

She smiles, and then, closes her fingers in a hard fist. Her eyes leave mine, and I turn back to watch. The spear fades away into particles of light. Then the holes close, one by one.

CHAPTER 45
SAPPHIRE
MIKAL

A gasp ruptures the silence, sharp and sudden as a winter's break.

His eyelids flutter open, revealing the world in hues of gray, as if color has yet to be reinvented. Mikal stirs, an involuntary shiver coursing through his blood-soaked limbs. His fingers, cold and numb, curl instinctively around something soft. With a dawning realization, he sees the wild dark brown curls, partially matted with blood and rubble.

The cold he feels is a stark contrast to the warm, sunny mountain they were now sitting on.

A long wooden spear connects the two of their bloody forms together, and the sight makes his insides churn with awful panic, especially when he sees the metal cuffs and his raw wrists.

"Este?" His voice is a ghostly whisper, barely disturbing the air.

A presence greets him in the silence—*Death*. They are dead. Gone from the earth.

It has been an elusive specter, always lurking at the periphery of life but never quite touching it... until now. He had imagined it as an eternal sleep or perhaps a journey to some far-off place where souls wandered, lost and disconnected.

But death isn't some awful darkness, a rest after a life of pain. It is gentle. Full of song. His memories of the last few months are fragments, blurred around the edges like a dream upon waking.

The boy tightens his hold on his sister, the one who has protected him since birth. This closeness, this warmth—it is life after life.

"Estela," he repeats, a fervent whisper, waiting for her eyes to open and see the beauty around them. "Wake up. There is no more pain."

This would make her happy. She'd been through so much hurt, and, somehow, he could tell that he had been, too, though the memories were blurred and charred.

Just then, the world pulses anew, a gentle rhythm beckoning him. He feels it first in his fingertips, then coursing through his veins like the first flush of heat from a hearth. Every beat of his heart is an echo in the emptiness that death leaves behind, filling the void with whispers of color and sound.

Eyes still closed, he listens intently to the symphony of existence playing softly beneath Estela's deafening silence.

And then she gasps.

The sudden movement puts strain on the spear connecting them. She looks around, tears already tugging themselves out her eyes, despite the surrounding beauty.

"No," she sobs.

He reaches up and touches her with one hand.

"Este, please. You're... hurting me," he grunts.

She shakes her hand, her own hands placed on her stomach. She looks up at the sky

"Rholker was supposed to die!" she screams. "Not me. Not us."

"Este, please. We need to remove this. Then there will be no more hurt," Mikal says fervently, trying to refrain her from moving. "We will be free."

Estela jerks her shoulder away, ignoring her brother. It is as if she were possessed, staring at the golden sky, streaked with cozy colors of summer sunsets.

"Put me back in the fight! *Let us live,*" she sobs to the empty sky. "*Please.*"

Light flashes.

Before him, a blood-soaked troll warrior stands, reaching across time and space for Estela. His arm strains, and his face is streaked with tears.

She reaches back, screaming words Mikal does not understand and jostling the pain in his chest. The troll's silver braid falls over his shoulder, swinging toward them.

The whispers in the wind grow louder, weaving threads of vitality into his being. They speak in a language older than time, uttering words that only the heart could understand, calling Mikal back to the land of the living with a tender insistence.

He can feel the energy of life's tapestry entwine with his own, stitching together the frayed edges left by death's sharp scissors. With each thread, the boy's spirit mends, piecing together the fragments of who he was, who he is, and who he might yet become.

He wonders if Estela feels the same.

And then, as if the universe itself has leaned down to murmur into his ear, the final word comes, a secret carried on the wind:

"*Live.*"

It is not a command, but a gift—a soft-spoken invitation to embrace the dance of the living once more. And with that single word cradling his heart, the boy's eyelids flutter open, revealing the dawn of his new beginning.

And, *gods*, is it full of pain.

CHAPTER 46
M☾NSTONE
TEO

The grey pallor fades. The slackened flesh plumps once more, and then the bodies rearrange themselves out of my lap. They lay next to each other, Mikal in Estela's arms.

I feel the second that her heartbeat sputters to life because it seeks out my own and matches my rhythm.

As my magic leaves me, I am left with my wounds and over-heated skin. I put my weight on the leg that was shot earlier and feel a crack. Pressure on the fracture makes the bone snap, and I cry out. I do not have enough energy to truly move.

My body is ravaged. Drawing both of them onto my lap, I can only weep.

The light is gone. Now, we are back in the middle of a destroyed manor. The air is heavy with dust and the stench of death. Surrounded by bodies, both fresh and decaying.

We are alive.

I look down at Estela and Mikal. The gaping wounds on their chest are gone, but they have left behind a mess of bloody clothes. I'm grateful not to have to gaze upon the grotesque spear any longer.

Every muscle in my body feels heavy, else, I would pull all of us away from the carnage.

The best I can do is brush Estela's hair from her face and cover their chilled bodies with my arm.

"Teo!" a voice chokes out in the distance, breaking through the eerie silence.

I look up and see Vann crawling towards us, his long legs dragging him effortlessly through the wreckage. In his arms, he carries the giant child, but his weapon is nowhere to be seen. A long gash is cut across his arm deep enough to showcase sinew and bone.

I hiss at the sight, wondering if his Fuegorra was simply too exhausted to heal further wounds.

As Vann approaches, he slows, his eyes wide and his blue skin ashen. He looks at Mikal and Estela, who are both lying on the ground, and his expression softens with relief. He kneels down beside them and checks their pulses as I clutch them close.

"They're..."

"Alive," I breathe.

He lets out a long breath and tears line his eyes.

"Praise the gods, from their stony thrones to their foresty shadows." Then he falls to his knees and hugs me. "Thank every greater being in the world. I thought you'd all..."

A wail from the small giant in his arms cuts him off. He tends to the young boy, but his eyes find me a second later. They are red, and a tear slips down his cheek.

"I thought I couldn't save you this time. I am sorry. I love you, brother," he cries.

I pat his back, bringing him close, baby and all. "We live on.

And you must bear the weight of my love and brotherhood, as well."

He laughs, and then slumps closer. Alive, in the middle of the ring of death. The word tastes sweet in a land of ash.

"I smell like shit," Vann groans.

"Yes, you do," I wheeze. My Fuegorra is working hard to repair the hole of my magic, and it makes me sluggish. I feel like if I close my eyes, then I'll be lost forever. I avoid the darkness.

"Tell me, after another meeting with death, do you have regrets?"

He shifts out of my arm so that his back is pressed against the rocks. "A million."

"Tell me one," I insist, needing to talk instead of closing my eyes.

My body is worn out, my magic hewn from my very body. My breath wheezes in and out of my chest, and I am relaxed only by the deep, rhythmic breaths of Mikal and Estela. The giant infant cries, but I have nothing more to offer him.

"You first," Vann shoots back, voice raw.

My eyelids sag, my back and ass burn against hot ground. My leg still feels broken.

"I regret not killing my father sooner," I say.

Van lets out a shocked huff, and then wheezes.

"Your turn," I insist.

He laughs once more. "I regret not listening to Adra... And I regret never tasting Arlet's lips."

Then he grunts and winces while shifting to accomodate the child.

My lips curl up at the corners, my burned skin splitting open. "You bastard. I knew it."

He laughs. "How well you know me."

"Well, to that I say: we aren't dead yet." I then choke on the smoke billowing around us.

Vann laughs. "You know better than most that battlefield confessions are hollow."

"Sometimes."

That is met with silence. I do not mind. My throat is too torn up to speak anymore.

It's hard to tell how many hours we stay like that before the elves start to search through the dead. We rest, exhausted as voices call out, saying they've found us.

It hurts when they drag us away.

CHAPTER 47
IOLITE
ESTELA

When I come to consciousness, there is a weight across my legs. Every part of me hurts even worse than before.

Ugly nightmares come rushing in. Ones of Mikal's dying body, hanging above me, and I remember... *Dying*.

My eyelids fly open, and I find myself in the back of a wooden wagon. Mikal and Teo are sprawled out on either side of me.

"Oh gods!" I exclaim.

Mikal is here. He is filthy, but he is alive. And with me.

I pull his face close and kiss his head, despite the fact that all moisture has been leached from my mouth and lips.

"Easy, *amor*[1]," Teo's grumbly voice says from behind me. I turn to see my husband holding a giant child.

Another breath pushes past my lips.

We are there, a stinking, bloody mess of limbs.

"He's alive, and..." I press my hand to my stomach.

"The child is fine," he murmurs. "We are all fine."

Such fierce joy takes over me, but then my stomach lurches.

The smoke and ash take their toll, and I lean over an empty space of the wagon and vomit.

"Easy," Ulla's voice cuts through my thoughts. "You are all right." She brings a rag to my mouth.

Another voice calls from the front of the wagon. I look up to see Liana through blurry eyes.

"You are weak. You need to rest more," she says. "This wagon will take us back to Enduvida."

"My baby is really alive?" I say, my breath still rushing in and out of my mouth.

"Yes. Teo saved you both," she says.

I let out a sob. "I—"

"Sleep, or I will make you sleep," Liana grits out. I almost miss the fear in her voice.

The wise woman withdraws an enormous crystal, hands it to Ulla, and they begin to sing. My eyelids grow heavy. I clutch my brother to my chest.

And then I sleep once more, despite the cart's jostling.

MY CONSCIOUSNESS COMES IN AND OUT OVER THE NEXT FEW DAYS. Gentle hands force-feed me water and soup.

In the end, that fades, too.

IT ISN'T UNTIL THE WARMTH OF ENDUVIDA'S AIR HITTING ME THAT I wake once more.

My eyes blink open, and I feel like I've come back from death itself. Everything is stiff and... disgusting. I try to swallow, and my throat burns.

My eyes open, and I recognize the ceiling above me. My

arms are wrapped around an immense weight, and I look down at the filthy black hair.

"Mikal," I say.

He stirs, then rolls over and lets one leg flop over the side of my old bed. I smooth his hair away and wince when I think of how they had him hanging in chains.

"Are you in pain?" my mate's groggy voice rumbles next to me.

I look over to see Teo's head peeking at me from his seated position on the floor of the room. From the looks of it, he's just waking up, too.

We are all still stained with the remnants of the battle.

"I'm fine, but why are you on the floor?" I demand.

A ghost of a smile crosses his lips. "There wasn't room on the bed, and you wouldn't let him go."

I look at Mikal and realize that he had grown since I'd seen him. I forgot how sixteen-year-olds grow like weeds.

I sit up to get a better look and find a basket on the ground next to my mate. In it is the giant child.

More emotion wells up. A part of me is shocked to see a giant in the under mountain.

They are synonymous with pain, but the baby is dirty and sleeping peacefully. It's hard to believe this child is the heir to the giant throne.

"That's... Keksej's son," I say weakly.

Our sound wakes the babe, and he immediately starts to cry.

Teo's eyes snap open.

For a second, fear is stricken into my heart. He could be as much of a threat to us as that child was to Rholker. And yet...

"Please, don't kill him," I plead.

The lines on Teo's face scrunch up.

"What? My star, I would never do that. I'm awake because

he started crying." As if to emphasize his point, he turns and then scoops up the whining child. Something new pings inside my chest. It was what I felt the first time I saw him holding Sama in the caves.

My eyes widen as he presses the baby to his chest and begins to gently pat its back. I realize he's been caring for it while I slept.

"You... have a tender space in your heart for the enemy," I say. Gods, that is just like Teo.

He nods. "I'm afraid I do."

I think of what I discovered about Sama—that Teo wanted to care for him, too, but thought it best to give him to a mated pair.

The child burps and makes a contented coo that causes my heart to squeeze again. And then, the voice of reason inside of me reminds me that the babe is helpless. It knows nothing of the giants or their cruelty.

"Do you think me mad for wanting to raise a giant in an Enduar family?" Teo asks, softly.

"I've... raised a half-giant baby before. What's a fully giant one?" I say softly. "But... giant lords will come for him."

The thought of putting the Enduares in danger again feels like peeling my skin from my bones.

Teo looks up at me. "I don't think we need to worry about the giants for a long while. We destroyed their court."

We are interrupted by a knock on the door. Then, the door swings open anyway.

Liana strides in, and her nose curls up. "Gods, the stench in here is unbearable."

Behind her, Svanna, Iryth, Vann, Arlet, Joso and Ulla follow.

My face brightens, and then I attempt to hide because I am utterly filthy.

"None of that," Arlet says. "We've all seen worse these last three days."

"Three days?" I repeat.

Liana nods. "Yes. You all have been sleeping, and it's now time to air out the room, scrub you clean, and fill those bellies up with food."

Svanna comes over and begins to extricate Mikal from me. I look at her, thinking of the way she hacked through her enemies.

"Were you wounded?" I ask.

She grins. "I broke my arm. But, thanks to Ulla and Liana, I'm all healed up." I watch in awe as she picks up my enormous sibling like he weighs nothing. I feel a little jealous.

"I'll take the big stinky half-giant," she says proudly, and then takes Mikal to the tub in the corner.

Joso follows her over.

"Let me clean him," he insists. "He's nearly a man. He doesn't want to wake to a woman washing his bits. Especially one inexperienced with male anatomy."

Svanna rolls her eyes. "I have a son, remember." But she concedes.

"Why hasn't he woke yet?" I ask no one in particular.

Liana looks at me. "He's still very wounded. His giant blood helps, but the process is slow."

My brows furrow. "Why haven't you put a Fuegorra in him?"

Arlet and Liana share a look.

"We didn't know if you would want that. You were very upset when we gave you one in your sleep."

I grit my teeth. "Give him one as soon as you can. He needs to heal faster."

"If you want it done soon, he won't be able to pick it, and neither will you," she says. "You're to stay in this room until you can walk without falling over."

"I. Don't. Care. I want him healed," I insist, wincing in pain. It's then that I remember they don't know about who is growing inside of me.

Liana nods and tells Joso to fetch Ulla and have her get a stone. Then Arlet is next to me, helping me to my feet.

"Can you walk?" Arlet asks, gently.

I nod as they support me underneath my arms. I feel how disgusting I smell, but they don't so much as cast me a wayward glance. I look back to see Iryth and Liana take the babe.

"Be careful," I call, and Iryth gives me an understanding smile.

"Of course, My Queen."

Then I see Vann help Teo to his feet.

One by one, we are navigated to the baths, stripped and washed. Our small army of friends heal us, feed us—and *gods*, it makes my heart overrun with joy.

I never thought I would have more than Mikal and Arlet in my life.

And now...

I have a whole village.

When I sink back into sleep, I am cleaned, watered, fed, and... healed.

Whole.

CHAPTER 48

TOPAZ

ESTELA

I t's much later when a sound rouses me from my sleep.

"Este," a parched voice says.

I bolt upright.

It takes a moment to realize I'm back in the king's suite, and there is a baby basket hanging near the bed. The hallway between the king's and queen's suite is open.

I hear sound from the other room. I wish I could say that it doesn't jerk the tears straight from my ducts, but it does.

"Miki," I say, wiping away the moisture and nearly sprinting into the other room.

He's propped up on the bed, clutching his sides. He looks awful, but he is clean and alive.

I rush to the bed.

"*¿Qué pasó?* Did you hurt something? Are you hungry again?" I ask in our language.

He smiles, and then coughs. "I... I am okay. Where am I?"

I take a deep breath. My mouth opens, but I don't know how to explain everything to him. It's been so long since we were together.

537

An entire lifetime.

I am a new person.

I take his hand, and he groans.

"Oh no. What's happened?" he asks.

I frown. "I don't only hold your hand when something's wrong."

He grins through his split lip. "Yes, you do. You do it when I'm hurt, when you told me you were coming to the mountains, when my fox Friji ran away..." He winces.

And I purse my lips. "Maybe you are right."

He takes a stuttering breath. "I already know I'm hurt. So the news can't be that bad."

"We're in Enduvida. The Enduar city."

His eyes go wide. "We aren't with the elves?"

I shake my head.

He looks so confused. "I... gods I can hardly remember the last few months."

I think of the witches, who Rholker had said had been tending to him. Smoothing some of the hair from his face, he jerks back, mock annoyed.

"The elves are not so great. Be grateful we didn't end up there —though I do like some of them. Mikal, we are free, with the trolls."

He blinks. "We are captives of the trolls."

I shake my head. "No. We are *free*."

He goes still.

"But the trolls..."

I shake my head. "I am married to a troll—not that they call themselves that anymore. I am..." My voice catches on the words, feeling ridiculous saying them outloud. "I am the Enduar Queen. And we have been liberating the slaves."

He looks at me like I've gone mad, and then his eyes go wide.

I look over my shoulder to see Teo standing in the doorway,

carrying the baby. Any fear he might've inspired in Mikal is ruined by the rough cloth thrown over his shoulder for spit-ups. He looks between me and Mikal and dips his head slowly.

"Mikal. My name is Teo. I am your sister's mate," he says slowly.

Mikal looks at him, and I see the protectiveness there. He doesn't respond to Teo, just looks back at me.

"You married a king," he says flatly.

"I did." I reach down and touch the Fuegorra on display. "You have one, too."

He reaches to his own breastbone, and his eyes grow wide.

"*Hostia puta*[1]," he curses.

I smack his arm. "Don't curse in front of the baby."

He gives me a lopsided grin. "Do I have powers now?"

Teo cracks a smile. "Perhaps. Your sister does."

Mikal gives Teo a more assessing glance. "She has always had the power to annoy everyone who spends more than three seconds with her."

I groan. "Gods. I spent *months* trying to save you, and that's one of the first things you say?"

He laughs, and then grunts in pain.

Teo smiles. "How does eating sound?"

I like how he directs the question to both of us.

"I'm fine," I say just as my stomach growls.

Teo scowls.

"Let me change." I look back to Mikal. "You're coming," I say, pushing a finger into his chest.

He smiles but still needs my help standing. I pick out his clothes as he walks carefully.

I don't know if it is a blessing or a curse that his memories are more faded than mine, but I hope, for his sake, that it is for the best.

THE NEXT MORNING, MIKAL WANTS A TOUR OF THE CAVES. TEO COMES, holding the enormous baby, which I've given the nickname *Peque*, or small one.

Mikal keeps glancing over him, and I nudge him slightly.

"What's wrong?" I ask finally. Mikal looks at me with his large yellow eyes and smiles.

"I just keep thinking about how that child could be... my half nephew," he says.

I blink. "He is your literal nephew," I say after a few more moments.

Mikal nods, and we walk to the Ardorflame.

We are once again stopped by no fewer than a hundred curious eyes. They greet Mikal, bowing to him as if he were royalty.

It's rewarding to see how he takes each step in stride, looking around the cave like a blind man seeing light for the first time. As we approach the temple, he reaches out and touches it.

Then he smiles. "I like this light. Does it come from the lava below?"

Teo perks up and furrows his brows. "Perhaps it is a part of the same magic, but no, it isn't lava."

Mikal asks another question I don't hear as the patter of little feet sound behind me. I turn just in time for Rila to launch into my arms.

Worry splashes over my skin, for the Ardorflame is near the edge of a very large cavern.

"*Mi vida,* be careful," I chide.

The young Enduar girl doesn't listen, her hair coating my face as she looks over my shoulder at my brother.

"Who are you?" she says in perfect common tongue.

I smile, somehow already missing her broken attempts from earlier.

Miki comes over and holds out his hand. "I am Este's brother."

Rila grabs his hand. "Rila."

I turn just in time to see Mikal smile, and I set the girl down. She reaches into the pocket of her tunic and pulls out one stone the size of her fist.

"For you," she says to Mikal and then disappears.

When I turn back to my brother, he's looking at the stone with a confused look on his face. "What's this supposed to mean?"

I laugh. "She wants to be your friend."

Mikal looks up at me, and his eyes are tortured. I've spent so long watching over my brother, and he's spent most of his time around men much older than him.

It breaks my heart to see how his childhood had been snatched from him, and now he gazes down at the stone with such a boyish face.

Gods, he's so young.

I grab his face and pull him down to kiss his forehead. "Welcome to your new life."

He jerks away from me in mock irritation and gives my shoulder a little shove.

"You don't have to keep doing that," he says.

I grin. "Of course I do. I couldn't for so long."

We are interrupted yet again by another voice. "Your Majesties." This time, it's Svanna.

When I turn, I find her attention is fixed on Mikal.

"You have the look of a future hunter about you. Do you know how to hold a weapon?" she asks.

Mikal puffs out his chest. "I have chopped trees since I was eleven."

Svanna laughs. "Excellent. Would you like to join us today?"

Mikal nods once.

"Good." She jerks her head toward Hammerhead Hall. "Go help with lunch, and we'll find you later." Then she turns to me and says, "There's need for a meeting in the throne room right now."

I look at Teo, who bobs alongside with the sleeping child. Without thinking, I reach up and tuck a bit of hair behind the child's ear.

We don't even have a proper name for the boy yet.

"Very well," I say and follow her through the rooms.

Everything is a blur until we walk in and find... two thrones.

I suck in a breath and then look at the others in the room. Teo hands me the child as we walk up the steps and sit.

Those before us look on, but Thorne has a small smile playing on his lips.

"Congratulations," he says with a bow. "Parenthood suits you."

I blink, somehow shocked to hear the words on his lips.

"Thank you, Lord Thorne," I return.

Mrath laughs.

"Thorne isn't a lord. He's just my favorite assassin," she says.

Thorne's face darkens but he doesn't say anything more, so I press my lips together and avoid responding.

"It is good to see you all alive and well," Teo says, taking over the conversation. "What is the matter?"

Ner'Feon raises his hand. "From what I gather, King Ma'Teo, a lot is the matter. Permission to speak first?"

Teo acquiesces with a nod.

Ner'Feon begins to speak, and I'm struck with how good it feels to be back here. The weight of the child in my arms is almost welcome.

"We have nearly finished evacuating the ninth battalion from the ocean," Ner'Feon starts.

"Excellent," I say just as the baby burps onto my arm. Mrath curls her lips, but Fira grins.

"We have discovered... another group underwater," Ner'Feon continues.

Teo freezes. "Another? How? Did you not see them during the five decades you spent underwater?"

Ner'Feon tenses. "Apologies, My King. They were in a different section of the ocean. One of them was injured, and he brought us back to meet with the other soldiers."

"How many?" I ask.

Ner'Feon takes a deep breath. "Five hundred."

I blink, but Mrath smiles. "If there are five hundred of them, surely there could be other battalions."

Ner'Feon nods. "It is... possible."

Mrath looks gleeful, and Teo's attention turns to her. "You look awfully pleased, ally."

She grins. "I very much am. The more of you, the better our plans for my brother's city, Shvathemar."

I take a deep breath, frowning. The war continues.

I'm not ready for that again, but... that was the price for our relationship.

Teo nods. "Is that what you hoped to speak about today?"

"You might call me presumptuous, but I think it's in our best interests to act sooner rather than later," Mrath insists.

"Mrath," he starts.

Her smile fades and cocks her head to the side. "What is that tone you're using?"

"We have every intention of helping you with Arion, but surely you must know that we need at least a few months to recover," he says.

Mrath's lips curl downward. "Do you think word will not

spread of the help I gave you? All it takes is one survivor, and he will hunt me to the ends of the earth."

Teo takes a deep breath. "You are right, but still we need time. You have the artifact now. Won't that help you keep him off your borders for a short period? Besides, we have begun to speak with the swamp ogres. Do you not want time to try and enlist their help?"

Her face flushes with annoyance. "No more than three months."

"That isn't enough time. Do you wish to end this war? Or merely thwart your brother's advances," Teo asks.

She takes a deep breath. "We must be prepared—"

"And we will be. We have done much to help you, and I have given you my word that we will assist you in what is to come. Ogres and all. But please... my wife is with child."

Mrath sneers, pointing at me. "That is a damned giant."

Something primal rears up inside of me.

"He is mine to care for," I spit at her and press my hand to my stomach. "But Teo doesn't lie. There is another babe."

The Enduares in the room go silent, and then, one by one, begin to bow.

Mrath looks at them, exasperated, but misses how Thorne bows his head in a soft smile.

"Fine. I will give you the time you ask for. Use it to train these underwater dwellers and forge on with the ogres, but I will not leave you unsupervised." Then she turns to Thorne. "Would you stay and be my blade once more?"

My eyebrows rise, as do Ulla's.

I see her eyes cut straight to him, but he doesn't take his eyes off of Mrath.

"I will be your blade."

The leader of the sisterhood nods, and then, calling Ayla, leaves the throne room without the silver haired-elf.

With them gone, the meeting goes quiet.

"How far along are you, My Queen?" Liana asks, her eyes unnaturally glassy.

I smile and place my hand on my belly. "Perhaps a month."

She grins, then pulls a chunk of quartz out of her robes. The words pour out of her mouth, a chant at first, and then a melody when Ulla joins in.

Tears fall out of my eyes.

When it is over, the hugs start. First from Ulla, then Fira. Liana and Vann come right after each other.

Even Thorne. It's a stiff embrace, but I am appreciative of his friendship, nonetheless.

"Thank you for staying," I whisper. "I wouldn't want any other elf slicing my throat."

He pulls back, smiling. "I have a few crystals I haven't had the pleasure of harvesting quite yet."

"Now, if that's enough celebration for the moment, I propose a feast this evening," Teo says.

I grin at him, and every member of the council raises their hands in agreement.

"Done!" he says. "Now, a few things have been on my mind. First, any word from Ra'Sa or Melisa?"

Liana shakes her head. "No, but we won't until they arrive. They used the last of their speaking stones to send us Rholker's plans, and the crystal only shows me visions of snow and dirty feet. Have faith, my queen."

A pit forms in my stomach, but I push it aside.

"Are there enough houses for all these new men?" Teo asks.

It's Lothar who steps forward next. "Currently, no. But we have six months to build up this city. It once housed thousands of our people."

Teo grins, stands, and claps the quiet diplomat on the back.

"Yes. And so it shall again!" Then he looks at everyone else, his eyes landing firmly on Vann. "That reminds me. Any new mates?"

Ulla nods excitedly. "Yes. Of the thirty-three human women who arrived with Estela a month ago, all have decided to stay. Eight of them have begun the mating song."

My eyebrows lift, and the small sleeping boy on my chest takes an opportunity to start crying.

The sound shocks the rest of the sleepiness out of me. And then, I am scrambling while a flurry of people come over to help me situate the boy.

Eventually, he's taken to Iryth to be fed, and I am pushed out of the room to go get ready for the feast.

When Teo comes up behind me, I find us pushed together in a way we haven't been since before the battle. Our eyes meet, and heat spreads through my core.

In a second, he scoops me up and carries me back to the king's suite.

CHAPTER 49

ENARGITE

TEO

E stela's laughter follows us through the caves. Someone cleaned my suite while we were out, and I absently wonder who had shown us this kindness while we were at our meeting. The curiosity fades as I slam the door and cross the room to throw her onto the bed.

The shoulder of her dress goes askew, and she looks up at me with pure heat. It makes my own desire pique, and I admire the flush of her cheeks, the wildness of her hair, and the heave of her chest.

"I told you that you would never be taken from me again," I say as I grab the hem of my shirt and pull it over my head.

Her eyes trace the movement, and I feel the flurry of emotions passing between us when she bites her lip.

"But I was taken," she admits for the first time since we woke. "I died."

I shake my head. "You were never going to be truly gone."

Tears well up, and I decide that the time for tears has long since passed.

Tearing at the laces that hold my pants, I pull them off while simultaneously kicking off my shoes. Then I kneel by the bed, like a man prepared to meet his deity.

Estela props herself up on her forearms, watching me with hungry eyes.

I push up the cloth covering her ankles and then begin to remove her shoes. Each touch is possessive, but I feel how my pretty woman enjoys the attention I lavish upon her. I smile when her chest catches while taking a breath.

We have time, I say through the bond, and I mean it. Every second spent together will only be multiplied.

Estela bites her lip. "But—"

I lean forward, pressing a finger to her mouth.

She sends me images of elves and darkness and every other harsh thing that swirls in the world outside.

Shaking my head, I begin to ease her out of her clothes. At the point of each undone fastening , I plant a soft kiss and whisper a promise through our bond.

At her shoulder, I say, *I will protect you until the end of our days.*

At her hip, *I'll hold you tight throughout the months to come.*

At her knee, *You need not fear for my life either.*

A part of her lurks on the other end, wanting to contest each promise. So I grab each of her arms and put them above her head. She gasps at the sudden movement, but her heart races and her legs press together.

Harsh movements are not something I use often with my star, but perhaps I should move quickly more often.

For a second, I take her in.

Her skin glows in the dim room, and I memorize every curve of muscle and substance. My unoccupied hand skims across her skin, stopping to rub my thumb over her nipple.

She writhes beneath me.

"Teo," she mews helplessly, grabbing my tail.

I shudder at her touch, but she pauses at the since shaven tip.

Her gasp is delicious.

I smile and brush my thumb over her lips.

She bites me.

Pulling back in mock outrage, I hiss and lick the pain away.

She watches hungrily.

"Are you the kind of man to leave his wife waiting?" She grits out, frustrated.

I smile and then place my hand back on her midsection. Beneath it, I feel the first flicker of a heartbeat. It's as if a switch is flipped under my skin, unlocking some primal part of me I had never seen.

This woman holds our child.

I have sacrificed much for us to be together, and so had she, but this ultimate sign of commitment lights something tender and primal. My sense flies away to some unknown place as I use one knee to push open one of her legs, taking time to enjoy the glistening readiness that is awaiting me for a second before pushing myself forward, lining up our bodies, and sinking in.

Estela moans and grips my sustaining hand with the tips of her fingers.

She presses her feet into the bed, meeting the angle of my hips stroke for stroke, connecting our bodies and hearts with each moment.

When I claim her lips seconds before we come, I pull her on top of me. She looks tired, but she gives me a frustrated look. With her hands now free, they slide over my biceps as her braid curls around her shoulder and breast.

"Why did you stop?" she asks irritatedly.

I smile. "Because I am not in a hurry."

She moves her hips to show her displeasure, and I reach up to grab her braid, twisting it around my hand. She stills as I hold tight. Then she begins to move once more, and I can feel the way that she pleasurably aches at the new angle. The gem in her chest glows brightly, and a flicker of fear passes.

"Don't stop," I coax her on. As the magic between us builds, it is a symphony. We harmonize every melody, and I curve my hips upwards the second she gets closer.

Her back arches, and she cries out seconds before I find my release tumbling after hers.

"I love you," I whisper as she collapses atop me. Her skin is flushed and soft.

"*Te amo*¹," she returns.

Grabbing her mouth once more, I press another passionate kiss to her lips.

And then we fall into each other, resting and waiting for the next moment to come. I won't admit it aloud, but it brings me great pleasure when she doesn't move to put on her clothes once again.

I would have her skin on mine every day until the end if allowed.

"Teo, what did you give up to save us?" Her hand is on her stomach, and I stroke her shoulder.

"Not much. Honestly, I got the better end of the deal," I say.

She looks up at me. "I don't believe that."

I brush a kiss to her forehead. "Believe it."

When she continues to stare at me, I sigh. "I gave back the ability to control the volcano."

She freezes, and her heart rate picks up in a way that has nothing to do with passion.

"Why did you do that? We are defenseless without it." Her words are fast and tumble past her lips.

I shake my head. "I still have magic. I still feel the earth rumble beneath me, as you can, too, now that we are so connected. Besides, even if I had none of that... I have you. You are the Daughter of the Light Weavers. *Drathorinna*'s rider. The next wise woman. We have more than enough."

She looks up at me, wide eyed. "I... I am glad I have you."

I press another kiss to her lips, feeling as she eases back into our bond. There is a beauty in a partner that I never knew before her. Alone, we each had our own plans and schemes, but together we are greater than the sum of our parts.

Thank the gods for my beloved.

I smile.

"Besides, even if I don't have the same power, I feel... lighter. Happier. And nothing can stop me from *insinuating* that the power still is nestled within me." Then I place my hand on hers. "And who's to say our child will not have the same power?"

I feel her consider this, and then, when she accepts the idea, she snuggles closer.

"Tell me what you think our child will be like," she asks softly.

I smile wide enough for my face to hurt.

"Strong, stubborn, and incredibly well proportioned. None of the other younglings will have a chance."

She laughs, and I notice a tear sneak out of the corner of her eye. I wipe it away, and she catches my hand.

"I hope you know that this is from happiness, not pain," she says solemnly.

"Believe me, I know."

CHAPTER 50
OCEAN JASPER
ESTELA

The music of the feast swells around the hall. It's been decorated almost as elaborately as it was during my wedding on the Festival of Endu. A second wall was opened to look out at the Ardorflame Temple, and there is a group of singers sitting at the other end of the space.

Ulla and Thorne have joined Velen to create waves of music that would please the gods themselves, while several elves have brought instruments. I think of the ogres at Rholker's coronation, and all the great many things that I have passed through since I was taken from the cave a handful of months ago.

It strikes me that I never realized instruments weren't used under the mountain as I watch the musicians play. It spikes my curiosity.

That is, until a cry comes from the basket next to me. Mikal and the new baby were placed on either side of our table.

Mikal holds a dagger in his hands, and he practices twirling around his fingers and wrists.

"Be careful," I chide as I adjust the small babe's blanket, and my brother looks up at me.

He *grins*.

"Svanna said I have excellent blade instincts," he counters, and I snort a laugh.

Just as I'm about to snatch the blade away, Teo stills my hand. "She's right. Have you spoken to Vann? He's always happy for a sparring partner. I would be, too."

Mikal's whole face lights up. "Really? Would you like to practice tonight? War on the horizon means that you can never have too much practice."

I suck in a sharp breath.

He's young, so he's always been so full of energy, but I don't luxuriate in the idea of my husband taking my brother off to be a soldier. Teo has made promises to me and our family.

Knowing how to use a blade is wise, mi amor[1]*, he says through our bond.

I want to make a comment about his invading my thoughts. "Tomorrow, perhaps. Tonight, you should enjoy yourself. Go, there are others your age over near the roasting bear." Teo raises his hand to gesture where the other younglings play and run. I see mostly small children, but there are a few teenagers swaying about. One or two looks like they could go perform the *dual'-moraan* tomorrow.

Mikal stiffens. I look at him, leaning forward as he watches. After a few moments, his eyes find mine. I see his life spent cutting wood among men twice his age. He looks unsure, tugging on his tunic.

I worry that he won't find what he searches for with them. Rejection is more painful than self-imposed isolation, but the fear of success can't hold him back forever. Especially when most of that fear is mine.

They accepted you, they will accept him in time, Teo says calmly.

I purse my lips.

"Yes, Miki. Go and make friends."

He gives me a lopsided smile, and then stands, still twirling his blade before he walks over to join them.

I watch him with a heart two sizes too big. For a second, I can't help but marvel over the life the stones have sung for me.

We escaped death, and though I feared the worst, we both survived. Teo gave up some of what he was before to get us back, and I worry about how that will play out in the years to come.

Liana had once told me in our training that a wise woman's burden was the ability to see the future, and yet still be bound by the fears of the present. It's an imprecise magic, to be sure, but there's something about knowing that Teo and I have a future that is enough for the moment.

I pull the giant babe out of his basket and sit back, bouncing him on my leg. He nestles into me, and I look around the room. It surprises me just how many pairings there are, and the room is filled with laughter, kisses, drinking, and dancing.

Niht twirls one of the elves around the room, and I am pleased that they have stayed. It only takes a few to change the course of a relationship between two peoples.

The mood is ambient and joyful, and I let the crystals amplify the peacefulness that is harbored inside of me.

It isn't until a loud crash sounds through the room that I bolt upright.

There's a flurry in the crowd, and a few hurry off, leaving a clear view of the altercation.

In the middle of the room is Vann, shaking his hand.

On the ground in front of him is Joso.

Teo moves to the side of me, standing up and charging over to see exactly what had happened. I scan behind the two men to see Arlet with her hands pressed to her face.

"What the hell is wrong with you?" Vann roars.

Something wasn't right.

Joso was gentle and kind. He wouldn't have done something on purpose.

Just as I stand up to inspect what was happening, the sound of heavy footfalls crowds behind me.

I turn to the forms emerging from the tunnel to the outside. My breath catches, and I fear a horde of red eyes.

Except... they aren't the vaimpír.

It's Melisa holding Ra'Sa's arm while he carries twin girls.

Though they head the group, dozens continue to swarm inside behind them, clad in brown and grey slave rags. My hand flies to my mouth as I start moving.

We hadn't heard anything from them since their speaking stones had run out. A team was going after them, but I just hadn't expected that they'd show up like this. How had neither Liana or I seen this?

It's a *miracle*.

Teo is next to me in a second as they try to come across the cavern. When we meet at the bridge, I look over to still see hundreds pouring in. Old, young, men, and women. I let out the longest breath, and then, embrace Melisa the best I can manage with a baby still in my arms.

"My friend. You made it home," I say, grinning.

"We escaped," she says breathless. Her face is haggard, and her hair is a mess. I can't resist reaching up and tucking a lock behind her ear. She offers a weak smile. "We took as many as could walk. There are more on the road. We were just the fastest."

"How long were you walking for?" I ask. It took us four days to get to the mines, and we've been back at least four more.

"For over a week," she says.

Teo inquires, "How many all together?"

But before she can answer, Ra'Sa's eyes trail behind, to where the Enduares congregate.

His mouth drops open, and he gasps.

"*Pater*," he breathes, using the Enduar word for father.

An older Enduar, one brought out of the ocean, comes forward, pushing through the crowd with a woman on his arm. And then he hugs Ra'Sa.

My eyes track the movement, but it's not just us who take in the joyful reunion. Instead of stopping the festivities, Velen's song starts up once again.

I look at Teo, and then back at the humans. Liana has already joined us, as has a furious-looking Vann. Soon Svanna comes up, gazing at all the faces.

"Well, shit," Vann murmurs.

Svanna hits his arm.

"Be useful for once in your life." Then she raises her hand and points at a group of hunters hanging nearby. "Get another bear from storage!"

People begin to move around us, and a list unfolds in my mind. Clothing, homes, food, baths, everything.

The only calm in the storm is my mate.

I look at him, enjoying his tight jaw. My lips quirk up when I see the spectacles perched on his nose.

Without speaking, he reaches out for the baby. I give him to his arms, then straighten my dress.

"Are you ready?" he asks, finally looking down at me with those brilliant, blue eyes.

As the humans move past us, I take in the extent of some of their wounds and roll up my sleeves. This would be hard, but it is a good kind of hard.

If something like this had happened to me a year ago, I would've run from such a challenge.

But the cruel voices in my head are gone, banished by the light of the Enduares and my husband's kind words.

It's not the time to mourn what is lost; it's time to thrive.

"More than ready."

It's time to get to work.

EPILOGUE
TEO

I f there is one thing I know, it is that giant babies are heavier than Enduar babes.

Liana stands at my side, and the early morning light shines down on us with such gentle warmth. Towers of quartz surround us, ones that were used only weeks ago to play the deadly battle beat in the mines.

The last time I blessed a child, it was a sad occasion. A handful of us stood next to the ocean, trying to pretend that Sama was not nearly orphaned.

Now, a new orphan is nestled in my arms, one with skin the color of rose quartz and a Fuegorra in its chest.

The heir to the giant kingdom.

With no king, no royal family, and no slaves, their court is barely limping along. They do not know he is still alive and likely won't for a long time.

Thousands are standing on this snowy beach. Many humans, and even many more of the stony faces from those left underwater for half a century. They all look on with thinly veiled curiosity and... *hope*.

"I think it's time to start," Liana says at my side. "The singing is nice, but I don't think my coat is thick enough for this."

I look at her impractical dress, more crystal than leather. "That is your fault."

She glares at me, and then Estela steps forward out of the crowd. My mate is resplendent in a golden dress—it's a color that suits her very well, either in gown or armor.

Her belly is just beginning to round out, for Enduar babes come along much faster than human children. The sight of my sweet wife distracts me enough that I don't realize she's carrying something.

My head cocks to the side.

"What have you brought, my star?" I ask gently.

She smiles widely and holds up a large circlet. The band is gold, like the ones I usually wear, but this is studded with dozens of gems. Most of them are blue.

My mouth parts.

"This is a grand celebration. I know what an important day it is for you, so Flova helped me make you a gift."

My eyes are glued on the crown. Instead of geometric shapes, there are swirls that twist around the stones. It reminds me of... *her.* Another moment of inspection reveals the forty-eight gems artfully set next to each other.

When I look back at Estela, her smile has faded.

"Do you like it?"

"Of course," I practically choke. How long had it been since I had received a gift? I couldn't remember, and yet, here my small human stands with one she crafted.

My, the fates the stones sing for us...

"I would wear it today."

"Really?"

I let out a laugh and adjust the child so that I can kneel.

She comes over, smile fully returned, and gently places the circlet on my brow. With the singers' voices still filling the air, they bounce off the stones in the headpiece. A song I've never heard falls over my ears—it is bright and hopeful.

Unshed tears sting my eyes.

"I should've finished it sooner, but I am a poor metal bender," she murmurs.

"Enough. It is *perfect*."

"Your majesties, I think my feet have good and truly frozen," Liana grumbles. "Can we start now?"

Estela laughs, and I stand. Then my wife places her small hands over mine, and we step forward together.

We raise the child high in the air.

"Your mother and father have given you the name Kai!" I call up.

I have searched the scrolls and found that it means *Forgiveness* in some human dialects. I thought it was fitting for a child who would once have been called an enemy.

The crowd erupts in joyful chants, singing in time with Velen and Ulla.

My throat tightens.

"Today, you join your people." My voice catches.

Estela looks at me and smiles.

"Your people, the Enduares!" she calls out, laughing a little when he kicks.

Just as it has been for every other naming blessing, the crystals our people hold are raised higher, and the volume increases. The overwhelming feeling is almost painful, but I wouldn't change anything.

"I bless you in the name of our gods, Grutabela, Endu, and Ashra," Estela intones, adding in her own goddess.

A tear slides down my cheek.

"Be strong, little one. Grow with the stone." Another tear.
"May your eyes one day see Vidalena."
And then we all are swallowed by the light.
For underground dwellers, it feels... right. It's like this was
always meant to come to pass.
When I look at the sky, I thank any god who will listen.

THE END... FOR NOW.

If you enjoyed To Ignite a Flame, *please take a moment to leave
a rating or review—it really makes a difference!* Book three, To
Defend a Bride, *will be releasing in October, 2025! Join me for Ra'Sa
and Melisa's standalone story.*

NOTES

3. UVITE

1. Love
2. My love.
3. Shit.

4. HENMILITE

1. Good morning.

6. AZURITE

1. Mom, help me.
2. Leaf ball.

8. EMERALD

1. Get off!
2. By the gods.

10. MOONSTONE

1. Hello.
2. You shouldn't do that.
3. Leaf ball.
4. Thank you.

12. AQUAMARINE BERYL

1. Open.
2. My door is always open for you.

13. NUUMMITE

1. I feel fucking furious.
2. Thank you.
3. By the gods.
4. Thank you.

15. NEPHRITE

1. Holy fuck.
2. My life.
3. My love.
4. Love
5. My love.
6. I love you.
7. My gods.

17. WILLEMITE

1. Hello.

19. YUGAWARALITE

1. Shit.

21. HAUYNE

1. Love.
2. Love.

22. EUCLASE

1. By the gods, Este, I am so sorry.
2. My love.

24. RICHTERITE

1. Love

25. TOURMALINE

1. By the gods.
2. Meat soup.
3. Does everyone have food?
4. What the hell is that?

27. OBSIDIAN

1. My love

32. ELIAT STONE

1. Good morning, my little love. (Diminutive term of endearment.)
2. My love.

33. YUGAWARALITE

1. Literal translation: my life. But it's another way to say "darling" or "my love."
2. My love.
3. I love you.

34. OSMIUM

1. My love.

35. NUUMMITE

1. My love.
2. My life.

36. DUMORTIERITE

1. My pulse.
2. Fuck off!

NOTES

38. HAUYNE

1. Shit.
2. By the gods.
3. My love.

40. EUCLASE

1. Damn it.

42. TANZANITE

1. Holy fuck.

43. AQUAMARINE BERYL

1. By the gods.

44. RICHTERITE

1. My love.

47. IOLITE

1. Love.

48. TOPAZ

1. Holy fuck.

49. ENARGITE

1. I love you.

50. OCEAN JASPER

1. My love.

ACKNOWLEDGMENTS

When I wrote my thank yous for *To Steal a Bride*, my audience and circle was much smaller. In the last seven months, my life has been changed and I am literally an overflowing well of gratitude. LET'S GET INTO IT.

First, to my husband. Josué is the wind beneath my wings. Te amo con todo mi corazón. Eres mi razón de ser. You bring me food (because I am a gremlin artist who forgets to eat), support my wildest dreams, build my bookshelves, and even let me use your hands for videos. (Ugh, those gorgeous hands.) You are the reason I write about love.

To my dog, Biyuel, who healed a small part of me. She can't read this and that makes me cry. I also love that the fellow Mexican Swifties named her. (Yeah, her name is essentially Bejeweled.)

My mom, Jaqulyn, for being a supportive parent who cheers me on. I don't know if you knew how impactful all those years reading bedtime stories were, but it's shaped who I am today. My sister, Victoria, who loves to make jokes about my Sexy Big Blue Men books, but still recommends them to all her friends. To my brother, for always being so willing to get nerdy. Most of the technical knowledge I have comes from you. If it weren't for your video and research recommendations, my books would be 85% vibes.

To Margie, my PA. You are a creative genius. I appreciate your gorgeous, vibey reels, your designs, trope maps, and your willingness to talk about ideas and life. Your support keeps my sanity.

Sydney Hunt, Kourtney Mitchell, and Elayna R. Gallea. My dedicated writing group has been such a special blessing. These women are incredibly supportive, and I look forward to our riotous partying. Thank you for the endless help I've gotten with art, covers, and writing.

Kourtney, thank you for being my first beta reader. You are everything. I always look forward to your reactions, and for you to tell me, "hey this is good" when I can no longer see straight. Even if it's not good, I'm so glad you always help me get there.

Sydney and Chelsea, thank you for editing my book. Like—I CAN'T TELL YOU THANK YOU ENOUGH. Writing is a painful, soul-altering process and having a strong support team behind me to help catch my bilingual brain nonsense or my dyslexic spellings/grammar structures is vital. You two do it with such flair.

Elayna, I love you. With my whole heart. You are my work wife. To a lifetime of writing retreats, spa days, and success!

To Nisha J. Tuli, I appreciate you. I am so grateful for our friendship and how it pushes me to improve and achieve so so much. You are an incredible author.

Cassie, thank you for being my plot muse. Thanks to our friendship, there never seems to be a plot hole big enough that we can't fix. I adore your stories and I appreciate our friendship deeply.

To Ophelia Langsley Wells and Fleur DeVillainy for our HILARIOUS CHAT. We are menaces. Self-care goddesses. Groups of author friends are so important. Thank you for talking through everything from sentence structure to art to plotting ideas.

To the artists who have brought my Enduares to life. Hillary Bardin, Jaqueline Florencio, Brina, Covalienne, Amira, Agnieszka

Gromulska, Beth Gilbert, Artscandre, and several others—thank you. Your art is the perfect harmony to my writing and I feel so honored to show off your stunning skills.

To the narrators for Teo and Estela, Mason Lloyd and Ruby Corazon. I listened to your narration of book one while reading book two, and your added interpretation brought so much to life for me. I thank both you and Podium for giving my story a new medium.

And finally, to my readers. It's impossible to list all of you, but I want to say a special thank you to a few IG handles in particular. Thank you for being so supportive and vocal about TSAB. Namely, reesiecup08, polvodeletras, evenromanceisnerdy, tempest_reign_book_reviewer, noribooreads, _bethsbookcollection_, kiaras_booknook, kels.lovesbooks, bookish_selenovert, tairen_soul, badwitchesbookcoven, de_boekenplank_van_floor, arielrosereadsandwrites, emeph.writes, balancing_books_and_beauties, spookymess_, taylor.bilyeu, danii_ramage, readingtomyplants, emvz.woodandbooks, spaghootlesreads, thenarnianreader_, zelspov, and countless others.

It took a village to write this novel. I am so grateful I had you all.

No thanks go to: insomnia, imposter syndrome, and the USA healthcare system.

ABOUT THE AUTHOR

Daniela A. Mera was born into a royal Fae family in Scotland. She was a free spirit who loved traveling and cloud watching while laying velvet-soft grass. When she came of age, her Spanish Scottish mother forced her to travel to Las Vegas in order to kill a dragon and conquer a neighboring kingdom.

The dragon turned out to be a man, whom she fell wildly in love with. The couple ran away to the gentle hills of Mexico where Daniela ate lots of tacos and fruits the size of her head.

Something along those lines, anyway.

She writes whimsical tales full of lore all around the world, full of emotionally available men and women who run the world. She can be found listening to sappy romance ballads while writing scenes meant to emotionally damage her readers.

When not writing, Daniela can be found doing yoga and playing video games. Join her newsletter for freebies!

Visit: http://danielaamera.com/

f facebook.com/AuthorDaniela.A.Mera

⊙ instagram.com/authordaniela.a.mera

ⓐ amazon.com/~/e/B09JDDZQX7

g goodreads.com/authordanieaamera

Made in the USA
Coppell, TX
27 December 2024

43542080R00331